Praise for Lynn Hightower

'A cracking tale told at a stunning pace . . . the chartacterisation is great, the suspects are 10 a dollar and the dialogue worth a million' – Frances Fyfield, *Mail on Sunday*

'Hightower has invented a heroine who is both flawed and likeable, and she knows how to keep the psychological pressure turned up high' – *Sunday Telegraph*

'Suspenseful and psychologically sound, with a fierce, frazzled quality to the writing which gives it edge and credibility. Astonishingly good' – Philip Oakes, *Literary Review*

'Genuinely fresh and exciting' – *Observer*

'Cleverly crafted crime story from an exciting new writer . . . frightening . . . gutsy' – *Daily Mail*

'Good frissons of psychological terror . . . Sonora is a lively and sympathetic addition to the ranks of fictional female coppery' – Marcel Berlins, *The Times*

Also by Lynn Hightower

Flashpoint
Eyeshot
No Good Deed
The Debt Collector

About the author

Lynn Hightower lives in Tennessee, works full time
writing fiction, loves canoeing and horseback riding,
and is witty after two glasses of wine. She is the
author of four highly acclaimed Sonora Blair novels,
Flashpoint, Eyeshot, No Good Deed and
The Debt Collector, all available in paperback
from New English Library.

HIGH
WATER

LYNN
HIGHTOWER

NEW ENGLISH LIBRARY
Hodder & Stoughton

Copyright © 2002 by Lynn Hightower

First published in Great Britain in 2002 by
Hodder and Stoughton
A division of Hodder Headline

The right of Lynn Hightower to be identified as the Author
of the Work has been asserted by her in accordance with
the Copyright, Designs and Patents Act 1988.

A NEL Paperback

1 3 5 7 9 10 8 6 4 2

A CIP catalogue record for this title is available from the
British Library

ISBN 0 340 79241 8

Typeset in Great Britain in Sabon by
Palimpsest Book Production Limited, Polmont, Stirlingshire
Printed and bound in Great Britain by
Clays Ltd, St Ives plc

Hodder and Stoughton
A division of Hodder Headline
338 Euston Road
London NW1 3BH

Dedicated with love to the memory of my brother,
Jay Christopher Simmons,
1953–2000

Do they play kick the can in heaven?

Acknowledgments

My heartfelt thanks to Captain Stan and his lovely wife of Ace Basin Tours for their kind hospitality, and the thoroughly enjoyable and fascinating tour of the Ace Basin Sound.

To the proprietors and the staff of The Beaufort Inn, for my very wonderful stay in the Rosehill Plantation.

I was very impressed with the professionalism of the Beaufort County Sheriff's Office, and am grateful for their assistance. In particular, I would like to thank Midge Scott, the Beaufort County Sheriff's Office Public Information Officer, who was kind enough to spend an afternoon answering all of my questions and queries.

My thanks to the people of Beaufort, South Carolina, who were invariably gracious, hospitable and happy to give directions to lost writers.

My absolute gratitude to my agent, Aaron Priest, for believing in this book, and to Lucy Childs and Lisa Erbach-Vance.

Much appreciation to my editor, Jennifer Barth, whose editorial help was invaluable, and who gave me the time and encouragement to get it right. I am delighted to have the privilege of working with my US publishers, Henry Holt.

My thanks to my sister, Rebecca, to my kids, Alan, Laurel and Rachel, to Kay and Amy for early readings and opinions, and to Matt, for the same.

To Phil Pride, Karen Geary, Georgina, and the sales reps, publicity, marketing and production staff at Hodder & Stoughton, my very wonderful British publishers.

'This falls into the category of things you put up with if you don't have a gun'

—Michael Davidson, attorney-at-law

HIGH
WATER

PROLOGUE

I never dream about my father. But there are dreams, rare and precious, when my mother appears, bathed in sunlight so bright that I squint, even in my sleep. These feel more like visitations than dreams, and it gives me comfort when she hugs me and smiles, and makes me feel like I am still my mother's intelligent, pretty, good daughter, with a future that is unblemished and ripe with possibility.

I was born to that southern tradition of beautiful eccentric mothers who submit their talent, potential and happiness to raising children – three in our case – beneath the shadow of dark men. Men dark in nature, not in looks. Men with moods that hang over the household and pass like shadows when they leave.

A man like my father would not dream of raising a hand to his children – in fact, he would pride himself on his personal vision as strong but fair, strict but reasonable. By the talk-show measures of parenthood he can even be seen as landing on the side of the angels. We were fed, clothed, disciplined. We were never physically or sexually abused. My father worked hard his whole life, giving up the University of Virginia, the southern man's Harvard, to enlist in the Marine Corps at the beginning of the Vietnam War – this due to the impending birth of my brother.

I think control starts as a defense mechanism. I've

studied pictures of that young man my father was, and he seems as unsure as he is skinny and raw, a boy carrying the weight of the world. But somewhere along the line the control became an addiction, fed, perhaps, by years of command as he worked his way up the ranks of enlisted men, and landed, a seasoned veteran of war, as a drill instructor at Parris Island, South Carolina. And there he settled us, his wife and three children, into the small community of Beaufort.

I was a judgmental child. My father's rages, moods and small cruelties triggered in me an overabundance of defiance, rages and moods of my own, as well as a secret fear that I would grow up to be him. Shakespeare says that fault is not in our stars but in ourselves.

I miss Beaufort. I am miles and years away from what I think of as my home. I see another coastline and live in the rhythms of other time zones, my home at the foot of stark, brown mountains, surrounded by dry desert soil.

Each morning I wake in sun-drenched exile, and if my heart is hungry for the visual ease of live oak trees and green grasses, I have learned to love the raw un-fettered vistas of the mountains, and my soul is soothed by the cool relief of nightfall, when the temperature drops and brings absolution to the sun-seared land. It is wild here. I have seen coyotes ahead on the pathway, blinking back at me over their shoulders, wondering if I pose a threat. I know there are rattlesnakes in the thickets. I keep a hand on my dog's collar when we cross the prints of a mountain lion on the trail.

But the things I fear are not in these mountains. They are two thousand miles away in a small southern town.

I dream of the low country. The South is woven into the landscape of my mind so deeply that, whatever is bad and good of it, I miss like a physical pain.

If the South misses me, I cannot tell.

I was angry with my mother the night that she died. Angry because I had been made to feel guilty, frustrated and helpless. Guilty because her life seemed to me a form of undeserved hell; frustrated and helpless because she would not change it according to my dictates.

The drive to the hospital is etched in my memory – the flat, tarry pavement, a straight stretch down Highway 17, the newly settled dark riding softly on the treetops and sandy soil. I think of that drive as the last normal moment before the slow, heart-nailing realization that the things I took for granted, the things everyone takes for granted, did not hold true.

But I did not look, then, to find treachery among my own. You don't look for bloodstains, or double-bolt the doors, when you know it's only family coming.

There is a softness in the night when full dark comes over Beaufort. I notice it this night, as I notice everything: the moss in the trees beneath the beam of my headlights, the unreal sense I have that tonight is not really happening. I feel I am drifting through a dream.

I know that my mother is dying. I turn the radio off because it only plays one station – 98.1 THE BULL – which doesn't seem like the right kind of music for a time like this. I crank down the window. Big Mama is my Ford pickup, and as much as it is possible to love an automobile, I love Big Mama – a 1987 F-150, black with gray trim, oak side rails installed in the back so I can carry furniture, which I refinish and sell for a living. It's a stick shift, with gray vinyl seats that are murder in the summer sun. My air conditioner only blows hot air. Wear shorts on hot days and you will leave a layer of burnt hide on my upholstery, which is ripped on the passenger's side, exposing dirty yellow foam. What I do have is a 350 V-8 engine, a scratched-up trailer hitch and huge chrome side mirrors, so I can pull a trailer if I have a lot of pieces to move. There's no door on the glove compartment, which is stuffed with some things I remember putting there and some things I don't. The heater works, and the tires are Michelin, though they need to be rotated. Big Mama gets ten miles to the gallon and holds forty, and between the seat and the back is a convenient open space that right now is cluttered with an old flannel work shirt, a pair of work gloves, some balled-up maps and a tarp.

I don't owe any money on this truck.

The Beaufort Hospital parking lot is nearly empty. I put Big Mama in park and open the heavy door, which creaks no matter how much I oil it. A Coke can rolls off the gritty black floorboard and hits the pavement with a clank. I'm out in a heartbeat, grabbing the Coke can and looking over my shoulder to check if anyone has seen and disapproved – one of the realities of small-town life. I hate to be thought of as trashy.

But I am alone in the parking lot, thirty-four feet from the emergency entrance where my mother has been brought in, heart-stilled and cyanotic. It is Sunday night and the good people of Beaufort are tucked in front of their television sets, boats docked, beer or highball in hand, lazing through the last dark hours of their weekend.

The first person I see in the hospital is my father, Fielding Smallwood. He has retired from the Marine Corps and works in a bank as a loan officer, lending money to good old boys and retired marine officers. Active enlisted men cannot afford the rates.

He is wearing, as always, his off-duty, off-work jogging-suit uniform. He has two of them, a soft gray cotton with blue piping, and the one I hate, a navy blue polyester ensemble that has a slippery look and makes raspy noises whenever he moves. He is wearing the gray cotton one.

We look each other over, my father and I, bristling like territorial dogs, and neither of us likes what we see. I have worn my high-heeled black boots and slung my black leather jacket over my shoulder for effect, and because I know I will need to be tough. I am wearing my favorite 501 Levi's and my lavender T-shirt, because it is my lucky T-shirt and lavender is Mama's favorite color.

My father is compactly built, muscles running to fat, his exposed flesh raw with the freckled burn he maintains religiously on the golf course. His crew cut is a yellowing gray, short and spiky, and I know he is incensed that his haircut is back in style.

He puts a hand toward me but stops when he sees my frown. 'Georgie, those things I said on the phone.'

His face strains for sincerity. It looks real enough. To give the man his due, he probably is sorry. That is the tragedy of men like my father.

6

'I don't know why I screamed at you like that, sugar. I was upset about your mama, and I just took it out on you.'

'It's okay, Daddy, forget it.' But it is not okay, and my distance ensures he knows it. I was, after all, raised by this man and I don't accept excuses any more than he does. Too much alike, my mother used to say – an observation that chills me.

'What is it, Daddy? A heart attack or a stroke?'

'They're not sure.'

I lean against the wall and fold my arms. I am waiting for an explanation.

My father motions to a chair and I ignore him. This puts him in a bind. He cannot sit down unless I do and I have no intention of settling in. As soon as I am up-to-date I will storm the doors to find Mama.

He sits anyway, and I am as shocked by this breach of etiquette as I was by his vicious and unprovoked attack over the phone, my father's gentle way of breaking the news. His face takes on the distanced air of a man looking inward.

'She went to bed around – oh, I guess four o'clock.'

He looks up to make sure I get the message. Mama had been depressed. When Mama is depressed, which is often, she goes to bed, pulls the covers over her head and listens to country music on the radio. Mama has a crush on Garth Brooks.

'I checked on her around four-thirty-five, and she was fine. Sleeping; I guess she took a pill. I checked again at five-oh-five, and she was okay. I checked her again at five-thirty, and again at six. Six-thirty she was fine, and at seven I went in, and Georgie—' My father rubs a meaty hand over his eyes, voice going up an octave and a half. 'She was blue. She wasn't breathing, and she was blue.'

I cannot help myself. I lean down and hug my father, who is as close to unraveled as I have ever seen him.

'You want a cup of coffee or anything, Daddy?'

'No, sugar, I just finished a cup.' His eyes are wetly grateful and he clearly feels forgiven.

Deep in my heart I keep hold of my grudge. It is crowded in my personal grudge chamber – I have hostilities left over from kindergarten.

'Did Mama feel bad? Did she complain or say anything at all?'

He shakes his head, eyes going narrow. 'The only thing she said was last week. She said she'd seen her mama and daddy, sitting beside her on the bed.'

'She told me,' I say, fiddling with the zipper on my jacket. Mama, so practical and down-to-earth, occasionally did come up with these kinds of comments, speaking so casually you just kind of let it go. Still, it is common knowledge in the South that your dead relatives will come for you when you die.

'Where are you going, Georgie?'

'I want to see Mama and tell her to stay away from the light.'

'Don't make jokes, Georgie. And they said we can't see her right now.'

'They can say all they want.' Heading toward desks, nurses, swing doors and officialdom, I catch his look of approval out of the corner of my eye, and I wonder why he isn't storming the doors himself. His litany of time checks on my mother echoes in my head, and I have my first moment of nearly incomprehensible suspicion.

A year from now I will imagine going back in time and catching that girl I was in the hospital corridor. But I still won't know what I'd tell her.

✦

The nurses are kind. If nothing else, this alone tells me that my mother's condition is hopeless. It is clear that in their minds I am *grieving daughter of dying mother* and they bring me blankets, Coca-Colas and endless cups of coffee. Clearly frustrated over how little they can do for my mother, the nurses are making up for it with me.

My mother's name is written in strong black ink and slotted over the top of her bed: Lena Smallwood. She is cocooned in sheets, a tube running sideways out of her mouth like a deprecating half smile. The tube allows a machine to breathe for her, and the thought of her waking, confused and choking, makes me afraid to leave her side even to go to the bathroom, in case she miraculously wakes.

Her hair is tangled and spreads over the pillow in a halo of dark roots and Ash Blonde by L'Oréal. I touch her hair and it is stiff and sticky from the White Rain hair spray she applies every day like a fresh coat of paint. Her makeup regimen is the simple nice-girl ensemble of creamy ivory foundation and dark red lipstick, but the foundation is gone and the lipstick is a faded memory on her lips, which are painfully cracked and chapped.

I notice a dark spot coming up under Mama's collarbone and lean in close to find a rounded, thumb-shaped bruise imprinting the tissue-thin skin.

I know by now she is gone. The sense of her, the

9

presence, is starkly absent. She is not going to open her eyes or say, 'Hi, sugar babe,' or pat my arm and smile. I squeeze her hand, but the flesh is cold, lacking the emanation of warmth and the curl of fingers you get from those who are unconscious but still in the fight.

I am too stunned now for tears. The anger toward my mother I have lately been feeling is gone, replaced by the recognition of its absurdity. Only when it is too late do I understand that it is not about me. I was my mother's child and she loved me, but her decisions, her mysterious lack of logic, which contrasted so inexplicably with the undeniably lightning-quick intellect, are forever beyond my comprehension.

In our own way, my brother and sister and I have all tried to rescue our mother. We never understood that it was not up to us. We were blind with our love for her, sure that all the years with my father had somehow rewired her brain in such a way that she was not able to escape on her own, convinced in our incomplete understanding and limited experience that the conventions of her life were merely to be discarded because they did not match the conventions of our own.

I will always be that child, mystified by my mother's motivations and decisions. My sister, Claire, says that the women of our generation will never understand the women of my mother's.

The door to the ICU cubicle opens gently. The nurse is thick-waisted, and her long red hair is knotted into a blue scrunchie. She leans toward me, whispering gently.

'The doctor is here. She'd like to talk to the family.'

There is something about your siblings that sets the world to rights. The familiarity, the shared gene pool, the presence of recognized comrades in the war against the parents. I feel the weight come off me the moment I see them; Claire, hunched sideways in a hard plastic chair, arms wrapped around her knees, and Ashby, back to the wall, legs wide, hairy and sun-darkened. My brother, for all his natural beauty, has the hulking, shaggy air of a man just in from the woods, and grief sits oddly upon him. It is not his fault that he has a father who cannot be pleased. My brother loves dogs, fishing, picking up lizards, practical jokes, and every sort of reptile on the planet. It is because of my brother that I am not afraid of snakes, after years of having them thrust into my face and hidden beneath my pillow so he could savor my screams. It has always been my opinion that Ashby is the kind of son any father would be proud of, except for his one aberration, the genetic wiring that makes him love men.

Claire is on her feet the minute she spies me, legs trembling in what Ashby and I have cruelly labeled her earthquake walk. My sister has the metabolism of a small rodent and must always be in motion. She has an impish way about her, absent tonight, and an energy that is a magnet to young children and dogs. Her air of sweetness is deceptive. People are astounded at the flare of her temper.

Claire gives me a tight, clingy hug, then releases me to Ashby's awkward, reluctant embrace. Like many men, my brother does not like to show emotion. In this and many other ways, he has none of the homosexual advantages. He is not sensitive, cannot cook anything more complicated than frozen microwave meals, and is at a loss when decorating goes further than a stuffed fish glued to a plaque on the wall.

Ashby does not know how to dress and clings to the traditional like a life ring. Tonight he wears the usual loose khaki shorts that reach below his knees and a faded yellow sweatshirt with the sleeves torn out.

'How is she?' Claire keeps her voice to a whisper, which I secretly find annoying.

An orderly ambling down the hallway gives Claire a second look. Even with no makeup and wearing a pair of loose navy sweats she turns men's heads. Part of it is the hair. Red-gold and curly, she wears it cropped just over the back of her neck. My sister is that rare redhead who tans, and she has a perpetual sprig of tiny brown freckles that bridges her nose and cheeks.

Claire is oblivious to the attention she draws. She was born curvaceous, to her sorrow, though she tells me that she accepts the reality that her body will never fall into the supermodel category of thinness by which all women are judged. She swears she has no aspirations to such emaciation, but this is a frequent lie among women. I have spent a lifetime watching Claire diet and work out, attacking her food with fork and knife as if it is the enemy, despairing over the furtive look that comes into her eyes with every bite.

'Is she awake?' Ashby asks me. He is furiously chewing his nails.

I do not know what is the matter with me, that I feel the urge to tell my sister to speak up and my brother to keep his fingers out of his mouth. I see the reflection of my fears in their faces and the flash of anger is gone.

'She's not real good,' I tell them.

Ashby, at six-two, has no difficulty looking over my

12

head to scan the hallway. 'Where the hell is Dad? We thought he was in Mama's room with you. They told us at the desk that she could only have two people at a time in there with her.'

'Excuse me. I'm looking for the Smallwood family?'

There is command in the soft female voice, and we who are used to obeying our mother turn instantly around. This doctor is a surprise. Beautiful, despite the grim expression, at least a good six months pregnant, belly a solid healthy mound, long brunette hair curling softly to her waist. Her makeup is flawless but unequal to the task of concealing the red-rimmed fatigue in her eyes.

'I'm Dr Hayden.' She presses her back to the wall and gives Ashby a second look, as all women do.

My brother's smile is tight. He is weary of his effect on women, who go understandably weak over the heavy pelt of blond hair flecked with early gray, the puppy-soft brown eyes. He is big-shouldered and thickly built, tree-trunk legs invariably scraped and scabbed, face brown and weathered. Women feel safe with Ashby. Which they are, to their eternal chagrin.

I cannot help but admire Dr Hayden's manicure, pearly pink nails, white-tipped and square. I hide my hands behind my back, because my own nails are cut to the quick and stained with the residue of varnish and glue.

'How long has your mother been this overweight?' Hayden asks, and we are stung by the insult.

Claire's hands go to fists. 'She didn't *gain* that weight till you *idiots* put her on the prednisone.'

The doctor presses ever deeper into the wall, voice ostentatiously calm and measured, the tone the professional uses to address the lunatic.

'I am not insulting your mother. I'm trying to figure out what's caused her current condition.'

'Which one is it, a heart attack or a stroke?' Ashby puts a hand on Claire's shoulder, and she loosens the fists.

The doctor shakes her head, and the puzzled look on her face is as genuine as it is disconcerting. 'Frankly, we're not sure what it is. We've ruled out stroke. It may be a heart attack, it may not.'

'How can you not know?' Claire's question is breathy.

'Her heart doesn't show any damage – that we can detect, anyway – which is what we'd normally expect. It's possible she has damage in areas that don't show up on our tests. But I need a comprehensive list of any medications your mother is on.' Dr Hayden looks over my brother's shoulder, and he moves sideways, but what she wants is clearly not in the hall. 'Where is your father? I told him to stay close.'

Ashby heads up and down the corridors, and Claire and I check the waiting room, but my father cannot be found.

2

It is decided that I will drive home to my mother's house and gather up all her medications, while Ashby and Claire take their turns visiting Mama. I do not miss Dr Hayden's point when she urges me to get back quickly and stay close. Nor does she miss mine when I question the bruise on Mama's throat.

I check Big Mama's gas gauge, weighing the cash in my wallet against the gas in the tank before I put her into second gear and head over the two-lane draw-bridge that spans the deep, dark intercoastal waterway along Beaufort's town center. Even after dark, I can see how the water's surface wrinkles with the shim of waves.

I drive on autopilot. I roll the window down and inhale the musk of mildew and the briny scent of salt water, twin companions of coastal life. Out of the side-view mirror I catch a glimpse of a teenage boy crossing the road behind me, and I glance back over my shoulder, heart squeezing in a flash of hope that drowns in immediate and weighty disappointment.

It has been two years and two days since my son Hank walked off our front porch with nothing in his pockets but pride. His eighteenth birthday is five weeks away.

The memory of his leaving lives at the edge of awareness of every single moment of my life, and the sight of that boy on the road has me once again looking out the front bay window at Hank, who sits on the porch, rain pouring, dusk imminent, that five o'clock dreary time of day. We had hit the wall with the inevitable teenage ultimatum.

Follow my rules.

You can't tell me what to do.

If you want to live under my roof—

I don't.

In hindsight I realize that teenage boys need a way to back down gracefully, a chance to save face. I can see him now, jaw set, shoulders hunched against the downpour, walking off that porch into oblivion.

No jacket. A pair of Abercrombie and Fitch jeans with the left knee worn through. Worn-out Vans on his feet, no socks, a Smash Mouth T-shirt under a blue and gray flannel shirt, hair going dark and slick with the rain.

No phone calls. No letters. A private detective got my hopes up sixteen months ago, but the boy he found turned out to be from New Orleans and over twenty-one. I have caller ID on my phone and every anonymous call makes my heart jump. I know Hank is out there somewhere, and I can't believe he doesn't want to come home.

I built a life around my son, playing both father and mother since I gave birth in the Beaufort Hospital ten months after my sixteenth birthday. I was unmarried and a recent reject from Beaufort High School, which had thrown me out like bad milk. Hank's absence has left me numb. I have no memories since he ran away.

My parents have moved and I miss the turn that leads to their new home and have to backtrack, losing time. Big Mama's headlights catch the metallic glint of a small sign that reads PRIVATE RESIDENCE and hangs from the black wrought-iron gate that gapes open across the dirt-and-gravel drive. I drive slowly, winding through the overhang of live oak trees and bougainvillea, fragrant in the warm humid air.

Up until ten months ago this house belonged to my mother's great-uncle Dill, a nervous, slender recluse who gave the appearance of destitution in the years before his death. Mama used to buy him groceries and leave them, a Sunday ritual, on the steps of his front porch. He has rewarded my mother's respect and quiet kindness with the house and a figure just shy of one million before-tax dollars.

I cannot look at this house with anything short of awe. The paint is flaking, the roof questionable, and there is no central air. But a whitewashed veranda wraps the upper and lower levels, giving the house that confectionery wedding-cake look that is the signature of Greek Revival architecture and low-country charm.

I slam the door to the truck and run up the six wooden steps in the center of the porch, automatically skipping the second step from the top where the wood is rotting softly away. This is an old house, built before the Civil War. It has a root cellar that requires more courage than I have to enter, and nothing is left of the old slave quarters save a burnt chimney and a foundation wall that looks east, barely visible behind a choking snarl of ivy, saw grass and the twisted limbs of oaks. Three people I trust have told me that they have heard the faint but unmistakable ring of a dinner bell, coming from the direction of that foundation wall, and that it only sounds on moonless nights when the wind in the trees presages a storm to come. I myself have never heard it.

I ring the doorbell, feeling like a stranger at my parents' door. There is no answer. Wherever my father has gone, it is not here. I dig the key my mother has given me out of the dregs of my purse and open the door with an awkward lump in my throat.

I myself was raised in a split-foyer – sixteen hundred square feet, give or take – in a middle-class neighborhood that catered to the families of marines. I shared a room with Claire until we went our separate ways – she to dorm life, sororities and the University of South Carolina, and me to unwed motherhood and adult-education classes held at night in the warm over-breathed air of the high school where I had so recently spent my mornings and afternoons.

I sometimes miss that little house, the pattern of ugly linoleum, the avocado-green appliances, the pencil marks on the door frame between the living room and the kitchen. Those marks chart names, dates and measurements for myself, Ashby and Claire, with newer marks for Hank and newer ones still for Claire's three.

In truth, I am the family outsider. Ashby is a shrimper and makes a comfortable living on his boat, returning each night to the Charleston town house of the man he loves. Claire, newly poor in the midst of divorce, has been sweating out a dreary but financially comfortable marriage to a tight-lipped engineer. And I, who have seen the photo albums of my parents' youth, am well aware that bologna, macaroni and cheese, and furniture from Sears, Roebuck were not the mainstay of their childhoods, as it has been mine.

I open the front door shyly, immediately missing Cousin Beauregard, my mother's ancient black and odoriferous cocker spaniel.

'Hello? Cousin? Here, pup; here, little girl.'

The house has a hushed air, drained and quiet. My gaze settles on the Duncan Phyfe couch that my mother has crammed into the foyer in order to honor an heirloom that no one actually wants to sit on. I have a love/hate relationship with this couch, which used to dominate my grandfather's living room. It makes a torturous bed.

The couch has been slung sideways. A blue plastic wrapper has been wadded and tossed to the floor, and there are tracks of oily dirt across the cracked and yellowed marble foyer. In my mind's eye, I see the ambulance gurney and the controlled panic of EMTs trying to call my mother back to life.

I pause outside my mother's bedroom. She lives downstairs now, apart from my father. My parents hired workmen to frame and install a new oak door across the parlor at the front of the house, where my mother can close herself off from the mainstream of the household without wearing her arthritic knees on the sweeping bi-level staircase. It seems to me that my mother is awfully young for such crippling, but degenerative arthritis respects no generational conventions, and the hard truth is that more and more often my mother cannot make the stairs.

Her bedroom door is locked, dead-bolted at the top. It stops me. The only reasonable conclusion is that somehow, in the midst of a medical emergency, my father has seen fit to shut and lock my mother's bedroom door. Something here is wrong. I am wondering how to get through that door when I hear the unmistakable growl of a Harley-Davidson and the sputter of gravel in the drive.

⇊

A Harley-Davidson means one thing to me – Johnny Selby, the Beaufort chief of police.

Selby is a local history buff, and he is forever informing one of odd little facts. It is from Selby that I know Beaufort's first chief of police was employed in the late 1800s, with the job title Town Marshal, one that Selby would prefer. I know this because my mother has often called him Marshal, with a particular smile, though Selby will allow this familiarity from no one else. Selby will tell you (in fact, cannot be prevented from telling you, more than once a year) that the Beaufort police department purchased its first Harley in 1958. Although these vehicles are currently earmarked for patrol only, Selby will ride nothing else, rain or shine. Selby understands Big Mama.

He shuts down the engine, kicks the stand into place and leans back in his seat, peeling off his helmet. I have seen this ritual a thousand times and never tire of watching the practiced grace of his movements as he peels away the chin strap of his headgear, runs a hand through his sweat-soaked hair and balances his helmet on the arms of his bike.

The front door is wide behind me, and I stand under the porch light, batting a circle of moths from my head. Selby looks up and catches my eye.

'Hello, Georgie.'

Selby has a rough face, thick brown hair and the sad eyes of a spaniel, his best and most telling feature. He had one child, a son, Vincent, a childhood friend of mine and a wild card from birth. About the time Vincent smoothed out and seemed to be finding his way at last, he became a teenage statistic on the side of the road after flipping his Camaro and landing upside down in a ditch. He was seventeen and it was a bad time. Mama was close to Vincent and she took his death to heart. As did we all.

Selby swings a leg sideways and dismounts. 'I was running the dispatches, and Franklin Pierce tells me there was an ambulance out here this afternoon. Nothing wrong with your daddy, is there?'

This is wishful thinking. Selby has never said a word against my father that I have overheard, but I am aware, and have been for years, that a mutual animosity runs deeply between them. It is one of those things you understand from childhood, one of those things that no one will explain.

'It's Mama, Chief Selby.'

His boots are noisy on the porch and I wince when he hits the bad step, but it holds beneath his weight. 'I know, honey.'

Men like Selby are the reason people get nostalgic for small towns. I cannot think of him without remembering an awful party one hellish teenage night when he brought me home and let me off at the curb in front of my house, never saying a word, even to Mama. I can even laugh now at the time he caught me on the railroad tracks, a fourteen-year-old runaway in the making, and another dark secret kept forever.

'I just talked to the hospital. They need you to get back with those meds.' Selby squeezes my shoulder but there is a distance about him, an air of distraction, and he scans the porch and the driveway with a twitchy, nervous movement that I have seen him use when surveying a crime scene. Then he turns and gives me the full force of his attention, as if I am a favorite dog who deserves a pat. 'What did the doctor tell you about your mama?'

I brace my legs. 'They said they don't know what's wrong with her. They don't think it was a heart attack, and it's definitely not a stroke.'

I hear it in my voice, the tang of outrage overlaid with a relief that I am handing this trouble to a higher authority – as if the chief of police can command my mother's doctors to sort things out, or else.

Selby turns away from me, but I catch a glimpse of the seamed face exposed beneath the sixty-watt bulb. I see his eyes crease with a grief I have witnessed only once, and this at the funeral of his son. I know, suddenly, what should have been obvious to me years ago. Johnny Selby is in love with my mother.

'You got her pills rounded up yet, Georgie?'

'No, not yet.'

He gives me his squinty-eyed look, then motions me through the doorway ahead of him. 'What's wrong?'

'Well, two things. Mom's bedroom door is dead-bolt locked and I can't get in.'

'And?'

'Cousin Beauregard's gone.'

He shrugs away the dog. 'Cousin probably got out when the ambulance came, Georgie. She'll show up.

22

She's too old and too fat to go far – and don't you dare tell your mother I said Cousin is fat.'

I cannot help a smile. Three years ago Mama voted a very nice lady out of the Low Country Bridge Club for comparing Cousin to a potbelly pig.

Selby examines the bedroom door and I notice he is chewing gum. A sign that he has resumed the battle of the cigarette.

'Got a key?'

I shake my head.

He frowns at the heavy oak frame and brass lock with some disgust. 'Stay put.'

I scratch the back of my neck, shift weight from one foot to the other. Selby makes me feel young but safe. There comes the chink of breaking glass. Selby has broken a pane of glass in my mother's window. I hear heavy footsteps and the noise of a lock. The door to my mother's bedroom is solid and swings open with heavy grace.

Selby waves an arm toward the crowded nightstand. 'I hope you got a wheelbarrow.'

I glance over his shoulder to the bed, which has remained unmade for weeks. It is a tangled king-sized welter of cream-colored sheets, an assortment of one-hundred-count-thread cotton percale, slippered bed pillows and crocheted toss pillows, magazines and boxes of tissues. I know for a fact that the bedsheets are clean and the room has been recently vacuumed and dusted by the service my mother hires, but every surface is crammed with glasses in various stages of Diet Coke decomposition, with the occasional relief of Diet 7-Up. There are four open boxes of Luden's cherry-flavored cough drops, two paperback Harlequin romance novels and stacks of newspapers ranging from the *National Enquirer* to *The Wall Street Journal*.

I find plastic bags in the kitchen cabinet under the sink and take them to Selby, who is squinting under the light of the bedside lamp at a bottle that, when rattled, clearly contains one pill and one pill only.

'Bring your young eyes over here, Georgie, I can't read this date.'

I move across the room, thinking that I like it that Selby does not wear his uniform too tight over the comfortable paunch of his stomach, which gives him a cuddly quality that evidently appealed to my mother. I cannot get this idea of a romance out of my head, and my mind races backward to cast a new light over certain memories.

I am secretly thrilled. You cannot grow up in a small town like Beaufort without being subjected to the subtle and infinitely cruel innuendos of adults reveling in smug judgment of your father's infidelities. The notion that my mother had a secret love somehow salves those old wounds.

Selby pulls a pair of half glasses out of his shirt pocket. 'Does that date say May the eighth?'

I take the bottle from his hand. His fingers are warm.

'May twenty-eighth.' My mother's name is neatly typed on one line, Xanax on the other. Tranquilizers.

'Sixty count?' Selby asks, and I realize my mind has wandered.

'What?'

'How many were there? Pills, Georgie, in the prescription.'

'It doesn't say.'

'Yes, it does.' Selby's tone is patient but persistent, and I study the label.

'Sixty count, yes.'

'One pill left from a bottle of sixty she picked up on May twenty-eighth And this is June third.'

I see it in Selby's eyes. I can do the math as well as he can.

'Maybe she dropped the bottle and it spilled. That happened once before.'

Selby stoops and looks under the bed. He comes up, starched uniform rustling, a tiny matching pill between his thumb and forefinger.

'One. That makes two left and thirty-seven missing.'

'Look. I know my mother was depressed, but so's half the known civilized world. She didn't take an overdose.'

Selby is staring into space. 'That's not what I'm thinking, Georgie.'

'It's not?'

'No.'

'Then what are you thinking?'

He shows me his poker face, impossible to read, and I wonder if he knows things that I don't know. It dawns on me that I know things he doesn't. I am remembering the bruise on my mother's neck and my father's odd litany of check-in times that preceded her collapse.

Selby's eyes narrow. 'What is it, Georgie?'

'Just worried about Mama. I better get back to the hospital.'

'Leave me the house key,' Selby says. 'I'll look around for the dog.' He hands me the plastic bag, pill bottles clacking.

'If you find Cousin, don't try and pick her up, she'll—'

'Bite. I know. I've got the scars to prove it. Hey, Georgie?'

'Yes?'

'Nice boots.'

3

My hands shake as I park Big Mama in the hospital lot for the second time tonight. The sky is still dark, but sunrise will come within the hour and there are more cars in the lot. I see my sister's vintage '68 Cougar and Ashby's '88 Land Rover, a vehicle that actually increases in value every year. There are people who swear by these Land Rovers, and my brother is one. Perhaps it's genetic. We are all of us passionate about what we drive, though Big Mama garners little respect from my siblings, unless they have something to haul.

I leave my jacket in the car and make my way to the ICU. My senses are raw to the point where the hair stirs on the back of my neck. One of the fluorescent lights is humming and the corridor seems over-bright, my boot heels embarrassingly loud. I can hear the ding of elevator bells to my left. Someone behind me is rolling a cart. Heavy, from the noise of the wheels.

I turn the corner of the corridor and hear the murmurs of another family, clustered outside intensive care – tourists with sunburns, tear or sweat-stained cheeks and the stunned air that says accident, boat or car.

A woman is crying, and her sobs echo in the corridor. I stop and clutch the bag of medicine close to my chest. The woman sounds very much like my sister.

I see my brother around the bend. He is scanning the

hallway, looking for me. He is sweating and his face is a livid red, as if he has run a mile in the afternoon sun. I duck sideways around a sharp corner and press my back to the wall. This corridor is dim and mercifully vacant. It seems to lead nowhere. My heart pounds.

'Georgie?'

I hear Ashby's voice, see him pass. What the hell is the matter with me?

'Over here, Ashby.'

I hear his footsteps as he backtracks. He sees me and his shoulders sag.

'Georgie, I'm sorry.'

I put a hand on his arm, feeling awkward. 'She's gone?'

He nods.

I look down at the bottles of pills, so many medications. 'Where's Claire?'

'Next door. Dr Hayden gave her a tranquilizer, one of the orderlies is getting her some coffee, and that older nurse – the one with the glasses? – she's sitting with her for now.'

Impossibly, my brother grins. I understand his feelings completely. This phenomenon is peculiar to Claire.

She hit a car broadside while making an illegal left turn the week after she got her driver's license. The cop on the scene let it go, and the couple she hit brought her a bouquet of flowers the next day because she was so upset. She once went through Atlanta airport with luggage in both hands, off balance on ridiculous high-heeled shoes that I had bought her for her birthday, and was saved from plummeting down the steep escalator to the concourse train by a man who reached out and caught her just as she lost her balance. He told her that he knew she might trip and wanted to be there to catch her if she fell.

That is the way life goes for my sister. People adore her, and I am no exception. The only one impervious to her charm is her husband, who has finally been given notice to vacate her life. It took her ten years to make a decision I would have made in ten minutes.

I clear my throat, which is sticky. 'You saw Mama before she died?'

My brother nods. Something in his eyes is disconcerting, and I wonder what's on his mind.

'Did she ever wake up?'

He shakes his head, unable, it seems, to speak.

'So she just . . . did her heart just stop or—'

'Daddy had her taken off the life support.'

'*What?*'

'Georgie, she was already gone. Dr Hayden said her internal organs were deteriorating, there was absolutely no hope.'

'I've been gone, like' – I glance at my watch – 'an hour and a half. Getting her medications. He couldn't have waited till I got back? When did he do it?'

'Twenty minutes ago, just about.'

My muscles ache with rigidity. 'Did it occur to anybody that I might like to tell her good-bye?'

'Georgie, I *tried*. Believe me, Claire and I both wanted him to wait.'

My brother's face is easy to read – sorrow, remorse, the need for me to forgive. He tries to hug me and I push him away.

But I know I am blaming the wrong person. I make the effort to pat Ashby's shoulder. 'Not your fault. Go take a number and see about Claire.'

'What are you going to do?'

'I'm going to talk to Daddy.'

'Don't . . .'

'Don't *what*, Ashby?'

'I don't agree with what he did, okay? But in his defense, he didn't want mother to suffer. This is a bad time for all of us, Georgie. It's done, okay? You might want to cut him some slack.'

'*You* might.'

'Always the family hard-ass.' He says the words under his breath, but I hear them. Take sides, I want to tell him. But what I mean, of course, is 'Take my side'.

The hallway is getting crowded. This accident has been a big one. I feel sympathy for these strangers who look so anxious and lost. But they avoid meeting my eyes and stay well out of my way – this is how I know how angry I look.

How could Claire and Ashby have stood by and let this happen? How can a matter that seems to me so clear-cut, so black-and-white, be to them a murky decision of shifting pros and cons?

I will remember this moment. It will mark the beginning of an ever-widening chasm between myself and Ashby and Claire. And I will look back and wonder if we were really so different. What I met head on and confrontationally, my siblings handled with the confused actions indicative of conflicted love, loyalty, betrayal and rage. I will one day decide their reactions were more typical, more human. And I will understand that because of this, they suffered more.

I find my father just inside the swing doors to the ICU. He looks wonderfully fresh. Somehow he has managed to shower, shave, change into sharply creased khakis and a white polo shirt and end the life of my mother.

He is talking to a doctor, a tall, thin, chinless man I don't recognize. My father turns to me with clear discomfort in the sudden tensing of his muscles. He will not look me in the face.

'Georgie, honey, did Ashby tell you?'

'You took Mama off the life support.' I can hear the shock in my voice, and I clutch the bag of pill bottles in my fist. A sudden downpour of tears soaks my cheeks and trickles down my neck.

'I don't think you would have wanted your mother to suffer, would you, Georgie girl?'

My father's voice is schooled to a patient kindness that is as much for the benefit of the doctor and the nurses swarming the horseshoe counter as it is for myself.

'You could have waited.'

The doctor gives me a look of such unmitigated pity that I feel guilty for labeling him chinless.

'I did what was best for your mother, Georgie.' There is no trace of anger in my father's voice, and it is hard not to believe in his confident conviction.

I am unsure suddenly and do not know what to say. Years of obedience kick in and I know I was quick in my condemnation of Ashby and Claire.

'Mr Smallwood?' The doctor jumps into the uncomfortable silence, and I feel that he is rescuing me as well as conducting his business. 'I'd like your permission to conduct an autopsy on Mrs Smallwood.'

My father flinches and the doctor suddenly steps backward.

'Understand this. There will be *no autopsy* conducted on my wife.'

'Sir, please understand that with the irregularities and the lack of a concrete diagnosis—'

My father's neck has gone red. 'My wife is dead. That's enough for one man to deal with; don't you add to it. This hospital will not be allowed to . . . you couldn't *save* her live, and you sure as *hell* won't be allowed to cut her up.'

I press my back into the wall, the doctor's low, placating tones washing over me. But the doctor is losing ground, and he knows it. I can see defeat in the way he raises a hand, as if to rid himself of all of us.

I take the almost empty bottle of Xanax out of the bag and stow it in my purse. I have no plan in mind, just an instinct to safeguard the bottle. A pill bottle proves nothing in a court of law. There is no chain of evidence, and there are a million possible explanations – even, eventually, the suggestion that Mama emptied the bottle herself.

When the doctor walks away in disgusted defeat, I wonder if I will ever know what really killed my mother.

Southern children are imprinted early. Families stick together and keep their private business private. This is not the sort of thing you blurt out if you are unsure. I know only two things for certain – that it is up to me to protect my family, and that my mother would be appalled to be subjected to the indignities of an autopsy.

I am startled when my father squeezes my shoulder

before he walks off down the hallway after the doctor to make whatever arrangements need to be made. I can see from the sag in his shoulders and the slow, heavy footsteps that his anger is gone and he is weary to the bone.

For the second time in a long, long night, I feel sorry for my father. And I remember how differently he walked when he was younger and not so beaten down.

Picture me all of five years old. It is summer-hot, the morning light is brilliant, and a tiny red-brick Baptist church is absorbing heat. I am wearing a daffodil-yellow dress with a skirt that swirls when I spin and has a white daisy on the pocket. The dress is sleeveless and has straps that button at the back, and I am wearing white leather sandals and crew socks that fold over my ankles and are edged in white lace. My hair is long and fine and has been washed with violet-scented shampoo, but I am not entirely dainty. My knees are scraped and scabbed over, and the sandals, being new, are raising blisters on my raw, slender heels.

I am small for my age but mouthy. I do not like Sunday school, except for the snack, which is two shortbread cookies and a tiny cup of red Kool-Aid. Sunday school is a drag, unless we're doing crafts. You can make amazing things with rubber cement and Popsicle sticks. The part of Sunday school I find frustrating is when we sit in a circle on our blond wooden chairs and talk about Jesus. This Jesus is evidently a pretty extraordinary man, and I have a lot of questions. Children in the Southern Baptist Church are not encouraged to ask questions, so don't ever let anybody tell you different.

My Sunday school teacher is a tall, scrawny, dark-haired woman with an air of fatigued exasperation. Even at the unformed age of five I disappoint her in some way that is as mysterious as it is clear.

I don't remember this woman's name, but her face is a solid memory, as well as the pointy black-cat glasses that hang on a chain around her neck. Other than my questions, which are simply ignored, I don't believe I was disruptive. I was only ever a problem child during the first grade in elementary school, for reasons I can't recall, but it was my sole foray into juvenile delinquency.

Perhaps Cat Glasses is simply exasperated with my mother, who, as always, is late picking me up. My mother teaches Claire's Sunday school class and can't leave until her own charges are claimed.

I know I am hanging at the edge of the door, scanning the basement hallway, which is growing quieter and emptier as most families leave for the sanctuary upstairs. I have a sudden and paralyzing fear: my mother isn't going to come. The hallway is empty now. It is cool down here in the basement. In the nursery next door, most of the babies have stopped howling; the parents have all unloaded their offspring and gone upstairs to the service. I can hear Mrs Adams cooing to some lucky infant child.

Mrs Adams sits in a rocking chair by the window that opens out onto the grass, and she can fit three babies on her lap. One night a rattlesnake crawled in the nursery window during a Wednesday night prayer revival, and we could hear Mrs Adams scream all the way up in the sanctuary.

The organ starts up and I am all alone with Cat Glasses. My mother has not come.

'You'll stay with me then,' Cat Glasses says. She turns off the lights and closes the door.

I am stunned. Life, as I know it, is over. If my mother does come for me, I'll be gone. She won't be able to find me. I'll be living with Cat Glasses, who wants me as little as I want her.

Looking back, I cannot explain the conviction I had that I would never see my family again, and that I was doomed to a life of strict and unaffectionate upbringing by my Sunday school teacher. But I remember to this day following the woman into the airless sanctuary and sitting beside her on the wood pew. I suppose most children are like Alice in Wonderland, able to believe six impossible things before breakfast.

Hard as it is, I accept my fate. I will never see my family again. Adults are inexplicable beings when you are five years old; decisions are made without your consultation. On the other hand, I want no part of life with this cranky Sunday school teacher, so I decide to strike out on my own.

I am cunning. I wait for a prayer. Baptist prayers are tedious long and I sneak away, small and silent, when all heads but mine are bowed.

It is cooler outside. Sunny and already pretty hot. I look around, deciding which way to go. The woods have always interested me. I will head down the hill, through the parking lot and back up the grassy slope to the South Carolina pines. The preacher's house is on the right, so I'll veer left.

I am halfway across the parking lot when I hear my name. I should have kept on going but I turn and look, and there she is, that Sunday school teacher, standing at the top of the hill. She is at a serious disadvantage.

Her high heels will not take her down that hill with any degree of speed or comfort, and I'll be long gone before she catches up.

'Come up here,' she says. Pretty firmly.

I am indecisive. I do not want to live with this woman. I stand still, not running, but I'm not going back up that hill. Strictly reared as I am, I stand politely while she has her say.

It's a tough one. I spend a long agonized time making up my mind. But in the end, Cat Glasses is an adult, and I am military-trained to obey, and I go back up that hill.

Cat Glasses stays close to make sure I don't bolt and is right behind me as I go through the double doors toward the sanctuary. I feel a tap on my shoulder. I turn and see my father sitting in the short hall between the front doors and the last row of pews. He is perched on a metal folding chair like all the other deacons, six on one side, six on the other.

I have never been so happy to see anyone in my life.

He's not angry. He smiles at me and sets me on one knee, then winks at the Sunday school teacher, who miraculously surrenders custody.

The man sitting by my father hands me a butter-scotch candy. I look at my daddy, who smiles and nods his head. My mother never lets us eat candy in church, and I open the wrapper with slow care, staying quiet. I am getting away with a hell of a lot.

I sit on my father's lap for the entire service. I am quite proud to have such a handsome daddy. And today he has on his best dark blue suit and is clean-shaven, hair cut in a close new burr, and when he has to rise for deacon duties he sits me in the folding chair with a wink, and I wait with ladylike patience, hands folded in my lap, until he returns and sets me back on his knees. I never in my life loved my daddy more than on that day.

There in that hospital hallway, watching my father walk away, the simple truth is that even I cannot believe that my own father would kill my mother.

There's really not much you can do about death at 6.45 a.m., and my brother and sister are anxious to leave – Claire to break the news to her children and Ashby to find solace at home with his significant other, Reese.

I stand in the doorway of my shop. The sun is fully up, but the interior of my workroom is dark. I'm surrounded by the ghostly shapes of works in progress. On my left, lying on pads on my ancient oak work-table, is the leg of a George III ormolu-mounted mahogany wine cooler. I believe it to have been made in 1765, and my researches have revealed that three years ago a similar object sold at private auction for $77,550. I have told no one about this treasure, discovered six months ago at a flea market in Athens, Georgia.

The small knife box set to one side I will clean and sell for $500 to $1,000. Under a canvas dust cover is a leather-topped walnut library table, made in the 1850s. It is Victorian, an intricate mix of rococo C-scrolls and Elizabethan motifs, and worth anywhere between $2,500 and $4,000.

My eye grows keener and keener. The treasures come

slowly and unexpectedly and I have learned to mask my excitement behind a ditsy demeanor that is a no-brainer to pull off for a person of my age, sex and hair color. I have more money – assets, to be precise – than anyone in my family, or in Beaufort, imagines. Not riches, but a growing collection of antiques that will at long last allow me to own my shop and overhead living quarters, and to finally sleep at night knowing I can pay my bills.

I have my mother to thank for this.

She wanted to send me to college, after I finished my high-school work by correspondence, where I graduated by mail with a respectable 3.2 GPA, scoring 1,230 on my SATs. The family rows were enormous, my father smoldering at the idea of paying tuition for a ruined child with a ruined life.

Instead, I moved out of my parents' home and settled in a tiny, depressing apartment that had ants, a failing air conditioner, and permanently warped floors. Every Monday, Wednesday, and Friday my mother arrived to take care of Hank while I attended adult education classes in reupholstery, woodcraft, and small business management.

There is something about the tactile art of woodworking that calls me. I trace this back to the summers I spent in Paris, Kentucky, sun-drenched months of ease in humid, hot bluegrass country, where the burden of my father's presence was lifted from us all. We felt a quiet happiness and contentment in the presence of my grandfather, Herbert Strickland, who owned a small furniture factory.

The comfortable lie we lived was that Mama was there to take care of her father, lonely since the death of our grandmother, who was felled with unexpected finality by a massive stroke at the age of fifty-two. Only now do I see that it was my grandfather who took care of my mother by allowing my brother and sister and me the run of his home and workspace.

Ashby and Claire spent their days wandering through the crumbling local cemetery, the shadiest place in town on hot afternoons, swimming and canoeing the still waters of Stoner Creek and getting ice-cream headaches at Dairy Queen while racing to see who could eat their chocolate-dipped cones faster.

I spent my time with my grandfather, learning how to hold and use his woodworking tools, being taught the respectful treatment of valuable woods, which are often best left alone, and inhaling the giddy fumes of glue and varnish. These fumes, toxic in unventilated workshops, ravaged my grandfather's liver and led to his early death.

I would give anything to sit once more in the pine-paneled kitchen of Granddaddy's small whitewashed wood-frame house, to sink my bare toes in the rag rug beneath the round oak table, and to see again the pine corner cabinet he built by hand to display my grandmother's orange, blue, green and yellow Fiesta-ware.

If my mother missed the big house on Lexington Avenue that had been her childhood home, the country-club dances that highlighted her teen years and the life her father gave up after a fire destroyed his first shop, she never said. I have seen pictures of her then, a pretty bright-eyed girl, well loved. She sits at cloth-covered tables that are littered with flowers and expensive drinks, and she wears strapless gowns and corsages and is flanked by clean-cut boys in white summer tuxedos.

My mother never questioned my choices, though I know she was heartbroken over my refusal to go to college. She brought ant spray for the ants and hid money in the cheap jewelry box with the pop-up ballerina, a holdover from my girlhood days. She left rolls of dimes, nickels and quarters in my silverware drawer for the Laundromat. And best of all, she was a proud grandmother – showing Hank off at her bridge club like the Hope diamond and carrying photo albums stuffed with his pictures in her monstrous purse.

It was she who found me this shop on a side street in downtown Beaufort. On the second floor, where I live, I can open my windows in the evening when the breezes come up and smell the brine of the sea. The shop sits on the corner over a crumbling concrete curb, an ancient clapboard building with a big bay store-front window, faded white shutters and battered oak floors.

My mother paid the rent for three years, negotiated the lease with an option to buy and then co-signed the mortgage, five years later, on this piece of property that grows more valuable by the day.

I fumble up the stairs in darkness. You can read a person's mood by the way they walk up and down stairs. I remember my father's heavy, slow tread, and tonight my footsteps match the memory of his.

I am normally impatient. I run rather than walk, trip more often than not. I think of my mother, who has lately found stairs such an agony that she has given them up, and of Hank, who always ran and then jumped over the final three.

The light is on over the sink in my kitchen. A cereal bowl of warm milk and a handful of swollen, sugar-caked Rice Chex sit in a sticky ring next to an open carton of juice. I stop, set my purse down on the counter. My heart beats quickly. There are cantaloupe rinds and seeds in the sink from a melon that sat intact on the counter when I left just hours ago. I am suddenly aware of the flicker of the television in the living room.

My knees are shaky. I am almost afraid to look. I have imagined this day. I have never given up. I walk on tiptoe, holding my breath, and stand by the side of the couch.

He is here. He is home. My son lies sideways, arms curled up beneath him, sleeping hard in the sanctuary of our home.

I catch my breath. How different he looks. I hear the low murmur of Gene Wilder in *Young Frankenstein*, playing for our late-night pleasure on the Night Owl Movie Channel. My son has changed. He is taller, thinner, with a worn look about his face that makes my heart contract. The beautiful golden boy, blond-haired and blue-eyed just like his mother, needs a bath, a haircut and, shockingly, a shave.

I stand weightlessly and cry like a baby with a joy that is pure and unmatched.

And so it is that the winds of change blow though my life this night, and at the same moment I lose my mother, I find my son.

It would not be possible to convince me that this is coincidence. I see it for what it truly is, a parting gift from my mother, and an assurance that she will watch over Hank and me always. I cannot tell you that I lead

41

a charmed life, or that I am immune to the dark things that lurk. But deep in the core of my being there is a current, like an electric hum, a flow of assurance that I never face my troubles alone.

4

I sit cross-legged next to the couch. I am still crying; I cannot help it. Hank's eyes open and he wakes with a jerk and a raised arm, as if to ward off trouble. He looks confused and exhausted, like a sleepwalker.

'Mom?'

He lets me hug him.

How thin he is, whippetlike, all muscle and bone and tensile strength.

'It's okay, Mom. You don't have to cry.'

'But where have you been? God, Hank, why didn't you ever ever call me? I have missed you and worried myself crazy.'

I cannot find my voice. My throat is too tight, too thick with tears. Hank sits up and squirms, and tries to come completely awake. He bends down, finally, and gives me another awkward hug.

'I need tissues,' I say.

Hank looks around, flustered, a stranger in our living room.

'I'll get them,' I say. 'You stay here.'

I watch him over my shoulder, afraid he will disappear, that I am dreaming him or imagining him. But no, he is still there on the couch when I come out of my bedroom. He is sitting up now, watching me with a wary, closed look that lets me know I need to calm down and tread with care.

'Hank, sweetie, I have missed you so much.'

He nods, but there is something in his eyes. Reservation. He is not going to say he has missed me too. He isn't going to give me that.

'Where have you been, for God's sake?'

So much for treading warily.

My son raises his eyebrows. He has the same look on his face that Ashby gets when he is being questioned about something he doesn't want to discuss.

'Uh, well. The first couple weeks I stayed with friends.'

'Who?'

'Just people.' He is not going to tell me. 'Then, um, I camped out some over on Hunting Island. Near the lighthouse.'

I nod. Why is this so difficult? How can he expect me not to want to know? 'And then?'

Hank shrugs. 'And then I hit the road.'

'Hit the road?'

'Yeah.'

'Where'd you go? How'd you survive, how'd you eat?'

Hank settles deep into the couch. 'Hitched down to Fort Lauderdale. Places like that – where there were lots of kids. Met some good people, helped me out. Met some bad people. Did some dumpster diving around the McDonald'ses. A little panhandling.'

I look at him.

'I didn't trick, Mom. The guys that do that are dopers or lazy or just stupid.' Hank clearly resents my suspicions. 'I went to Miami and looked for work. Figured since I been out with Uncle Ashby since I was old enough to walk, I could crew a shrimp boat.'

This makes such sense I wonder it never occurred to

44

me before now. Ashby was taking my son out on *The Graceful Lady* as soon as Hank was out of diapers.

'Brothers,' Ashby used to tell me, 'don't do the diaper set.'

'Didn't have much luck in Miami.' Hank grimaces, as if he has no fond memories of the place. 'Some guy told me there was work around Corpus Christi, so I hitched up there and got on a crew working the outside waters. Worked a crew in San Antonio Bay; Mosquito Point. Loved it *there*. Did some work in Galveston. If I liked the captain, I stayed. He pissed me off, I walked.'

Hank's face is brown, and his forearms have that deep tan you can only get doing outdoor work.

'Let me see your hands,' I say.

Hank holds them out, palms up, revealing scar tissue and heavy red calluses. The hands of a fisherman.

'How did you get jobs with no ID?'

'It's fishing boats, Mom. Half the guys there didn't even have a driver's license. A lot of them didn't speak English. We got paid in cash at the end of every day.'

'So you've been in Texas this whole time.'

'Mostly.'

'Mostly? I mean, they've got phones in Texas, Hank?' The question hangs between us and I know it is time to ease off. 'You hungry?'

My son nods. He definitely *looks* hungry.

'Waffle House sound good?'

Hank nods again. We have a favorite one, not two miles away.

I am up and moving to the kitchen. 'I'm going to call Ashby and Claire.'

Once, on a vacation to Cincinnati, Hank and I tried to eat at every Waffle House between South Carolina and Ohio. By the time we hit the Kentucky border, we could no longer bear it. But if I remember anything about those ten days, it is the tired waitresses in polyester, the white china coffee cups, the jukebox with country music and Hank's favorite breakfast order.

He hesitates when the waitress comes and gives me a look that squeezes my heart. This is a boy who has had next to no money in his pocket for two years and two days.

'Anything you want,' I tell him. I know his order by heart.

'T-bone, rare.' Hank looks to me for the grimace – I hate anything not well done – and I squinch up my face. 'Eggs over easy, double hash browns smothered in chilies and cheese, waffle, large orange juice and a cup of hot chocolate.'

'Whew. Ma'am?'

I do not think I can eat, but I know this dance and will not miss a step. 'Hash browns with onions, Texas toast, large orange juice and coffee with lots of cream.'

The waitress grins at us, sticks the pencil in her hair-netted bun and heads through the clatter of dishware to the sizzling grill, calling out our order in a singsong alert to the cook. Waffle House is lively at 8.30 a.m., and cigarette smoke curls through the aroma of coffee and bacon. In the parking lot, next to Big Mama, is a silver Porsche. Two big rigs hog the back of the lot.

I dig through my purse for a quarter.

'Oh, God, Mom, no.'

But it is part of the ritual, and I head for the jukebox to select the one song guaranteed to embarrass my son.

By the time the coffee and hot chocolate arrive, Conway Twitty is singing about a woman in tight-fitting jeans. Hank and I are on the watch, and we exchange looks when two waitresses and the sweating cook join in the song. Hank and I used to make bets on whether or not the staff would sing.

It is unspoken, but somehow agreed, that my son and I will keep our conversation away from the danger zones while we eat. This leaves us with surprisingly little to say. Even the most commonplace remark is fraught with trouble. Did you see that movie? No? Were you homeless then, or what?

So we eat, we smile, we feel awkward. He gives me discreet, wary looks, as if he expects me to rage, and I try not to stare at him, in spite of my fear that he will suddenly disappear. The prodigal son has returned. Hank and I are beginning where the fairy tales end.

He has been homesick for Beaufort, he tells me. Ashby and Claire still have not arrived, and knowing how long it takes my siblings to do anything, and having drunk all the coffee I can hold, I pay the bill and Hank and I drive to the drawbridge and park near the town center, where we can walk and look at the water. I settle on a bench, feeling a fatigue that grinds. It is early enough to still be cool. Traffic is slowing down, people are settled at work and all will be quiet until lunchtime.

Hank has his back to me, and I wonder how the world looks through his eyes. And I wonder, as I study him – would I know, in a crowd, that this is my son?

'I'm glad you're home, Hank.'

He looks at me over his shoulder, and the smile on his face has that polite edge that lets me know he fears an excess of emotion. But I see it in his eyes, that he

47

is relieved and reassured and these are words he needs to hear no matter how embarrassing. He sits beside me on the bench and ducks his head and grins, and I know he is turning on the charm – after all, I am the one who taught him these ways.

'So, like, am I grounded?'

I smile and try for wisdom. I am afraid that words will set him off and make him run again, but I cannot be blackmailed by a threat of flight. Control is a hard thing to release.

'Hank, I don't think it's possible for you to understand how glad I am to have you back. I have had these huge fears and worries, because I don't know where you've been or what you've gone through, and I have been imagining terrible things for two years. I'm here to listen to anything you want to talk about – anything, Hank.'

'Mom, I *told* you—'

'I know.' I stop to think. 'I have to say, I *don't* understand. I hired private detectives. I put out flyers. I wore out the Internet. I drove up and down the interstate so much I got to know the truckers by name. *Why* did you never even call me? Okay, at first you were angry. Fine, so was I. But after that? Two years and no word? Not even an anonymous card just to let me know you're okay? I was as good a mother to you as I knew how to be, and I didn't deserve that.'

Hank studies the knees of his jeans and picks at his cuticles. 'Didn't Grandmom tell you?'

He doesn't know his grandmother is dead. I dread telling him. 'Tell me what?' I say.

'I did call. Three days after I left. What, I took off on a Tuesday, and I called Friday morning.'

'Hank, I stayed by that phone for weeks.'

'I called her. Grandmom.'

'*What?*'

'She wasn't there, but I talked to Granddad.' Hank's voice lowers, and there is darkness in his tone. 'He told me not to come back. He said everybody was really mad at me and totally fed up, and that *you* said not to bother to come home.'

'He told you I said that? My father?'

'*Hell*, yes.'

'That makes no sense. It's not true. You have to know I wouldn't say that, you have to.'

My son looks at me with a cynicism he developed at twelve.

'How could you have believed something like that? *Hank!*'

He blinks and gives no answer. I am up off the bench, pacing, chewing my nails. I, who never smoke, crave a cigarette. Hank watches me with a curious detachment. He has had months to mull these thoughts.

'Let me get this straight. You called Grandmom, she was out, you got my father and *he* told you not to come home.'

'In so many words.'

I look at Hank, and I am thinking of the 'so many words' I myself have heard from my father, and I know their effect.

'So what brought you home?' I ask him.

'I found out you were looking for me.'

'How?'

'I just did.'

He is closed, eyes blank, face unyielding. The past is a secret he keeps from me, something he holds in

49

check against the chance he might want to go back. It makes me angry, but I can see the humor here. We are on each other's nerves already. We have an interesting road ahead, my son and I, but I am two years wiser now and I know that this is life.

The rest of the story comes out. How he called my mother, three days ago, and she set him straight, and sent her love and a wire transfer of money.

I am astounded. 'So why didn't she tell me?'

'I told her not to.'

'Why not?'

'It was a long bus ride home. I needed to think.'

And wanted the chance to back out. I see it in his face and it wounds me, and I, who am so often driven to severe independence by my own anger, can now see it in my son.

I hug him again and he endures it. 'I'm just grateful you're safe and alive and you're here.'

'Can we go see her? Or do you think we shouldn't wake her up? Is Cousin okay – you guys have been taking care of my dog, right?'

'Hank, I have some really bad news. Honey, I am so so sorry.'

It is almost unbelievable, the words I have to say, the timing so awful that I have to clamp down hard on a bizarre urge to laugh. I know it is nerves. I'm still ashamed.

'Grandmom died last night, Hank. She's gone.'

Hank's jaw is rigid, and he blinks nervously, again and again. 'What happened?'

'They don't know.'

'How can they not know?'

So I tell him. Something in my voice, my eyes, tips

him off to my suspicions and he questions me closely. And I, who should smooth things over with philosophical bullshit, am tempted by this developing camaraderie and closeness, this vision of my son as almost adult, and I tell this child way too much.

'I bet your father killed her.' Hank is half serious, half blowing steam, but he catches my eye and frowns at what he sees in my face. 'Do you think there's any chance he did it, Mom?'

'I don't know, Hank, not for sure. I only know that a man who does what my father did to you and me – a man like that has no limits.'

I wish the words unsaid the moment they are out of my mouth. Such knowledge is too heavy for a seventeen-year-old boy. And a male of this age is full enough of anger without fueling the private fires. I will look back and think that, as a mother, this day, I failed him.

A door slams and I look up and see Ashby's Land Rover. The car is packed. He has stopped to get Claire and all three of her children. My brother rolls down the window and leans out.

'We checked at the Waffle House, but you were already gone.'

Claire opens the door and stands with her hands on her hips. 'We've been driving all over town looking for you two.'

'Beaufort isn't really all that big,' I say.

The back doors of the Land Rover open and Claire's kids pile out. Jared is eleven, a slim boy, fair hair cropped close. Sylvie comes next, nine years old, with round serious blue eyes and inscrutable thoughts. She holds her hand out to Cece, who is six, opinionated and quick to get her feelings hurt. I am watching them for signs of grief. They have a stunned air and are unusually quiet.

Jared is relieved to see Hank, and I see the look pass between them, admiration and hero worship on Jared's part, tolerance and affection from Hank. Cece runs to Hank, who has been her hero since she could toddle over and pull his hair. Sylvie hangs back shyly, but Hank grins at her.

'What happened to all your hair?' Hank asks her. 'Last time I saw you, you could sit on it.'

'You been away too long then, haven't you?'

I see how angry she is. Sylvie is not going to let Hank off the hook.

Ashby approaches slowly, and Hank turns and offers a hand, which my brother shakes before he pulls Hank to him in a rough masculine hug. 'You look good,' Ashby says matter-of-factly. 'Did you come back with a couple million dollars? Are you famous? Wanted by the FBI?'

'Nope.' Hank shoves his hands in his pockets and rocks back and forth on the balls of his feet.

'You're too skinny, boy,' Claire says. Her next words are muffled because she is standing on tiptoe to hug my son, but whatever she says makes him smile suddenly and chuckle.

Hank is easing back, beginning to relax. I do not know what kind of homecoming he expected, but it was not this.

Ashby stretches. 'I don't know about anybody else, but I want breakfast. Come on, Hank, you could probably eat again right now, couldn't you?'

'I can always eat. But Mom's got to promise not to play the jukebox this time.'

'I'll ride with Georgie,' Claire says. 'Ashby can take all the kids.'

I am on the verge of suggesting we call my mother; then I realize, of course, that we can't.

My sister and I climb into the truck. I am watching, sideways, as Ashby drives away with Hank and his cousins. Claire buckles her seat belt and sticks her over-burdened purse on the seat between us. I shove it back toward her so I can shift the gears.

'Can you believe it?' I ask.

'It's been a weird twenty-four hours.' Claire stares out the window. 'Maybe Mama brought him home, Georgie.'

'She works fast. I'd have figured she only just now got to heaven. How'd the kids take it?'

'Stoic. Weird. They're numb, I think, like you.' Claire leans back in the seat and closes her eyes. 'I have cried so much my pants are loose.'

'I don't get the logic of that.'

'I'm losing weight.'

'From crying?'

'Yeah.'

'If you say so.'

'Is there anything you won't argue about? Speaking of which, did Hank even say anything? Like where the hell he's been all this time?'

'In Texas.'

'Texas? What's in Texas?'

'He's been fishing. Making a living on shrimp boats.'

'That's what he's been doing for two whole years?'

53

'So he says.'

'I suppose that beats heroin addiction, prostitution or robbing banks.' My sister tucks her head on one shoulder. She has no energy at all. 'He could have done his fishing here. Why didn't he ever call us? Why didn't he ever come home? And what made him come home today?'

I rest my forehead on the steering wheel. If I look my sister in the face she will know I have things I want to tell her, and even I can see she's had enough. And I want to keep this to myself for a while.

'And by the way, Georgie, I think you *should* play the jukebox. Hank can't just run off for two years and then come back bossing you around. You just be as embarrassing a mother as you want.'

I put Big Mama in gear. Claire reaches around to the back section and finds the dented box of tissues. She has a good blow, while I let out the clutch and head toward the Waffle House.

'Oh, God, tissues,' Claire says.

I keep my eyes on the road while turning right, then glance at Claire. 'Are you laughing or crying now?'

'You remember Mama's Revenge?'

'Which one?'

'The used-tissue trick. Come on, Georgie, you have to remember.'

And I do remember. How my mother had a thing about people parking too close to her car. How she always made a point of finding large roomy parking spaces so she could park the boats she always used to drive, which usually meant we parked at the back of the lot.

'You know, Georgie, how mad she used to get when

she'd come back with her grocery cart and find somebody had parked real close to the car even though we
were all the way at the back?'

'Yeah, I couldn't forget that.'

'She never ever even said a word. Just got a tissue
out of her purse, blew her nose, and tucked it under
the driver's door handle of the car. God, that used to
be so embarrassing. And me and Ashby would be hiding
and pretending like we didn't know her, and you'd be
laughing your ass off and cheering her on. Mama really
wasn't your average bear, was she, Georgie? And there
we were, growing up, thinking we were normal.'

I wake early the day after my mother dies, and see that
it is just on 5 a.m. Hank is asleep in the next room,
and if I get up and stand outside his bedroom door I
will be able to hear him snore. I have already done so
three times since midnight.

Hank was different around the cousins and Claire
and Ashby. He ate another breakfast, not quite as big
as the first, and drank more hot chocolate. My son and
I were easier together. We had a whole family gang to
buffer us from our tensions, particularly Ashby, who
would be matter-of-fact during an alien invasion, and
Claire, who can make anybody laugh. Our only weird
moment came when Claire wondered out loud why
Daddy wasn't there. No one noticed the sudden look
that passed between me and Hank, and I smoothed it
over quickly, explaining that I had left a message
because Daddy wasn't home.

But today, this morning, I am ready to talk to my

father. Thinking about him makes me anxious, and I get out of bed to make coffee and think.

My father will go to work today, for a few hours, no more. He will walk into his office, and not because he is prey to the routine of his life, although he is. He will be well dressed. Reserved. Brave and strong, with a dash of bathos, and eager to bask in the glow of attentive sympathy that will avalanche over the mountains of his grief. We are good at death in Beaufort. My father will be greedy for his due.

After putting a pot of coffee on and standing once more outside my son's door listening to his snores, I open the balcony doors. It is dark still, warmer outside than in. I catch sight of my favorite picture on the bookshelf that is built into the far wall. I pick up the frame and wipe the dust away with the ball of my thumb.

I'm not exactly sure when the picture was taken. Sometime early in my parents' marriage, when they were still in their twenties. It shows the four of us – Ashby, Claire, me and Mom – standing outside on a sandy South Carolina lawn, underneath a young oak tree. We are posed in front of our old green and white Buick and the sun must be in our eyes, because we are squinting. The three of us kids are in the foreground, with Ashby, the oldest, in the middle, me on the right, holding Ashby's hand, and Claire on the left, Mom just behind her holding both of her hands, which are raised over her little head. Claire's diaper hangs below her tiny skirt and she is clearly just walking.

Ashby is thin and wears shorts. His hair is clipped close to his head, and he is smiling. My hair is cut short, with plastic barrettes on either side, and I have my tongue stuck out, like I do in nine out of ten family pictures. My mother is smiling. Her hair is short and flipped up, and she wears a shirtwaist dress, belted, the skirt full and the hem just below her knees. She is slim and years younger than I am now, closer in age to Hank than to me. Daddy must be the one with the camera.

I see no shadows here. We look normal, happy, middle-class and mundane. Why the picture, I wonder? We are a family that poses mainly on holidays and at large family gatherings. But here we are. It looks sunny out, not too hot. My guess would be April. Our clothes are clean and neat, and we are all wearing new shoes and socks. We are casual but slick.

I almost convince myself this scene is as much memory as picture. I know the car. The house is unfamiliar. But the little skirts my sister and I wear – my mother has for some reason dressed us just alike – these skirts I remember. The picture is black and white but the skirts were candy-apple red, with a circle of white piping two inches above the hemline. I loved those skirts. I remember them. I almost remember the day.

My father's silver Lincoln is parked in its designated spot at the Beaufort Federated Bank. Inside, the lobby is chilled by air conditioning in full swing, the heat of the afternoon still to come. The atmosphere is hushed by thick carpet and rich walnut countertops, and I wonder what kind of bank fees it takes to keep this sort of thing up.

There are two tellers this morning. One of them is balding, tall and hostile to the young woman cashing her child support check. An elderly woman stands with stoic calm behind a green velvet rope while the other teller, a female under twenty-five, runs sums on an adding machine. I hear the chunk and click of its grind.

I make my way down the corridor to the heavy door that has my father's name engraved on a polished brass plate. My father is on the phone. He sits sideways behind an empty desk, ashtray studded with the butts of stale cigars. His suit jacket hangs on a wood rack in the corner. A brass stand holds his crow-black umbrella. The walls are crowded with framed photographs of all the platoons he has trained, as well as the one platoon he did not: the doomed platoon that saw the loss of seven marine recruits, boys who came to be known as the Hardigree Seven, boys who died during a night hump over treacherous terrain while following a drunken drill instructor who should have known better. I would like to ask my father why he keeps this picture on his wall, but he would not answer. Though my father is the man who led an expert rescue mission that kept the death toll down to seven, he was also the man who could have prevented the tragedy, which left its mark on the entire town of Beaufort, as well as my own family.

I circle my father's desk, press a button and disconnect his phone. 'I need to talk to you about something, Daddy.'

My father never takes his eyes off me as he hangs up the receiver and leans back in his chair. 'What's the matter, Georgie?'

How do I begin? Maybe there really is an explanation.

'Daddy, I need to ask you about something, and I want you to tell me what happened straight up.'

'Okay. You want to sit down?'

'No.' I run a finger along the edge of my father's desk. There is no dust. 'Two years ago, after Hank ran away, did you talk to him and tell him never to come home?'

My father frowns, but this is clearly not the question he expected. He rubs a hand over his face. 'Georgie, I'm sitting here trying to decide what color coffin liner your mother would want, pink or blue.'

'Did you do it? Did you talk to Hank right after he left? Daddy?'

My father stares across the room. There are circles beneath his eyes, deep and dark. 'I did, yes, Georgie. I talked to the boy. Did your mother call you, then, before she died?'

'And you told Hank not to come home?' My voice sounds tinny and weird.

My father's tone is matter-of-fact. 'Yes, I did. I was mad as hell, can you understand that? Your mother was upset, the whole family was in a roar, we had the police on the lookout. Hell, we had the whole damn town of Beaufort in our business. All because of a spoiled teenage brat. Horse shit. There's no damn *excuse* for that kind of boy.'

'What do you mean, "that kind of boy"?'

My father blinks and his eyes look oddly elliptical, like those of a lizard or a snake. 'Come on, sit down, won't you, and let's talk this out.' He waits. 'Fine, then, don't sit. Look, Georgie, that boy of yours had a good home, which is more than some boys can say. He was taken care of, well loved, and he had no business not to be grateful.'

'He was fifteen. How many grateful fifteen-year-olds do you know?'

'Georgie, I'm tired. We'll have to talk about this later.'

'I don't think so. I don't think you and me are going to be talking anymore.'

'Don't be so damn dramatic.'

'Dramatic? Hank's been gone two years, thanks to you.'

My father stands up, the chair knocking into the desk. 'Don't blame *me* for that boy of yours. I told him what was what and it was long overdue. The thing is, he was a spoiled brat, just like you.' My father's face goes dusky red. 'Do you even know that the people in this town talk about you? You come in here and speak to me like I'm dirt the day after your mother died. It's just exactly what I'd expect from a child who's never been anything but a public embarrassment to me *and your mother*. Did you ever even try to get yourself married or put a Mrs to your name? Running your little business, your mother giving you money on the side and paying your rent so you could raise your little bastard boy.'

'I found the pill bottle.'

This stops him and his face goes gray.

'What pills are you talking about?'

'Mama's Xanax. Maybe you can tell me why so many of them are missing.'

I don't see it coming. My father hits me with a brutal full-fisted punch that explodes across my nose and left eye and knocks me backward, and I am falling, catching the sharp wood corner of the credenza behind my right ear before I sprawl to the floor. It won't be long before I forget the pain, but for the rest of my life I will remember the humiliation. I am a grown woman with a teenage son and my father has punched me in the face.

My mouth is full of blood. I touch my cheek where my father's class ring has flayed the delicate skin and torn a strip of flesh that will scar. Blood pours from my nose, making a bib of red on my shirt.

I won't look at him. I hear him breathing hard, but I don't look up. He offers a hand, but I wave it away and he has the grace to step backward and say nothing. I know without question that my father will decide he had no choice but to do what he did, and he will never even doubt that he and I will get past this incident and all will once more be well. Men like my father live in a charmed world, where they never truly pay the consequences.

5

When I stumble into my living room, I see that Hank has taken the George III wine cooler off my workbench and refitted the broken leg, I shudder to think how. He is using it as a TV tray. He glances at me over his shoulder, and I see he has microwaved a carton of macaroni and cheese. I can only imagine what the heat is doing to the cooler's mahogany finish.

The television is loud, and I see a wadded T-shirt draped over the kitchen table and my son's discarded shoes – pathetically worn and full of holes – in the center of the living-room floor.

'*Mom?* What happened? Did you wreck the truck?'

I shake my head. My face is swelling and my shirt is covered in blood, but my nose has finally stopped dripping.

'You look like you got shot.' Hank peers at my face and winces, which has the effect of making my nose hurt even more. 'You want me to drive you to the hospital?'

'No, thanks.' Hank has been able to drive since he was thirteen. I make a mental note to see about getting him a license.

He stands over me, puzzled. 'Did somebody hit you?'

'Yeah.' My voice sounds funny, like I have a cold. My face hurts like hell.

'Who?'

I ease carefully onto the couch. 'My father.'

'God damn. Where is the fucker? I'll beat the crap out of him.' Hank heads to the kitchen. 'We got an ice pack anywhere, Mom?'

The 'we' makes me happy. 'Just throw some ice in a dish towel, that's good enough.'

I put the latest copy of *Rolling Stone* under the macaroni while Hank is in the kitchen. The initial subscription was his, and I have kept it going these last two years.

Hank comes back with Advil, a bottle of water and a dish towel stuffed with ice. 'Were you talking to him about me?'

'Yeah.' I swallow the Advil. Lean back on the couch and put the ice to my nose.

'What'd he say?'

'Nothing worth repeating.'

'What'd he say, Mom?'

I shake my head. Not a good move.

'Where are the keys to the truck?'

'Where are you going, Hank?'

'Are you going to ask me that every time I head out the door?'

'Damn right.'

'I'm going to see Granddad.'

'Hank, stop and think. If you hit him, he'll have you thrown into Juvie so fast you won't know what hit you. And he'd love it, don't kid yourself. Then what? You're seventeen, and he's an old man. You won't have a chance in juvenile court, and once those people get their hands on you, Hank, it's a runaway train even your mother can't stop.'

Hank sits on the couch. 'Fine, then. How about I

go look for Cousin. She's too old to be out on her own.'

I know I should say no. 'Okay, Hank. But stay away from my father. Promise me, I mean it.'

'I'll stay away from him.'

'Keys are in my purse.'

'You sure you don't want to go to the hospital? Looks to me like your nose is broken.'

'No. And don't talk about this to anybody.'

'Who would I tell?'

I close my eyes, clock my son's progress by the doors that slam until I hear the truck engine and the sound of Big Mama pulling away. The ice pack is so cold my nose is going numb. I lean back against the pillows of the couch.

Good southern daughters are cherished beings who look to their fathers for rescue and protection.

Picture me six years old. A second-grader, one year younger than the other kids, small for my age, and mouthy.

My family has moved here to Beaufort, South Carolina, where we have strong ties and family, in the middle of the school year, a hazard of military life. It is my first day in a new school and I have just been introduced to a new class and a new teacher who has stated in a loud voice, in front of all the other students, while glaring at the school secretary who holds my trembling hand, that she does not want another student in her class and she does not want *me*, a little Georgia cracker, for a student.

This teacher, Miss Tarant, has problems that I am unaware of. She is single and eight weeks pregnant and afraid she will lose her job, which used to happen to single elementary school teachers who found themselves in the family way. Later in the year she will introduce us to her fiancé, a blond man with a sunburned forehead and a weak chin. We, a class full of bright but self-absorbed seven-year-olds, with the exception of myself, a self-absorbed six-year-old, will never realize she is pregnant. We will have no idea why Miss Tarant brings her future husband to class and we will assume she is just being friendly. We obediently learn to call her Mrs Bernurt after the March wedding that takes place over a weekend. We are glad to meet Mr Bernurt. We are glad to meet anyone.

But Miss Tarant is not glad to meet me. I look up into the face of this woman, who has fine features, a pert nose, arched brows, dark-blond hair swept into a complicated arrangement that used to be called a beehive, and I understand that we are at war.

She marks my math problems wrong when they are right. She makes fun of me in front of the class because I don't know where the bathroom is in a school that is new to me. She will not let anyone lend me paper or a pencil when I forget to bring what I need, which is often. And while she likes to punish all of us, she particularly likes to punish me.

She likes to draw a chalk circle on the board, and I often stand with my nose in one of these chalk circles for half an hour at a time. She particularly likes to dole this punishment out after recess, on hot days, and the sweat rolls off my nose onto the blackboard, smearing the white circle of chalk. I often sit in a corner on a tall wooden stool wearing a dunce cap, but I quite like being up on a stool where I can see over everyone's head, and as the dunce cap looks very like a headdress in one of my books of fairy tales, I always pretend I am a princess. This punishment does not faze me.

Miss Tarant seats me in the back row behind Brenda, who is as quiet as she is tall, then sends home notes to my parents recommending eye exams because I can't see the board.

I am vengeance-oriented even at the age of six.

I leave pieces of chalk in Miss Tarant's chair, so there will be yellow and white marks on her expensive skirts, and we snicker whenever she turns her back. I spill pencil shavings all over the floor when I empty the pencil sharpener, which I do at least once a week, pretending to be helpful. I tell everyone who will listen what a witch she is, and after one particularly loud session in the girls bathroom Miss Tarant informs me that she hears every word.

I decide she is bluffing. If she really hears every word, something awful would happen to me, and it never does.

Miss Tarant's absolute favorite punishment is assigning sentences – five *hundred* sentences – in cursive, which is a hell of a lot of sentences when you are only six years old. It's a lot of sentences even if you're seven.

I could probably use Miss Tarant as an excuse for my abysmal handwriting – my mother certainly blamed her – but if you saw my father's handwriting you would understand that such things are probably genetic.

I spend many hours writing sentences, and on one particular day, a fall afternoon that is growing dark, my father comes walking in the door early, way before dinner. I lie on my side, with a tablet of paper under my arm. It is that thin gray paper with fat lines made for those of us just learning to write, and I am only on sentence number twenty-three.

I will not forget to bring my pencil to class.

'What are you doing there, little doll?'

The television is turned on cartoons, but I am not watching. I want to sleep, but if I could subtract large numbers in my head, which I can't, I would know I have four hundred and seventy-seven sentences to go.

'Don't you feel good?' My father puts a hand on my forehead. 'What are you working on, anyway?'

My father picks up one of the papers lying loose by my hand. The shame is overwhelming, and I burst into tears. I can barely say the words, my throat is so tight.

'I was bad in school.'

My father takes my papers and pencil. He is furious, but not at me. He tells me to curl up on the couch and that I don't have to do any more sentences today.

'Miss Tarant will kill me.'

'No, she won't.' His tone of voice tells me this is true.

Even over the noise of the cartoons – Mighty Mouse, come to save the day – I hear my father on the phone. Probably the neighbors can hear him around the block. He has caught Mr Lonnie Gayles, the kindly school principal, at home having an early dinner.

I learn, from snatches of overheard conversation, that I have a fever, which promptly cheers me up, because I love the orange-flavored Johnson & Johnson children's aspirin and I am hardly ever sick, so I consider them a rare and cherished treat. I also know I am likely to get Popsicles for dinner, something else that cheers me up.

I find out that five hundred sentences is a ridiculous and outrageous punishment for a child in the second grade. Now, the truth is, even at six I don't consider myself a child, because I am in something of a hurry to grow up, and this makes me burn. I also learn that my father has had enough of Miss Tarant, and that there will be some changes made or I will be put in another class. I don't want to be put in another class. The unknown scares me more than Miss Tarant.

To wrap it all up, there will be no repercussions for me when I am well enough to go back to school. I gather from the general conversation that this means Miss Tarant has to be nice to me and there will be trouble if she holds it against me that my father complained.

At this point I know I am doomed. Miss Tarant will never ever be nice to me, and if she finds out even half of what my father has said to Mr Lonnie Gayles, I'll spend the rest of the year with my nose in a chalk circle.

But here I am all wrong.

I never again write sentences, not for Miss Tarant anyway, or sit on that lovely stool wearing my princess headdress, or stand with my nose in a circle. Miss Tarant still does not love me, but she picks on me just once more, in a spelling bee, telling me that I must say too-mah-to instead of too-may-to. When I explain to my father why I asked him to pass the too-mah-toes at dinner, he goes to the school in person *the very next day*, and Miss Tarant, who is now Mrs Bernurt, never bothers me again.

One of the worst things about leaving home in disgrace, an unrepentant unwed mother, is that my father never rescues me again and I am left to fight all my own battles.

Two days after my mother's death and one day after my father has hit me, I can no longer be alone with the things I am starting to think, and I call a sibling meeting in our secret childhood place. It takes me twenty minutes to drive to the lighthouse on Hunting Island, which rises from the flat coastal marshland.

My father phoned me early this morning, wanting advice on what dress my mother should wear on the occasion of her funeral, which will be held in just two days. I did not pick up the phone while my machine recorded my father's voice, but instead contemplated how it was that he could sound as if nothing unusual had passed between us.

It did occur to me, however, what I wanted my mother to wear: a dress the color of chocolate, one my mother used to wear years and years ago on special occasions. This dark dress, not my mother's usual blue or green, made a striking contrast to her pale blond hair. It had a heart-shaped neckline and was cut low and off the shoulder. The dress was sophisticated, and my mother looked extraordinary when she wore it. And when I curled up on her bed while she got ready to go out, and she consulted me on the evening's choice, this was the dress I would always pick.

I can see us now, my mother and me, all those years ago.

I help my mother select the right earrings – small pearls are her favorites. I go to the closet to get her shoes, always the black stiletto heels. I still believe that a real woman is defined by black stiletto heels. I clomp around in front of the full-length mirror in those delicate shoes, something my mother tolerates with steady good humor. My grandmother wears stiletto heels, my great-grandmother wore them, and I cannot wait to grow up and wear them myself.

My mother will only wear clear nail polish – a rebellion, I always think, against my grandmother, who paints her long nails red. But my mother's lipstick is red, and I find it dramatic, ladylike and womanly.

My mother is always nervous before she and my father go to parties. She is shy of new people and crowds. She makes it clear how valued and essential my opinions are and insists she cannot get ready without my help. I get to go shopping with her when she buys new clothes and have a strong vote in the decision making. I love shopping for my mother almost as much as I love shopping for me, because she gets to wear the good stuff.

And after the parties and the dinners and the invitations to the local country club, where we are not members, my mother comes to my bedroom, no matter how late she's been out. She is relaxed and still smelling sweetly of perfume and sits smiling on the end of my bed. We don't turn on any lights because Claire is sound asleep just a few feet away. My sister sleeps like a hibernating bear.

My mother kicks off her shoes, tucks her feet up under the pretty dress and tells me every detail of her evening. I stay snug under the blankets, enthralled by my mother's voice. She begins with who she and my father met on their evening out and follows with a description of the most magnificent restaurants imaginable. Mama describes each and every course, from the appetizer to the dessert, and I am lost in a vision of my beautiful mother eating in such a fancy place.

Whenever she goes to a wedding, she brings my sister and me a thin slice of wedding cake to put under our pillows, so that we will dream of the men we will marry. At least, that is what we are supposed to do. I always eat mine, but I save the wedding napkin, so I can admire the scalloped edges and trace my fingertips across the gold or silver lettering that spells out the names of the bride and the groom.

I close my eyes, because right at this moment my mother feels very close. I listen for the memory of her voice, but what I hear is the ocean, no more than a hundred feet away, hidden behind the trees. It is going dark now. I am aware of shadows and movement behind me. Claire and Ashby are parking their cars, the tires grinding against the spray of sand that coats the asphalt. Ashby is missing dinner with Reese, and Claire is having a night of freedom while her children stay with their dad.

I shine my flashlight at the door of the lighthouse, take a screwdriver from my pocket and pry the door latch free with a practiced flick of the wrist. I have done this a hundred times. Flakes of rust shower the lip of the concrete stoop. The door hinge creaks.

It is hot inside, the air stale and heavy. I aim my light and look around with a proprietary satisfaction. The spiral staircase wraps the inside of the lighthouse like a ribbon on a gift. I cling to the skinny black rail.

Halfway up, the stairs pull away from the wall. I clutch the six-pack of Coronas in one hand and hold tight to the rail with the other. The stairs swing away from the wall. The sensations hit me in quick succession, the paint flaking into the creases of my palms, the lurching of metal as it loosens beneath my weight, then finally, blessedly, holds.

I fall forward on my right knee. More bruises to match the ones on my face. But the stairs, loose in the joint, are steady now that the slack is gone. I take deep breaths and lower myself to the damp metal step, looking to one side at the drop.

Voices drift my way with the clarity sound acquires near water. I hear Hank's name and someone says *Shush*. Downstairs the door creaks and echoes and a shaft of light appears at the bottom of the well.

'Watch out below,' I say softly.

Ashby drops his flashlight. '*Shit*. Georgie, what are you doing just sitting on the steps?'

'The stair up here is loose. You better watch it, coming up.'

'Beer okay?' Claire asks me.

It is getting very dark outside. I hear canvas soles on metal as my brother and sister climb. I go up to the third-level platform and shine my light. The black metal floors are dusty over the scars of hard usage. I set the beer down and peer out the tiny four-paned window. It is gluey with dirt. Outside, the reflections of light tunnel into the depths of the coastal waters below.

Claire and Ashby come up slowly, and I shine the light where the staircase has pulled loose from the wall.

'Do you think this is safe?' Claire asks.

'Not really,' Ashby says, but he keeps coming up.

I hear both of them panting, out of breath from the delicate climb. We are older now, and their leg muscles will be burning just like mine. They stop to catch their breath, and someone shines a light my way.

'God in heaven, girl, take a look at your face.'

I see them exchange significant looks. I sit on the floor and wrap my arms around my knees as my brother tends to opening the beers with the seriousness of a demolition expert defusing a bomb. We have set our flashlights on the floor, and I watch him as he passes in and out of the light, a giant shadow on the whitewashed walls. He wears khaki shorts and a thick cable-knit sweater. He is unshaven, and his cheeks are rough with the sandy stubble of his beard. Claire is wearing jeans with a hole in the knee, flip-flops with fake rhinestones and a loose long-sleeved T-shirt that says ROXY GIRL.

Ashby hands me an open beer, and I almost drop it in the dark. I hug my knees even tighter. It is weird in here with just flashlights.

I take a small sip of beer and it tastes bitter and cold. My brother and sister settle on the metal floor. Ashby gives Claire his sweater, and she folds it in a square to make a soft seat. They sit side by side and face me. It feels kind of scary and important, meeting like this in the dark. We haven't trespassed in the lighthouse since we were kids. Back then it used to be bright and hot in the cabin at night. The lighthouse was fully functional until just recently, when the essentials were shipped off to Charleston.

'What happened to your face, Georgie?' My brother speaks softly, but his voice still echoes.

The question I have been dreading. 'Daddy hit me.'

I hear one of them catch their breath. I sit quietly. The beer is cold in my hand.

'Daddy told us Hank did it,' Claire says.

I sense them staring at me. It is too dark to see their faces. I am secretly surprised that even my father would stoop this low.

'It's not that we don't believe you,' Ashby says, 'but Hank has probably been going through a lot of things we may not know about. You don't have to protect him, Georgie. Not with us. We love Hank no matter what.'

'I'm not protecting him.'

They are silent, my brother and sister, and I know they watch me.

'Tell us what happened.'

I shed my sweatshirt and drape it over the rail. I have promised myself that come hell or high water I will protect Claire and Ashby from the things I know about our father, as well as the things I suspect.

Instead, I spare them nothing, and in so doing I change all of our lives.

'Do you think Dad ever really loved us?' Claire's voice is so full of alcoholic woe, there can be no doubt that she believes me.

Ashby scoops something up off the floor and opens his hand under the light.

Claire is up on her feet. She moves away from Ashby and settles close to me. 'Dammit, Ashby, kill that spider and get it away.'

'Come on, Claire, she's a beauty. Fat too, probably looking for a place to lay her eggs.' Ashby lets the spider mince her way down his fingers to darkness and safety by the wall. 'I wish I could say what I think of all this, but I just don't know.'

Claire pulls her legs up and rests her chin on her knees. 'Even if Daddy didn't hurt Mama, or mean to hurt her, I think we should talk to Johnny Selby and get this settled once and for all.'

'Johnny Selby?' My brother snorts. 'Yeah, that's a great idea, since Selby and Mom have been doing it the last twenty years.'

'*Doing* it?' Claire says.

'Come on, you didn't know that? Why do you think Dad and Selby always hated each other?' Ashby turns and looks at me. 'You figured it out, didn't you?'

'I suspected.' I don't say that I only just started suspecting.

Claire puts her chin on her knees. 'Ashby, you are so full of shit. Mom wouldn't mess around on Daddy. She wasn't like that.'

'Everybody's like that, sooner or later. Hell, you can't blame her, with Daddy gone all the time and having affairs all over town.'

'You don't know for sure,' I say.

'I guess I do. I saw them one afternoon when I came home early from soccer practice. It was the day I quit the team, and I knew Dad would kill me, so I kind of came in quiet, and I saw them in Mom's room.'

'You saw them?' Claire asks.

Ashby nods.

'What did they say?'

'Nothing, they didn't see me. I just went down to the 7-Eleven and hung out till my usual time to come home.'

I look at Claire.

She is shaking her head. 'I can't believe it. Mom having an affair.'

'How come you never told us?' I ask Ashby.

'At the time I was really weirded out. I didn't tell anybody.'

'But *Mama*,' Claire says.

Ashby looks at me. 'She can't believe Mom ever had sex.'

'Oh, shut up,' Claire says. 'So we don't go to Selby. But we need to talk to somebody.'

Ashby looks in Claire's direction. 'If worst comes to worst, would you put your own father in jail?'

I set my beer on the floor. 'I think we need to just know. I think we ask for an autopsy.'

'Nobody's cutting Mama up.'

I realize Ashby's words are slightly slurred. 'You're not driving,' I tell him.

'And you are?'

'I haven't been drinking, have I? Just one sip?'

Claire starts collecting bottles, and she is making too much noise. Both Ashby and I look over our shoulders, as if we can see the park patrol at our back.

But Claire is oblivious. 'Georgie's right, Ashby, we need to find out for sure. I can't just live not knowing one way or the other. And I tell you both this. If Daddy did kill Mama, if he really did do it? I'll push his butt down these lighthouse stairs myself and pray he breaks his damn sorry neck.'

The phone is ringing, but I can't open my eyes. My head aches and my mouth is dry. My face is sore and throbbing, and by the time I reach blindly for the phone the ringing has stopped.

I feel like I could sleep straight through the day. Ashby and Claire and I wound up in a Mexican restaurant last night after we left the lighthouse on Hunting Island. I drank coffee over dinner, watching my siblings swill margaritas and listening to Claire rant about what she would do to Daddy. It took four Excedrin PMs to settle my caffeine-hopped body to sleep.

Hank appears in the doorway. He is shirtless and skinny, hair sticking straight up. 'Mom? Uncle Ashby's on the phone.'

I put my arm over my face. 'Ashby? What time is it?'

'Six-twenty.'

'I can't believe he's conscious.'

'He doesn't sound too good.'

I pick up the phone.

'Georgie, it's Ashby. Wake up and listen. I have something really bad to tell you.'

'What's wrong?'

'I just got off the phone with the police. Hell, Georgie, I don't know how you say stuff like this.'

I open my eyes and stare at the wall.

'It's Dad, Georgie, he's dead. Are you there? Georgie, are you there?'

'I'm here.'

'He died in the lighthouse – our lighthouse, on Hunting Island. He fell down the spiral stairs. Selby says it looks like he severed his spinal column and broke his neck.'

My brother sobs, and I close my eyes.

6

The days are beginning to blur in my mind, and I feel
peculiar and unreal. I am driving to Hunting Island at
the break of dawn, and this time it is my father who
is dead. I am not alone this morning. Hank is beside
me, in the seat.

The first thing I notice is that Selby is here. His back
is turned and he does not see us. The police cars parked
at angles and the flashing lights and the yellow barri-
cade tape form a backdrop to these upright men and
women in uniform. All of this I notice, but what strikes
me, what grips me, is Claire's car – parked where we
left it so innocently the night before.

'Aunt Claire's already here,' Hank says, following
my stare. There are pine needles on the hood of Claire's
Cougar, and the windshield is fogged with dew.

Ashby's Land Rover pulls up beside us, Claire in the
front seat beside my brother. Hank frowns and looks
at me. My son asks no questions, but his mind is
working. He lives behind the impenetrable reserve of
the adolescent male, and I have no idea what he is
thinking.

Claire, innocent heart, goes straight to the Cougar,
brushing the pine needles away. Her red curls are
disheveled, edging over the neckline of her hooded cotton
jacket. A man in a suit says something to Selby, who
frowns and heads toward Claire. Selby looks different

somehow, and seeing him makes me uncomfortable. Part of it is the idea of dealing with him in a professional capacity, civilian to cop, and part of it is the sure knowledge that he has been sleeping with my mother.

Two men in pressed khakis and golf shirts are talking to a man in uniform who is clearly a presence in the Beaufort sheriff's department, which will be handling my father's case. I learn later that his last name is Markum. The perfection of his uniform is clear even from a distance, and the tall hat looks new, though I'm sure it's not. He is black and broad-shouldered and has the unsmiling demeanor and rigid posture of an ex-marine. The Beaufort sheriff's office is full of them – men who come to Parris Island, South Carolina, and decide not to leave. For a small town, we have high-caliber law enforcement.

A uniformed officer is carrying a plastic bag toward Selby.

'*Those are mine.*' There is a lull in activity, and my sister's voice comes through loud and clear. Claire glances at me and Ashby. 'These guys found my shoes.'

I exchange looks with my brother. Claire got her flip-flops stuck in the mud as we left last night and abandoned them for a pair of boat shoes in the trunk of her car. Unfortunately, Ashby and I are too far away to shut her up. Out of the corner of my eye, I see Hank wince and glance upward.

I jog over to Claire but am distracted by the bump of a gurney coming out of a morgue van. The gurney is empty. Two men wheel it toward the lighthouse. I change direction and am halfway across the parking lot when I hear Selby's voice.

'*Georgie.*'

I can tell from the tone that this isn't the first time he has called.

We are frozen in place – Ashby, two steps behind me, Hank and Claire standing close to Claire's car. Selby's look takes us all in, and he motions us away from the lighthouse and into a huddle. I hesitate, but the others are going. I glance through the trees toward the lighthouse. Uniformed officers are walking the area in a five-hundred-yard perimeter. Clearly, there is no quarter given to my status as family of the deceased. I move with reluctant obedience. I am being handled and managed, and it makes me feel small.

Selby gathers us to him like a star quarterback plotting strategy with the team. But this is a Selby I don't know, and he is looking us all over with a cool professionalism that smells and tastes like cop. We pretend not to be aware of the attention we draw. Small as Beaufort is, I do not recognize all these uniformed women and men. Clearly, they are all excited. My father's death is a very big deal.

I will soon learn that appearance is everything when dealing with the police. I would like to talk privately to my siblings, but Selby has short-circuited this option. Hank has become very silent, and I see with a mixture of pain and pride that life on the streets has made him wise. I wish to God my sister were half as smart. I would give anything to have taken her car with us last night.

Selby tucks a finger under my chin and lifts gently, eyes narrowed as he studies my face. 'Where'd the bruises come from?'

I know I am blushing. 'I fell. Bad step on the back of my porch.'

My sister glances at me and I think what a terrible liar she is. I'm not sure why I don't tell the truth. Actually, I am sure. It is self-preservation as well as family reticence that keeps me mute.

Selby does not challenge my explanation, but neither does he believe me. His face seems as creased and tired as the uniform he has no doubt worn all night.

'You all have had way too much to bear.'

In my heart, I think Selby means it. But inside, layered deep, is the recognition that this abrupt shift to family friend and sympathy will topple all our defenses. We are vulnerable and looking for a friend. Oddly, I begin to notice small things. I can hear the ocean. I can hear the wind in the branches – pine trees and palms. The sand underfoot is white flecked with black, like a pound of salt defiled by a shake or two of pepper.

Ashby throws his shoulders back. The man of the family, taking charge. 'I still don't understand how this happened. What you've told us doesn't make any sense. And I want to see my father, before you take him away.'

'From what we can piece together, Ashby, your father came out here to the lighthouse late last night or early this morning. We don't know why he was here or what he was doing. But it was an odd time for him to be out.' Selby looks to us for an explanation.

'We were all out here too, but earlier, right before dark.' Claire talks quickly, breathlessly, as if the words are exploding from her chest. 'And that's my car.'

Selby nods. 'We ran the plates. What were all of you doing out here last night?'

I try not to frown. Surely the proper thing for Selby to do is separate us and see if we give the same

81

explanation. Instead, he is asking us questions while we are all together, all within earshot. He is giving us a chance to get our stories straight.

Claire puts a hand on Selby's arm and whispers, standing on tiptoe. 'We were drinking beer in the light-house.' She sounds so much like a guilty teenager, even Hank smiles.

'Why in the lighthouse?' If the police have found telltale evidence of our party last night, I can't read it in Selby's face.

'Sibling meeting,' says Ashby.

'That doesn't explain what you were doing in the lighthouse.'

I manage a smile. 'Like you haven't known we've been hanging out there since we were kids.'

Selby permits his one-sided smile, which answers my question; he does know. 'So your dad came out here with you?'

Claire shakes her head. 'No, it was just us. Us three. Hank was at home.'

'When did you leave the lighthouse?'

'About an hour after dark. Around nine.'

'Together?'

I take over the story. 'Yeah, together, that's why we left Claire's car. I was the designated driver – and Claire and Ashby needed one last night.' I glance at my brother and sister. 'They had a lot of beer. Then we went to eat and they got even more drunk on margaritas at the restaurant, so I took them both home. Believe me, the staff will remember us. We were pretty loud.'

'When did you come out here and pick up your car?' Selby asks, looking at Ashby.

'I didn't have a car; Claire picked me up.'

The gurney wheels slam down the bottom concrete step of the lighthouse, and I turn and see the thick black bag that contains the mortal remains of my father. Claire catches her breath.

Selby takes her shoulder and turns her head. 'Don't look, Claire.'

But I have to look, and so do Ashby and Hank. It is really my father there in that bag.

'Did he suffer?' Claire's voice is so tight my throat aches just to hear it.

Ashby gives her a hug. 'He didn't suffer, Claire. If he fell all the way down the stairs—' My brother looks a question at Selby, but gets no response. 'He would have died on impact. It was over before he knew he'd hit.'

Claire's sobs are contagious enough to bring tears to my eyes. Her voice is muffled, but the words 'my fault' and 'so guilty' emerge.

Selby pats Claire's back. 'Why is it your fault, Claire?'

'I was just so *mad* at him.'

'Hush, Claire. Just because you were mad at him doesn't make it your fault.' Ashby is thinking what I am. That we don't need Claire bringing up the exact details of our last conversation – particularly the part where she threatened to push Daddy down the stairs.

Selby steps closer. 'What do you mean, Claire? Why should you feel guilty?'

'He knew we were all mad at him. It might have been the last straw after Mama dying. Isn't that why he jumped?'

'What makes you think he jumped?' Selby says.

Claire's mouth opens and closes.

'We thought he committed suicide,' Hank explains.

Does Hank think that, I wonder? It is my opinion that people like my father don't take their life.

I look to Ashby. 'Remember where the railing was pulled away from the steps? Maybe he lost his balance up there and fell.'

'Your father didn't jump,' is all Selby says.

Claire tilts her head, looks over her shoulder at the gurney that rolls my father away. 'But then what do you think happened? Georgie's right, we were up there last night, and the railing was broke on that third set of stairs. Go up and look, you can see for yourself. That's got to be what happened. He just fell.'

'I'm sorry, I know this is hard to hear, but your father was still alive this morning when he was discovered. The park ranger was driving through, doing his rounds, and he noticed your father's car and saw the lighthouse door was open. Your father was conscious then, Claire, and what he said led us to believe he was pushed.'

Claire's voice is rising. 'So you're saying it wasn't an accident? That somebody *pushed* Daddy down those stairs?'

'I'm saying we're treating it, at present, as a homicide, pending results of the autopsy.'

The roof of my mouth feels like a dry wad of cotton.

'Did he say who?' I ask.

'Ranger says he died before he could name names.'

'What exactly did he say?' Hank asks.

Selby shakes his head. 'Sorry, son, I can't tell you the details just now.'

We are silent, all of us. Wondering about these words.

'I want to see him,' Ashby says.

'I'll let you know later when you can view the remains.'

Ashby's muscles are going rigid, and I wonder if he is going to hold his temper. Claire is turning away. Selby is still talking to Hank, welcoming him home, I think, but I can't make out the words. The only thing I hear is the hum in my ears.

Selby takes a sudden step in my direction. 'You okay over there, Georgie girl?'

'Just fine,' I say, but it is a lie, because my knees turn soft and Selby manages to catch me just before I fall.

Ashby, Claire and I invite Hank to go with us to our parents' house, but he wants to go home for a while to get some sleep. He plans to spend the rest of the day tracking down old friends, many of whom are still in the post-teenage time warp of working low-end jobs to fund their evenings of drinking and smoking out.

Ashby and Claire arrive ahead of me. My brother's Land Rover is parked right by the front porch of the house. The wind is feathering through the trees, making the leaves hiss, and from time to time I hear the faint clang of the wind chimes that hang from a rusty chain on the porch.

The front door is unlocked, and I find my brother and sister settled around the cheap marble table in the kitchen. Claire is crying softly, and Ashby is slumped in a chair. There is a rinsed water glass in the center of the table, yesterday's paper, still rolled tight and unread, a sixty-count bottle of Walgreen's aspirin, lysine capsules, a packet of Tagamet and a wad of grocery-store coupons.

'Hey, guys.'

'Hi, Georgie.'

'Hey, you okay?'

I go to the kitchen pantry and, sure enough, my mother has stockpiled boxes of Kleenex bought at Kmart on sale. There are over a hundred rolls of toilet paper in the basement. I put a fresh box of tissues on the table for Claire.

My sister sniffs and grabs three tissues, *slip-slip-slip*, so they make a wad in her fist. She blows her nose like a trumpet and nobody blinks. We have shared bathrooms, playpens, chicken pox, toys, cars and money.

'Georgie, tell Claire that just because she said something about Dad falling down the stairs, none of this is her fault.'

Clearly, this is an ongoing conversation.

'Oh, come on, Claire, this isn't about you.'

Ashby glares at me.

'What I mean is, it's just a weird coincidence. You have nothing to feel guilty about.'

I haven't had my morning coffee, and my head aches with caffeine deprivation. I am the only coffee drinker in my family; my father gave up caffeine seven years ago. I wander through the kitchen, grimacing at the avocado-green appliances that have been here since the Seventies. My mother does not have a coffee pot, but somewhere there is a stainless-steel percolator that she drags out for bridge parties. God knows where she's stashed it. I open all the breadboxes, five in all – my mother was something of a collector – but there is nothing but old bread. There is a little yellow teapot on the stove, and I rinse it and fill it with water and put it on to boil.

'Is there anything to drink in the fridge?' Ashby asks me.

I find Diet Coke in the fridge and set a can each before Ashby and Claire. We were raised on Coca-Cola and there is nothing I like better, but it is no substitute for coffee, plus it makes me gain weight.

'It's so unbelievable,' Claire says. 'I can't believe they're both gone. This house is just full of their presence, or their essence, or whatever you want to call it. It's like they're still here. Like I can just open the bedroom door and Mama will be there.'

I open the pantry and unearth a jar of instant coffee. I think it best not to speculate on its age, especially if the greasy smudges on the label are any clue. It is entirely unfair that my head is aching when it was Claire and Ashby who swilled liquor like pigs last night.

My brother opens the tab on his Coke, and it snips and hisses and I imagine the cold crisp tang of cola syrup and fizz. My father's kitchen is clean. My mother's housekeeping was indifferent. On his own, my father is neat.

I slump down in the chair across from my sister.

'Why does all this stuff keep happening to us?' Claire says.

I close my eyes. I can see the future, and in it Ashby and I are going over and over this with Claire when we are all ancient and sitting in rocking chairs on the front porch. I hear a hiss from the stove. The teapot is already boiling. I get up to make my coffee.

'*Georgie.*'

'What is it, Claire?'

'Stop slamming cabinets, will you please?'

'What are you looking for?' Ashby asks.

'A coffee mug, if that's all right.'

'There were forty-five mugs in the cabinet you just slammed. Are you looking for one in particular?'

Claire rolls her swollen, red-rimmed eyes. 'You have to ask?'

It is true that I am picky about coffee mugs. I also think orange juice tastes best in some champagne flutes that I bought in an estate sale in Charleston. I find what I want in a cabinet next to the sink. It is an orange mug with a crack down the side from the time I froze Coca-Cola in it the summer I was ten. Coffee tastes especially good in this cup.

I pour water over coffee crystals. 'The problem with you, Claire—'

Ashby shushes me, and my sister freezes. Someone is fumbling the lock on the front door. There is a pause, then the unmistakable squeak of a hinge. Then footsteps, slow, uncertain and soft.

'It's Daddy,' Claire whispers.

A figure appears in the doorway. Claire sobs and I catch my breath.

'Hello there, Mrs Blanchard,' my brother says. 'This is certainly a big surprise.'

Carla Blanchard does not look like a typical mistress, but she is clearly my father's type – intelligent and well endowed. Her hair is blond and gray, and her eyebrows are heavy and dark. She is widowed and works at the bank with my father. Her late husband, Clive, was something of a son of a bitch, which explains her attraction to our dad. She has two grown children, a son and a daughter, both of them active in the Tazewall Baptist Church.

'Lord, Ashby, you kids like to scare me so bad I had a stroke.'

'I'm afraid we have some bad news,' Ashby says.

'Oh, sweethearts, I know all about Fielding.' My father's current mistress wipes her nose with a wad of Kleenex, and I see her face is red. She walks into the kitchen, the heels of her navy Pappagallo flats clomping on the linoleum. She is wearing a khaki raincoat over a navy skirt that lands a neat two inches below her knees, and a beige blouse that has a long loop of bow on the neckline and is buttoned tightly.

'I thought you-all would be at the hospital.' She stares at each of us in turn. She seems to have a lot of confidence for a woman who has barged into the kitchen of our house. 'Now, you kids, I want you to know that I'm here for you. I know how hard a time this is going to be. I know how Vicky and Ben took on when we lost our Clive.'

'You want to sit down? Can I get you a cup of coffee or a Diet Coke?' Claire would be polite to a burglar.

'No, honey, thanks, I've got to run. I just came to pick up a few things.' She goes to the stove and grabs the handle of the teapot, which is still hot with the water I've boiled. '*There's* that teapot. Hot, isn't it? I guess I'd best get it another time.'

She opens a kitchen drawer, the second one, where my mother kept the lacy for-company tea towels we hardly ever used, but my brother is up on his feet and somehow manages to close the drawer without slamming Carla Blanchard's overly manicured fingers.

'What are you doing here, Mrs Blanchard, if it's not too much to ask?'

Carla Blanchard puts her hands in the pockets of the raincoat. She is the kind of woman who actually wears a raincoat on a cloudy day, even if it's hot outside. Her propriety likely appeals to my father. He has always preferred the classic female to the young one.

'I told you, Ashby, I'm here to pick up a few things, and there's no need for you to be rude. You children know how things stood between your father and me. You know he and your mama were going to get a divorce. You need to be adults about this. Lord knows, I told your daddy I didn't want it, but he wanted to make sure I was taken care of all of my life. He knew how hard it was for me, going back to work after Clive left me with all those debts.'

'What is she babbling about?' Claire asks my brother.

'I'm talking about your father's will.' There is a hard note in Carla's voice.

'Daddy put you in his will?' Claire says.

'I pretty much am his will, but I tell you like I told him I didn't want it. But he said, "Carla, I want you to be taken care of," and he made out a new will the day after your mama passed away. And no matter what any of you think, he was completely devastated over your mother, and I think he really understood, then, what I went through with Clive.'

'Carla.' I figure we may as well be on a first-name basis. 'I can't find my mother's Fiestaware. It was always in that cabinet next to the stove. Do you happen to know where it might be?'

Carla puts her hands on her hips. She has a trim figure and nice legs. 'Oh, yes, I know exactly where it is. Your father asked me to take it. I gave Vicky my set of CorningWare and, frankly, I took that Fiestaware as a favor to your father to make him more at home in my kitchen. I always think you should take the time to create a festive table setting.'

'Those dishes belonged to my grandmother,' I say. 'I'd like to have them back.'

'Well, Georgie, I just told you I gave my Corning-Ware to Vicky. It's not like those old dishes are worth very much. They're full of chips and cracks.'

'Give them back, Carla.'

'Georgie, those dishes are special to me. Fielding brought them over himself, right before he died.'

'They belonged to my mother and my grandmother, and my father had no right giving them to you.'

'That's not the way the law reads, honey, not as I understand it.'

Ashby stands slowly and puts himself between me and Carla Blanchard. 'Okay, then. We've cleared the air here, and I think we all know where we stand. You were Dad's fuckbuddy, and he had to sweeten the pot. We get that. It's time for you to leave now, Mrs Blanchard, and I'd like to have your key.'

Carla Blanchard goes very red in the face. 'There is no excuse for such language, Ashby. And I'm sorry, but I have every right to have this key. This house belongs to me, and everything in it is mine. Out of consideration for your feelings, I won't ask you for *your* key just now, but I will be consulting Mr Wilbanks about changing all of these locks.'

Carla Blanchard leaves with the last word.

'Do you think it's true?' Claire says. My brother gets up and opens the kitchen drawer. 'Ashby, what are you looking for?'

'Trying to figure out what that woman was after.'

'The teapot,' I say.

'She came over here for more than a teapot.' Ashby methodically unpacks the drawer, setting items on the stovetop and kitchen counter. Lace tea towels, a tablecloth, also lace, a red oven mitt in the shape of a rooster, the box of small crystal-and-silver-topped salt and pepper shakers, a small manila envelope.

Ashby reads the preprinted address: 'Beaufort Hospital'. He rips the end off the envelope. 'This is it. Daddy must have set these aside when the hospital gave them to him.'

Ashby spreads Mama's rings out on the kitchen table – a thin gold wedding band, a matching band with three empty slots that used to hold diamond chips, and a solitaire half-carat diamond ring Daddy gave Mama on their twentieth anniversary.

Claire rubs a finger on the maple tabletop. 'How'd Carla Blanchard know where the rings were?'

'Don't be stupid, Claire. Daddy told her.'

Claire picks up the solitaire. 'This is what she was after. It's a perfect diamond, no flaws. Daddy paid a mint for this thing.'

Ashby gets that silly quizzical look he has when he's upset. 'Do you think she's right? Do you think Dad really left everything to *her*?'

'We can ask his attorney.' Claire's comment is punctuated with a largely unattractive snorting noise. Daddy's attorney and best friend, Eugene Wilbanks, is likely executor of the estate. None of us like Wilbanks, but he has been a presence since we were kids.

'I bet there's a copy of the will in his desk,' I say. 'Let's go take a look.'

My father's office is at the top of the house, on the third, attic level. My brother and sister wonder out loud, as we climb the third-floor staircase, why Daddy didn't have his office downstairs. I have always had the opinion that it is because the attic is the one place in the house my mother would never go.

I run ahead and am first in the attic, which is dark and shadowed. My father's presence here is strong. Light filters in through the grimy windows beneath the eaves at the back of the house. If this were my office, I would wash those panes. I feel nervous and glance quickly at my father's chair, to reassure myself that it is indeed empty. I stand on tiptoe and strain my fingertips to reach the light cord that dangles from the ceiling. My brother, who is right behind me, reaches easily over my head and pulls. The seventy-five-watt bulb sends light lapping over the massive and scarred walnut desk that sits in the center of the room, leaving the corners of the attic in shadow. The cord swings from side to side in a gentle easy motion.

I look sideways at my brother and sister, and I know I will always remember how lost they look as they stand in our father's attic office. They want so badly to believe that our father loved us. I wonder how long they will be able to stay convinced.

The stench of old cigars, cheap acrid Tampa Nuggets, is thicker than the dust. The ashtray on my father's desk is a Sixties relic, green ceramic and shaped like a giant leaf. It still holds a half-smoked cigar loosely wedged in the center, and there must be ten stubs and enough ashes to fill a small urn. If we decide to cremate Daddy, there will be more ashes left over from the cigars he smoked than from his mortal remains.

The floor creaks as we circle my father's desk. The floors are solid oak, soft with the patina wood acquires from years of wear and use. I would fill this room with bookshelves, add windows and light, and a red-gold oriental rug. But if Carla Blanchard isn't lying, this beautiful house will go straight into her grabby, beringed and manicured hands.

Ashby picks through the papers on the desk. I am careful not to step forward and take them from him. Ashby is so severely dyslexic he came out of high school unable to read. He once told me that to him the printed word looks like a page of black fleas that move in and out of focus. Ashby's big dream was to graduate from college and make a splash in the business world. I think he really wanted to be an attorney. Instead, he fishes for shrimp just outside of the Ace Basin Sound, and every year his profit is choked back by government regulations. Ashby says that in forty years the shrimp fishermen of today will be a memory. He says the average fisherman can't afford the new boats, and the old ones are deteriorating. And in Ashby's opinion, the South Carolina legislature and the federal government are more concerned with the pleasure of wealthy sportsmen than the livelihood of those who fish.

Claire reaches for the framed picture on my father's desk, a shot of my father and Eugene Wilbanks. Daddy and Wilbanks are inseparable, lifelong ex-marines who formed a concrete bond at an early age. Wilbanks is a lawyer, and though he works in the local district attorney's office, he takes care of all my father's legal business. No doubt he drew up my father's will.

I am struck by how at home my father and Wilbanks look in the perfect-pressed Marine Corps-issued cammies, posing on the golf course at Parris Island, where they spent their happiest years terrorizing new recruits. They were trim then, hard-muscled and at the top of their game: the breaking and building of new marines. The way they stand and the way they smile make it clear that while Daddy and Wilbanks are not tied by blood, they are tied by something stronger. I have never seen my father look so content or complete.

The picture was taken before the incident of the Hardigree Seven. It was Wilbanks who stood beside my father when the rest of the world wanted his blood. It was Wilbanks, attached to the judge advocate general, who came to my father's legal defense. Wilbanks, who kept my parents' social life going, with invitations to country-club dances and backyard barbecues in the days when my classmates stared at me whenever I entered a room, when the grocery-store checkout clerk turned suddenly cool.

Ashby is frowning over the papers. 'Did you-all know that Daddy and Wilbanks hired a private detective?'

Claire grins. 'What, were they having Mama followed?'

I think momentarily of Selby.

'What is it?' Claire asks. Ashby tosses the papers down on the desk, and Claire scoops them up while Ashby starts opening drawers. 'Hell, Ashby, this is a huge bill. Daddy and Wilbanks paid this guy over five thousand dollars.'

I know that Claire has a shoebox of unpaid bills under her bed. Her divorce is coming at a tough time, and you can't run two households for the price of one.

She looks ground down and tired. I have attributed this to grief over Mama, but now I wonder just how bad her finances are. I take a quick look at her hands and I see what I need to see. Her nails are cut down to the quick. My elegant sister has given up manicures. Her hair is curling over her collar and I wonder when she last had it cut. These are the first things a mother gives up – I know from experience. I think back over the last few months. I can't remember seeing Claire buy anything that wasn't for her kids, and last night she said she hadn't been out to eat in weeks because she'd been on a home-cooking jag. I should have figured this out sooner. Claire would starve before she'd ask for help. But for the first time in my life I have a cushion of pieces to sell, and it feels good to know I can bail her out.

'Here we go.' Ashby pulls a folder out of the desk. He opens it deliberately, with his thick, scarred fisherman's fingers. 'Last Will and Testament of Lena Strickland Smallwood.'

Ashby hands the will over to me. It is clearly out of date, obviously written when my brother and sister and I were very young children. 'This isn't right. Is this the will Daddy filed for probate?'

Ashby nods. 'Filed at the courthouse the afternoon after she died.'

'But it doesn't make sense. This is years out of date. I know Mama had money set aside for all the grandkids, for college. Didn't she tell you that, Claire?'

'Only about a hundred times. But I always told her not to worry about it.'

'So did I, but that didn't stop her. And that was even *before* she inherited all that money from Uncle Dill.'

'Maybe she just never got around to it, Georgie. You know how people are about wills. And she wasn't getting out much, with her knees so bad.' Claire puts her head in her hands. 'We shouldn't even be doing this. Looking at wills when Daddy just died.'

'We better get on the ball, Claire, and be smart about stuff, with that Blanchard woman breathing down our necks. Think we can get a locksmith out here this afternoon to get the locks rekeyed?'

I sit on the edge of my father's desk, something I'd never have done while he was alive. I am aware, in a dark corner of my mind, that already his presence is going, draining slowly like the last bit of daylight goes as the sun drops and darkness falls. My father is dead. His presence wanes, unable to withstand the living onslaught of his children.

'Ashby? Did you hear me?'

My brother has an odd look on his face.

'There are copies of insurance policies here. Look at this. It comes to about five hundred and fifty thousand. Why on earth did Mama have so much life insurance?'

'Are you telling me Daddy was getting over half a million dollars of insurance money, in addition to all of Mama's estate?' Claire has her back pressed to the wall. She is in the shadows and I can't see her face. 'Because I went to Daddy for a loan two days ago, when the electric company cut my power off. And he gave me about twenty of those old boxes of Chef Boyardee pizza mix Mama had hoarded in the basement. He told me life was full of hard decisions and I might have to get rid of my dogs. And I asked him about Mama's college money for the kids, and he said there wasn't any. I had to cash in some of the kids' savings bonds to get the power back on. I mean, I know it isn't up to him to pay my bills, but all I wanted was a loan to see me through, just for the short term.'

'Claire, why didn't you call me?'

'Why didn't you call *me*,' Ashby says. 'Me and Georgie will look out for you, won't we, Georgie?'

'Of course.'

My sister shakes her head. 'I'm okay.'

'Claire, don't be absurd. We're helping you, you don't have a choice, so forget it. And throw those damn pizzas away, they must be a hundred years old.'

'The kids and I ate one of them and I have to say it was truly godawful.'

'We'll bury them in the coffin with Daddy,' I say.

My brother and sister exchange looks. I have gone too far.

⬇

As I turn the wheel and pull Big Mama out in front of my shop, I can't get over the image of Claire being turned down by Daddy for a loan. A month ago I would not have believed any of this.

'*Mom.*' Hank is on the balcony, waving his arms. I wince to see him jumping up and down on the sagging wood. I reflect on the peeling white paint and how great that balcony will look when I get the time and the money to fix it up. I have been living like a zombie since Hank's been away. '*Stay there,*' he shouts, and I wonder what's up. It is 11.30 a.m. on one of the worst days of my life, and I don't want to face one more thing.

'What is it, Hank?' But I am talking to the air. Mentally I follow my son's progress through the great

98

room, the hall, the stairs. He bursts through the shop doors and runs to the truck. He must have jumped the last six steps or gone over the side of the staircase. His shirt-tail is flying, and he runs to the passenger's door. We are in a hurry, whatever is up.

'Ribault Street and hang a right. Out Rodex Road to the pound, Mom, I think I found Cousin.'

My mother's missing dog. My heartbeat picks up.

'They're supposed to be putting her *down* this morning, Mom, I've got the janitor holding things up.'

I drive, making time, wondering how Cousin got so far from home. 'Are you sure you got the right dog?'

'Chester said an old black cocker spaniel who bites people when they try to pick her up.'

'That's Cousin.' She has stinky ears too. Yeast infections. 'Chester is who?'

'The maintenance man. He works nights too, at Beaufort High. He helped me out once or twice. He's a good guy.'

I wonder how Chester, who works at night at the high school, has helped Hank out, but I'm not asking. Right now I'm giving my driving 110 percent, noting the red car coming from the left-hand side of the intersection, the cement truck braking just ahead, the groan of straining discs. Hank is leaning forward in his seat, and his shoulders strain ahead like that will get us there faster.

'Fasten your seat belt,' I tell him.

Hank taps the windshield. 'Turn left, Mom. It's a short cut. Come on, it's faster.'

I swerve left in front of an oncoming Dodge pickup, and the man driving is making a gesture but he's eating my dust.

'God, Mom,' Hank says.

Approval? Disapproval? I have no idea. We are coming up on another intersection.

'Right here, at the light, then take the next left. Don't worry, I know where I'm going.'

'Okay.' I check my watch. Ten till twelve. The Humane Society opens at noon on weekdays. I asked Daddy once why they opened so late, and he said it was because they used the morning to euthanize the dogs.

Five till twelve. And I look up and see where I am.

'Damn,' I say, gunning it the last mile. I can't believe we got here so fast. 'I had no idea you could get there this way.'

'You've only lived here all your life.'

Gravel crackles under Big Mama's tires as we coast to the door. The lot is empty; employee cars must be out in back. Hank is out of the truck before we've rolled to a stop. He leaves the passenger door hanging open and runs to the cinder-block building that houses the Beaufort County Humane Society. He has on a blue flannel shirt over a white T-shirt, and it flies out behind him. One thing I can say for my son, he is quick on his feet.

I hear the drum of glass as Hank pounds the front door. Over Hank's shoulder I can see partitions and empty desks. There are no people, and the lights are off.

'*Dammit,*' Hank shouts, and I see his point. If we wait for somebody to come to the door we'll be too late, too late.

'Try around back.' I step sideways, otherwise Hank is going to mow me down. He is there ahead of me, slamming a fist into a rusty orange double-wide metal door that is locked by a banded hasp three quarters of the way up.

'Open up. *Police*.' There is sweat on Hank's forehead.

The door opens a crack and a girl peers around the edge. 'Hank Smallwood?' I hear dogs barking. The girl is grinning. '*Police* my ass. You like to made me pee my pants.' This girl is happy to see my son, and I am thinking that two years may have gone by, but some things don't change. I think Hank knows every female in Beaufort between the age of fourteen and twenty-one. They used to stop me in the streets and ask when he would come home. And once or twice, I would get the feeling one of them knew something she wasn't telling.

'Y'all killed any dogs this morning, Chrissy?'

She nods, sad but matter-of-fact. 'We've euthanized two already, got one more to go.'

'Show me quick, will you? I think they've got my dog in there.'

Chrissy's round little face seems to draw tight. Underneath the pancake makeup and eyeliner is a sweet young face ravaged by acne. 'Down that way, Hank, but you better come on.'

The two of them run ahead. I look at the clock in the hallway, one of the big round institutionalized kinds like you see in waiting rooms and schools. The second hand jitters and jerks and shows twelve o'clock on the dot.

I pass an open doorway and get a glimpse of sinks and stainless steel tables. The floor is concrete, still damp and dark around the edges, as if it has recently been hosed down. I hear the animals, a cacophony of barking and whimpering. On my left is another open doorway. The odor is strong here, animals, disinfectant and fear. I catch a glimpse of dogs in cages. They are afraid. Some of them bark, others are silent. Over the noise I am aware of the voices of men.

I turn the corner and see a man in a navy jumpsuit shaking his head at a guy in a shirt and tie who stands with arms folded across his chest. He seems to be guarding the entrance of a door marked AUTHORIZED PERSONNEL. A red light glows over the words NO ENTRY. I can hear Hank shouting, but I can't make out the words.

I pick my pace up to a run, blow past the two men, and through the double doors. I have the element of surprise, and a split second to see the look of satisfaction on Hank's face. He is right behind me.

I stop hard, the door swinging shut behind us. The seconds are stretching out like they do when everything happens so quickly it feels, perversely, like slow motion. A blonde, blue-jacketed technician stands over a small black dog lying quietly on the table. The woman's mouth opens wetly. In her right hand, raised over Cousin Beauregard, is a hypodermic needle.

'*No.*' Hank flings his body over the table to get between Cousin and that needle.

'What the hell do you people think you're doing?'

Hank reaches up and snatches the hypodermic out of the technician's hand.

'*Hey.*' The woman's face turns red.

'Did you use it?' I ask, moving in closer. Cousin Beauregard is so quiet I fear the worst, but her eyes are wide and her sides heaving. Whatever struggle and protest she made, whether she snapped or squirmed or whimpered in fear, those moments have passed. My mother's little dog has given up.

Hank unfastens the buckles that hold Cousin to the table, and I take the syringe from his hand, check the liquid level and realize I have been holding my breath.

'It's okay, Hank. She hasn't used the shot.'

'Is this your dog?' the woman asks.

Cousin's stump tail moves weakly, and I see from her wet brown eyes that two years is as nothing to a dog who has been waiting for her favorite boy to come home. Hank lifts Cousin from the table and she squirms like a pig, so he sits on the floor and holds her in his lap. His fingers fumble with the stubby blue muzzle over her mouth, and I unclasp the buckle behind her head.

Cousin is up in Hank's face, licking his neck, his nose, his ears. Hank talks to the dog in a kind voice I have never heard him use to mere humans. I bend down to pet Cousin Beauregard, and she licks my hand.

Hank stands behind me, glaring at anyone who looks his way. He keeps a hand on the dog, who sticks to his right leg as if she is attached by Velcro. The guy in the tie is going to charge me $72.50 to spring Cousin from the pound. He has had the grace to settle for a check.

'You understand, ma'am, the man who dropped her off, he said she was a stray he found. And she didn't have a collar. You might want to get a microchip put in her neck. That way if she gets lost again, we can find her. We have a scanner, just like they have at the Piggly Wiggly, and your name and address come up.'

He is talking nonstop while I write out the check, and he keeps looking over my shoulder at Hank and Cousin.

I sign my name and look up. 'This guy who dropped Cousin off. Did he give you his name?'

The man frowns at the record. 'It says here Henry Simmons.'

'Henry Simmons,' I say. I know this name. Henry Simmons was a cousin of my father's who died of a brain tumor when he was twenty-nine. My father used to laugh about how Henry Simmons used to go to all the family reunions calling 'Cousin Beauregard!' as a sort of in-joke, because Southerners were always supposed to name their kids stupid stuff like Beauregard and call each other Sissy and Bubba. That's how Cousin got her name.

I tear off the check. 'What's the date on your sheet there?'

'If you mean the day the dog was dropped off, it was the third of June.'

'You sure?'

'Absolutely. June the third, two o'clock in the afternoon.'

June third. The day my mother got sick.

I thank the man, for what I am not sure, and Hank carries Cousin to the truck and tucks her into the seat between us. She licks Hank's chin and shivers.

There is an image in my mind, a memory, of Cousin curled in a circle at the foot of Mama's bed, growling at Daddy. I hear my mother's voice, telling Cousin to hush, explaining how Cousin is getting confused and some days won't let anybody near. But the dog has no objection when I sit on Mama's bed and is happy to let me pet her, so long as I don't touch the chronically infected ears. My mother goes on and on about how Cousin has always had a difficult personality, that you can't pick her up or she bites, that she's never been good with kids, except for Hank.

'Mom?' Hank looks up from fiddling with the radio dial. 'We going?'

'Sure, son.' I am barely aware of my son sitting beside me in the truck. The vision is one I cannot shake – Cousin at the end of Mama's bed, growling at Daddy when he comes in the room.

7

Day four after my mother's death. Her funeral has been delayed due to my father's own mysterious death and I am on my way to Burgin's Antiques. I cannot overcome the slightly queasy sensation in my stomach. Outside, the sun is shining. This is very important. Big Mama is loaded down. Today I will have to part with a green Lloyd Loom chair I found at a flea market under a pile of old doll clothes and encyclopedias; a nineteenth-century mahogany bergère, also green; an eighteenth-century French caned beechwood chair; and the one that will break my heart – a hand-painted pine Dover chest, circa 1800, with the original locks, one missing hinge, and all the original legs. I have been hoarding and restoring these pieces with the intent of selling them in due time, to the right person, and for the right sum.

Like many good plans before it, this one is totally shot. I have looked under my sister's bed and I have seen the shoebox full of bills. I will spend my afternoon at the Beaufort Electric Co-Op, Bell South, and the Beaufort County Water Company paying past-due balances and averting utility cut-offs. I don't know how my sister has managed for this long without help, but I will show up on her doorstep later today with a check large enough to see her through the next few months with no worries.

The silicon-rich South Carolina asphalt sparkles like a layer of crushed diamonds over the flat two-lane blacktop road. I take Highway 17 out of town. The route is familiar.

I used to work at Burgin's, off and on, while I got started in my own restoration business. There weren't a lot of jobs in Beaufort then. There aren't now. This town consists of fishermen, truck farmers, marines and their families, have-nots, a struggling middle class, and the fabulously wealthy, who like to savor the sedate comforts of a small, occasionally elegant, southern town. We even have a movie star or two hereabouts. They come to Beaufort on location and fall in love. Beaufort is host to Hollywood more often than you might expect. *The Big Chill* was filmed here, and so was *Forrest Gump*. Julia Roberts and Lyle Lovett stayed at the Beaufort Inn, where the rooms are furnished with antiques and VCRs and the front desk can lend you a videotape of all the movies ever made in this town. It's part of our charm.

I turn on the radio. Hank's best efforts have yielded nothing but static, and as usual my only choice is 98.1 THE BULL. My son's tinkering has increased the bass so that the front dash throbs in accordance with the volume. While Alan Jackson sings 'Crazy 'Bout a Mercury,' I tap a nervous finger on the sun-baked steering wheel and run figures in my head. It's a given that Burgin will cheat me; I'm just trying to decide by how much. He is the last person in the world I want to do business with, a fact he is more than well aware of. By virtue of walking through his door, my desperation is apparent and he gets the upper hand. That's how it goes when you need money fast.

The turn indicator clicks as I pause to let a Mazda pickup go by in the oncoming lane. I turn left into the weed and gravel lot in front of a concrete block building that is graced by a hand-painted tin sign that reads BURGIN'S ANTIQUES. I haven't been here in over three years, but the place looks just the same.

I park Big Mama in the center of the lot, away from the canopy of pine trees that shed mounds of needles that turn brown and brittle and pad out the sandy soil. I want no pine sap on my carefully wrapped pieces.

For old times' sake, I wander down to the side of the building, my Keds slipping in the pea-sized gravel. No changes here. A rusted propane tank squats at the property line, camouflaged by weeds. The weeds have grown higher so you can see less of the tank, and I wonder how long it will take to completely disappear. A broken bottle of Bud Lite leaves a trail of brown glass scattered like lethal crumbs along the side of the clearance that serves as the employee parking lot and lounge. Someone has left a jumbo Wendy's cup on the picnic table where we used to sit, smoke cigarettes and eat our lunch. The picnic table was the official employee break room when I used to work for old man Burgin. We used to call it the Coop because it sits in front of a storage building that has seen better days housing chickens.

I shove my hands in my pockets and take a look at that old screen door. The metal plate across the bottom is still bowed in where Arlo Bradford kicked it the day he got fired. Arlo getting fired put the fear in us all. If the punctual, kind and talented Arlo, a lathe turner whose work was as much art as craft, could be fired without warning for reasons as insignificant as one personal call when Mr Burgin himself wanted to use the phone and a lost tool that turned up the very next day, what chance did the rest of us have? It is only now that I realize that Arlo was fired not in spite of his skill but because of it. Arlo was slow and methodical, a man with large hands, calloused but sensitive fingers and a standard that did not tolerate cutting corners. Burgin had been lying in wait for him, that was all.

Arlo works freelance out of his garage these days, and he seems to get by real well. When I can afford it, I use him to work on my best pieces, and local gossip has it he's going to be part of a special on PBS.

I hear the hum of a cranky refrigerator and glance through the back screen door. The same leaking, yellow Frigidaire. I wonder if those egg-salad sandwiches I left behind are still rotting away in there.

I take a clip out of my pocket and twist my hair up on top of my head. I go back to lock my purse up in Big Mama; for some reason, I feel that toting a purse over my shoulder puts me at a certain disadvantage. There are two cars in the lot that weren't there before. One is a Lincoln Town Car from Ohio – a tourist victim who has wandered off the beaten path – the other an '87 Cadillac Coup de Ville with Louisiana plates. While I was wandering around remembering the bad old days, two people have gotten in ahead of me. For an out-of-the-way hole, this place sees a lot of activity.

The front door is oak and heavy brown glass, and a bell rings as I push it open. The front room looks like a cluttered abandoned attic and smells like a mildewed basement. It's dim inside, the windows are dirty and the bulbs low-watt, and the visual impact of dust alone makes you feel like you're going to choke. There is a stranger to my left. He is standing in the shadows, but my impression is of big shoulders and dark hair.

Burgin stands in the center of the floor, pulling an earlobe. He is five feet ten, slender around the basketball belly, somewhere between fifty and sixty years old. His white hair is going yellow and is parted conventionally to one side. Burgin favors polyester: checks, patterns and pastels. Today his pants are robin's-egg blue, and his short-sleeved button-up shirt is spotted with old food stains that his wife dutifully irons in every day. His shoes are black lace-ups, polished till they shine, and a plastic pocket insert clasps two pens, one pencil and a tape measure tight to his puny chest. He is talking to a man with a formidable stomach, a short haircut and an intimidating air of success.

'You paid my great-aunt one hundred and eighteen dollars for two pieces that have been in our family since she was a girl.' The accent is Ohio, not Louisiana, and the voice is soft, but the tone and timbre reveal a man used to obsequious and instant respect. 'You bullied her and you cheated her, and I am here to get those pieces back. Your money I am happy to return.' Ohio reaches into his pants pocket and takes out a slim wad of bills.

Burgin is what's known in the trade as a 'knocker'; he roams the countryside knocking on doors, leaving notes in mailboxes and bullying the elderly into parting with their antiques for pennies on the dollar. He is keen as a tick hound for bankruptcy filings and funeral notices, and he circles old homesteads like a vulture. He is always happy, of course, to provide a handwritten receipt and a disconnected phone number, plus a promise that the customer has seven days to change his or her mind. This is provided that they can find him; the address he gives is a post office box in Savannah. Burgin is also a coward. If this man insists, I know Burgin will back down.

'I don't have the pieces here, sir, they are in my warehouse. I can retrieve them for you, provided they haven't already been sold. Perhaps you could come back later this afternoon.'

Ohio notices me behind Burgin and I catch his eye, shaking my head slightly. Ohio does not betray me with his expression, and his transition is so smooth I'm not even sure he noticed my shake of the head.

'I'm not leaving without them. I can follow you to the warehouse right now.'

'I won't be able to leave for a little while yet, sir. It would be best if you could just come back.'

'Best for who? If they're not here, you go get them right now.'

Burgin's little eyes disappear into slits. 'Let me just check back in the workroom. I marked your aunt's things for storage, but it's remotely possible they haven't been sent over yet.' Burgin turns and sees me for the first time. He purses his lips. I've never been a favorite, but I am holding the grief card and this is a small town. 'Hello, Georgie. I'm so very sorry to hear about your mother and your dad.'

'Thank you, Mr Burgin.'

'I'm afraid if you're looking for work—'

'I'm not. I've got a few pieces I thought you might

want to look at. To tell you the truth, I'm on my way to see Robard in Charleston. I just thought I'd stop in on the way and let you take a look, maybe save myself a drive.'

Burgin wavers and pulls at his lip, sticking his thick wet tongue out of thin lips. 'What have you got?'

'A mahogany bergère, nineteenth-century; a French caned beechwood chair and a pine Dover chest.'

'Hand-painted?'

I nod.

'Condition?'

'Original legs, original locks, missing a hinge. It's very nice. I hate to part with it. I've also got a Lloyd Loom.'

Burgin's nose twitches over the Dover chest. It's a piece he'll sell privately, and he'll make good money. Like I'd planned to do.

I glance around the showroom. 'But if you're busy, I can just head on out.'

'No, no, just give me a minute or two.' Burgin nods at the man in the corner. 'I'll be with you, sir, in just a bit.'

'No hurry.'

I am vaguely distracted as Burgin leaves for the back room. This dark stranger's voice has turned my head. The tone is in the lower registers, with an odd scratchy quality and an accent that's hard to place. Chicago, maybe? New York? I remember the Louisiana license plate and decide on New Orleans. The natives there sport an odd southern patois that seems to take more from the Bronx than the old slurry South.

I am intrigued by the face that will go with the voice, but Burgin will be back any minute, so I turn with some reluctance to Mr Ohio, who is trying to catch my eye. 'There is no warehouse,' I whisper. 'Don't leave without your stuff.'

Ohio looks more angry than grateful, and his face goes dark red so quickly I am sure his blood pressure will land him in trouble before the end of the year. He gives me a curt but friendly nod. I suppose in Ohio that must mean thanks.

A lampshade rattles as the dark man steps forward. 'Excuse me, miss?'

You could describe this man's voice as sandpapery, but it has a quality that is soothing as well. A cat tongue, in the physical world. He pauses to steady the lamp at the base, then steps out of the shadows and into the light.

I am not in the habit of indulging attractions to dangerous men. In spite of a Beaufort reputation earned by my fall into unwed motherhood at the age of sixteen, or maybe even because of it, I have not been one to tolerate the complications of difficult men or to negotiate the treacherous rapids of mad, bad love. I have no aspirations to marriage and, in truth, live in fear of a relationship that requires the permission of a judge to escape. I have never been on the catch for a substitute father for Hank, preferring single parenthood with its lack of interference, and I'm not looking for a man attached to a bank account bulky enough to make me feel safe. I'm never quite sure how to describe what exactly it is that I want, but I know it when I see it. And today I'm thinking I see it.

There is something very physical about this man, something predatory. He is not particularly tall, a couple inches under six feet, but his shoulders are broad, topping an almost stocky build. His hair is dark and parted to one side. He has brown eyes, a face used up by the sun and the kind of physical confidence that makes him a man you would not pick a fight with. He has an odd alert weariness, like an old soul who has seen and done things the average person never sees or does. He is guarded, like a man who has strong opinions but plans to keep them to himself. He looks like a man who can go to the dark places and find his way back.

He is walking toward me, smiling just a little, an odd half smile, reaching only one side of his face, with that mix of confidence and insecurity that men have when they like you.

'Those pieces you were talking about?' He stops a respectful distance away, as if he is used to intimidating people and wants me to feel secure. 'Mind if I have a look?'

I wonder if his interest is genuine. But it will do Burgin good to think there's a little competition.

'Sure. They're out front here, in my truck.'

I am self-consciously aware of him behind me as we head to the parking lot outside. Is he looking at my ass? These aren't my best-ass jeans, they are the comfy ones, with a split across the left knee.

Ohio watches us go out the door and I think he is glad that we are leaving, as if our presence inhibits him from saying to Burgin what he really wants to say. Burgin is in over his head with this one.

I head for Big Mama, checking the still-sunny sky for hints of rain as an automatic precaution. I am as careful of my pieces as a mother with a newborn. I untie the thick green pads over the caned beechwood chair, blocking this man with my back. I don't want any help unwrapping my pieces, and I am relieved when he makes no move to assist. He puts a proprietary hand on the side of my truck. I am impatient for Burgin to come out so I can get on with my business. I climb into the back of Big Mama, ever careful of fragile wood. Once I have unwrapped the padding, I perch sideways on the edge of the truck bed. I don't say a word. Either this guy is for real or he's not. The pieces speak for themselves.

The dark man meets my eye for a quick moment, considers me, then turns his attention to the back of the truck. He shoves his hands in his pockets. He is wearing jeans, a T-shirt so white I figure he took it out of the package this morning and a loose khaki overshirt, sleeves rolled halfway up his arms, shirt-tail loose. He has just a hint of sideburns, which give him an Elvis air.

'You do good work,' he says.

I wonder what kind of work he thinks I do. Furniture polish? Building from scratch? This man doesn't know shit about antiques. What the hell is he doing out here at Burgin's? Planning a robbery? I wonder if he knows that Burgin deals primarily in cash and there is probably at least $3,000 squirreled away on the premises. The screen door creaks, and I look up.

'Just pull around to the back and Alfonse will load you up.' Burgin is talking quickly, throwing words over his shoulder as Ohio follows him out to the lot. Clearly, he is cutting his losses and wants this Ohio man out of the shop and gone. It is the only thing I admire about my old boss. He knows when to walk away.

Burgin heads for Big Mama with the hint of an old limp – he is the sort of man people like to kick – and it is clear from his hurried step and his focus on the back of my truck that he is worried about New Orleans here getting the jump on a bargain. I shift my weight so I am sitting more comfortably. Things are starting to work out.

'What price are you asking on this one?'

New Orleans is pointing at the Dover chest, and he doesn't even know what it is called. What instinct is it, I wonder, that makes him select the one item Burgin cannot live without?

Behind us, Ohio has started up his car, but he pulls up close to Big Mama, turns the engine off and steps out. 'You mind if I take a look at what you've got?'

He is eyeing the Lloyd Loom, and he looks like he knows his stuff. It is a struggle to keep my face non-committal and resist the catlike smile. Mama must be watching over me, because I have an auction on my hands.

I am up early the next morning, working by half past six, stopping only to drink coffee on the balcony while the sun comes up. It makes me feel good, remembering the look on Claire's face when I handed her a check last night. Her kids were still awake, and we picked up Hank and went out for late-night doughnuts at Krispy Kreme, and Claire looked ten years younger when I left her at the door.

I know before I open the shutters in my shop that the work is going to go well. Sometimes you just feel it, a sort of power that flows in your fingertips and chest. The world is peaceful this early, and I feel the contentment of a woman whose son is sleeping safely upstairs in his bed.

The phone rings. I figure it is Claire. 'What you doing up?' I ask her.

But the voice is not Claire's. It is the dark man, the one who bought my Lloyd Loom chair. 'I just wanted to tell you how much I like the chair I bought yesterday. I hope I didn't call too early.'

'No, you didn't. I'm glad you like the chair.'

He pauses. Gives a little laugh. 'So how long you been in the antique business?'

'You interested in antiques?'

'I don't know much about them. This card you gave me. Second Chances?'

'That's the name of my shop.'

'You mind if I stop by, some afternoon this week?'

'You're more than welcome.'

'My name is John Wallace, by the way. And you're Georgie, that right?'

'That's right.'

'Pretty name. Look forward to seeing your shop.'

I am smiling when I hang up the phone but nervous too. There is always that little voice inside of me that says, 'Stay safe and stay alone.'

I try to get John Wallace out of my mind. As soon as I get my hands back in the glue there is a knock at my door. I ignore it. It is nine-thirty, and the shop isn't open till ten. I take a last look at the fabric backing I have just stretched across the bottom of this chair. This piece is not worth a great deal, except to the young woman who grew up with it in her home.

117

I find a thin scar where I have repaired the wooden arm, which will be easy enough to varnish into invisibility. I wash the glue off my hands and pull the banded mask off my nose. I should have opened the window.

The knocking is louder now, and there is the unmistakable scrabble of someone trying the lock. The early-rising tourist is often insistent. I open the front door just a crack.

'Ma'am, are you Georgie Smallwood?'

There are two men on my doorstep, and they wear sports jackets and khaki pants, short haircuts and an air. They are not smiling, which rules out religion and sales.

'Who's asking?'

The ID is out with a practiced flick, and the dark-haired man patiently gives me a chance to look, but his sandy-haired friend does not.

'I'm Detective Hutchins; this is Detective Click,' the dark one says. 'We're from the Beaufort County sheriff's department. Uh, ma'am, we've got a warrant to search your house.'

I don't know what to say.

Sandy-hair, Click, is about to elbow me aside, but Hutchins waits politely. 'Ma'am? May we come in?'

'What's this all about?'

Click hands me the warrant, like they do on TV. Hutchins nods at me and seems almost embarrassed. The noise or the smell or the presence of these men has penetrated the deep deaf sleep of my mother's dog. Cousin Beauregard sets up a fuss.

'Mom?' Hank appears at the top of the stairs in boxer shorts.

'Grab Cousin, Hank.'

'Son, put the dog outside,' Hutchins says.

'I'm not your son.' Hank looks at me, unhurried and cool. 'Mom, we can't put her out, she'll run away.'

'Put a leash on her, Hank, and hold her. But don't pick her up.'

'I know.' He bends down and holds Cousin by the collar. She is frantic now, ready to defend her house, and Detective Click's radio goes off. Hutchins is mouthing words at me, but I can't hear shit over the noise of this dog.

I glance up at Hank.

'What are they doing here?' he shouts.

'Searching the house.'

'What for?'

I shrug. I have no idea.

Hank looks at Hutchins. 'You think two of you are enough, or is your buddy pig calling for backup?'

The dog is still barking, and Hutchins is kind enough to pretend not to hear.

The detectives are asking me about shoes. Hank and I are sitting side by side on the couch with a tense Cousin Beauregard between us. Cousin frankly smells bad, and her eyes are draining, and she is so overweight she looks like a hairy sausage casing, but her head is up, ever watchful, and she growls low in her throat at regular intervals. Cousin does not like the police.

Click holds up a pair of worn white Keds. 'These the ones?'

I nod.

He considers my shoes. 'They're little.'

'I have small feet.'

'What size?'

'Five and a half.'

He gives me a hard look.

'Want me to put them on?'

He is clearly considering it. A new fairy tale is in the making. Cinderella and the police.

'How come they're so clean? These *are* the shoes you wore the night you father was killed?'

'Yes, they are. The very ones.'

'It was wet out. Kind of muddy. Should be some sand or mud on these, if you wore them that night.'

'Yes, there was. I told you; that's why I washed them. That is the whole point of Keds. You can throw them in the washing machine and they come out fine.'

Click is rocking back and forth on his heels. 'You hear that, Hutchins? She washed her shoes the morning after her father died. Now why would you do that, ma'am, at this particular time?'

'Because they were dirty.'

Click maintains stern eye contact with me while he puts my shoes in a plastic bag.

'Look, I've already told you guys I was at the lighthouse that night. You don't need my shoes to prove that.'

I picture a courtroom and a prosecutor who looks just like my father's best friend, Eugene Wilbanks. He is holding up my shoes in front of a jury of my peers. One thing I've learned in my years of selling antiques is that seventy-five percent of what people remember is visual. Do the police think this way? Do they want a shoe to hold up in front of a jury for visual impact alone?

My feelings are hurt. The sheriff's department is seriously investigating me, which is an insult to my family grief.

The detectives have so little to go on. It is scary, really, the way they think. It seems to be about patterns of behavior. Keep your actions within the normal range, and they will never look your way. Step outside the box at your peril. And my brother and sister and I are clearly out of the box. I am thinking that it might be easier for a careful murderer to go free than for an innocent caught in circumstance to explain.

Hutchins comes out of my bedroom holding a pair of sandals that are clogged with dust.

'Where did you find *those*?' I ask.

'Under the bed.'

'I've been looking for them for weeks.'

'They're sandy.'

'This is a beach town.'

Hutchins puts them in another bag. 'We'll be in touch, Mrs Smallwood.'

'*Ms* Smallwood.'

He tries to hand me a business card, but Cousin is growling, so he leaves the card on my coffee table.

I am sitting out on the front step of my shop when the New Orleans Cadillac pulls up and parallel-parks right there at my feet. The dark man with the scratchy voice is here as promised and I am suddenly aware that my hair is falling out of the comb that holds it up off my neck, there is varnish on my chin and I really ought to brush my teeth.

John Wallace gets out of the car and smiles down at me. He offers a hand and helps me to my feet. 'So this is your place?'

'This is it. Come on in, I was just taking a break.' I do not tell him that a visit from the police has left me so rattled I cannot concentrate on my work.

John Wallace stands just inside the shop and takes it all in. He walks to the wall and studies my grandfather's tools. 'You're happy here, aren't you?'

It seems an odd thing to say, but it's true.

The shop bell rings and Selby walks in. He is in uniform and I have not noticed the sound of the Harley.

'Hey, Georgie.' He stops mid-stride when he sees John Wallace. 'If you've got a customer, I'll come back.'

'No, no. I'd like you to meet John Wallace. John, this is Johnny Selby, policeman and family friend.'

Selby and John shake hands, and I do not like the look that passes between them.

'I won't keep you from your work,' John Wallace tells me.

'I'll walk you out.'

We head out to the sidewalk in front of the shop, and I am feeling awkward about this abrupt visit. Then John Wallace smiles at me.

'I'd like to take you to dinner next Friday night, if you're free. Will you come?'

'Yes,' I say. 'Pick me up here, around seven.'

I watch him drive away. When I go back in the shop I see that Selby has slipped out the side door and is gone. I take a quick look out the front shop window and see him writing in his report book. I have the uncomfortable feeling he is noting the license number on the back of John Wallace's car.

8

Some of the best places to eat in Beaufort are on the waterfront. The problem with eating there is you will see about five or six people you know, and it is impossible to have a private conversation. This explains why I am walking into the local Shoney's, looking up and down the rows of booths for my brother and sister. I know they will be in a booth. People in my family do not sit at tables in restaurants unless we have to. Mama started this habit when we were little. Sometimes, when I look out at the rest of the world, sitting at tables and doing just fine, I wonder what the big deal is. But I always sit in a booth.

My brother and sister are on my left down the center aisle. They are deep in conversation. At the booth on the other side are two men I don't recognize, but one of them has a friendly smile. He is dark-eyed and tanned, and I smile back and slide across the vinyl seat next to my sister. I never sit by Ashby. He takes up too much room.

The waitress, an older woman with a tired face and a smile, wants my drink order.

'Tea,' I say, looking at my siblings' plastic glasses. They're drinking cola; I can see the dark fizzy liquid through the opaque plastic. I really want a Coke. God knows I deserve one with the police in the house first thing. 'Make that a Coke,' I say. The cute guy in the booth catches my eye. 'No, sorry. Tea. Make it tea. Unsweet.'

The waitress pauses another second, then, when it is clear I am not going to change my mind, she scoots away.

'Hottie at three o'clock,' I whisper to Ashby and Claire.

My brother winks. 'This one's on my bus, Georgie.' There is something to be said for a brother you can man-watch with. He screens out the homosexuals so Claire and I don't waste time.

'No he's not, Ashby. He gave me a big smile when I walked in.' Gay men think *everybody's* on their bus.

'The dark guy with the tan? He gave me his phone number in the men's room.'

'Damn.'

Claire points her straw in my direction, leaving a trail of Coke. 'So what happened with the police?'

Ashby leans forward. 'Claire, can you hold it down? That's Eugene Wilbanks's cousin Butch over there by the salad bar.'

'He can't hear me from over here.'

I frown at my sister. 'We wouldn't have this problem if you-all would have met me in Savannah like I asked.'

Claire shudders. 'I told you, bad things happened to me last time I went to Savannah airport.'

'I didn't want to meet you at the *airport*.'

'What happened at the airport?' Ashby asks.

'Okay. On the way, a cop gave me a speeding ticket when I was having a really bad day, and *three* people pulled out in front of me and almost caused me to wreck, and one of them gave me the finger.'

'That's a normal day, Claire,' I say, but my sister ignores me. In the universe of Claire, roads begin and end with her personal experiences, and she drives torturous routes to avoid places she doesn't like. Twice, when giving directions, I have heard her tell people that a road ends, when in reality she simply has no interest in the road beyond a certain point. Like my mother, Claire really needs to be accompanied by an interpreter.

'The police took my Keds,' I say. 'And that Click guy—'

'The light-headed one?' Claire asks, and I think by that she means blond.

'Yeah. He thought me washing the shoes was suspicious.'

'It *is* suspicious,' Ashby says. 'You're kind of a pig. Of course, the cops wouldn't know that, unless somebody talked.'

'Shut up. They also took my sandals, Claire. You know, the ones I bought when we were Christmas shopping in Charleston?'

'The cute ones with the ties that go up your leg? I thought you lost those.'

'That detective, Hutchins, he found them under my bed. They're evidence now.'

'Evidence of what?' Ashby asks. 'Of dust?'

My brother always makes remarks about my house-keeping because I had the messiest room growing up. The truth is, Ashby is the real pig, and his bathrooms were toxic before he and Reese hired the Queen's Cleaning Emporium, which is a maid service run by a couple of older gentlemen who wear frilly aprons and make snide remarks. But Ashby says they're funny and they clean real well.

My tea arrives and we order.

'Slim Jim and fries.'

'Slim Jim and rings.'

'Rings and fries and Slim Jim.'

As far as Ashby and Claire and I are concerned, Shoney's has two things: Slim Jim sandwiches and hot fudge cake. It's the only place where all of us order the same.

In the booth over the partition, a man with an outdoor face and a stained baseball cap lights up a cigarette. I wrinkle my nose. Cigarettes have always made me queasy, even during the week I smoked the year I turned fifteen.

'Did they take *your* shoes?' I ask Claire.

'Just the flip-flops they found at the lighthouse.'

'The crime scene,' Ashby says.

I take a breath. 'You guys better sit up and start paying attention. This is getting serious.'

'Not really.' Claire shrugs. 'They were just flip-flops I bought at Wal-Mart, and they were caked with mud and sand anyway.'

'Did they take anything else?'

'The clothes I wore that night.'

I wonder why they didn't take my clothes. 'You know, it's not like we said we weren't out there.'

Ashby makes a noise that is a cross between a snort and a laugh and the dark man looks his way. 'They can't really think we killed Dad.'

'Are you guys just stupid?' I ask. 'They got search warrants.'

Ashby shudders. 'Not for my place. Thank God.' Like

most gay men, he has reason to be wary of the police. 'Maybe you're right, Georgie. You know what? Maybe we shouldn't be talking to the cops without a lawyer.'

'I can't afford a lawyer,' Claire says. 'And you have nothing to fear if you're innocent.'

'God help her,' I say, looking at my brother.

'Claire, promise me you won't talk to the—'

Claire folds her arms. 'I feel like shit about those things I said that night, Ashby, but I don't have anything to hide. And if that Carla Blanchard is right and Daddy left her all his money, what's my motive?'

My brother looks glum. 'I talked to Eugene Wilbanks.'

'You called him?' I ask.

'No, he called me. He's executor of Dad's estate. And I talked to Walt Prichard, that insurance guy? Dad's life insurance and estate all go to Carla Blanchard, just like she said. Prichard wants to know if we're going to contest. The insurance company will hold up her payments if we do.'

The waitress is carrying a heavy round tray with our sandwiches. We wait while she delivers the food, pulls a full bottle of ketchup out of her apron pocket and inquires after drink refills.

'What do you think?' Claire asks me.

I take a bite of sandwich. Swiss cheese, ham, special secret dressing that tastes a lot like Thousand Island. I chew slowly, and bits of shredded lettuce fall from the side of my sandwich onto the white ceramic plate.

'I don't know. Part of me wants to fight it, and part of me wants to say, If that's what Daddy wanted, forget his damn insurance.'

'I would go that way too, except I need the money.'

Claire is looking at her food but not eating.

'Fight it,' Ashby says. He is aggressive about money. 'Carla Blanchard was just the flavor of the month. Most of that money was Mama's. Do you all want Vicky and Ben Blanchard getting Mama's stuff? What about the Fiestaware, Georgie?'

Ashby knows how to push my buttons. I put my sandwich on my plate.

'Fight it.'

Like most funeral homes in small towns, the Sutter Funeral Parlor on Ribault Street in Beaufort is located in the kind of house people dream of owning – over a hundred years old, this one with classic Georgian architecture, and a front porch for people to congregate on but not enjoy. A discreet sign out front makes it clear that this is a commercial establishment, located in the ever-changing Demilitarized Zone that straddles the business and residential district. There is plenty of parking out back in a lot that is smooth with recently laid asphalt. This is a home that has no need for a backyard. The circle drive makes it easy to pull a hearse around to one side, load a casket, and then pull into position at the front of the drive to lead the funeral procession on.

My mother, spouse of a retired marine, will be buried in the National Cemetery here in Beaufort. The thought makes me sad. I don't want my mother placed beneath the small white cross, one of hundreds, fanning out like sculpture in the grass. The effect is symmetrical, even pleasing, and appropriate, I suppose, for military personnel, but my mother does not belong there. I want her to have a large headstone of rose-colored marble and the random charm of irregular lots and family sections. The National Cemetery is like those Nazi neighborhood communities in Southern California, rife with rules, regulations and the need to conform.

But my father made the arrangements and paid the bills and, as executor, holds all the cards, even in death. And I am tired, preparing to sink my finances into the rescue of Claire, and just not up to the fight.

Hank is with me, in new khakis and a sports jacket. If his khakis are oversized and loose, it is, after all, the fashion of the day. He has new boots, Timberlands, because he balked at shiny leather dress shoes, but he did compromise and allow a tie. His hair is newly cut. Large and regular feedings have not put any weight on my son, and he is thin and wiry but looks well.

Hank and I are an hour late to my mother's visitation, thanks to Cousin Beauregard, who wandered out in the street as we were leaving and had to be chased down and coaxed back into the house. I know Mama will understand – she loved her smelly dog – but this town is another matter.

Hank looks nervous. We don't talk about it, but we both dread walking into the fishbowl of a small-town visitation. The rumors are flying fast and furious. Between Hank's return, Mama's sudden death and the irregularity of Daddy's own demise, the stir we endured over Claire's imminent divorce in concert with the backdrop noise of my brother's homosexuality, my father's military scandal and my own unwed motherhood seem like background music from the past.

'You look good,' I tell Hank.

He smiles politely and nods. A mother's opinion rates low on the scale.

'So do you,' he tells me, and we make our entrance. The floor in the funeral home is hardwood, and it creaks and gives way at the joints. I can hear it and feel it through the thin green carpet and my black sling-back shoes. I suppose I am lucky the police left me any shoes. As the door swings gently shut behind us, I hear seagulls. Then the sound is cut and I hear the murmur of voices and note the scent, ever faint, of old furniture, mothballs and Lemon Pledge. On my right on a wooden podium is a splayed guest book, the pages exposing each unique scrawl where the names have been penned by my mother's family and friends.

I pause at the edge of the parlor. In a horseshoe-shaped section at the back of the room rests Mama's coffin, open at the top, the midsection burdened by a blanket of yellow roses that I now know is called a coffin spray. My father favored yellow roses all his life, and it was a shock to me once when my mother, recipient of a recent bouquet, rolled her eyes and expressed a preference for red.

I am being eyed discreetly with sidelong looks. Ashby is deep in conversation with a woman in royal purple and a black hat with a net, and they have drawn the attention of my son. Hank looks at me and hides a smile.

'The South,' I whisper, leaning close, 'and certain New Orleans drag bars, are the only two places where you can get away with a hat with a net.'

'Probably helps to be over a hundred,' Hanks says.

'And attending a funeral. Let's be tacky and go see who sent the best bouquets.'

As Hank and I move close to the flowers, I see Claire's ex-husband, Clark, sniffing into a handkerchief and acting bereaved. You would never know from his tragic demeanor that he and my mother rarely spoke, and he is so thick-skinned and oblivious I'm not sure he ever knew how little she liked him.

His sad, wishful voice carries across the room. 'I'm sure I've been as good a husband as I know how to be, but I guess I wasn't good enough.'

I don't recognize the woman he has cornered. She pats his hand. 'These things are very hard.'

Clark folds his handkerchief and tucks it into a pocket. 'What worries me is what effect our divorce may have had on Claire's mother. I would never forgive myself if I thought we were one of the reasons her heart gave out like it did.'

Claire catches my eye, and I know she has overheard.

The crowd formation shifts. My father's mistress arrives with her children. Carla Blanchard, Vicky and Ben are dressed with self-conscious formality and go straight to my mother's coffin, to eye her flower arrangements with critical eyes. They have had the effrontery to send my mother a wreath.

Ben is sadly unimpressive, being afflicted with slack, doughlike white skin and protuberant pale eyes. He is painfully thin and angular and I mark him down as an ascetic, a man who enjoys few earthly pleasures and resents those of us who do. The daughter is a study in envious hauteur and insecurity and wears a judgmental air like cologne. Vicky's conversation is usually dull beyond belief, and she often snubs me in public. She fingers the roses on Mama's casket spray with an expression of resentment that convinces me she is imagining how much better the flowers would look in a vase at her house.

Vicky has a certain long-faced prettiness and is the kind of woman tortured by her devotion to leading a perfect life. I have no doubt that her house is clean and tidy, with no pets allowed on the couch, her underwear drawer neat, her diet low-fat with plenty of fruits and vegetables. Her lawn, need I point out, will be mowed, weed-eaten, precisely edged and trimmed. The milk in her refrigerator will not go past the sell-by date. And she has a heart like a peach pit – small, poisonous and hard.

The three Blanchards stand by my mother's coffin and stare at her mortal remains. My mother seems vulnerable, exposed to their gaze. Carla Blanchard picks up my mother's hand and closes her eyes as if in prayer. I take a step in their direction, but a hand on my shoulder breaks my stride.

'Don't start something, Georgie.'

I turn with a rush of relief to Johnny Selby, disconcerting in a new suit that is that color that hovers between navy and black. Selby looks at me with steady clarity, the way those of us who are survivors of grief learn to look without comfort at the world.

'I'll see to it.' He gives me a brief and desolate smile and heads for the Blanchards.

His mere presence breaks their conversation. Vicky and her brother, Ben, edge close to their mother, who braces her legs and mouths some social pabulum that I'm luckily too far away to hear. Johnny Selby gives them no smile and no encouragement, and he tucks my mother's hand back into the coffin so that we can imagine her comfortable there in the upholstery of her burial box.

The Blanchards fade backward into the crowd. I know they will work their way over, and I will do my social duty and nod and smile. But for now I watch Johnny Selby, as he stands by my mother's side, his back to me. He takes two roses from the top of the casket. One he presses into my mother's hand, the other he keeps for himself.

This is a good man, a handsome man, with brown eyes, a good heart, brains, humor, all the right things. I am glad that he loved my mother, and proud in a way that is hard to explain.

A shriek heralds the arrival of little Annette Wilbanks. My father's best friends have arrived.

Annette is the only child and Barbie-doll daughter of Captain Eugene Wilbanks, retired, USMC, Judge Advocate General, now a practicing attorney with the Beaufort County DA. He is currently running as assistant district attorney on a ticket with Sondra Mannelli, the incumbent DA. The newspapers call them 'the Bulldogs' and Mannelli is leaning on Wilbanks's years with the Marine Corps JAG to give her office a stronger law-and-order flavor and counter claims that she is in the habit of turning a blind eye here and there, to pay back the good old boys.

Wilbanks certainly has the right presence, honed to a fine edge by the smug esprit de corps of the USMC and instilled at an early age by old family money and a fine education at the University of Virginia. He is the perfect complement to Sondra Mannelli, and the man that my father always wanted to be.

Annette looks slim and brittle pretty in a shell-pink dress that is sheathlike, expensive and the color of your inner ear. She clings to her father's left arm and takes small mincing steps in outrageously high Gucci heels. I envy those shoes with a burn in my heart. Behind her walks the wifely Maureen.

Annette gobbles the room with a gaze that registers handsome men and female rivals. Claire gets a second look – my pretty sister – but Annette avoids looking at me.

Annette and I went to all the same schools, growing up here in Beaufort, Annette a staple with the cheerleader crowd, me rounding up outcasts, artists and theater kids. She and I made a habit of preying on each other's boyfriends. She once 'accidentally' sloshed paint over my beloved black velvet blazer on an ill-fated afternoon at Beaufort High School that had me painting scenery for the senior play and Annette meeting with the planning committee for the prom. If she accused me of painting a hot-pink Barbie on the door of her new white Mustang, she was never able to prove a thing.

For now, she abandons Daddy dearest to run to my brother, who holds her at arm's length to ward off the perfumed hug and tentacle-thin arms.

'Ashby, honey, I just can't believe it. How much can one family bear?'

I catch my sister's eye again. Claire looks tired but gives me a small smile. Annette Wilbanks is probably the only person in Beaufort who doesn't get that my brother is gay.

'Hello there, Annette.'

'Oh, hello, *Reese*.'

Annette once confided to Claire that she thinks Reese has a thing for her. Reese is my brother's roommate and life companion. He is a big man with a thick head of hair and a knack for getting along. Mama considered him her other son.

Reese sees me and abandons Ashby to Annette. No doubt he will hear of this later.

'I like *your* shoes better,' he says. 'Yours are sexy and hers are grotesque.'

I laugh, attracted, as always, to liars. 'If you weren't on Ashby's bus, Reese, I'd take you home with me.'

'If I was that kind of guy, you'd be my kind of girl.' He gives me a hug. He is broad and well padded and looks handsome in his suit, but I like him best in sweatshirts or sweaters. Hugging Reese is like clutching a bear. He has a shoulder a girl can get lost in.

Reese played football in college, which always put my father in a bind. Daddy worshiped football players all of his life, so on the subject of Reese he stuck to the sidelines. Ashby always says it was worth dating Reese just to make Daddy squirm.

'Are you okay?' Reese asks, like he means it.

I nod, like it's really the truth. 'Tell me how my brother's holding up.'

'He'll get through it okay,' Reese says, but his words seem forced, and when he looks over my shoulder at Ashby there is trouble in his eyes.

'He's taking it hard, about Daddy?'

'And your mother. And what happened to Hank. And everything else that's gone on.' Reese glances over at my son. 'That just by itself – what he said to your kid – that alone makes me want to wring your father's neck.'

'Too late, Reese, he's already dead.'

'I'm sorry,' he says. 'I shouldn't say bad things right now about your father.'

'Don't worry about it, Reese. It's nice to know that somebody feels like I do. I just can't see why . . .'

'Why what?'

'Why Ashby still defends him.'

Reese takes my arm. 'Georgie, the one thing a man never gets over is wanting his father's approval. Now you and I both know that no matter what Ashby did, he would never please your father, but at least when he was alive there was always the chance. Now it'll never happen. That's a hard thing to face.'

'He'll get over it,' I tell Reese, and he smiles down at me, but from his look I'm not sure he agrees.

He bends close to my ear. 'Wilbanks at three o'clock. Shall I make way for the captain?'

I am aware of silence and a rise in tension. I turn in time to see Eugene Wilbanks headed directly my way.

No drama queen could do it better. He takes two steps toward me and pauses, flanked by the regal and ever silent helpmeet, Maureen, his arm extended to his Barbie-doll daughter, Annette. The resemblance between father and daughter strikes me anew.

'Captain Wilbanks,' I say, beginning the polite dance of the bereaved, but I am forcing a smile and preparing conversation for nothing. Wilbanks sails past me as if I were dirt and it takes me a moment to recover.

It is a brutal snub and it takes me by surprise. My smile feels like a grimace and my face feels hot. Is it my self-consciousness or has the conversation around me died? I swallow, feeling like I might cry.

I have always known that Eugene Wilbanks was never overly fond of us Smallwood kids, but because he was so deeply and surely my father's friend, I considered him in some way ours. Clearly this is not the case. And though the feeling is mutual, I am oddly wounded. If anything will make people speculate about the circumstances of my father's death, it is this sudden coldness. And Wilbanks is a high flier in the office of the district attorney.

Claire, sensitive as always, is turning from her conversation, looking at me, at Annette, at Wilbanks, her mind moving at warp speed. 'Captain Wilbanks,' she says, in a very loud voice. 'Of course we knew you would come.'

In one easy sentence she has forced the issue and put him in place. People are watching.

It takes one fluid motion to bring him to her side, so smooth is he that it appears Claire was always his destination. He wraps both of his hands around hers and bends down to let her kiss his cheek, which she does with a certain reluctance. And I think again what I have speculated many times – that Wilbanks has a thing for my sister. I remember, when we were kids, the pains my mother took not to leave the two of them alone. Claire says it is all a crock, but she is never comfortable around Eugene Wilbanks, as if, on some subconscious level, she can sense the nature of his thoughts.

I do not like to see her command him this way, or to see him obey. It degrades her to exert this feminine power, like a princess summoning a reptile. This is a man who lives for power and control, and he is dangerous to sweet, pretty girls. A man like Wilbanks will like you the way a spoiled child breaks a favorite toy the minute it makes him mad.

I have forgotten Maureen, a tall woman with shoulders that work like hangers for her clothes. I have often wondered how she feels, running silently in the captain's wake. My sympathies have never gained her affection.

She taps my arm with long fingers thickened by icy white gloves, and her fingertips feel like soft paw pads on my arm. Softly, softly she touches me, but in her eyes flickers the thinly concealed desire to bruise. Her face is drawn with intelligent dislike, and her mouth purses, like a smoker inhaling the sweet toxin of her vice.

'So sorry, Georgie dear, about your mother. And your father too, of course. We thought you might have planned some sort of joint ceremony.'

'Daddy made all the arrangements, Mrs Wilbanks. We're just following through.'

Maureen Wilbanks allows herself the bad manners of a smirk. Gracious she is not. The idea of myself as a dutiful daughter seems to amuse her, and I am aware of her dislike pulsing toward me with every beat of her heart.

This woman is a mirror to her husband. His likes are her likes, his dislikes she takes as her own.

I wonder how the Wilbankses can be so close to my father and so completely dislike all us kids. They have money, the big house, country-club membership, even a boat. Yet they are competitive and watchful, stirred to resentment if good fortune comes our way, full of sour gratification when it does not. Did my father know this? Did he care? Do his friends reflect his true feelings about us all, or do Maureen and Annette dislike my father as much as Ashby and Claire and I dislike theirs?

Perhaps it has always been Mama who held the Wilbankses in check. She entertained them, when it was unavoidable, with a grace that was somehow aggressive, as if she knew things about Eugene Wilbanks and he'd do well to behave. The captain, unfailingly polite to Mama, always had, in her presence, the air of a man who has been burned and now fears the fire.

But their envy I will never understand.

The nicest thing about a funeral visitation is that you can set a time for people to leave. The last to go is Gertrude Tessaro, Mama's best friend since we moved to Beaufort.

I walk Gertrude to the door, and she puts an arm around my shoulders, out of affection and for support. She is limping a little, as if her feet hurt.

'I would kill for a cigarette.' Her voice is almost masculine, deepened by years of a pack-a-day penchant for Chesterfields.

'Hold out, Gert, you're almost to the parking lot.'

Our footsteps make the wood floors creak. The air inside, still heavy with the presence of too many people, is cooling now, empty and stale.

A hushed, stately silence is rising in this house, deepening the creepy-crawly aura that clings to funeral homes, no matter how elegant and carefully kept. The dead, drained of bodily fluid and animation, still have presence, and this house makes its living by mourning, a fact that hangs as thick as the paint on the walls.

'Claire said you're to ride with us tomorrow in the hearse.'

Gert pats my arm. Her face is pale under the foundation, which stops in a line at her neck and smudges the collar of her lavender silk blouse. Her eyebrows, heavy and straight, are knit, either in grief or a frown.

'Can I smoke?'

'In the hearse?'

'No, dear idiot, out here.' She stops on the porch, watching the last few cars put their lights on and pull away. It is dark now. I take a deep breath and lean against a white stately column.

'I guess I'm not afraid to die anymore,' Gert says.

I give her a look, a real look, not the gloss we daughters tend to apply absently to our mother's friends. It would be indulgent to call Gert handsome, but she has a certain something, in spite of the unflattering polyester ensemble of heavy dark maroon. Her hair is white and cut short in the *I no longer give a shit* mode that is sometimes adopted by long-married women.

She has been a regular in Mama's Tuesday-night bridge game, a fixture since I was a child. I think of those nights I would lie in my bed, unable to sleep, listening to the women's laughter, the voice and manner of my mother, changed subtly by the presence of her friends. The Diet Cokes, the bridge mints, peanuts and chips and dip – later replaced by carrot sticks, celery and dip – ending with a fancy dessert and always extra for the kids. The bridge players alternated houses, endured cranky, neglected husbands, and their children were kissed good night and tucked into bed when their mothers had the dummy hand and could spare the time.

I liked it best when they played at our house. I liked the excitement of guests, the way the house looked when we cleaned for company and the fistfuls of pastel bridge mints and peanuts we'd sneak back to our beds.

Gert sighs and faces me. 'The only regret I have, Georgie, is that your mama didn't get a chance to end things with your daddy once and for all. I thought she'd tied everything up, but now I hear that horrid Carla Blanchard gets all the loot, and I have to say that really stinks. But at least you kids will get your Uncle Dill's house and most of the money.'

I shake my head.

Gertrude frowns me down. 'What do you mean no?'

'I mean Mama left everything to Daddy.'

'The hell she did.'

'Everything.'

A look comes over Gert's face, a mask of toughness as she looks over her shoulder and walks me off the porch. I have never, before now, thought of my mother's girlfriends as formidable. It bothers me how superficial I have been, how oblivious to the qualities of the people right under my nose. I have an odd surge of hope. I suppose it is the natural order, that one generation looks to the one before it for help. It hits me, for the first time, that both my parents are dead and the last line of defenses has been breached. No one stands between me and the hard, uncaring world.

'Georgie' – Gert is leaning close, her voice hoarse in a stagy whisper – 'explain all this. And forgive me for getting up in your business, but—'

'That's okay. We found a copy of the will in my father's office. It's so old, Gert, she appointed you as our guardian.'

'What do you mean, she appointed a guardian? How old is this will?'

'About twenty-three years. She wrote it before we left home, before all the grandkids. It's ancient.'

'That's the one your daddy was putting through probate?'

'As far as I know.'

'Georgie, your mother made a new will; she told me about it. She told me everything, honey. About Hank, and how she had finally had enough of your father.'

'Did you *see* it? The new will?'

'No, but think, Georgie, this other one *can't* be right. Remember how she'd go on and on about money for college for the grandkids?'

'Do you know for a *fact* she made a new will?'

'She said she was going to. She told me she didn't want to go to somebody local; she didn't want your daddy to interfere. Wilbanks and your father were pressuring her to put her estate in a joint trust, so that if either of them died everything would go to the one who was alive, without even going through probate. They've been trying to set that up since she got that money from your Uncle Dill, but she was digging her heels in. And when that business with Hank came up, she called me, and I drove her to Charleston and took her to wire money to Hank, and then we went to some lawyer's office downtown.'

'So you knew about Hank?'

'Don't get mad. I had to swear I wouldn't tell.'

'Do you remember the name of the attorney?'

'It'll come to me, give me some time.' She squeezes her eyes shut with a hand to her head, and the ritual works like magic. 'Carmichael and Hubert, on State Street. Right by that Bank of America that's got the fountain out in the front. Now, you get yourself over there directly after the funeral.'

Excitement is buzzing in the small of my back. My inner voice says hurry, hurry. 'I'll go first thing after the funeral.'

'If you *don't* she'll haunt you, Georgie. You think

she wants Carla Blanchard getting all her stuff?'

'Did you see that woman in there earlier? Holding Mama's hand?'

'Looking for her rings, Georgie, that's what I think.'

Gert opens her purse, takes an open pack of Chesterfields and taps out a cigarette. She lights the end with a disposable Bic in a practiced motion that reveals the grace of a longtime addict. She pauses to enjoy the first lungful, and the look of satisfaction on her face makes me wonder what I'm missing.

'See you tomorrow, sweetie.'

I watch her climb into the old Cadillac Seville, and she waves and drives slowly away. I think of the endless possibilities in a new will and feel more hopeful than I have in a while. There is no denying that my mother's money would make all our lives easier – college for Hank, a safety net, less worry for all of us three. Not to mention keeping the family treasures away from Carla Blanchard and her two grabby kids.

Inside the funeral home all the guests have left and the employees are discreetly tucked away. My footsteps are loud and the wood floor groans, so I walk on tiptoe into the parlor.

My brother and sister sit side by side in chairs they've pulled close to the coffin. Candles lit on either side sputter and burn, and I'm distracted by the wax that rolls down the tapers in slick round drops. Without the coffin, the room would be acceptable in the home of nine out of ten grandmothers in the South.

Claire has her shoes off. My brother is crying. I can't

remember ever seeing Ashby cry before, even when he was eight and dropped the storm sewer cover on his toe. They look lost, my brother and sister.

'Where's Hank?' Claire asks me.

'I sent him home with Big Mama ages ago.' License or no. 'Where's Reese?'

Claire smiles. 'He took my kids to McDonald's and then dropped them off at Clark's apartment.'

'How about a ride home?' I ask them.

Ashby says, 'Sure, I'm already driving Claire.'

My sister is putting her shoes back on, tugging at the thin leather straps. But Ashby does not move. He looks up at me and Claire.

'It's just – is this the last time we're going to see her?'

'You can see her tomorrow, if you want. You can come early and spend some time.'

He nods and gives Mama a final look. I know that tomorrow will be arrangements and social practicalities, and it is unlikely he'll see her again. Ashby and Claire say their final good-bye. I study my mother over their shoulders, but that is as close as I get. She is gone, Lena Smallwood, and there is no comfort for me in that coffin.

Outside, the crickets are noisy, and I can smell pine trees and magnolia in the night. The windows of the funeral home glow with light, sending their comforts out to the dark.

'Let's have dinner,' Ashby says. 'Just us three.'

I feel curiously light and unencumbered. There is a freedom in mourning that exhilarates because you tell the world to go to hell, and well and truly mean it.

⬇

The post-funeral gathering is hosted by Claire. She lives in an eight-year-old split-foyer house in a suburb off Jacks Creek Pike, close to where we lived as kids. As much as any marine family can say they grew up somewhere, this is where we grew up.

I have never seen Claire's house this clean. Her husband, Clark, has finally moved out and taken with him his clutter, the curio cabinet full of junk, a recliner and a plethora of odds and ends. The house seems open, if stripped down, and twice as big. It is only now, as I stand in the living room, noting the absence of their ugly coffee table, that I realize how heavy Clark's presence has been.

Claire's children are very quiet, very polite. Their clothes are crisp and a touch oversized, the way children's clothing looks when it is new. Starched, pressed, with room to grow.

The dining-room table is crowded with the platters of food that have been arriving since Mama died: fried chicken, lemon cake, broccoli casserole, corn pudding, an entire spiral sliced ham, brownies, chocolate-chip cookies, a peach pie. The smell of coffee emanates from Mama's stainless-steel percolator, which Claire has finally unearthed. The kitchen counters are lined with paper cups, two-liter bottles of cola, napkins, stacks of used and food-strewn paper plates, sugar, creamer, salt, pepper, margarine for the hard beaten biscuits, cutlery with which to eat. The funeral feast.

I wonder when Claire had the time to get the house so clean, buy the kids new clothes, gather the napkins and plates and cups. I picture her scrubbing bathrooms at midnight. Death is an awful lot of work.

146

The phone rings. Claire has her hands full with Cece, who has torn her new tights at the knee. Gert signals she's got the phone.

My son puts a hand on my shoulder. 'I'm leaving, okay?' Hank has changed out of his funeral clothes and hands me a plastic grocery bag containing his funeral attire. 'You mind taking these home?'

'Where are you going?'

He looks at me. Shrugs.

'How are you getting there?'

'Marvin and Ritchie are waiting out front. I called, and they came to pick me up.'

'They're here now?' I go to the doorstep and see the boys. One has a magnificent Mohawk, the other a shaved head. They are wearing loose jeans and large shirts, jewelry only where they are pierced. But I have known these boys since kindergarten and I can see the children beneath the camouflage, as well as get a sense of the men they will become.

My feet hurt.

'Hank, honey, bring me my Keds out of the truck before you go. Marvin, Ritchie – lots of food in the kitchen. You got time for some fried chicken or a piece of pie?'

Ritchie grins, and Marvin is already on his way up the steps. To Hank's annoyance they troop through the door.

'Shoes?' I remind him. He wanders away. I walk the boys to the kitchen, in case they are shy.

They are awkward here in the realm of well-dressed adults. I take my shoes off, toss them under the kitchen table and lead the boys to the dining room to fill their plates.

Marvin waves to someone sitting on the couch. 'Hey, Mr Barret.'

'Hello there, Marvin. My wife made the peach pie, be sure and give it a try.'

Hank appears in the doorway and hands me my Keds. He folds his arms and grins at his friends, relaxed in a way he can be only in the company of his peers.

'Smallwood,' Ritchie says, 'eat something. Got to be a ton of stuff here you like.'

Hank takes a chicken leg from a platter. I feel good, here and now. My boy is home and it is like old times, his buddies in the kitchen.

Gert is waving at me. 'That was the funeral home, Georgie. Did you-all arrange for anybody to bring the flowers home?'

'I didn't think of it.' Ashby, in the hallway, has come at Gert's call.

'Neither did I,' I admit.

Gert puts her hands on her hips. She has taken the liberty of donning an apron, and she looks ready to tackle the kitchen mess. 'You better both go, and take Big Mama.'

Claire becomes one with the huddle. 'What's up?'

'We're going to the funeral home to pick up the flowers.'

'Why don't the three of you go together?' In my mother's absence, Gert has taken command.

'*One* of us has to stay.'

Gert shakes her head. 'Listen, Claire. This thing has been winding on all afternoon. You've been a great hostess, but you got to be worn out. Me and Ruthie will take over.'

I peep in the kitchen and wave at Ruthie. I'm not

listening while Gert talks Claire into doing what we all so badly want to do. My mother's friends will handle the kitchen and the rest of the guests, see to the kids, let the dogs out. They'll put the food away and take out the trash, because they want to do these things.

I stand in the hall where I can see cousins and neighbors, with plates of food perched on their laps as they sit on the couch, or I can look the other way and see a kitchen full of my mother's best friends. They are not particularly beautiful, these people. They have lines in their faces and moles on their necks, and they run the gamut of body shapes from string beans to pears and the occasional melon. I feel more affection for them than I have ever felt, but at the same time I feel miles away, as if I stand on a mountaintop looking down.

I pull on the Keds and knot the laces. Sheer stockings, silk dress, tasteful pearls and tennis shoes.

'Come on,' I say to Ashby and Claire and we are running down Claire's stairs and out the door like children on the last day of school. It makes no sense, being happy right now, but as the three of us crowd into the front seat of my truck and I shift Big Mama into gear, there is no doubt in my mind that I am.

'I heard you snicker, by the way, little missy.' Ashby is squeezing in next to Claire.

'I didn't.'

'Did too,' Claire tells me.

'Nobody heard.'

'*We* did.'

'Mama would have laughed too,' I tell them.

'She would not have.'

I replay the scene in my head. The church is filled, the minister has ministered, and Cousin Alma has sung

149

every verse of 'Amazing Grace'. The curtains above the pulpit open slowly to reveal . . . an empty space. The minister turns his head with a frown. The creak and groan of hydraulics heralds an impending arrival, and, shoved by unseen and tardy hands, my mother's coffin slides with more haste than dignity into the niche.

9

I am on the road the day after my mother's funeral, just like I promised Gert. The drive is tedious. When you live in a tiny town like Beaufort, the Charleston traffic is really a bitch. I have found the firm of Carmichael and Hubert near the Bank of America building on State Street, just like Gert said. I circle the block for the third time, looking for a place to park.

Rain drills the streets and my depression rises along with the humidity. The afternoon is almost over – 3.47 as I check my watch, and the sky is dark and edgy, just the way I feel. I glare at a red Ford Escort, which is straddling two spaces, and circle the block again. No scrunchy little slot is going to do for Big Mama.

Half a block down, a man in a sky-blue Suburban pulls out in front of me into traffic. I snag his space, then unfasten my seat belt, but that's as far as I go. The thing is, I am self-conscious to be out will-hunting like this. But it would be ridiculous to sit by and let those Blanchards swipe Mama's personal family pieces, not to mention her house and money market fund. I open the truck door.

I check over my left shoulder for a break in traffic, step out onto the curb and unfurl my red umbrella. I don't usually bother with umbrellas, I prefer the simplicity of a baseball cap and a brisk walk, but today I have on a black skirt and blazer and the last thing I want is rain all over my outfit. Bad enough that the humidity takes the fluff out of my hair.

I notice that two spokes of my umbrella are broken, like the injured wing of a bird, and rainwater runs down the slick red dome onto my foot. I hold the umbrella to one side and move down the sidewalk as fast as heels allow. The sidewalk is wet and slick and water spatters my ankles, making them itch. I pass through the heavy glass doors of 137 State Street with great relief.

The floor, a tile mosaic, is streaked with dirt and water, and I walk carefully, so as not to catch a heel between the tiles. The building is old, with high ceilings, and involves a substantial amount of mahogany crown molding. The absence of linoleum and Sheetrock makes it evident that Mama has selected a fairly successful firm.

The directory by the elevators indicates that Carmichael and Hubert are located in a third-floor suite. I eye the narrow doors of the elevator with serious reluctance. My fear of heights has lately been jarred by an increasing sense of claustrophobia, and elevators are fast becoming one of my least favorite things. The doors open. Inside are men in suits, a thinly carpeted floor and a row of gold buttons labeled B to 4. The men regard me with mild interest.

'Are there stairs?' I ask. One of the gentleman has been kind enough to push the button that will keep the door from closing on me as I cross the threshold into that dark and airless space.

The gentleman jerks his head to the left. 'Right past the water fountain.'

Six flights of stairs shouldn't wind me, but they do. I take a minute standing outside Suite 302 just to catch my breath. The door is heavy, dark wood with frosted glass in the top panel. It makes me think of those old *noir* private-eye movies, though I doubt many investigators could afford the rent on these digs. I knock shyly, then open the door.

Even a polite person could not describe this office with any word except cluttered. Cardboard file boxes are stacked in every corner, and there is paperwork on one of the leather chairs next to the couch. A coat tree is so heavily laden with men's raincoats and umbrellas it looks in danger of toppling over.

A secretary sits in a horseshoe-shaped fortress. 'Good grief, is that elevator on the blink again?' She hasn't looked away from her computer screen, but I'm the only other person in the outer office, so I'm guessing she's addressing me. She looks up and smiles. 'You seem out of breath, so I figure you took the stairs.'

'I don't like elevators.'

This secretary is a pretty girl, on the up side of thirty, in a gray cashmere sweater, narrow-leg khakis and high-heeled black boots. She wears glasses that hang from a chain around her neck, and with such an air that I wonder if this piece of what I consider old lady jewelry has defied all odds and come curiously into style.

'I'd like to speak with someone about my mother. I believe she made a will here not too long ago.'

The cashmere girl's smile takes on a wary air. My decision to dress carefully and do this in person was clearly wise. It's easy to blow people off on the phone. Most attorneys hire assistants who perform this function well.

'Do you have an appointment?'

'No. I wasn't sure who to make an appointment with.'

This, from her expression, is a shade too honest. 'If you'd like to sit down there and wait just a minute?'

I sit, and Cashmere heads out from behind the fortress and knocks on one of three closed doors. From the murmur of voices that escapes down the hall, there is a lot of business going on.

I glance through the tattered stack of magazines that rest on a dusty end table. There are no windows in this room, but the rain outside has nevertheless managed to inflict an interior gloom. Cashmere is back quickly. She retreats behind the desk.

'Ma'am, I'm awfully sorry, but even if your mother did use our services, it would be a breach of client confidentiality to discuss it, even with her daughter.'

'I understand, but here's the situation. My mother died unexpectedly several days ago, intestate.' Okay, a small lie. 'A friend of hers remembers driving Mama here to Charleston to make out a will. This friend was pretty sure my mother had an appointment with someone in your firm. Obviously, if that's the case, you should have a copy of the will in your files.'

Cashmere is frowning. 'Did the friend actually come in with her?'

'She had errands to run, so she dropped my mother off.'

'Are you executor of the estate?'

I think about this. 'I can't be sure until I see who she named as executor in her will.'

'Makes sense.'

'I do have a copy of her provisional death certificate.

154

As you probably know, it takes forever to get a final certificate from the state.' I hand the document across the desk and the woman puts on her glasses and takes a look.

'Who is Fielding Smallwood?' she asks.

'My father.'

'He's listed as next of kin.'

'He died too, right after my mother.'

'My Lord, how awful. You poor thing.' She looks up and scrutinizes me carefully.

People are fascinated by the survivors of grief. This sort of attention makes me uncomfortable because I'm not exactly sure how it is I'm supposed to look.

Cashmere glances over at the closed door of the office and grimaces. 'Hang on a second, will you, I just want to check the computer.' Her fingers move over the keyboard like a tornado. She taps her toe and squints, leaning close to the screen. Whatever she sees there or doesn't see, I get the impression I am out of luck.

'Do you know when she came in?'

'Not precisely. But I think it was some time around May eighteenth.'

'Umkay. Umkay. Smallwood, Smallwood, Lena . . . oh, here we go.'

I smile and lean forward.

'Yep, here it is. Now why can't I find that file? Maybe . . . umum-um. Oh. *That's* what happened.' Cashmere looks up, and the expression on her face says *I'm sorry*. 'She did have an appointment, and it was on the eighteenth, but she was a no-show.'

I sink down lower in the couch.

'Just a second, let's see what I put in the notes. Maybe

she rescheduled. Here it is.' She squints again. 'It says she called in at one-fifty on the eighteenth, canceled, and said she'd call back if she wanted to reschedule. But she definitely called and canceled her two o'clock appointment.'

'She called at one-fifty and canceled an appointment for two?'

'That's what the notes say.'

I am most definitely confused. 'Thank you so much for all your help.' I get to my feet and shake her hand.

'I'm really sorry,' she says, with enough sincerity to make me embarrassed at what must be showing on my face.

I hear the rattle of the knob from one of the closed wooden doors, and I scoot out the door. I'm in no mood for a cranky lawyer.

It hits me on the last flight of stairs. *Is that elevator on the blink again?* I run back up five flights of stairs, knock, then open the door to Suite 302. Grumpy lawyer is standing over the horseshoe, flipping through typed pages while Cashmere is taking notes.

'Sorry to interrupt,' I say, 'but can you tell me if the elevator was out of service on May the eighteenth?'

From the troubled expression on Cashmere's face, I can see she is going to be of no help. But cranky lawyer is a man of precision.

'Yes, it was. Out on the eighteenth, the twelfth, and from the fifth to the seventh a month before. Are you here about the elevators?'

I can see he's winding up.

'Actually, no,' I tell him, just as I shut the door.

I stand outside the law office of Elspeth Dougall. It is the timing that clued me in – Mama canceling a two o'clock appointment at one-fifty, Mama who was invariably thirty minutes early for every appointment she kept. She always said I balanced the equation by being thirty minutes late.

I see her walking slowly into the lobby, carrying the suitcase she liked to call a purse. Still a blonde after all these years, wearing pale foundation to match her ivory skin tone and dark red lipstick, freshly applied. She'd be nervous. Mama's knees have been so painful the last few years, she rarely leaves the house. I know her well enough to see that, standing in the lobby, she'd be feeling fairly shy.

I see her in front of the elevators – is there a sign that says OUT OF ORDER? She will never make those stairs.

But Mama is a problem solver, and she's on a mission and full of purpose, and she's not going home till she gets what she wants.

There is one attorney with a suite on the first floor listed on the wall directory: Elspeth Dougall. I say a small prayer and knock on her door.

The voice that welcomes me in is youthful, and when I open the door it comes within an inch of hitting the desk. A woman is scrambling to attention; her feet come off the desk, and she drops a magazine to the floor.

'I'm looking for Elspeth Dougall.'

She beams like I'm her long-lost sister and shakes my hand. 'I'm Elspeth Dougall.' Sure enough, that is the name on the plate on the empty, shining desk. She is a pretty girl, with a deep Georgia accent, and I can see from the diploma on the wall that she went to law school in Atlanta. She is blue-eyed and blond and her hair flips up like the Breck girls in the old commercials. 'How can I help you today?'

'My name is Georgie Smallwood. I'm Lena Smallwood's daughter. My mother died a few days ago, and I'm wondering if she came here to make a will.'

Elspeth Dougall's eyes are very wide and kind. 'You're Lena Smallwood's daughter?'

'Yes, that's right.'

'I'm sorry to ask, but could I see some ID?'

I dig through my purse for my wallet and driver's license and hand them with my mother's death certificate across the desk to Elspeth Dougall.

'Of course I remember your mother. She was only my third client since I opened my office. I warned her I was a newbie, but she said I needed to start somewhere and it might as well be with her. She actually waited right here while I put together the will, so she could sign it and not have to come back. The two secretaries next door were good enough to witness it for us. I can't believe your mother passed away. I'm so sorry for your loss.'

Elspeth Dougall is up on her feet opening the top drawer of the filing cabinet. From the hollow sound the drawer makes when it opens, I get the feeling the rest of the cabinet is fairly empty. 'Let me get you a copy of her will. Did she not leave a copy with your dad?'

'He died too, a few days after Mom.'

'Oh, my goodness.' Elspeth Dougall looks at me over her shoulder, and I know she is eager for details. She pulls a file from the cabinet and opens it up. 'Okay, here's a note. Your mother said she was leaving my name and number with Ashby Smallwood, her son, so that if something happened, he'd know where to come.' She smiles at me. 'Did your brother send you?'

'Yes.' My throat goes dry. Maybe Mama never talked to Ashby. Maybe Ashby forgot. I reach for the papers Elspeth is handing over.

'Read it through at your convenience. Most everything is divided between you kids.'

'She didn't leave it all to Daddy?'

'She left him fifty thousand dollars and any items he wants from the house, with the exception of her family pieces, which she wanted to go to you and Ashby and Claire. There's a list on the back – it's attached.'

So it's true. Our father has betrayed us. I find it is one thing to suspect treachery and another to be perfectly sure. I decide not to think about Ashby until he and I get a chance to talk.

And this is good news, really. Enough money to keep all of us safe, and the comfort of knowing Mama thought of us before she died. I wonder if I can get back the stuff Carla Blanchard already took.

'You know, I think I may need to hire you, Ms Dougall. Do you have a few minutes for me to explain?'

Ashby brings *The Graceful Lady* in at low tide, which comes today around four o'clock in the afternoon. I sit and wait, engine idling. *The Graceful Lady* comes in with outriggers down and doors out; no netting can touch the water in the Ace Basin Sound. The boat is more stable this way. When the outriggers are up, the boat will be top-heavy and vulnerable in rough water. There are ice docks on Coffin Point. My brother sells his shrimp to the guy who runs the dock.

These days the ice that keeps the shrimp fresh is blown in chips from a machine, but when Ashby and I were kids the fishermen used to load three-hundred-pound blocks on board and shave the ice by hand.

There are seagulls perched on *The Graceful Lady*'s mast. The birds stay close to the boats to feed on the by-catch, and while Ashby is fishing they are as thick as snowflakes in the air.

My brother maintains his boat fastidiously. If you study *The Graceful Lady* you will find all the equipment in harmony. The lines come up in efficient synchronization; Ashby won't tolerate a block that's jammed.

Ashby fishes alone, or did until Hank came home. The boats go out at three in the morning, and today Ashby has worked a grueling fourteen hours. Hank is not fishing today. I would worry about my son with anyone except Ashby. Shrimping is one of the most hazardous occupations in the world, though most injuries and deaths are caused by carelessness or poorly maintained equipment. If a line slips off the gypsy head it will sever whatever gets fouled: your arm, your shoulder, your head. Beaufort loses two or three fishermen every year.

I can tell from the way my brother moves around the deck that today was a good day. I'm relieved on his behalf. Ashby's rule of thumb is an annual gross equal to the initial cost of his boat. Insurance rates are rising, fuel costs a dollar fifty a gallon, and with *The Graceful Lady* using ten gallons an hour, a fourteen-hour workday comes with an overhead of two or three hundred dollars. I know that last year Ashby ran into significant repair costs and took a second loan out on the boat.

I cannot watch these boats come in without a twinge of sadness. Once the old boats are gone, so will be the industry. A used boat like *The Graceful Lady*, which cost my brother in the neighborhood of fifty thousand dollars, would take half a million to replace. Half a million is too much investment for a man to turn a profit. Just to break even, you'd have to double or triple your catch.

Good day or not, my brother is happiest when on his boat. I fish with him from time to time and am always impressed by the grace and balance of his routine. Ashby fishes almost every day and is an artist at finding the shrimp. When I ask how he knows where they are, he shrugs and says you have to consider the tide patterns, how the winds have changed, where the shrimp were last, and at what time of day. The tides are the key, Ashby always tells me, and Reese says Ashby wakes up in the middle of the night, thinking about them.

My brother sees me and raises a hand. His smile is the one I remember from childhood, uninhibited, happy. I hear seagulls and the thud of the wooden dock planks beneath his feet.

Ashby slings a denim shirt over his shoulder. His T-shirt is wet with sweat and his hair is soaked under the ball cap. He's dirty and has that look of weary satisfaction worn by a man who's put in a full day.

'What's up, Georgie Porgie?'

'Can we talk? I know you're tired and you wanna

go home. But if you hop in quick, I'll take you to Sonic for some jalapeño poppers and a Coke. My treat. I've got cash.'

'Okay.' Ashby moves to the passenger's side of the truck. Raises a hand at one or two of the other fishermen as we drive the short stretch that takes us to Sonic.

I order from the speaker at the drive-in restaurant: jalapeño poppers and Diet Sprite for Ashby, Coke and Tater Tots for me. We do our best talking over junk food.

I open my purse and extract a folded copy of Mama's will. Ashby takes the paper and frowns over the words. I wait, wondering how much my dyslexic brother has read and absorbed.

'You found the will?'

'Yeah.'

'Good for you.'

'So you're happy? About me finding it?'

Ashby lays the papers in my lap and turns to face me, eyebrows raised. 'Sounds like you got something on your mind.' In spite of his southern upbringing, or perhaps in rebellion to it, Ashby prides himself on being direct.

'Why didn't you tell me that Mama made another will?'

'I would have told you if Gert hadn't brought it up. I was actually hoping you wouldn't find out I knew. But remember, at Shoney's, I did say we should look for it and fight.'

Ashby looks over my shoulder and smiles and I crane my neck to see the smitten waitress holding a plastic red tray with our food. One smile from my glorious brother and she'll be walking on air all day.

But at least when I ask for ketchup, she's happy to give me all I want.

I balance the tray on the half-open window, and Ashby takes off his shoes, puts the seat back as far as it will go and stretches out his hairy, sun-drenched legs. I see the scar on his chin where he had a cyst removed when he was twelve.

'Yeah, but Ashby, you didn't say Mama actually told you when she made the will. That you knew who the lawyer was and probably what Mama left to who.'

'Don't you mean 'whom'?'

I cannot read his face. 'Ashby, you made it seem like you only thought we should fight it after Daddy died.'

'I know.' He is chewing steadily, eating those jalapeño poppers.

I put my Tater Tots down. 'You didn't even tell me I had the attorney wrong.'

'I didn't *know* you had the attorney wrong.'

'Oh, okay. So all of this is in my head.'

'No, it's not all in your head.' Ashby pauses; what's coming next is clearly difficult for him to say. 'I really don't want to explain this to you.'

'Why not?'

'I don't want you to hate me, or quit speaking to me, or get started on one of your grudges.'

'Ashby, you're my brother; you know I could never hate you.'

'No, I don't know that, Georgie. Remember that time two years ago when you wouldn't talk to me for three weeks?'

I look at my hands. 'I was upset.'

'And now you're not? You know, you make me feel like I *have* to take sides, to choose between you and

Daddy. The way you talk about him. You're so full of anger, Georgie.'

'Ashby—'

'I won't say you don't have every good reason in the world. I won't say you aren't right, you may be *more* right, really. But I can't just write my father off.'

Does Ashby not realize that Daddy wrote him off years ago? That the more you tried to please Daddy, the harder he was to please?

'I mean, you may well be the most honest and realistic one of all of us, but Claire and I – no, don't *look* like that, it's not like we're ganging up.'

I swallow and stay quiet, but my throat is tight and I hand the Tater Tots to my brother because there's no way in hell I can eat them.

'Georgie, you make me feel like if I admit that I love Dad, you'll never talk to me again.'

'That's not true.' My voice cracks. But he's right.

'I don't mean that you—'

'Ashby, just don't dredge it all up, okay? You're right. I'm not sane when it comes to Dad. And I know that how you and Claire feel is more normal and more morally correct.'

'I don't know about that.'

'Whatever. I'll back off, okay? I won't let it interfere between you and me, I promise.'

He looks at me.

'Honest.'

'You won't quit talking to me? You won't pretend everything is fine and avoid me like the plague? You do that, Georgie, and I'm not going to have a sister who won't talk to me.'

'I won't. I promise.'

'Prove it. Eat a jalapeño popper.' He hands me the fried pepper and I hold it in my hand.

'But you did know about the will, didn't you, Ashby?'

My brother rolls his eyes. 'I did know about the will. Here's what happened. Dad came to me. He said he made some bad investments. He was afraid there were going to be layoffs at the bank. He was scared, Georgie, no kidding. He was worried about money. So I promised not to bring it up, about the new will. Some of that money should have been his anyway; he's worked like a dog all his life.'

Which is true, even I admit.

'But see, he also promised to take care of you and Claire if you ever got in a tough spot. I know, don't look at me like that. I still can't believe how he treated Claire. I was going to make it up to you guys. I'm actually having a pretty good year. I was going to give you all part share to make it all up.'

'You don't need to do that, and you know it.'

'I want to. Reese makes good money and I want to share with my sisters, what's so wrong with that?'

I study my brother because I have been of the opinion he's been having a bad year. Now I'm not sure.

'Ashby, I appreciate it, really, but I can't take it. I just won't. You might want to help Claire. Except it doesn't matter, because now we've got the right will.'

'Mom said she was that attorney's first client. Wilbanks will eat that kid for lunch.'

'Third client. Don't roll your eyes. Her name is Elspeth Dougall and her father's been an estate attorney for thirty-seven years. He's going to help her – he helped her draft the original – and I think with him at her back she can kick Wilbanks's butt. She's sure game to try.'

'Push that speaker button. I want a grilled cheese sandwich and another Diet Sprite. And by the way, Hank has the makings of a hell of a shrimper.'

'I really appreciate you taking Hank out. I know it means a lot to him.'

'Hell, Georgie, it's a pleasure for me. I like having him with me. You know I'll never have kids of my own. I decided years ago to help raise yours and Claire's.'

He is crafty, my older brother. Reminding me how good he is to my son.

'Promise me, Ashby, you won't just let those Blanchards get Mama's money.'

Ashby frowns. 'Don't you worry about that.'

Years from now I will regret that I don't hug my brother this day and tell him everything is okay.

I stand on my sagging balcony, arms resting on the railing, and look out into the twilight at the world's prettiest small town. The moment has come for my long-awaited date with John Wallace. Will I need a sweater tonight or not?

Behind me the door is open to the living room, all lamps blazing, attracting insects from Savannah to Charleston. A palmetto bug inches along the railing. He is as big as a mouse – up north he'd be called a cockroach – and I am just grateful he is crawling in the opposite direction from me. I don't want to make him mad. I know people who keep a gun in the house just to shoot these bugs, and in my experience they are damn hard to kill.

Behind me, I hear Cousin Beauregard contentedly munching. She is a creature of regular habits and has somehow let me know that she likes her food in the bowl by five o'clock at night, though she feeds continually in small portions as the urge strikes. I did not realize, until lately, how much I have missed having a dog. I like to hear the rustle of Cousin's snout in the ceramic food bowl with dog paws painted on each side which I rescued from Mama's kitchen floor. I like to hear the delicate crunch of kibble in her needle teeth.

This dog has peculiar eating habits. She fills her cheek pouches with tasty bits, spews them in a cluster of brown chunks on the oriental carpet and delicately lips each crunchy pillow, sorting and choosing till everything is eaten; then it's back to the food bowl again. According to a show I once watched on Animal Planet, this is instinctual pack behavior. Take your food away from the feeding ground so you can finish it undisturbed.

I hear the clink of Cousin's dog tags as she jumps from the carpet to the couch. She noses a cushion and settles in. I hope Hank did not feed her any junk food this afternoon because she will throw it up all over the couch.

There are footsteps on the sidewalk. The light is failing, but I can see John Wallace through the branches of the tree that grows beside my house. The trunk is twisted and is as smooth as bone. It sheds long strips of bark, like curls of lathed wood, and the limbs are layered like muscular tissue, raw and rippling beneath the skin. The branches bear leaves like latticed wicker, three quarters of the way up. I have looked at this tree every day for years. Like me, it accumulates layers of life, some of it easy and weightless, some of it heavy, like scars.

The footsteps stop, and I peer sideways around the tree. John Wallace is on the curb across the street, pausing beneath a streetlight as if trying to decide the way. He wears dark dress pants, a crisp striped shirt and dark suspenders. There is a bouquet of flowers in his hand, and even from here he gives the impression of being well scrubbed and oddly vulnerable.

I back away softly, careful not to run my stockings, which are eleven dollars a pair. I still have to put on lipstick and find my shoes. I pat Cousin's head and glance at the clock. I have been daydreaming on the porch forever and have completely lost track of the time.

I run an eye over my living quarters. Immaculate, as things can only be when Hank is off fishing with my brother. I have no intention of asking John Wallace up after dinner, but on the off-chance I always prepare.

My hair is up tonight, caught loosely in a clip, and the silver of my earrings catches the light. It's been a while since my last dinner date, and I had a Victoria's Secret halter dress Fed-Exed to the shop. I have the grace to feel guilty. There are bills to pay and Hank's future to plan, but I know my sister is safe with money in the bank, and the guilt refuses to take.

I slip into open-toed sandals with disastrously steep heels. I will be comfortable for exactly two hours, then the watch towers that report pain in my feet will start screaming like a three-alarm fire. Tiny purse, cash, key, tissues, lipstick, breath mints. A woven silk jacket in case it's cold in the restaurant, and I'm ready to go.

I clomp carefully down the stairs, hanging on to the rail, and shut the door to the second floor just as the front bell rings and sets off the barking Cousin alarm.

Beaufort in general is a courteous town populated by mannerly people, but if it has a fault it is that the locals are prone to stare. John Wallace sits across from me in the dining room of the Beaufort Inn and graciously endures. He is a stranger and I am well known, and the people at the tables around us are easy to separate into categories of tourist and local. The tourists are hungry for their dinner; the locals, for information.

They are particularly interested in who is sitting across from me at this table drinking a beer.

John Wallace raises a glass and smiles at me, his Budweiser to my Miller Lite. We have ordered the coconut shrimp and dirty rice, and the waitress has set a basket of bread by the candles between us, with a serving of sweetly pungent maple nut butter.

'It's good,' I tell John Wallace, offering up the basket of bread.

'What is it? I didn't catch what the lady said.'

'Maple. It's like butter mashed with maple syrup, and it's perfect when you're drinking beer.'

He looks dubious but spreads butter on the bread, and I wait for the satisfied smile.

'I've never had anything like this before. I didn't think it would be this good.'

Our awkwardness eases as we work through the beer and the bread. I look around me at the small dining room, which has thick carpet, heavy gold curtains, white linen napkins and several women clearly admiring my date. It surprises me how happy I feel. I'm not going to worry about anything tonight.

John Wallace is staying in a cabin on Hunting Island, one of the busiest state parks in the Carolinas.

'So how are you liking Hunting Island?' I ask him.

'I like everything but the bugs.'

'You check for holes in the screens?'

He gives me that half smile. 'I did think of that, yes.'

Salads arrive. He eats blue cheese dressing, while I prefer the raspberry vinaigrette. 'Girl dressing' is what Ashby calls it.

'Just doing some fishing and passing through?'

John Wallace's expression is good-natured. How he

answers this question will determine whether or not I disappear immediately after dinner. I've been single all my life and if this guy seems even a little bit hinky I won't hesitate to find my own way home. I have already broken my first-date rule by not driving my own car. It was the flowers he brought that did it. That and the new dress – climbing in and out of Big Mama in stockings and heels is at the very least inelegant. And I always run my hose.

'I'm not fishing, but I am a fisherman. Used to shrimp down in Louisiana. I've got a stake, and I'm looking around to see where I want to put a boat. It's tough down in Louisiana these days, and I wanted to see how matters stood here.'

There is not enough vinaigrette on my salad. But you can't order extra with a guy you hardly know, so I eat the best parts out of the middle. It's more salad than I'll want anyway.

John Wallace takes a small bit of lettuce and chews, wiping his mouth with the cloth napkin. His manners are fine, but he has a hesitant air, as if he is not at home in this sort of place. This dinner will not come cheap. I would have been fine drinking beer in the Shrimp Shack, but he is trying to impress. And so far I am impressed. I try not to worry about the bill.

'Don't you-all have shrimp of your own down in Louisiana?'

He shakes a finger at me, but he is amused. He knows I am testing him. 'Did you say you grew up here in Beaufort?'

'I don't remember. Did I say that?'

He smiles and waits me out.

'Okay, yes, I did grow up here.'

'Then you know that when the shrimp boats come in at low tide they take their catch to the ice docks, sell them to the dock owner, and *he* sells the shrimp to the highest bidder. If you look at the trucks that come to haul that catch away, a certain percentage will be heading for Louisiana.'

'And the other half goes to New York.'

'So you do know.'

'My brother's a shrimper. Been working the Sound since he was a kid.'

'From what I understand from talking to the locals, nobody works the Sound anymore.'

'They closed it to commercial fishermen. I meant he works around it.'

John Wallace looks across at me. 'Who was behind getting it shut down? Environmental groups?'

'Sport fishermen. First they said the commercial fishermen were catching the game fish in their nets. *Then* they said, Well, no, but the by-catch was full of fish that the game fish were feeding on, and the commercial fishermen were screwing up the food chain.'

A waitress arrives with a heavy round tray and two plates of shrimp and rice. She works with precision, serving from the left, with the glass and silverware arranged just so around the plate. The shrimp is coated in a light coconut and cornmeal batter. South Carolina has the best shrimp in the world.

John Wallace settles his napkin back in his lap. 'So it was the money boys, then? Local politics?'

I nod, thinking of how it now takes Ashby over an hour to get *The Graceful Lady* into the shrimp grounds when it used to take at best fifteen minutes. How he is facing the chop and churn of the ocean in a small boat better suited for the calm surface waters of the Sound.

John Wallace takes a bite of shrimp and smiles.

'Admit it,' I say.

'Very good.'

'The best.'

He gives me a stern look but can't hold it. 'The best.'

John Wallace is intent on pleasing me. I feel approved of. Like he will be interested no matter what crazy viewpoint I come up with.

'Here's my problem with all of this.' I pick up a shrimp and point it across the table, which is possibly not the best etiquette, but I am on a roll. I've had just enough beer to relax, which is about four ounces. 'I'm not against taking care of the ocean, the Sound, the islands – South Carolina, for heaven's sake. But I want my *community* to survive. I want the people who live here to be able to make their living here. And the way it's going, if you have to have half a million dollars to buy a boat, the sheer economics will never pan out.'

John Wallace takes a sip of beer. 'In order to survive, you have to at least pull in an annual gross equal to the cost of your boat.'

'That's what my brother says. He goes out at three a.m. every morning and works till low tide every single day. He probably spends three hundred dollars a day on fuel alone.'

'And some days you don't catch three hundred dollars' worth of shrimp.'

'I see him working harder and falling behind. If they keep going the way they have been, the only people who are going to fish here are the huge corporations. And if you don't think they'll fish these waters out and move on to the next place, you're living in a dream world. This is *our* town. And they'll come here and take all the shrimp and leave us with no way to work our own coast. Do people in this country think that when the big boys kill us off, community by community, this country can survive?'

Our eyes meet. If he patronizes me I will throw a shrimp at him, but he isn't giving me an amused smile or squirming in his chair. He waves a shrimp back at me. I meet his eyes across the table and he smiles, and I notice how closely he has shaved, and wonder what it would feel like to trace a finger along his jaw. He leans close. I never do find out what he was going to say.

'Georgie *Smallwood*.'

Annette Wilbanks is making her way to my table while the hostess finds a spot to please her father, Eugene. I have been too wrapped up in John Wallace to notice them come in, which is pretty wrapped up. This is an intimate dining room. No more than fifteen perfectly set tables.

'Honey, how have you been?' Annette faces my dining companion with wide eyes and a tremulous smile.

John Wallace is on his feet, which pleases me as much as Annette's intrusion does not.

'I'm Annette Wilbanks; my daddy is Eugene Wilbanks of the district attorney's office?'

My daddy is, my daddy is, my daddy is.

'John Wallace.'

They shake hands, and Annette turns to me, friendly as a puppy. 'I just had to run on over and show you this T-shirt I bought.'

The shirt is aquamarine to match her eyes, stretched

tight over a small but well-shaped figure. She has on black Lycra pants, high-heeled gold sandals and a silk jacket thrown over the T-shirt that reads *GRITS – Girls Raised In The South*.

'They do serve grits here,' I tell John Wallace. For some reason he laughs. Annette gives me a sideways look as if she is suspicious of an insult, and I can see mascara clumped on her naturally long lashes.

'You'll have to excuse us here.' Annette rests a hand on John Wallace's arm. 'But being such a small town, we just visit around from table to table.'

John Wallace remains standing. Annette wants to join us, and he doesn't want her to.

Annette glances across the dining room toward her father. 'I guess I better not keep Daddy waiting. Nice to meet you, John. Georgie, I'll see you later, I guess.'

Eugene Wilbanks is sitting down and the waitress is bringing his bourbon and ice. When Daddy was alive, Wilbanks would have come over and said hello, and even Annette seems bewildered by the latest snub.

John Wallace's gaze sweeps the room before he sits, and I get that feeling again, that this is a man you treat with care. But then he sits down and studies me over the table, and the way he looks at me makes me feel safe.

'Let's order dessert and coffee and walk it off afterward down by the waterfront.'

'I don't think I can eat another bite.'

'Then eat half a bite. Come on.' He looks up and the waitress miraculously appears. He smiles at me across the table. 'Help me pick something out.'

We drink coffee in tiny china cups while we wait for dessert. The coffee is too strong, like they always serve it here. 'Man coffee' Ashby calls it, whenever we splurge on a Beaufort Inn breakfast – though what he would know about it, I don't know, since Ashby doesn't drink coffee.

I get a white-hot jealous gaze from Annette, who can't seem to resist looking over more than would be considered polite. She is talking loudly to her daddy and laughing a lot, such a fun-loving girl, but Wilbanks seems to have a lot on his mind, and he sips one bourbon after another.

Later, John Wallace and I walk down by the waterfront in Beaufort's town square, listening to crickets and watching cars cross the drawbridge. It is hot and humid. My two hours are up and my feet hurt and I have to go to the bathroom.

But we are walking close, almost touching hands. My head reaches his shoulder and he keeps having to slow down for me to catch up.

'Pretty shoes,' he says, with just enough awkwardness in his voice to make me think he's sincere.

Pretty fucking agonizing shoes, I think. 'Thank you.'

'You're getting quiet on me, Georgie. Are you tired? Should I take you home?'

'I've got a day of it tomorrow.' And I do. 'But I have really enjoyed tonight, and I can't thank you enough.'

The ride home is short – in better shoes, I could almost have walked. John Wallace sees me to the door. The porch light is on and moths are circling beneath. John Wallace stands very close and looks at me, and

176

when I don't move away he puts his arms around me, pulls me away from the pool of light and sucks my bottom lip into his mouth. My world spins. He cups my face in his hands and kisses me deeply, and I know he would happily follow me upstairs if I led the way.

'Good night, John.'

'Good night, Georgie.'

I open the door to my shop, smile sweetly and wave good-bye, a woman in no hurry without a care in the world. As soon as the deadbolt shoots home, I peel off my sandals and run like a banshee up the stairs. Cousin Beauregard has started barking and I really have to pee.

When the phone rings early the next morning, I wake with no trace of a headache and something of a glow.

'I know I shouldn't have called you this early. I woke you up, didn't I?'

John's voice is easy to recognize, and it's a nice one to hear first thing in the morning.

'I was awake.'

'You sound sleepy. Still in bed?'

'Maybe.'

'What are you going to do today?'

'Work.'

'I just wanted to tell you I enjoyed seeing you last night, and I woke up thinking about you. If I call you later, will you tell me about your day?'

'It's bound to be boring.'

'Not to me. I'll call you.'

I stretch and get out of bed. The last thing I want to do is work. I decide to delay and take Cousin for a walk. She is building her stamina, and when we get time I'm going to take her walking on the beach. Maybe we will walk over on Hunting Island. Maybe we will invite John Wallace.

After a quick shower and some coffee, Cousin and I are out on the town. We go slowly with frequent rest breaks. She likes to sniff every tree, and I am in no hurry. I am thinking about my wake-up call, and about my mother and my father, and I wonder how things were for them at the start.

When I was growing up, my parents had a private date together every Friday night. Saturdays were for bridge clubs and couples gatherings, and Sundays were for church. Friday was just for them.

The tradition went like this.

My father comes home with a huge sack of McDonald's hamburgers. Claire and I clear off the coffee table, because Ashby, being male, never does kitchen stuff. On the other hand, I don't have to mow the lawn. I pour the drinks and the three of us, Ashby, Claire and me, start our Friday night off with *The Flintstones*. Because it is the weekend, we can stay up as late as we want, all night if we choose, so we don't care where our parents go or how long they stay, we are set for the night. My sister will tell everyone how she is going to stay up all night, but she'll be asleep by nine. The only glitch is that my brother, being the oldest, is always in charge. He never lords it over me, but I can hardly bear it. I'm bossy and I want to be in charge. Ashby knows this very well, and he knows how much I want to be the oldest sibling, and all his life he introduces me as his big sister, mainly because I am so short, and he calls this humor.

As we get older, we have friends over from the neighborhood. We are approaching our teens and we get into enormous trouble, holding séances, putting on shows, playing kick the can or going to war – boys against the girls. Whatever we do, the evidence is usually destroyed before midnight. My parents never have any idea what we are up to, except the time I get mad at Ashby and kick a hole in the wall, and we manage to hide that until we move out of the house, by propping Claire's large stuffed donkey against the wall. When my mother asks what Claire's donkey is doing on my bed, Claire says she gave it to me.

But one thing my mother always knows is when we are in trouble over our heads. She is psychic about this kind of stuff. It is not something we talk about much, or a matter of believing or not believing. When we need her she is there.

A typical example would be the night when she calls from a phone booth on her way out to dinner. Ashby takes the call, reassuring her that all is well. Within minutes of hanging up, there is a knock at the door. A neighbor boy, Stanley Jefferson, who lives across the street, has carried Claire home. A stream of blood gushes from her knee where she has gone over the handlebars of her bike and torn a triangle of flesh all the way to the bone. Claire is crying hysterically, and Stanley Jefferson is clearly relieved to hand her over to Ashby. I look out the front door and see a trail of red drops on the sidewalk.

Ashby carries Claire to the upstairs bathroom. We are well trained and aware of where it is and is not acceptable to bleed. I follow my brother and sister up the stairs, but I am worried. My parents will be out of

179

reach for hours, and Ashby and I are on our own. That minute the front door opens and I look over my shoulder down the dark hallway. My mother has arrived.

Before cell phones, we used to make do with psychic mothers.

The sun is getting hot, and Cousin and I cut the walk short, happy to get back home to the air conditioning. I have put a quilt down on the floor of the kitchen, but she piles her toys there and does her day sleeping on the right-hand side of the couch. This used to be my favorite spot, but I've moved to the left.

I feel good this morning, and I have half a mind to kidnap my sister for a girls' day out. It is time for the big analysis, where we examine every moment of my date. Women are natural anthropologists. We read a man's every comment and facial expression with an intensity that compares to a researcher sifting a historical dig.

As it turns out, I will not have to work today, but the shopping trip and the girl talk are out. My shop bell rings, and whoever is beating on the door is not impressed by the sign that says CLOSED. I am being visited a second time by the police.

I sit in the back seat of the unmarked Ford Taurus and my hands are shaking, which is humiliatingly hard to hide. I am cooperating with detectives Hutchins and

Click in their investigations into my father's death. I find that I now look at policemen in a new light. No longer are these the men I call for protection if someone is trying the door of my shop. These are different men, men I think may be trying to put one of us Smallwoods in jail. Hutchins and Click are homicide detectives, after all, which means that no one is thinking that my father has died an accidental death, and I realize we all better get that through our heads. Ashby and Claire have been oddly unfazed. Score points for denial.

I rub the knee of my khaki pants, wondering if I was wrong to agree to 'go downtown'. Policemen on the doorstep are intimidating. One has the most incredible urge either to appease them or to run away. What would have happened if I had refused to come along? Should I call an attorney when I get there? Will they think I am guilty of something if I do? Have they talked to Ashby and Claire?

Hutchins parks across the street from the modern well-kept building that holds the Beaufort sheriff's department. They lead me through a side door, so I don't have to trail behind them through the lobby. On the other hand, no one sees me go in, so no one knows where I am. Hutchins holds the door for me and smiles. Is he being a gentleman, or does he want me sandwiched in between?

My Keds are quiet on the clean linoleum floor until we hit a newly waxed patch, when the right one starts squeaking with every step. I am embarrassed. I tell myself I am Jane Q. Citizen and that my family has lived in this community for years. I own a local business, I have friends in town and both my parents have just died. I straighten my shoulders. If I do not get treated with courtesy, I will make them arrest me or I will go home. At least now I have a plan.

I am led into a small room with a table and four metal chairs. It looks like a conference room in a school or moderately successful accounting firm. There is no two-way window. Hutchins waves a hand, and it is clear I may sit wherever I want. I do not think I am going to be tortured, at least not yet. This is more like a meeting with an insurance salesman, where you feel kind of trapped and wonder how long it's going to take. The sheriff's detectives join me at the table. Click looks impatient, Hutchins relaxed.

Hutchins smiles. 'Can we get you a coffee, Ms Smallwood – Georgie? Do you mind if I call you Georgie?'

'Certainly not, Doug. We both live and work in the same town.'

Detective Doug Hutchins grins at me. I have amused him. I feel easier now and settle back more comfortably in my chair.

'Georgie, we're just trying to figure out what happened to your father. You got to admit, it's weird, him being there at the lighthouse so late at night.' Hutchins waits in vain for me to agree. The less said the better, I think. 'But you know your father better than we do. You got any theory on what he was doing there so late?'

'No.'

'None at all?'

'No.'

'Care to speculate?'

'Not really. It makes no sense to me.'

Click gives me a hard look. 'So what were *you* doing

there that night? Or doesn't that make sense to you either.'

'What do you mean?'

'Are you saying you weren't there?'

'No, I told Selby I was there. I told you guys the same thing. I've been clear about that.'

'Make it clear to me.'

I take a slow breath. 'My brother and sister and I met at the lighthouse to drink beer and talk.'

Click leans back and folds his arms. 'That's trespassing, I guess you know, and frankly, Ms Smallwood, it still makes no sense to me.'

I stare at him but have no comment. It takes a surprising amount of effort not to talk.

Both detectives watch me. Are their minds made up? Are they playing games?

'Why the lighthouse, Ms Smallwood? It seems like an inconvenient place to meet.'

'Sentimental reasons, Detective Click.'

'How so?'

'We used to go there when we were kids. After my brother got his driver's license. Actually, it was Daddy who took us there the first time. He's the one who showed us the little side road where you can get around the gate.'

'But why this particular night? The same night your father wound up there?'

'For us it wasn't a particular night. It was just a night. I don't know why Daddy went there. Ashby and Claire and I went just for the hell of it. We were feeling nostalgic. Our mother just died.'

'Sentimental enough to drink beer, then go out to dinner and drink margaritas?'

'That's right. But I wasn't drunk. I had one sip of a Corona, and then I stopped drinking. That's why we all went to the restaurant in my car and left Claire's car at the park, and that's why I drove everybody home.'

'They remembered you at the restaurant, Ms Smallwood. That part of your story bears out.' Clearly, in the opinion of Detective Click, the rest does not. But he is still talking, and I do not like the look in his eyes. 'The waitress remembers all of you. She says you had a lot to drink and were pretty loud. She said your brother, Ashby, had muddy shoes. She remembered him in particular.'

'Yes, women usually do.'

Click frowns at me. He neither understands my remark nor likes it. He pushes his chair back from the table. 'We have a statement from the waitress who says she overhead one of the women at your table make a remark about 'pushing Daddy down the stairs'. Do you remember that comment, Ms Smallwood? Or do you deny it was ever said?'

I look down at my feet, but there is no help there. My hands are icy cold. 'No, I remember the remark.'

'Can you speak up please, Ms Smallwood? I can't hear what you said.'

'I said I remember the remark, Detective. I'm the one who made it.'

'Is that so? I have a statement from your sister that she's the one who said it. How do you explain that?'

'Claire was drunk, I'm afraid. I doubt she remembers either way. Check with the waitress; she'll confirm it.' I am gambling here, hoping the woman will not remember. This damn person has remembered too much as it is, and I would take back my generous tip if I could.

Hutchins swivels back and forth in his chair. I would like to tell him to be still.

'You want to lawyer up now, Ms Smallwood?'

Lawyer up. It's a good question. But I am still thinking everything can be explained. I am thinking that it is the guilty who need attorneys. I am thinking that all this can be stopped, if only these detectives can be made to understand.

Click is staring. 'Tell me please, why you would make this kind of remark?'

'I was angry with my father.'

'How so?'

I am on the verge of telling them about Hank, but the protective instinct of motherhood stops me cold. I won't drag my son into this, so I tell them exactly what I really think, which is that my father killed my mother. I tell him that Ashby and Claire disagree.

There is a long silence in the room. Hutchins and Click look at each other.

'And your brother and sister?' Click asks. 'They don't think your father killed your mother?'

I pause. 'I don't think so, no.'

'Do you have any hard evidence?'

Hutchins raises a hand. 'Click, hey. Hold on here a minute.' He leans across the table and smiles. He is wearing a short-sleeve polo shirt and there is a thin half-moon scar on his arm. 'Obviously, if you knew something definite you'd have come to us earlier. Now look, I had a pretty raw deal myself with my old man, so I understand how it is, you know?'

It is hard to resist the sincerity in this man's eyes. It

makes me want to cooperate with him; I want his approval. They are playing games, I tell myself. I know how this works, I watch TV. But it is a hard thing to resist, in real life and face-to-face, here in this small room with both men.

I lay it out. I begin with my father's affair with Carla Blanchard. I point out that this part of my story is backed by the contents of my father's will. I mention my father's fraudulent filing of an old will of my mother's that grants him her entire estate. I give them the details of Mama's death and am rewarded with considering looks when I mention my father's temper tantrum preventing an autopsy to determine the exact cause of death.

This at least interests them. This much even I can see.

'And you really believe this?' Detective Click asks. 'That your own father would kill your mother?'

'Hey,' Hutchins says, giving me the nod. 'It happens every day.'

'If that's what you really think, Ms Smallwood, you'll let us exhume your mother's body, and see how it checks out.'

I look at both men, pretending to consider their request with care, but in truth my decision is already made. Ashby and Claire are going to kill me when they find out.

'Show me where to sign.'

John Wallace calls me as soon as I am back in the house. The warmth in his voice affects me like a glass of champagne.

'Where are you?' he asks. 'You sound like you're down a well.'

'I'm taking a bubble bath.'

He sighs. 'So tell me about your day, Georgie Smallwood.'

'Just the usual. A little varnish, a little glue.' A little interrogation by the police.

'Would you like to go to a movie? I'll buy you some popcorn if you promise not to throw it at me.'

'Why would I throw it at you?'

'You threw shrimp at me last night.'

'I did not. I waved it at you.'

'I'll buy you popcorn if you promise not to wave it at me.'

'I can't. I'm supposed to meet my brother and sister.'

'Oh. Okay. Can I take you out tomorrow for ice cream then?'

'Yes, you can.'

'Good then. I'll call you.'

I am smiling as I towel off and put on my favorite jeans with the rip under the left back pocket. I can't wear these jeans out and about because my underwear shows, but I can wear them to my mother's house to meet Ashby and Claire. I throw an oversized white shirt over the jeans and slide my feet into white flip-flops. My hair is damp, so I twist it into a quick chignon.

I am halfway down the stairs to my shop when I realize I forgot my keys and that I should leave a note and some cash for Hank. I don't know who is distracting me more, John Wallace or the police.

Cousin looks at me sadly from her nest on the couch. She's depressed and missing my mother. Just as well I came back.

'Get your leash,' I tell her.

I spent too long in my bubble bath and am late to met Ashby and Claire. I lift Cousin Beauregard out of Big Mama and walk up the creaky front-porch steps of my mother's house, remembering belatedly that Ashby asked me to bring something for our dinner, but I can't remember what. We are going to have a shrimp boil, with the fresh catch from Ashby's nets.

Cousin runs to the front door, ears flapping, joy in her rheumy eyes. Claire has been looking for me. She opens the door wide.

'You brought Cousin! Hey, baby, hey, girl.' Claire leans down and Cousin licks her face. The dog's back end is wiggling, nub tail on the go. Then Cousin Beauregard is off and running, heading to the couch in the den where my mother used to sit. She stops to jump up and kiss Ashby, who comes in out of the kitchen, hands sticky. He has been heading the shrimp.

'Hey, Ashby.' He comes after me but I avoid the sticky hands.

'Where's the bread?' Claire asks.

I put a hand to my head.

'Georgie, you space cadet, don't tell me you forgot

the bread.' Claire is thinking of sopping up cocktail sauce and the butter that will drip from the fresh corn we will boil with the shrimp.

'Oh, it's okay,' Ashby says. 'Don't worry about it.'

I have forgotten to apologize too. I watch Cousin Beauregard sniff at my mother's favorite chair.

'We've got peaches, tomatoes and corn. Beer, cocktail sauce and shrimp.' My sister has a check list in her mind. 'That's plenty. We should be fine.'

Ashby rubs his hands together. 'I'll put the water on to boil.'

I know I should go help my brother and sister in the kitchen. Officially this dinner has been called to pick out a burial suit for my father, but in truth we are celebrating reclaiming the family house. Elspeth Dougall is hell on wheels.

I sit on the couch where my mother used to sit, and Cousin jumps up beside me and lays her head in my lap. From the clatter of pans in the kitchen, I know Ashby is pulling the iron Dutch oven out from the lower cabinet. I hear the faucet running. Ashby is filling the pan with water and getting ready to put the spices in to boil. When the water is roiling and full of steam he'll add the fresh ears of corn and, for a few short minutes, the freshly headed shrimp.

More dishes rattle, and the refrigerator opens and closes. I hear the murmur of my brother's and sister's voices. They are up to something. I hear an energy and excitement in their tone, and I wonder what they are discussing. I feel separated from my siblings by the paper I have just signed.

My mind wanders. Cousin lays her head in my lap and I stroke her head. We are both missing Mama.

My mother graduated summa cum laude from the Institute of Genteel Female Martyrdom. My sister carries on this tradition, a trait that runs as strongly in my family as blue eyes and blond hair. Now, a true southern female martyr is an exquisite creature who hints and sighs and will not tell you until after you have served the strawberry pie that berries give her migraines, but she ate it anyway so as not to hurt your feelings. She will assure you that the pain is well worth the pleasure of your pie. If you are so foolish as to criticize the martyr for eating the pie in the first place, you will get a tolerant smile, and the martyr will clam up and not bring the subject up *ever* again. If you try to force the issue, the martyr will not have the vaguest recollection of what you are talking about. At this point there is no turning back, and it's too late to apologize. But make no mistake, you are going to be punished.

I once skipped the whole family deal on one of my birthdays, celebrating quietly at home with a young Hank, and the next two relatives that died were long buried before I got the news. My mother simply 'assumed' that I would not be interested in the news of these deaths, as I was so clearly distancing myself from family affairs.

Ashby, who makes no secret of distancing himself from the family on a regular basis, finally made a pact that when someone we know or are related to dies, we tell each other right away. In the event that we were both in disgrace, we have to rely on Claire.

For the last five years, my mother's knees were always swollen to the point that even looking at them made you wince. She would never complain about the pain. For relief, she would go to a family doctor right outside of

Savannah, a doctor my sister and brother and I dropped like a rock as soon as we were out on our own. My mother said she went to Dr Wagner because my father liked him, but I am wondering if the truth was more on the order of a thinly veiled death wish. This doctor is a pretty large man. He smokes cigars and has a burr haircut – which may be why my father liked him. He has been reprimanded once by the AMA that I know of and views women in the same regard I hold palmetto bugs. My mother always hated him. He is rude, impatient, sloppy and uncaring. He has the bedside manner of a Nazi and is as obstinate as a pig. But on the plus side, he gives my mother unlimited opportunities to be a noble victim, so this doctor is martyr-made-to-order.

'Mom,' I would say to her, while sitting on the edge of the footrest where she has propped her legs, which clearly are hurting like mad, 'Mom, you're too young for this. You need to get this taken care of. You need to go to a specialist. You need to let me find you another doctor. If I find you somebody good, then will you go?'

My mother looks over my shoulder at Vanna White, who is spinning the Wheel of Fortune.

'Look, if I find somebody, will you go? I'll take you myself. One visit.'

'Dr Wagner says there's nothing we can do till I lose some weight. Though how I can lose weight if I can't walk, I have no idea.'

'Dr Wagner has no room to talk, plus he's an idiot. Also, Mom, why would you listen to him since you know he's an idiot. Why do you go to him at all?'

She sighs. 'Your father trusts him.'

'You're the patient, Mama, not Daddy. Dr Wagner

191

is not helping you. You're in pain every minute of every day.'

'Dr Wagner doesn't want me to get addicted to painkillers.' My mother smiles at me and pats my hand. 'Don't worry so much. How is little Hankie?'

'Hank is fine, don't change the subject. Just say yes. If I find somebody, you'll let me take you to see him. Will you at least do that?'

'We'll see.'

I do find someone. I nag and cajole and worry her till she finally goes. The doctor talks her into replacing both knees, and I am right there, pressuring her into the decision. The surgery is a nightmare. Six months later, one knee is much improved, and the other is worse. Did I help?

The sound of whispering brings me back. Ashby and Claire stand in the doorway. I cannot make out their words or see their faces. Dusk has settled in heavily and I have not turned on a light. Cousin snores like a piglet, and her head is heavy in my lap.

'Dinner's ready,' Claire says softly, and from Ashby I hear the whisper, 'Do you think she's asleep?'

I reach over to the lamp on the end table and twist the black plastic switch. Light pools into the den, and in the glow the shabby green rug seems merely comfortable.

'Not asleep,' Claire says.

They separate, my brother to Dad's old leather recliner and Claire to the other end of the couch.

'We know something's bothering you, Georgie.'

'I talked to the police today,' I tell them.

'No wonder you're upset,' Ashby says. 'We talked to them too, both me and Claire.'

'What did you tell them?'

Claire shrugs. 'Hell, Georgie, we told them the truth.'

'What did they ask you?' Ashby says. I tell them about the lighthouse, the restaurant and nothing more.

'They asked us all the same questions,' Claire says. 'Particularly that awful thing I said about Dad.'

'You didn't say anything awful about Dad.'

'I said something, didn't I? I mean, in the restaurant? About pushing him down the lighthouse stairs? And that bitchy little waitress overheard and parroted it all back to the police? I hope we didn't leave a good tip. Hey, is that why she ratted us out? Did we forget to leave her a tip?'

'I left her a great tip, Claire. And she wasn't sure which one of us said it, and I told the police it was me.'

My brother and sister exchange significant looks.

'Why would you say that?' Ashby asks.

'It's bad enough Claire's car was there all night.'

'But we told them—'

'Claire, the policeman is not your friend. Don't you and Ashby get it? These detectives, Hutchins and Click, they're *homicide* guys. The sheriff's department thinks Daddy was murdered and they're looking at the three of us. The best thing we've got going is they don't know which one of us to accuse.'

Ashby leans forward and puts his elbows on his knees. 'Georgie, Daddy cut all three of us out of his will. Do they think we killed him because he was a grump?'

I look down at Cousin, snoring in my lap.

'Did they ask you why you said it?' Claire says. ''Cause I told them I was drunk and pissy and don't exactly remember why.'

Ashby picks at the sole of his shoe. 'What did you tell them, Georgie?'

'I told them I thought Daddy murdered Mama and that's why I was mad.'

My brother opens his mouth, and Claire stands up, then sits back down.

'Look, I know neither of you want to admit it, but I happen to think that it's true. What? Why are you two looking at me like that?'

Ashby rubs the bridge of his nose. 'How'd they take the news that you think Daddy murdered Mom?'

How odd these words sound here in this den where my parents read books and watched TV.

'They wanted to do an autopsy. On Mama. So I told them to go ahead. I know you guys will hate me for it, but I see no reason to protect Daddy from the truth. He's dead now, anyway.'

Ashby blows air through his lips. 'It's not Daddy I'm worrying about. You just handed the cops a motive that applies to all us three.'

Claire stands up and motions us into the kitchen. 'Dinner's ready. Come on, you guys, don't let the cops screw up our meal.'

Ashby and Claire are annoyingly cheerful considering the bombshell I have dropped, and their appetite does not seem impaired. My brother has made his special cocktail sauce, which includes just a hint of habañero pepper, horseradish, tomato sauce, Worcestershire and a hint of something sweet. I dip the white chunky flesh of a peeled shrimp into the red sauce and take a small bite.

Claire hands me a plate of fresh sliced tomatoes. She looks at Ashby, who is sitting wide-legged with his elbows on the table, methodically working over his third ear of corn. He looks at me warily.

'Tell me what's up.' I set my fork down.

Claire leans across the table. There is shrimp sauce on her chin. 'We think we've figured out what may really have happened to Dad.'

Ashby puts his corn down and licks his fingers, ignoring the napkin in his lap. 'I've been going over Mama and Daddy's accounts. By the way, you were right about that Elspeth Dougall; she's been kicking Wilbanks's ass. She's got her daddy and his buddies in Charleston as backup and she's got old Wilbanks tied up in knots. Seems like we're about her only clients, and she spends all day churning out paperwork on our case. The upshot is, Mama made me executor, and since Daddy and Wilbanks have committed possible fraud, Wilbanks got removed as executor of Dad's estate. Actually, they can't prove Wilbanks knew about the will, but he agreed to hand the executorship over to the state, so long as they didn't give it to me. He tried to give it over to Carla Blanchard, but he had to back down, and Elspeth got Carla Blanchard's key. She's worked out a sort of a deal.'

I wipe my mouth with a napkin. 'What deal?'

'Carla Blanchard has agreed to sign off on every-thing else if she gets Daddy's insurance; since she's on there as beneficiary, there's not much we can do. And if she gets to keep the stuff Daddy gave her after Mama died.'

'Hell, no, I don't agree.'

Claire puts a hand on my wrist. 'Georgie, Mama left Daddy whatever personal items he wanted from the house. If we fight it we'll never win, and if we win it'll cost us a fortune. If we take the deal, Carla Blanchard will totally back off.'

'Then why ask if I *agree* with you if I don't have a choice?'

'We didn't ask you if you agree,' Ashby says.

'Something's funny here anyway, you guys. It's not like Eugene Wilbanks to give right up.'

'He's not stupid, Georgie. He could lose his license over this.' Ashby turns away from the counter, where he has been rinsing his hands in the sink. 'And listen. I've been going through Dad's bank accounts.'

'And?'

Claire pushes her plate away so she can rest her elbows on the table. 'Daddy has been making big cash withdrawals over the last eight months, $12,000 at a time. He's pulled out $96,000, and the last withdrawal he made was two days before he died.'

'You got any idea why?' I ask.

'We think he was being *blackmailed*,' Claire says.

I snort and fling down a sauce-slick shrimp. 'Maybe he was betting on the dogs.'

'When did Daddy ever gamble?'

'Then it was for a new mistress.'

'Daddy's too damn cheap to give a mistress £12,000 a month.'

'Maybe he was giving two women $6,000. For all we know he's got a piece of ass in every county in South Carolina.'

'I don't think there are $96,000' worth of women in the state of South Carolina who would put up with him,' Claire says.

Ashby leans across the table. 'The thing is, Georgie, we have more than just the money. We think we know who's been squeezing him. Come on up to the attic, and I'll show you what I mean.'

My sister and brother and I leave all the mess behind in the kitchen, and Ashby settles behind my father's desk. When Claire pulls the light cord, I can see they have spent a lot of time up here. There are papers scattered on my father's normally neat and shipshape desktop, and half-filled cans of Diet Coke decorate the windowsill and the top of the old oak filing cabinet.

'Daddy had a safe deposit box at a bank in Charleston.' Claire sits on the edge of Daddy's desk.

'Look at this.' Ashby holds up a swatch of camouflage material. It is a shirt pocket with a last name, Pickett, stenciled in fading black. Ashby hands me a brown envelope that still reeks of cheap cigars. 'Open it,' Ashby says.

The letter is dated 18 March.

Dear Mr Smallwood

Please consider this a written confirmation of the information I passed on to you earlier today on the phone concerning Marine Recruit Stephen Pickett. To the best of my knowledge and the scope of this investigation, Recruit Pickett has not been seen or heard of since the incident in question.

His social security number has not been used. No one has used the name Stephen Pickett in tandem with the corresponding birth date to secure credit, college enrollment, government benefits, federal employment, or state employment in South Carolina, North Carolina, Georgia or Tennessee.

I have interviewed Mr Pickett's family, in particular his grandmother, Verna Pickett. Ms Pickett lives at 5801 Montgomery Avenue and is the maternal grandmother of Stephen Pickett. Ms Pickett still grieves for her grandson, in point of fact maintaining his room as it was when he left for boot camp fifteen years ago. Please note, Stephen Pickett lived with his grandmother from the age of fourteen through his eighteenth year, up until he left for Parris Island. Ms Pickett was the beneficiary of Stephen Pickett's death benefits.

While I am happy to continue my inquiries, I question whether it is a wise use of your money. Please advise on whether or not you wish for me to continue my investigations. As things stand, I will send you a final accounting of my fee, minus the money order I received last week in partial payment of the account.

Regards,
Preston Meyer, Meyer Investigations

'Pickett's name familiar?' Ashby asks.

I nod. 'He was one of the Hardigree Seven. He was one of the recruits who got swept out with the tide.'

Ashby shakes his head. 'No, Pickett fell down a trout hole. Remember? They found his pack.'

'He's the one who went to Daddy for help,' Claire says softly.

I close my eyes, imagining Pickett's last moments. He did not die an easy death.

It was Pickett who went to my father when Staff Sergeant Hardigree decided, after a long night of drinking, to rouse his recruits from their deep sleep and lead the exhausted would-be soldiers in an impromptu night hump through the swamps. The recruits wore sixty-pound packs and heavy boots and were additionally weighted with flak jackets, helmets and guns. In boot camp, marine recruits are taught to trust their commanding officers and fellow marines. There is no greater offense than to betray that trust. And that night this trust was betrayed. Motivated by fear, and the newly drilled in instinct to follow orders without question, sixty-four recruits followed their sergeant into the night, seven of them never to return.

Staff Sergeant Hardigree led his recruits past the obstacle course, Bayonne's Challenge, and straight through the deadly ground between the shoreline and the trees. It was a pitch-dark night, and after the first miles of marching the recruits became exhausted and disorderly and began to string out, many of them falling behind. They began to bunch up into small groups and, predictably, to separate and get lost. It was not until early the next morning, during head count, that it was discovered that eighteen recruits were not in their bunks.

My father led the search-and-rescue, which was efficient and thorough, an amazingly quick and organized response. Five recruits were found treading water, where they had been swept out to sea. Six were found wandering in the woods, some of them still hiking, some of them sitting under a tree waiting for rescue. The final seven, known as the Hardigree Seven, were never found.

Some of them drowned in the ocean, according to

the final report. The unluckiest ones fell down trout holes while wandering the treacherous swampland after dark. Weighed down by heavy equipment and boots, arms restricted by pack and weapons, these recruits never stood a chance.

My father became an instant hero, celebrated for the swift rescue he engineered, until a preliminary investigation revealed that recruit Stephen Pickett had gone to him for help with a drunken drill instructor who looked to be leading his platoon into trouble. My father went from being the man who rose to the occasion to the calloused hard-line sergeant who turned his back when he could have prevented the tragedy. It was Wilbanks who saved my father from a court-martial for dereliction of duty. My father retired soon after, military record tarnished, personally haunted by the loss of seven recruits and the ruin of his friend and fellow marine, Staff Sergeant Hardigree. Hardigree died six years later in military prison.

I look up at Ashby. 'I still don't see how all of this connects.'

Claire sits down on a box under the window. 'Frankly, neither do we. But there must be some reason Daddy thought Pickett was alive. Something Pickett knew that he could blackmail Daddy and Wilbanks with.'

'I don't know what it would be,' I say. 'Daddy took more than his fair share of the blame.'

Ashby nods. All three of us are quick to defend our father when people bring up the Hardigree incident.

'Maybe somebody besides Pickett knows something about what happened that night,' Ashby says.

'You're talking about monthly bank withdrawals of

twelve thousand dollars. What could have happened that would be worth that after everything else that happened?'

'I don't know,' Claire says, 'but I bet Mama did.'

'But why now?' I ask. 'After all these years?'

My brother shakes his head at me. This is a discussion he and Claire have already had. 'Everybody in the county knows Mama inherited Uncle Dill's money. Nobody bothers you when you're poor.'

Claire nods. 'Think about it, Georgie. The withdrawals started about three months after Uncle Dill died and left Mama the money and the house.'

I frown. 'It's not just that. Don't forget, Wilbanks is involved.'

'Maybe it's the election,' Claire says. 'Wilbanks is on Mannelli's ticket, right? As assistant District Attorney.'

'Now would be a bad time to dredge up the Hardigree thing. Whoever is blackmailing Dad must have something on Wilbanks too.'

Ashby nods. 'I think Dad must have gone to meet this blackmailer the night he died. And I think they got into an argument, not too difficult with Dad involved, and whoever it is killed him.'

'We should go to the police with this,' Claire says.

My brother shakes his head. 'We stay away from the cops. Let well enough alone.'

My brother and sister look my way.

'I'm inclined to agree.' I close my eyes. It's been a long day. 'Look, you guys, it's late. Cousin and I want to go home, and we've still got to clean up the kitchen and find Daddy some clothes.'

Claire shudders. 'I'll do the dishes if you'll pick the suit.'

'Okay by me. What are you going to do?' I ask Ashby.

My brother seems rooted to the desk. 'I have some stuff to look at up here.'

Claire and I exchange looks. Ashby never helps with the dishes.

My sister heads for the kitchen, and I go down one flight of stairs to the left of the second-floor landing. My father's bedroom is carpeted in blue. The dresser is walnut, and dusty. There is a picture of my mother in a small metal frame next to a stack of change, a coiled black leather belt, two credit cards that expired in the Eighties and a roll of butterscotch Life Savers.

I glance into the bathroom. Toothbrush, razor, Rolaids and a hairbrush of my mother's that looks about thirty years old. My father's closet is open and full of clothes he has not worn in years. I smell cigars and Mennen aftershave. I choose quickly: a navy blue suit, a pale blue cotton shirt and a dark maroon tie. I lay the clothes on the neatly made bed and sit down in order to give Claire time to finish in the kitchen. I wonder if I am supposed to provide underwear with the suit.

The clock by the bedside ticks audibly. It would keep me from my sleep.

One of the things I always admired about my father was his ability to sleep anytime anywhere. The other thing that always impressed me was that when he was a boy he had his very own horse.

Like lots of little girls, it was my greatest dream to have a horse of my own. My father knew this, and whenever he was gone for a long duty call, he would bring all of us kids a present. He always brought me a model horse. Every night I asked my parents for a horse, and every night they said no. I also asked for a kitty of my own. My mother did not like cats, and I figured I was as likely to get a cat as a horse.

Picture me in the kitchen of our three-bedroom single-story house. I am eating Sugar Frosted Flakes. I hear loud voices coming from my parents' bedroom, then my father storms to the front door and tells me to hop to it and get in the car.

'Where are we going?' I ask.

'To the pet store to get you a cat.'

The pet store is in a shopping center between a Safeway grocery store and a People's drugstore, and they only have one cat today, a bruising tiger-striped Tom, who is one year old, big for his age. This cat is free of charge, but there is one catch. The lady who dropped him off promised to come back and get him in an hour, so we have to wait that hour out before we can have the cat.

This will be the longest hour of my life. I don't know what the store clerk and my father know – that the lady has dumped her kitty and the pet store owner has kindly taken it in. In my opinion, no sane person could abandon such a magnificent tiger-striped cat, and I decide that if life is good and I am lucky, I will name him Timothy the First.

I sit on a concrete block outside the pet store, turning occasionally to peer in at the cat, who paces with a look of great annoyance in a metal cage, but mostly I keep my eye on any women coming close to the pet store who have the look of a person coming to claim her cat. But the woman does not return, and my father and I take Timothy home in our big green Buick, where he immediately scrambles out of my arms and under the front seat. I am a study in frustration. At last, my very own kitty, who is God knows where in the coils of the upholstery of my father's precious Buick.

At home, we roll down all the windows on the Buick and wait for the cat to come out. It takes hours. He is one year old and perfectly behaved save for a strong opposition to being housebroken. Timothy poops under the beds, in the bathtub, in the corner of the pantry, and anywhere else he pleases, and it soon becomes clear why he was abandoned that day in the store. Timothy, under orders from my mother, becomes an outdoor cat.

He doesn't mind. He catches fish in the creek, climbs trees, lets me dress him up in doll clothes and push him in a toy stroller, loves me with a tolerant affection and worships my father. Every night, when my father works late, Timothy leaps up on the ledge of the kitchen window, which my father opens so they can say hello. On cold or rainy nights, Timothy mysteriously winds up cuddled next to me in bed, though my father will never admit to sneaking him in.

It is a wonderful thing, a kitty of my own, and it is clear from the outset that I was meant for feline companionship. Now the only thing I pester my father for is a horse.

Inside the Ribault Street Presbyterian Church a funeral service is in progress. My father will be buried today.

This morning I got up and put on my black silk dress, my slingback shoes and the delicate pearl set – earrings and a necklace. My hair turned out especially well. I look pretty in a sober way, and the black dress lends me an air of dignity. I critique my reflection in the mahogany cathedral mirror I bought at an auction in Lexington, Kentucky. My eyes are sad.

I walk up the concrete stairs to the church with Hank on one side, Claire trailing behind with her children, and Ashby opening the heavy wood door to usher us in. And there on the threshold of this church, I falter. I stand before the cavelike entryway and see that it is dim inside. The morning light makes it look like midnight in the sanctuary. Cool air rushes out of the church, along with the scent of old wood and musty hymnals. I get a glimpse of the stained-glass windows that bracket the sanctuary.

'Hank?'

My son bends close to hear my whisper.

'Go on in, will you? Tell Ashby and Claire not to wait.'

'Where are you going?'

'I don't know. Probably just the bench out front.'

Hank looks behind me at the bench. He is wearing his funeral clothes and he looks handsome. If anyone else dies, my dress and his suit coat will need a trip to the cleaners.

'Are you sure?' Hank is considering me, weighing my actions, coming to conclusions at which I can only guess. He sees my look, nods and heads without hesitation into the church. My son is possibly the only person I can rely on to take me at my word. Ashby and Claire would question, probe and argue. Hank, who is determined to go his own way in all things, will at least grant me the consideration he expects.

How he handles my brother and my sister I do not know, but handle them he does. I sit on the wooden bench, smell the flowery dogwoods and magnolias and hope my bowed head and stiffly turned shoulders will keep the world away.

The noise of conversation, the click of heels, the purr of engines and the slam of car doors die down. I listen to the music emanating faintly from inside the church. I take a breath, easier now.

How did we come to this, my father and I? Did he ever really love me? Was my mother's influence so strong as to keep his calloused tendencies in check? Was he snapping this last year, under extraordinary pressure? Or was he simply tired of being my father?

What is it, I wonder, that separates me so definitively from Ashby and Claire? How can my brother and sister see my father with such an anguished mix of love, loyalty and confusion? Am I incapable of love? But I know that no mother could love a son more than I love Hank, that I would do anything to make life easy for Ashby and Claire and that I miss my mother like a part of me is gone. I love my pickup truck, Cousin Beauregard, mahogany and Beaufort, South Carolina. My father I do not love.

It is common myth, here in the South, that your relatives come for you when you die. I believe this is true. Who came for Daddy? Was it Mama? Did she come with forgiveness or an accusing stare?

I think on what I know of my father and realize it is not a lot. My impression of his childhood is of a past thick with shadows, bad tempers and tired old grudges. My father was selfish with his memories, both good and bad, as if his past was a party to which his children were not invited. I close my eyes and the stories come to mind. The cake he ate out of his father's bag lunch. The picnics where Henry Simmons called for the mythical Cousin Beauregard. But the memories are few and far between. What I really remember are faces. Ashby, rejected and disapproved of, masking hurt with sarcastic indifference. Claire in grade school, crumbling beneath my father's angry tongue. And Mama, seemingly unaffected, gently placating with a smile and a solution, seeing that my father's life went smoothly, so we children would be shielded from his frustrations and rage.

We were happy enough, growing up. The Smallwood household endured my father's storms like a seaworthy ship, and if he spread a certain dread among us, we assumed this was merely the way of fathers and went about the business of our lives. We were provided for, we were protected from hardships we were too inexperienced even to imagine and through our mother we were unconditionally loved. And when she told us, as she often did, that our father loved us dearly, we believed her because she said it was so. This must be the key to my brother and sister. They both still believe.

I admit to myself how much I want my brother and sister's approval, how much I need them to be on my side. And I face the truth – that whatever this approval of me will cost them, it is a price they cannot afford.

Behind me, a car door slams, and I hear the muted voices of men. Footsteps crunch pine needles and gravel, and I turn and look.

The police are attending my father's funeral. They're moving quickly because they are late – Hutchins and Click, the detectives who have searched my home, as well as Ashby's and Claire's, and who still have two pairs of my shoes. They notice me, here on the bench.

They pause and speak to one another, careful not to meet my eyes.

They will think it strange if I do not go inside. Still, I sit on my bench, oddly peaceful. My mother's death has given me a sense of freedom I did not expect. It enables me to sit with this inexplicable contentment on a city bench in Beaufort, when family duty and social conditioning demand I be present at the death services inside that church. What is the good of pretending, when God surely knows my heart?

12

The police wait until the day after my father's funeral to request my presence downtown. I am becoming more and more familiar with the conference rooms in the Beaufort sheriff's office, and I am here once again for what I have been assured is a mere formality. I have brought a sweater this time, as they keep the air conditioning turned high.

There are no questions this time, just a long wait. I keep my hands folded in my lap, while I wonder if I am truly alone or being watched from a secret spy hole somewhere in the room. I tell myself to act normal; then I wonder what normal is. Cross my legs, or feet flat on the floor? No nail biting, and thank God I'm not some big burly guy who sweats at the drop of a hat. If I were in advertising, I would film deodorant commercials in the conference rooms of the police.

I think of John Wallace, who is making a habit of a morning wake-up call. He never talks long, just starts my day with 'Hello' and 'What are you working on?' It is a small thing, but I look forward more and more to the sound of his voice. He is not overly smooth and has the startling and unsouthern habit of saying what he is actually thinking. I compare my conversations with John Wallace to the ones that used to pass between my parents.

A typical conversation between my mother and father goes like this.

Say we are driving along, my father at the wheel. I cannot recall one time when my mother drove my father. Even on long trips, my father always drove.

The three of us kids are sitting in the back. If it's that old Ford Fairlane, there are see-through plastic covers on the seat. These covers are patterned with little round balls that make red marks on the back of your legs when you wear shorts on hot summer days. My dad ordered these seat covers out of the Fingerhut catalog, and I fault Claire for this discomfort. She was a messy child. Every ice-cream cone she ate dripped over her fingers and down her arms and onto whoever and whatever was in range – often the upholstery of my father's car.

Everyone is starving and everyone wants to eat out, everyone except my father. He wants to eat at home, like always.

'Do you want to eat out, Lena?' my father asks.

'Whatever you want to do.' My mother's stock answer to any question. It drives me insane. Say it, I will her. Take a stand. Tell Dad we're going out.

'Well, what do *you* want to do?' my father counters.

He knows the question is safe to ask. Never in a million years will my mother actually *say* what she wants. My father knows as well as we all do that she wants to go out. We kids want to go out, but our opinions don't count – which, speaking as a parent, does not seem to me a bad thing. My son's generation gets way too much leeway, and it only leads to trouble.

'Whatever *you* want, Fielding.' My mother sounds bland but slightly annoyed.

My father keeps his voice cheerful and pleasant. He knows he'll get his way, and so does my mother, which is why she's annoyed. My father is only trying to decide how much my mother will make him pay, later, with subtle coolness and vague punishments.

'I would love one of your special Lena-burgers.'

I groan. I hate my mother's hamburgers. They are big and fat and juicy and there's too much meat. I only like thin hamburgers, cooked on the grill.

'Let's just go out,' I say, from the backseat. I am ignored.

'Fine,' my mother says.

'Is it fine?'

'If you want Lena-burgers, Fielding, we'll have Lena-burgers.'

My father turns sideways to catch my mother's eye and winks. 'Even Eugene admits you make the best hamburgers in the South.'

My mother stares out the window. 'Well, then. If Eugene Wilbanks says it, it must be so. Eugene is as honest a man as I know.'

My father's voice goes flat, like it always does when he and Mama talk about Wilbanks. 'Lena, if you want to go out, just tell me.'

'Take me home,' my mother says.

My brother and sister are looking out the windows. I fold my arms and glare at the back of my parents' heads – my father's short burr, my mother's blond bubble.

Say it, I will my mother. Tell him we're eating out. Say it, say it, say it.

She never, ever does.

The conference door opens abruptly, and I am full of the kind of nervous anticipation one feels in the doctor's office, where you wait in a series of smaller and smaller rooms until you are graced by a visit from the demigod. It's funny, really, how alike they are, a visit to the doctor, or the police. Both involve vulnerability and the life-and-death evaluations of men and women who are near strangers in your life. Will they be kind and competent? Do they have a personal agenda? Are you screwed because they had a fight over breakfast at home? It is a helpless feeling, being dependent on the opinions of a person you barely know.

I am out of luck. My least favorite detective walks alone through the door.

Detective Click makes a noise in his throat that is evidently his Neanderthal form of a greeting. 'Ms Smallwood?' he says, taking a chair.

'Detective.' I have been silent and worried too long and I have to clear my throat. Ten points to the cops, I think, in this game where I don't know the rules.

Click shoves paperwork across the table. 'This is a statement put together based on the information you gave last week.'

I am wary. Mentally, I try to review everything that I said, then realize I'd better just read the statement. Carefully, I tell myself. The policeman is not your friend. I read the statement through quickly, then back again slow.

Click slides a pen across the table. 'If this a correct statement, Ms Smallwood, please sign at the bottom and date.'

I take the pen and make some small changes, giving Click a sideways look to see if he objects. He doesn't. He sits quietly, waiting, and I feel that there is a trap about to be sprung, but I don't know from what direction it will come. Amateur hour is over, I think. Any questions today and I'm going to lawyer up.

Click is intent upon the pen. He waits silently for me to sign. Everything in the statement is the absolute truth. I take the pen, sign my name and jot down the date. Detective Click leans across the table and takes the paper himself. I notice that he is very nicely dressed. No polo shirts today; it is crisp white cotton and a striped tie.

'I have one or two quick questions, Ms Smallwood. A couple of things to clear up.'

'I will be more than happy to cooperate, but I want an attorney present from here on out.'

I have said it. In my mind I have practiced this line a thousand times. Today I have recited it flawlessly, and I wait for the sky to fall.

Click leans back in his chair. He isn't smiling, but in my company he rarely does. He wears a wedding band. What is he like with his guard down – at home with his wife? Does he have children? A dog? Is it hard for him, making the transition from human to cop?

'It's a lot of expense and trouble to go to, just for about ten minutes of talk.'

'I am requesting an attorney.'

'I guess that won't be necessary, Ms Smallwood.'

'I beg your pardon, Detective, but it's my right.'

'It's okay, Ms Smallwood.' He stands. 'No more questions at this time.'

I swallow. 'Are you going to arrest me?'

He narrows his eyes and tilts his head. 'No, Ms Smallwood. You are free to go.' He waits patiently, almost sad.

'Then what happens? Do you have any suspects? Was it really an accident? Are you just going to let it go?'

He regards me for a long moment, and I can see he is making up his mind. Is it kindness, curiosity or malice that prompts the information he gives?

Click glances at his watch. 'We'll be making an arrest any time now. We're arresting your sister, Claire Smallwood Ryker, for the murder of Fielding Smallwood.'

⬇

I have been moved to another conference room, mainly because I won't go home. The tables have turned. The Beaufort sheriff's department wants to get rid of me, but I am refusing to leave until I talk to the man in charge. Whoever that may be.

I picture my sister answering her front door. I have called her house, but there is no answer, and my mind is circling. Should I go and look for her? Are the police already there? Do I want my sister on the run?

Will they arrest her in front of the kids?

I know in my heart that Claire is innocent of the death of my father. I know she is fragile and cannot tolerate jail. And Ashby would be a sitting duck in prison.

The conclusion I reach is clear-cut as far as these things go. My only concern is for Hank.

But he spends his nights and days, more and more often, on *The Graceful Lady* with Ashby, fishing for shrimp. As if whatever weighs his shoulders and robs his face of his smile lifts once he's on the water. I sometimes think that *The Graceful Lady* is the only place where my brother and my son are completely at ease.

Claire has three children. All of them under ten.

I check my watch, see I've been sitting for forty-five

minutes, and wait quietly now, hands easy in my lap. It is a relief, really, to have made a decision.

The door creaks and opens slowly, and Police Chief Johnny Selby walks through the door. Something inside me must feel safer, because my guard goes down and the tears start rolling onto my cheeks.

❖

Selby sits across from me, still holding my hand. His handkerchief, well used now, is tucked into my sleeve. Click has called on him to make me go home. Selby is officially uninvolved in this case. I try again to talk, but my throat is tight and the words have to be forced through the panic that makes me want to scream.

'Claire is innocent. I promise you, I know this for a *fact*.'

My voice catches and Selby is amazingly calm in the face of the hysteria that is rising with every word. He pats my hand. Does he understand, I wonder? Does he get what I am trying to say? Is this man, who loved my mother, who cherished her, I hope, is he going to be just another law-enforcement brick wall?

'It was *me*,' I tell him. 'I'm the one that did it, I'm the reason Daddy is dead. I'm ready to confess, to sign a statement. That detective – what is the matter?' Here I hiccup and swallow and start again. 'He didn't write it down, he didn't read me my . . . my—'

'Take a breath, Georgie. Come on, stop and take some slow deep breaths.'

'Are you *listening* to me, dammit?'

'If you hyperventilate and pass out on me, it won't help a thing.'

No one is making any sense.

'Now sit tight and I'll be right back. I'm going to get you a glass of water.'

'Did I *ask* you for a glass of *water*?'

'Georgie, sit here and be still.'

So I do. I hiccup and watch the second hand of the clock moving in tiny spasms as it tallies the seconds. In a silent room, those big institutional clocks give off a faint metallic hum.

Selby is gone such a long time. My hiccups turn into yawns, and my mouth is dry. This water may be a good idea. I have always wondered why people fetch endless glasses of water for those of us who are hysterical, but now it begins to make sense.

The door opens, and Selby is back. He hands me a small blue and white Dixie cup, placing it with both of his hands in mine. It is odd, the way he hands the cup over. The press of his fingers against my palm draws my attention to the scrap of paper tucked against the bottom of this cup.

'Do you need to use the ladies' room?' Selby asks me, with a look in his eyes that commands *yes*.

'Yes.' I hold tight to the cup of water and the piece of paper and follow him out the door. I feel the weight of unseen eyes, as I walk down the corridor.

Selby takes up a post outside the bathroom door. 'I'll wait here.'

Inside, I see a line of three sinks opposite three stalls and a woman with a badge on her belt, checking her makeup in the mirror. Is it my imagination, or does she watch me?

I open a stall door, lock it with hands that shake and sit on the toilet in case the woman is studying my legs. I gulp the water, crumple the cup and open the piece of lined notepaper, folded three times to make it small.

GO HOME is written in thick block letters. Signed A. And at the bottom, a message between brother and sister, so I may know the instruction truly comes from him, *Kick the can and run* is scrawled at the bottom of the note. Kick the can was the game we used to play every summer night until our parents finally called us home. A form of hide-and-seek in the dark.

I sit in the sheriff's department parking lot, wondering what to do next. The problem, actually, is not so much a lack of things to do as it is too many. My mind is frozen, and it is hard to suddenly change direction, when what I want to do is rescue my sister and go back inside and confess.

I feel weird and hot all over, and I know my face is turning red. My clothes feel tight, and I can't stand the weight of my hair on my neck. I have a heavy feeling, like something very bad is going to happen, except it already has. My sister Claire is being arrested.

Somebody is honking his horn, and I look up in sudden venom – I am being interrupted in the middle of a panic attack – and I scream, '*Shut the hell up.*'

A familiar Land Rover makes a shark pass down Ribault. Ashby is here. I take a deep breath, put Big Mama in gear and follow my brother down the road. In a mile and a half, I see he is leading me to where *The Graceful Lady* is docked. Maybe Claire is there, in hiding. With all her children, Cousin Beauregard and

Hank. Maybe we will go far, far away and escape at last from the hell of confusing complications that make up all our lives.

⇊

The Graceful Lady sways gently at dock in the Sound. A rope hits against the side of the boat, and the old wood creaks and speaks the language of a ship in the water. There is a feeling here of being on tenuous ground. Boats are like horses – you have to trust them or you can't feel safe.

Ashby and I are secure together in the lower cabin of the ship. When I am in the mood to appreciate such things, I love the efficiency of a boat, where every last thing is miniaturized, stowed neatly, with no wasted space.

I sit on the very edge of the worn royal blue cushion in Ashby's galley, jumping at every sudden noise. He reaches into the tiny refrigerator and hands me a can of Coke. I take it without hesitation. When my life turns to shit, I fall immediately back upon the vices of the past. Days like today I wish I smoked.

My brother is full of purpose, and strong. 'I've called Elspeth Dougall; she's with Claire now, seeing if they'll post a bond.'

'If?'

'They usually don't, she says, in murder cases. Not around here, anyway.'

'She's a nice kid, Ashby, but she's not a criminal attorney.'

'First thing she told me.' Ashby opens a can of Diet Sprite. 'She's just pinch-hitting till we get somebody else.'

'Who does she think we should hire?'

Ashby swallows a huge gulp of Sprite. 'She has a guy in mind. A brilliant criminal attorney, and her dad says he's the best. She's trying to get us set up.'

'Trying? Just give me his name, I'll call him right now.'

Ashby shakes his head. 'He's eccentric, okay, Georgie? Late sixties, cutting way back on his caseload. Right now he's in a dance competition in LA.'

'A *dance* competition?'

'World-class tango. He won't come till he's done.'

I sit back on the cushions. Is this real?

'I've got it taken care of, Georgie, it's all under control.' My brother is looking at me with great confidence, and I want to believe that everything is going to work out.

'You did write me that note, right? The one that said—'

'Kick the can and run? I dictated it to Selby over the phone.'

'Why, Ashby? I could have gotten Claire *off*.'

'How? By faking a confession? It wasn't going to fly. It didn't work for me.'

'You?'

'I was an hour ahead of you.'

'Dammit, Ashby, that screws everything up.'

'I screwed everything up? What about you? Don't make faces at me, you look like a monkey. Look, I talked to Selby. You have to understand what's going on.'

I set my Coke can down on the little Formica counter-top. 'Selby told you what's going on? Do you trust him?'

Ashby's eyebrows go up. 'You don't?'

'I guess I do. Just tell me what he said.'

My brother leans forward, elbows on his knees. 'This goes no further than the two of us, Georgie, or Selby will be in a hell of a jam.'

'You want me to prick my finger and seal it with three drops of blood? Who am I going to tell?'

Ashby rolls his eyes, but he is making a visible effort to humor me. It hits me, how good it is to have him here to get me through this, because right now he is shouldering the load. Mama is gone. Thank God I have a big brother.

'Okay. The district attorney's office has been pressuring for an arrest, and they narrowed their list of suspects down to one of us three.'

'*What?* But why?'

'The cops have their suspicions, but they weren't ready to make an arrest. On the one hand, they have Claire's car at the lighthouse, her shoes and the statement about Dad she made at the restaurant. That really cooked it right there.'

'But *I* said that.'

'It's me – Ashby – remember? I was there, I know who said what.'

'Anyway.'

'Anyway. The circumstantial evidence looks bad, but the fact we don't inherit is very much in our favor. The only motive they can come up with is revenge. If we think Dad killed Mama.'

'And I'm the one who handed them that.'

Ashby is shaking his head, but his eyes tell me otherwise. What an idiot I've been.

'Somebody in the DA's office is after our ass. They would have come to it on their own.'

'Wilbanks,' I say.

'Selby wouldn't confirm, but you and I know.'

'So why Claire, and not you or me?'

'The night Dad got killed, he called Carla Blanchard. They were supposed to get together, but he blew her off and said he was going to meet Claire.'

'That woman is an idiot. Claire was with us.'

'I know. And another thing she said was that a big brown padded envelope he had was missing. He'd locked it in a drawer in her house, but she got in with a nail file and looked inside and she said it was full of cash.'

'She could have made that up. Or taken the money herself. Did she say how much?'

'No, she said she didn't count it, which I don't believe, but it was a lot. She estimated $12,000. She knew Claire was having money problems, so she figured he was giving the money to Claire. But that sum, $12,000. Doesn't it ring a bell?'

'So you were right. That really is what Daddy was doing at the lighthouse that night. He was meeting his blackmailer.'

My brother smiles at me like I am a dog who has learned a new trick.

'But Ashby, that's so weird. Us there that night, and then him. And he's meeting some nut who's sucking him dry.'

'A rich nut. And it's not so odd. Remember, Dad's the one who showed us how to get back there when we were kids.'

'Then what is the logic here, Ashby? What are the police thinking? I mean, if Daddy was actually giving Claire money, why would she push him down the stairs? And if he was doing something else with it, then he wasn't really going to meet *Claire*.'

'I don't believe he was giving Claire the money, do you?'

'No, of course I don't. I paid her bills, Ashby; I saw what food was in her house. Claire hasn't had money, I promise you.'

'Right. First the cops were suspicious because somebody paid all her bills.'

'I know, that cranky Detective Click.'

'Yeah. He traced the payments back to you, so he wondered where you got the money, but then he figured that out.'

'About the pieces that I sold?'

'Right. He talked to Burgin. Georgie, why didn't you come to me? You know I would have helped.'

'How's the shrimp business?'

'The shrimp business is fine.'

'Really? Look, I know you took out a loan on your equity in the boat. So even if the business is good, it's got to be double good to pay your loans.'

Ashby seems to sink lower in his chair. 'We're going to be in this for the long haul, Georgie. It's going to take some work.'

But I am shaking my head and rising to my feet. I know what I have to do.

'Georgie, sit down.'

I plug my ears and head for the stairs. Nothing he says will make me change my mind. 'Take care of Hank and Cousin for me, Ashby.'

'If you're going to confess again you'll just screw everything up.'

I glance over at my brother, who is leaning back and swiveling his chair.

'Says who?'

'Says Selby. Haven't you been listening to me? I tried to confess myself two hours ago, I told you. It goes like this. They wanted one of us for Dad's murder, they just weren't sure which one. With Claire, they've got the shoes and the car – physical evidence, which DAs love and have to have to make their case.'

'But she didn't do it. And how can they say Claire got all that money?'

'They can't. They've searched her house. And mine, and yours, but that doesn't mean we don't have it hid.'

Hidden, I think, but keep my mouth shut.

'So what the cops do, under orders from the Beaufort DA, is get you and me to sign a statement, part of which says that we didn't have anything to do with dad's death.'

'But—'

'To prevent us from doing just what we did. All three of us confessing, and saying we're the one who did it. They considered trying all three of us on conspiracy, but then went with making their best case against Claire.'

'Claire didn't do it.'

'Do you think the DA cares who really did it? Do you think this is about justice and truth? You know if Wilbanks is behind this, he's the one who picked Claire.'

'But he's got a thing for her. He'd protect her.'

'Wrong. God, Georgie, what did I tell you about never going wrong underestimating men?'

'For a gay man—'

'I'm a cynical faggot. Claire never gave Wilbanks the time of day, and this is his chance to get her right in his power where he wants her. They've got physical evidence they can hold up in court – the shoes, the pictures of her car. The waitress they can parade into the witness box. And think about this, Georgie. Wilbanks knows us all way too well. If he could bank on breaking one of us, you know it would have to be Claire.'

It makes perfect sense. Claire is easy to manipulate, and Wilbanks is an old hand at breaking people down.

'Which is even more reason for me to confess.'

My brother scratches his chin. 'You know that grumpy detective?'

'Click?'

'Yeah. Selby says Click doesn't like it. He's feeling railroaded by the DA. He saw the withdrawals from Dad's bank account, and the first thing he thought is what we did. Blackmail. So when he finds out that Dad withdrew twelve thousand dollars in hundreds and twenties just two days before he died . . .' Ashby waves a hand.

'And it's the same amount Daddy's been pulling out once a month for the past eight months.'

'Right. And it's clear that if any of the three of us have been getting it, we're hiding it pretty well. Might be some reason to hide it now, after Daddy is dead, but before? Of course, there's always the possibility that one of us was blackmailing Dad. Which puts us back in the middle. Selby hinted Click has that in mind. He definitely wanted to continue the investigation. Selby says he's a good cop.'

I rub my forehead. I'm not sure where to go with this. I still want to run in and confess.

'Selby says you and me need to quit confessing. He says the worst scenario is, the DA goes back to the conspiracy theory. The best is, we get prosecuted for obstruction of justice.'

'So what are we supposed to do? Sit tight and trust in the justice system? Excuse me while I puke.'

My brother just looks at me. Waiting.

'What?'

'*Are* you going to puke? Or should I tell you my idea?'

Ashby has that smile he gets when he is up to no good. And I can't squelch the surge of hope. This is the Ashby I know and love. The one who won't sit still and wait for the fates.

I lean forward. 'Come on, big brother. Tell me your brilliant plan.'

'Simple. We find Dad's blackmailer.'

'This is your big plan?'

My brother just sits there like an idiot, smiling like he's the greatest brain on earth.

'Ashby, we have no idea who else knows about that business at Parris Island. It could literally be anybody, or someone we don't even know. It's impossible. We'd have to get a list of all the recruits. Jeez, I don't even know where to start. It would take forever. And whoever it is, they've got almost a hundred thousand dollars. With Daddy dead now, the smartest thing they could do is disappear.'

'I agree.'

'You do?'

'Absolutely. Which is exactly what we want.' Ashby watches me.

Beneath that happy-go-lucky exterior breathes the world's most manipulative man. I brace myself.

Ashby leans forward and grins. 'Selby asked me if Dad had a safe-deposit box. I said I didn't know, but I'd look around.'

'Ashby, you know he does; you already looked in it and there wasn't anything much there. Silver spoons and some coins and medals. Big deal.'

'I know. I'm proposing we fill it up.'

'I'm not getting this.'

'Suppose we put five thousand dollars in the safe-deposit box. Cash. Along with everything else that's already there. We'll also put the report from the private detective we found in Dad's desk, the insignia from Pickett's uniform and the letters from Dad's black-mailer in that box.'

'But we don't have any letters from – oh. *Oh*.'

'Right. We make them from Stephen Pickett. We cut words out of magazines and newspapers. We're subtle, so we don't sign his name. It's perfect, Georgie. And since Pickett is dead, he can't show up and gum the works.'

'They'll never believe it, Ashby. The police know you've had access to the box. That letter from the private detective helps, but it says that Pickett is dead.'

'Right. They can only prove it if they find Pickett's DNA.' Ashby leans backward, opens the little refrigerator with his foot and hands me another Coke. 'I've been reading over all those copies Dad had, of Marine Corps confidential reports. The thing the newspapers didn't mention, because there was no point in throwing mud, was that this Pickett guy was trouble. He had a record of assault and drug use and he was walking a fine line in boot camp and on the verge of washing out. These days, the Marine Corps wouldn't even take the guy.'

'So this makes you feel better about pointing the finger at him?'

'No. It just makes it more believable to the police.

Think about it. The report from the private detective says Pickett lived in Beaufort with his grandmother, and she still keeps his bedroom the way it was when he died. So. You and me go into his bedroom. Take a hairbrush or something. Put hairs in the envelopes with the letters – bingo, we've got DNA.'

I look at my brother with awe. I am jealous I didn't think this up. 'You really think we can pull this off?'

Ashby crosses his legs the guy way, with his knee sticking way out. 'Tell me why not?'

'It's just . . . don't you have to sign in when you get into a safe-deposit box? And even if you don't, somebody at the bank might remember you. If there are women they'll remember you.'

'How about a bus locker?'

'Same thing. Somebody might see us. *We* could leave DNA. If we screw this up, it's over. Claire will look more guilty and we'll all go to jail.'

Ashby shifts sideways and purses his lips. 'So what do *you* suggest, Georgie? That we just let the whole thing go?'

'No. It's a good plan, just keep it simple. We stick as close to the truth as we can. Put the letters in with the files Daddy actually kept, right where you found them in the drawer.'

'They'll just think we put them there. Oh, I get it. Until they test for DNA.'

'And Wilbanks becomes an asset, Ashby. Because deep in his nasty little heart he knows most of this is true.'

Ashby rubs his knee. 'Pickett's grandmother is probably a very nice lady. Pickett's dead, and he's already been screwed once by this family.'

'If it's a choice between a dead man and Claire, for me that's no choice.'

'So we're in?'

'We're in.'

'Nobody can know about this, Georgie. You can't tell Hank.'

'And you can't tell Reese.'

'I'm not going to tell Reese. What about Claire?'

'Are you kidding, Ashby? We definitely can't tell Claire. She'll get all intimidated and guilty and confess just to make everybody go away.'

'Good point. We won't tell Claire. So Operation Deep Shit begins.'

My brother and I shake hands.

13

Jenkins Dennis Radcliffe, aka the Jinx, as he is not so fondly known by district attorneys in the tri-state area, has flown in from Atlanta, Georgia, to talk to the local district attorney, meet with my brother and me and see Claire. He will confirm, yes or no, whether or not he'll defend my sister. According to Elspeth Dougall, if we act nice and give him all our money, he will likely take our case. He's flying in because he's in a golf tournament in Hilton Head. Elspeth Dougall thinks we have a good chance.

In our favor, the Jinx has something of a grudge match going with the local DA, Sondra Mannelli, which can work very much in our favor. Even those who like him say the Jinx is a vindictive son of a bitch.

The man's reputation makes me nervous. Ashby, on the other hand, is pleased. We sit in the tiny but elegant lobby of the Beaufort Inn and wait for the Jinx's assistant to fetch us. The Beaufort Inn, a famous bed-and-breakfast in a Victorian house, deserves its reputation. The mahogany is polished till it shines, the wood floors are dark and immaculate, the carpets vibrant and new.

The inn is also as quiet as your great-aunt's parlor. There is no one behind the front desk, though we can hear the faint clatter of dishware from the kitchen. The deacon's bench we share is hard on the back, and I shift and cross my legs. Behind us a staircase sweeps to the second and third floors, and Ashby keeps annoying me by turning his head around to see if Jinx's assistant is on his way.

'Maybe we should hire somebody local,' I whisper. 'You realize, if we hire this Jinx guy, we'll be paying for all of this.' I wave my hand at all the elegance. I know what a suite upstairs costs.

'Georgie, there's no second chances here.' My brother sounds worldly. He's been in lawsuits before.

'But don't you think some hot-shit lawyer from Atlanta's going to piss all the locals off?'

'So what? We get some doofus that everybody likes, who bumbles along, and we hope the jury lets Claire off because they like the attorney? Look, the DA doesn't have much of a case, but the ball is rolling and we've got to get it stopped dead.'

I look at my feet.

'Georgie, we *want* a guy with an ego. We want a guy who knows what he's doing, who doesn't spend most of his time on divorce and personal injury. We want a guy who *needs* to win.'

I'm still looking down at my feet.

'Just meet him. That's all I ask.'

It is another twitchy fifteen minutes before Ashby and I hear the clatter of high heels and a quick step on the wooden stairs. The phone rings behind the desk, and a young woman in khakis rushes in to pick it up. Meanwhile, behind us, we see legs first, slim, with expensive stockings, then the hemline of a black pleated skirt that swirls around delicate knees. The assistant, in full view, is young. Her face is interesting, more than traditionally pretty, and she wears small round glasses. Her thick brunette hair has reddish tints and a shine achieved by good health and expensive haircare products. Her hair is collar length and expertly cut. She wears an open white blouse and a small strand of pearls – elegant, but rather much for a Beaufort morning.

'I'm Brenda Vasquez.' She shakes our hands. 'Would you like to come on up?'

The Jinx is occupying a third-floor suite, and our footsteps clatter as we follow her. She is silent, reserving all conversation, wisely, until we're behind closed doors.

Vasquez uses a key to unbolt the door – a real key in this inn full of antiques – and lets us into a small sitting room that has polished wood floors, Queen Anne side tables and a blue-striped Italian silk couch. There are windows in the turretlike sitting area that look out over the courtyard behind the hotel. The furniture is mostly reproductions, by my eye, but expensive for all of that.

There is a pot of coffee on the end table and a basket of fresh biscuits from downstairs.

'Coffee?' Ms Vasquez offers.

I am pleased and immediately say yes.

'No.' This from Ashby. But when Brenda Vasquez offers the basket of biscuits, I see him smile. It takes more willpower than Ashby possesses to pass up the homemade biscuits at the Beaufort Inn.

Ms Vasquez gets right to the point. 'Mr Radcliffe and I are both licensed to practice in Georgia, South Carolina and Louisiana. The majority of our cases center around the Atlanta and New Orleans area. Honestly, it would be more economical for you to hire someone local to handle your case. As I told you over the telephone, Mr Radcliffe is playing in a golf tournament in Hilton Head, and there will be no hard feelings if you prefer that he not take the job.'

I clear my throat. 'Do you find, Ms Vasquez, that there is a certain amount of hostility among the locals when the lawyer comes in from out of state?'

Ashby, beside me, is tense and watchful.

But Ms Vasquez smiles, and I get the feeling she's answered this question before.

'That's very true. On the other hand, Mr Radcliffe has no ties with the local district attorney's office. He doesn't have to work with them in cases down the road, he doesn't play golf with them on the weekends and when it comes to the best interests of his client, he's not afraid to make people mad.' She studies us, to see if we get the point. I know I do. 'Also remember, in a murder trial, it is possible to get a change of venue, if local sentiment is a problem for the defense.'

Ashby gives me a look. He might as well stick out his tongue.

'Do you want to proceed?' Ms Vasquez asks us.

'Yes,' I say.

'What is your financial estimate on Mr Radcliffe's representation?' Ashby's face reveals no trace of his gung-ho attitude from downstairs.

Inside I am cringing. Money conversations make me tense. But it is clear from Ms Vasquez's demeanor that the subject was next on her list. I am glad my brother is beside me. I would have been afraid to ask.

'A murder case, if we go to trial, can easily go to a hundred thousand dollars. And if we do go to trial, you'd best consider that your bottom-line base. If we need to hire investigators – and we have some regulars we trust, who give us a reasonable rate – it will go even higher. If we need to hire consultants, in forensics and the like, higher still. All those possibilities are very likely when trying a murder case.'

I try not to look upset. It is only Mama's estate and insurance that will keep us afloat at these rates. And we don't have an insurance check yet.

'We'll need thirty thousand dollars to get going on this,' Ms Vasquez tells us, as if it's an everyday sum.

Ashby, amazingly, haggles and in a short conversation has handed her a check for nine thousand dollars like he writes one every day. Arrangements for collateral are made; within twenty-four hours I will be handing them the mortgage on my shop.

Ms Vasquez is smiling. 'You've made a good decision,' she tells us. 'If it were my sister in that jail cell, Mr Radcliffe is definitely the man I would hire.'

In a part of my mind I know she has to say it. But in spite of myself I'm impressed.

She stands, and her skirt makes a soft noise. 'I'll ask Mr Radcliffe to come in.'

Jenkins Dennis Radcliffe bursts forth from the inner sanctum, and his steps, as he crosses the floor to greet us, are so precise and graceful that I am reminded he dances the tango. He is tallish, lithe and slender, a post-retirement Cary Grant. He has the slightest stoop to his shoulders, his hair is brown and gray, cut short and gelled carefully back. He gives Ashby a manly hand-shake, then clasps both hands intimately around mine.

It is as if the very air crackles around him, and his presence in the room makes Ms Vasquez recede.

'Not a coffee drinker?' is the first thing he says to

my brother. 'I wish I could say the same. But the biscuits are amazing, aren't they? Can we get you a soft drink or a cup of tea?'

There is something about this man that is relaxing even as he fascinates, and Ashby asks for a Diet Coke.

'How about you, Ms Smallwood. Is there anything you'd like to have?'

I shake my head but he waits, eyes full of good-natured humor, to be certain that I won't change my mind.

'Brenda, dear, would you get Mr Smallwood a Diet Coke?'

And Brenda dear, hovering behind him, says yes very softly, and he pats her hand.

It hits me that they are sleeping together. Given the age difference I would not have suspected, but after meeting the man I understand why. I would sleep with him myself. Brenda, no doubt, will work hard, stay loyal, but eventually tire of the arrangement, and the Jinx will likely help her find another job, some years down the road. They will part friends, and, to her benefit, she will have favors to pull from a man of influence and will also be very well trained.

Radcliffe settles in across from us, hands on his knees, and I get a faint whiff of expensive and masculine scent.

'Now look,' he says. 'Let's get on a first-name basis.'

'I'm Georgie.'

'Ashby.'

'Georgie. Ashby. You go ahead and call me Jinx. I've earned my nickname and I don't mind it, so long as you understand it's the prosecutors who run into trouble, not my clients, and the district attorney's office that gets all the bad luck.'

I laugh and so does Ashby.

'This is a bad time for your family. Believe me, I understand that. And I want you to put all of your problems in my hands. I want you to know right here' – he touches his heart – 'and here' – he taps his temple – 'that I'm going to give you a hundred percent.'

The relief I feel is amazing. To this day I cannot express why the Jinx inspires me with such confidence. The man is intelligent, warm and capable – and I believe every word that he says.

'What part of your sister's case worries you the most?' The Jinx has changed tack unexpectedly, and I blurt out the first thing that comes to my mind.

'They're going to bully her. The police. And even worse is there's a man in the district attorney's office, Eugene Wilbanks, and he knows my sister pretty well. She doesn't stand up to bullying. I don't know what she'll say or sign to get left alone.'

Jinx gives me a look over his glasses that is admiring and sharp. 'I know exactly what you're telling me. I was going to spend some time interviewing the two of you, but let's put that off. The first person I need to see is Claire. Brenda?'

'I'll use the phone in the next room.' Vasquez is off to the inner sanctum, greasing the skids behind closed doors.

'Claire needs to accept my representation in any case,' Jinx tells us, and stands up to shake our hands. 'Forgive me for cutting this short, but I'm going straight from here to the jail. If you can stay a bit, Brenda has some paperwork to take you through.'

An hour later, Ashby and I are clattering down the staircase with a decidedly lighter step.

'Let's go downstairs and get breakfast,' Ashby says.

'Unless you want to interview some more lawyers.'

'You know I don't.'

'When all of this is over, I wonder if we can get the Jinx to adopt us.'

'I don't think we'll be able to afford it. And speaking of which, the breakfasts here are awfully high.'

Ashby puts an arm around my shoulders. 'Then thank God for all of Mama's money. We're in the fast lane now, Georgie Porgie. If we're going to go broke, let's do it in style.'

The next morning, Ashby and I go together to visit Claire in jail for the first time. Afterward, we will decide to go separately so that Claire gets two visits instead of one. Claire prefers it this way also; I am the only one who doesn't. There is some special energy when the three of us get together.

My brother and I sit at a table and wait for our sister. There is no grill, no visitation carrels, no telephone because there's no glass to separate us. There is a guard in the corner of the room, and families, friends and children of the other inmates. I watch the other prisoners until my sister finally appears.

Claire stands out, looking graceful, refined and vulnerable. She moves nervously, like her knees will go out from under her, like a foal still finding its legs. People watch her. Families of prisoners look up when she goes by. I exchange looks with my brother. How is my sister going to survive?

The smile she gives us is painfully sweet. It will be the last one I see for a while.

'That attorney you guys sent is a *trip*. No, don't hug me, it's not allowed. Where did you find him? Georgie, *Jesus*, don't cry.'

'I'm sorry, I'm sorry.'

'He's the best criminal lawyer in the southern United States,' Ashby says. He's steady, which is good, because I can't talk.

'Thanks, you two. No, I mean it. Do you have any idea how many people in here get dumped by their families and just left to rot?'

'What can we bring you?' Ashby asks.

Claire waves a hand. 'Nothing for now, somebody will just take it away.'

'Who?'

But this is a matter Claire will not discuss. She changes the subject. 'Where is the money coming from to pay the attorney? This Jinx guy can't be cheap.'

Ashby and I very carefully do not exchange looks. 'Elspeth takes care of everything. We've got the insurance, and pretty soon we'll get all the money from Mom's estate.'

Claire seems to deflate, she is so relieved. 'I thought, you know, with all this jail and stuff, that might hold things up, with the insurance or the estate or whatever.'

In truth, Claire being in jail holds everything up, and Wilbanks has us tied in knots. The insurance company is dragging its feet, wary of impending lawsuits, and the probate is still in dispute. But Ashby and I have agreed that this is something we will spare our sister.

Claire props her chin on a fist. 'I miss my babies. Have you guys seen them? How are they holding up?'

I exchange guilty looks with my brother.

'We've kind of been working the attorney angle and the financing,' Ashby says.

'But we'll go today. We'll check up on them,' I promise.

Claire runs a finger on the edge of the table. 'Clark has them.'

'Okay, they won't be having fun, but they'll be okay,' I tell her.

'He wants to bring them to visit me. I don't want them to come.'

'Let them come,' Ashby says.

'Don't,' I say.

'I told Clark to have them write me letters. But I talked to them on the phone. Both of the girls cried.'

'I'll go over this afternoon,' Ashby says. 'I'll take them to a movie. I'll get them popcorn, and a candy bar, and a huge drink. I'll keep them out late on a school night and annoy ol' Clark.'

Claire actually smiles. She studies a spot over Ashby's shoulder. 'I've been afraid you guys might be mad.'

'Why would we be mad at *you*?' I know my voice has gone up an octave, and Ashby's quick look tells me to keep it down.

Claire drums a finger on the table. 'Maybe you thought I really did it. Maybe you think I killed Dad.'

'We don't think that.' Ashby's voice is solid. 'Do we, Georgie?'

'No, we don't. Not for one second, not in a million years.'

We could use my mother right now. She had a solution for every problem, no matter how big or small. I wonder how she would get Claire out of jail. Her methods were not always traditional, but they were effective and direct. My mother always thought outside the box.

Today my brother is the problem solver. Ashby rolls his eyes at Claire. 'Listen up, moron. The cops are idiots, and Wilbanks is on a hate campaign. Don't you know why you're here and we aren't? Because you're beautiful. You know damn well that pervert Eugene Wilbanks has always had a thing for you.'

'He does not.'

'Get real.' Ashby is cheerfully nonchalant, and his tone makes me and Claire take heart. My brother leans back and crosses his legs. 'Think, Claire. Didn't Mama always bend over backward never to leave you and that pisspot Wilbanks alone in the same room? Don't tell me she didn't take you aside and warn you not to get in a car with that man.'

Claire looks stunned, as if Ashby is reading her mind. 'How'd you know?'

'Because, unlike you, the rest of us don't live in the twilight zone.'

'Mom never warned *me*,' I say.

'You're *beautiful*, Georgie, you're a lot beautifuller than me.'

'I know that, honey. I just don't appeal to the perverts the way you do.'

'You'd think *I'd* appeal to perverts. But Mama never did warn me either.'

Later, when I think back upon this, our first visit with our sister, I like to remember how innocently upbeat we were, ready to take on the world.

⬇

A new phase begins in our lives. My brother takes three days off from fishing – a miracle, this – and sends Hank out with a friend of his, an Australian fisherman named Barney Jones. Hank will learn the trade from another viewpoint and keep Ashby informed. My son will follow the shrimp.

Ashby and I meet each morning to work on Operation Deep Shit and share a late breakfast at our favorite breakfast spot, the Lamplighter II. As far as I know, there isn't a Lamplighter I, though Ashby is convinced there must be one somewhere. The Lamplighter has a worn feeling, and there are rips in the blood-red vinyl of the booths, but they have fresh orange juice they squeeze on the spot, and the waitresses are like your favorite aunt – provided your favorite aunt always has a smile and an eye for what you need before you need it.

Ashby and I have spent the first morning cutting letters out of newspapers. We decided, after the first tedious hour, to start cutting out entire words, and so the work began to move faster. We both use the scissors, I compose the letters and Ashby wields the glue. We work in Mama's kitchen like two evil kindergartners, only our scissors are sharp on the end, not rounded. We begin work at seven, and stop for breakfast at ten. I am lucky Ashby lets me sleep past five. He is normally up and out by three or four with the a.m. tides.

Today I am eating corned-beef hash with two poached eggs on top. It is a huge order, and I can never eat even half, so I always give Ashby my toast. Ashby can eat more toast than anybody I know. He spreads the jelly so thick it makes me ill, and he has the waitresses here well trained. They always bring him between six and eight of those tiny tubs of strawberry jelly. In addition to my toast, Ashby has a breakfast sandwich with ham, cheese and eggs and three or four glasses of juice. The coffeepot belongs solely to me, and along with the strawberry jelly, the waitress knows to bring me eight of those little plastic buckets of cream.

'Can I ask you a question?' Ashby has jelly on the corner of his mouth, but I'm not his mother so I don't say a word. 'Don't you consider fishing a job?'

I smash the egg yellows into the hash and salt them heavily. 'Of course I consider fishing a job. A damn tough job.'

Ashby manages to smile *and* look perturbed. 'Well, then, I guess I don't understand.'

I roll my eyes. 'Make your point.' My brother is in manipulative mode. He has been impossible since he hatched his master plan.

'Hank tells me you want him to go back to school or get a job.'

'That's right.' I hear the belligerence in my voice. I'm not big on interference over the way I handle my son. It's probably just as well I'm a single mother. 'It's not going to do Hank a lot of good sitting around the house. He can take some time, rest up, get back into the flow. But he needs to be involved in something, and he needs to think about his future. You can't just let an eighteen-year-old sit around.'

Ashby makes a point of catching my eye. 'Take it slow with him, Georgie.'

'Why? What did he tell you?'

'If he did talk to me, it would be in confidence, wouldn't it?'

'I guess.'

Ashby takes a large bite of toast. 'Let's put it this way. How would you feel if Hank goes out on the boat with me at least three days a week? Any other days he wants to come out, he's welcome. But he has to agree to a minimum of three.'

'That'd be great. I'd love it, but are you sure it's all right with you?'

'Are you kidding? I love having him with me. Hank's a natural fisherman, and he's smart as hell. You wouldn't believe how fast he picks things up.'

'Thanks, Ashby.' My worries for my son are greatly eased. Ashby can look out for Hank and do all the guy stuff. Take a load off my mind.

In the past Ashby has kept a certain distance – always afraid Hank would figure out his uncle's homosexuality and reject him out of hand. Nothing I ever said relieved Ashby of his fear of that rejection, but I guess that's not an issue anymore.

'And Hank is definitely cool with this?' I ask my brother.

'Hank is definitely cool.'

I glance down at my plate and wonder what Claire is having to eat.

'We'll see her in a few hours,' Ashby says, reading my mind.

This is another reason for Ashby's time off. He wants to be there for Claire her first week in jail. There is no bail for suspected murderers in Beaufort, South Carolina.

'It's just I feel so guilty. We're all going out tonight while she's there in jail.'

'She says she's living vicariously through both of us,

242

so not to sit around. And she wants me to check out this new guy of yours.'

'Ashby, promise me you won't do anything weird.'

'Quit obsessing, Georgie. Hey, are you going to eat that egg?'

It strikes me that my brother's hand is shaking. I wonder if he is tired.

It was John Wallace who suggested that we all go dancing, and we left it up to Reese and Ashby to pick the place. I had my nails done yesterday. For me, the anticipation is as good as the date. But then, I haven't been out much lately.

It's hot. Outside, the humidity feels like you've been wrapped like a mummy in steaming towels. Inside, I stand enveloped in a cream-colored Egyptian cotton towel that I keep hidden from Hank, and rub lotion that smells like apples into my wet, glistening skin.

I slide into brand-new French underwear – a demi bra and lace, high-cut panties. I sit carefully in front of my makeup mirror and go heavy on the eyeliner, line my lips with a mauve liner and apply lavender lipstick and sticky gloss. Silver hoops for my ears and a toe ring. No panty hose tonight. It is too hot, and I have a good tan, freckles on my knees. I slip into a white, slinky tank dress that has a plunging V-neck in the front and back, and a high wide slit on one side. My dancing shoes are small-heeled white sandals, a little scuffed, but you'd have to look for it, and I know I can dance in these shoes for hours with minimal discomfort. I twist my hair and clamp it into a silver comb so that it is up off my neck but hangs loosely around my face, with little bits escaping here and there. No watch tonight. I grit my teeth and twist my arm like a pretzel to fasten a slender silver bracelet, which drapes loosely across my left wrist. When it is finally latched I look in the mirror, convincing myself that the bracelet gives me a small-boned, delicate look. It took me a full hour in that bubble bath to get the wood rosin out of the ridges of my thumb, but they are pink now, and you would never confuse me with a handyman.

John Wallace is not quite fifteen minutes late yet, but Cousin is barking and scrabbling at the door that leads out of my second-floor apartment; he must already be waiting downstairs. I kiss Cousin on her soft, smelly head, and my lipstick leaves a lavender smile in the fur.

John Wallace and I will drive into Charleston tonight, meeting Ashby and Reese at a place Reese just discovered. John Wallace assures me he likes the blues, and in fact he has the look and feel of a man who might have played the saxophone in another life. He will be on probation until the end of the evening. I am going to see how John Wallace treats my brother.

The bar is rough around the edges. The windows are painted black and layered with the residue of a million cigarettes. The ceiling is brown tile and cracked right down the middle. The floor is dark wood, dull, gouged and nicked, and whoever cleans here does it with a serious lack of enthusiasm. It is clear from the stale cigarette smoke, the smell of spilled beer and the electricity in the air that this is a great bar.

We are early because Reese insisted on coming early. He is convinced there will be a crowd tonight; a local favorite is playing – Memphis Motown. I have never heard of them.

The lack of conversation at our table bothers me, and the bar is temporarily quiet. The men are sizing each other up, and my stomach is cramping like it always does when I am nervous. John Wallace could easily be one of those men who think gays are for beating up in alleyways behind bars. And Ashby is quite capable of turning stuck-up and snobby with John Wallace.

Reese winks at me across the table, and I think he is reading my mind. Ashby and Claire have gotten so used to me being alone that they are hypercritical when I date, and Reese has warned me more than once that no human male can survive the sibling test.

A waitress stops in. She is wearing new white Keds and isn't tired yet; the evening is young. She's still smiling.

'Michelob,' Ashby says.

'Bud,' from Reese.

'Bud,' from John Wallace.

Ashby points a finger at me. 'And she wants some kind of big frozen daiquiri with a little umbrella and lots of chopped-up fruit.'

I ignore my brother and look at the waitress. 'Miller Lite, on tap, if you've got it.'

John Wallace frowns and touches my hand. 'Have a daiquiri if that's what you want.'

'I don't. Ashby's just messing with me.'

Reese, who has been frowning over the menu, opens both arms wide to include us all. 'I'm ordering the Splatter Platter, my treat.'

'The what?'

Ashby looks at John Wallace. 'Buffalo wings, nachos, mozzarella sticks, everything fried and bad for you. But if you want something else . . .'

'No. Sounds good.'

Ashby is trying to make John Wallace feel excluded. He is on his worst behavior tonight, and I am wishing we had not come.

John Wallace pats my thigh, and I see my brother notice the familiarity.

'Be right back.' John nods at Ashby and Reese and heads for the men's room. I watch him weave his way across the floor and disappear.

'Nice ass, anyway,' my brother says.

People are coming through the narrow front door in twos and threes and the tables are filling up. Cigarette smoke hangs in the tired yellow light. I try not to think what would happen if someone yelled fire. You can't live forever.

'I see the attraction.' Ashby looks after John Wallace and exchanges dark looks with Reese.

'That man is sex on a stick,' Reese says.

'Not gay,' I say. It doesn't sound like a question, but it is.

'Definitely hetero,' Ashby says.

Reese just sighs loudly.

'I don't think you like him.'

Ashby shrugs. 'He looks dangerous.'

'Dangerous? What do you mean, dangerous?'

My brother says nothing.

'If he's playing footsie with you under the table, Ashby, I want to know.' This happened once before, and Ashby didn't tell me right away because he didn't want to hurt my feelings. Life is complicated when you have a beautiful brother.

'No, I told you, Georgie, this one is definitely straight.'

'Then what's wrong with him?'

I catch sight of John Wallace making his way through the crowd. One of those annoying girls in tight jeans and a large belt buckle stops in front of him. She has long hill-woman hair, a terrible crunchy-fried perm, and I am reminded of the lyrics to a Jerry Jeff Waller song that goes, 'I like my women a little on the trashy side.'

The woman grins at John Wallace, but he gives her a quick look, finds me with his eyes and smiles. My brother can go to hell. I have a heart no one can steal, but tonight, when I look at John Wallace, I want to roll the dice and give it away.

John Wallace sits back down and reaches across the table, enclosing my wrist in his thick, large hand. 'They had Etta James here last fall. I saw an old poster on the way to the men's room.'

'You like Etta James?' Reese says.

John Wallace cocks his head. 'Seen her twice in Chicago and once in New Orleans.' He says *New Orlins* like a native.

Reese is grinning. 'When in Chicago? I was there in ninety-eight.'

The Splatter Platter arrives, blazing hot and heaped with fried banana peppers, sour cream, guacamole, fried pickles. I smile. I am out on a Friday night with three guys, and I can eat stupid like the men. I take a sip of Miller Lite. The waitress deals four small plates around the table, leaves a pile of thick paper napkins, and I feel the tension ease. The guys are halfway into their first beer, and the food clearly makes them happy.

'You like Etta James?' John Wallace asks my brother.

Ashby takes a nibble of buffalo wing. There is red hot sauce on his chin. 'I just go along to keep my sweetie happy.' He is using a more effeminate voice, and I kick him hard under the table.

I refuse to look up. I select a fried mozzarella stick from the platter, but it's just for something to do.

'So you guys are a couple?' John Wallace says, without batting an eye, which is frankly more than I can say for my brother.

'For eight years,' Reese says, and he is looking wary.

I take a bite of fried cheese.

'How'd you two meet?' John Wallace asks.

The cheese is hot and stringy. I burn the roof of my mouth and spit the cheese into a napkin with more self-defense than social grace.

'I picked him up in a sports bar.' Ashby leans back in his chair and looks at Reese with a slow smile. Everyone relaxes. The contest is over, for now anyway, and I think John Wallace won. He reaches for my hand under the table and squeezes it once, before he makes a dent in the nachos, and I feel like part of a couple.

The lights go dim. A spotlight illuminates the small raised stage at the end of the walnut bar. A woman walks out from a door near the men's room. She seems unaware of the stares. She reminds me of Tina Turner, not so much for the facial features as the self-confidence and the glorious legs. She wears a short, fringed black cocktail dress. One by one, five musicians move onstage. One behind a keyboard, another fingering a trumpet. A very old woman, hair in dreads, sits on a stool tuning a Les Paul electric guitar. She is joined by a young girl with a cello that probably weighs more than she does, and a man with a kinky gray beard who clutches a saxophone. He looks more like someone who has escaped from a nursing home than a musician.

A skinny man with age spots and a greasy gray ponytail dries his hands on a white apron and steps up onto the stage and behind a microphone. Applause breaks out. This crowd is relaxed and easy to please.

'Evening y'all.' The man looks around the room, so self-possessed he seems to live in an alternate reality, but he looks benevolently out upon all of us as if he is our long-lost grandfather, and then he smiles, and the light glints on a gold cap that covers his left front tooth. 'Let's give a warm Carolina welcome to some serious musicians. Please welcome Memphis Motown!'

Someone squeals, and the crowd is clapping and whistling. Memphis Motown is clearly a huge favorite in Charleston.

John Wallace and Reese sit like men in a trance. They have even quit eating the buffalo wings. Ashby gives me a tired smile, turns a troubled look on Reese and continues to eat like a robot programmed for food. And I realize that Reese has his chair turned on an angle, with his back to my brother, and the two of them have not really exchanged a kind word all night.

The low sweet notes of a lone sax draw my attention to the stage. I'm too short to see over the crowd. I look back once at Ashby, who is staring into space as he chews and seems oblivious to the music. He seems left out, somehow, and I remember the way it used to be for him in high school, deep in the gay closet but an outcast just the same. I want to talk to him, draw him into the fun, but the sax is no longer alone, and the music is too loud now for thinking of anything else, much less random conversation.

Maybe it is the blues, but I am twelve years old again, in my first year of junior high school, and my brother and I are walking into a 7-Eleven, no more than a few hundred yards from my school. Ashby has driven me himself, and I can't get over the thrill of having an older brother who drives.

There are five boys sitting on a low brick wall that divides the 7-Eleven from the dry cleaners. One boy swings his legs, and they all have that vacuous look in their eyes that every outcast immediately recognizes.

'Hey, hardo,' one says.

I recognize him. He goes to my school, one of the kids who smokes outside the cafeteria, rarely goes to class and is by all means to be avoided in the hallway. He is looking slyly at my brother.

'Hardo, hardo, hardo,' chants another boy.

Ashby is in high school. He is older than all of these guys, and in the social pecking order of teenage boys these guys are way out of line.

'Hey, hardo.'

'Hardo.'

'Haaaarrrrdooo.'

They sound like malevolent parrots with a new word that excites them, and I wait tensely to see what Ashby will do.

He ignores them. I follow him into the 7-Eleven, looking over my shoulder. The boys are staring and smirking, and my knees go shaky and I feel sick. I need to defend my brother, but I'm not sure what to do, and

I am afraid of the consequences. Me, afraid. And I always thought I was so brave.

Ashby pretends nothing is happening. He doesn't hurry. He gets what we want and pays the clerk, but his voice cracks once when he asks the cashier for ones instead of a five, and his hand trembles as he holds it out for change.

Outside, the boys are still chanting, so loud we can hear them from inside the store. The clerk is male and middle-aged and he punches away at that register like there is nothing going on. I watch him with fading hope. He is an adult but he is either powerless or un-interested. No one is going to defend my brother, not even me.

Ashby and I drive home together in silence and never once do we talk about what happened. But I know my brother has been humiliated and I have been shamed.

This is one of the most painful memories of my life.

14

It is day three, the final day, of Ashby's and my preparation for Operation Deep Shit. The letters are finally done. We are having breakfast at eleven today because we worked straight through until we were finished.

I had to cut the final words out myself. Ashby's hands are so shaky now he cannot hold scissors. He says for me not to worry, it's just some medication he is on.

We are treating ourselves. We sit at the Beaufort Inn eating homemade biscuits and maple butter, waiting for hash browns, ham and eggs. Ashby is having bacon too, but that's more than I can eat. In between bites his lips move oddly. He reminds me of a baby bird.

Maybe he is nervous. I know I am. This afternoon we move to phase two of our plan.

The butterflies kill my appetite, and I worry a lot about Claire. I crumble my biscuit into chunks on my plate. Ashby works his way steadily through his meal. There are shadows beneath his eyes and I'm wondering if he has slept. His face looks puffy and sad. My beautiful brother is gaining weight.

But he'll be better, we'll all be better, when Claire gets out of jail.

The heavy breakfast does not sit easily on my stomach as we pull out of the parking lot and head off to visit Stephen Pickett's maternal grandmother, Verna Pickett – Pickett because, like me, Stephen's mother never married. She lives in a small home built in the Forties. It is a white frame house, in need of paint, and it has a wide and shady porch. I park Big Mama out front.

The driveway is gravel, with tufts of grass here and there, and you can see the dirt showing through in the tread marks that cars make on both sides. Parked halfway down the driveway is a 1988 Ford LTD, gold, with plush brown seats. The car windows are open. The garage door is shut tight. Probably full of junk. It is the old-fashioned kind of garage, located toward the back of the lot with a heavy wood door that flips out.

The grass out front is newly cut and peppered with yellow dandelions and clover. Ashby follows me up the chipped concrete porch steps. On one side of the porch is an array of small black plastic pots of geraniums and violets that sit in a puddle of water. The other side of the porch is taken up by a rusted white and green glider, a metal two-seater that moves back and forth on a rail. Yesterday's newspaper has been scattered and then restacked and left underneath the glider. Ashby and I have visited four other houses on this street, knocking on doors and enquiring after 'antiques'. For appearance's sake I have bought two things already. The first is a record cabinet that a man swore belonged to his great-great-aunt. He told me he inherited the piece twenty years ago. She must have bought it the day before she died. I judge it to be circa 1973, and it is veneered in thin walnut, and made by Montgomery Ward. The other purchase I have made is a black metal floor lamp with a fringed rose-pink shade. They sell them in the old country store at Cracker Barrel and at Big Lots in Tennessee.

Ashby is sweating, and I want to go home and take a long shower. We've looked at a shitload of junk.

Now that we are here at 5801 Montgomery Avenue, however, I am no longer feeling the heat. I'm excited again, and not so tired. For Claire, I tell myself for courage, and ring the doorbell. Ashby, by my side, is still doing those bird lip moves.

The front door opens, a woman stares out and a fly lands between us on the screen.

'Mrs Pickett?' Ashby says, and I freeze inside. Ashby shouldn't have called her by name.

Mrs Pickett is a lumpy woman, with a frown on her wrinkled, disapproving face. Her skin looks pale, waxy and tissue-fine. Her hair is disastrously thin and ill equipped to withstand the frizzy perm that seems recently applied, and she has drawn her eyebrows on in a reddish-brown arch. She wears a floral housedress and black slip-on shoes, and her shoulders are hunched forward. For all her physical frailty, she seems intimidating.

'I am very hard of hearing. You will have to speak up.' Irritation drips from the tone of her voice, and she clearly has no patience for those who speak softly in this world.

'We're in the neighborhood, buying antiques. I sell them, from my shop in town.'

Mrs Pickett clearly does not understand what this has to do with her. I'm wondering if she heard what I said. I feel like an idiot, shouting on this woman's front porch. This is not going well.

Ashby edges me sideways, and I am relieved. He gets along with old ladies and dogs. I just get along with dogs. 'We've bought a couple of things here in the neighborhood. Some of this stuff we just sell at the flea market. That lamp there from Mrs Barret, and the cabinet from . . . what was his name?' And Ashby looks at me.

'Queensbury.'

Ashby nods. 'Anyhow, we haven't found too much, so we still got cash here, budgeted to spend. If you have anything you want to show us, we'd sure like to have a look. If not, we'll be on our way. My sister here is hot, and she wants her lunch.'

Mrs Pickett peers at me with a judgmental expression that makes it plain she is not surprised to find me the kind of female who goes off eating lunch when everybody else is working. She looks back at Ashby, whom she treats as if he's in charge.

'What kind of stuff you in the market for?'

'Oh, you know. Old stuff. Antiques. Stuff like we've got in the truck.'

I am cringing inside. Old stuff?

But Mrs Pickett finds his explanation completely adequate and opens the bent screen door.

'I got a thing or two you might want to take a look at up in the attic. If you think you're not wasting your time.'

'Thank you, ma'am.' Ashby is all over smiles as he steps sideways and lets me in first.

The living room is dusty and cluttered. The couch is a study in fading floral upholstery, covered with a crocheted afghan in a patchwork of Easter pastels: pink, blue, mint green. An old black-and-white television sits on a metal stand next to a piano that looks like it has not been touched since the police action in Korea. Yellowed sheet music slopes sideways in the center stand. I edge close and read the title: 'A Bicycle Built For Two'.

We have interrupted Verna Pickett's lunch. She is eating beets and turnip greens from a plate on a metal folding tray.

'Nothing in here is worth anything,' Mrs Pickett says. 'Stuff I want to show you is this way.'

She leads us to a staircase that goes up from the side of the kitchen. I get a glimpse of tired black-and-white linoleum and yellow counters and kitchen drawers. The curtains on the kitchen windows are fringed by little knitted pink balls.

'I'm not so big on climbing stairs these days. Most nights, I sleep down here. Head up them steps and go to the left. The attic is up that way. It's dusty up there, and hot, so I warn you. But anything you find up there, I would probably be happy to sell.'

I am excited, and it is an effort not to look at Ashby as we make our way up. We start in the attic, for appearance's sake, but on the way down the hall I pass two closed bedroom doors. One of them, I hope, belongs to Pickett.

The attic is only accessible by pull-down stairs, the kind of attic I hate. It is good that Ashby is here, because even if I jumped I would not be able to reach the dangling pull-down cord.

I go up first, feeling the heat as I stumble up the raw wood stairs. It is like poking my head into an oven. I won't say I haven't run across treasures in this sort of attic, but what I know I can count on is dust, heat, bad lighting and shaky floors of plywood laid casually over insulation and open studs. The ladder quivers beneath me – my brother is climbing up. Even though it is daylight outside, I can barely see. For once, the cord to the light switch is within my reach. I click it on – a dim bulb, maybe forty watts – and crawl sideways, making room for Ashby to come up. I know there are spiders. I can't see them, but I know they are there.

'Phew,' Ashby says, directly at my back. 'It stinks up here. What is that smell? It's like Vienna sausage, rolled up in a sweat sock.'

'Mouse. Male mouse. It's the male of the species that always stinks.'

'Am I supposed to take that personally?'

I crawl forward slowly to see if there is anything I can bear to buy.

'Pick something,' Ashby orders. 'We need to make this worth her while.'

'Um. It's crap, mostly. I like that old green trunk.'

'No way am I hauling that fucker down these attic stairs.'

'Then go open it up and I'll buy whatever you can carry. I'm going to take a look in the bedrooms.'

'Be quiet, Georgie.'

'Ashby, she's deaf.'

'Selective hearing, if you ask me.'

'Just go raid the trunk.'

'Why don't you raid the trunk and I'll do the bedroom. You're the collector, not me.'

'There's spiders in the attic.' I am ducking down the stairs so he can't take my place.

'*Georgie*. What am I supposed to look for?'

'*Old stuff.*'

The first bedroom belongs to a female – there are flowered curtains and bottles of pills and lotions by the bed. I can smell the faint odor of floral perfume and Vicks Vapo Rub. I shut the door softly and move on tiptoe to the next. The sound of the television – a game show, I think *The Price is Right* – wafts upstairs alongside the odor of grilled cheese. I open the door softly, peer inside and smile because I've hit the jackpot.

It is dim inside this bedroom, but I am not about to turn on a light. There is presence here, as if I have entered a tomb. I shut the door behind me. My hands are dusty, and the knees of my blue jeans are streaked with dirt.

Stephen Pickett had a thing for blondes in red one-piece swimsuits, if we can go by the posters on the wall. He liked Black Sabbath and had a subscription to *Popular Mechanics*. There is a dusty dismantled set of weights beneath the grimy window, and a model of a B52 bomber hangs from a string on the wall.

I stand before the dresser, and I feel sad. Next to a smudged whiskey flask and a stack of quarters and dimes is a hairbrush, a comb, an electric razor and a white glass bottle of Old Spice.

I wonder what that night was like for Stephen Pickett, after he went to my father for help and was sent back out to his death. Was he lost when he fell down that trout hole? Was he alone? How long did it take for him to die? I picture him confused, disoriented, getting a mouthful of water and grit when he gasped for air.

'Sorry,' I whisper.

I take an envelope from my back jeans pocket. Use the comb to pluck hair from the brush, and put the proceeds into the envelope, then open the razor top carefully, and am rewarded with beard hairs to sprinkle into the mix.

I hear a footstep outside the door, and it opens before I can get the razor back in place.

'*Dammit*, Ashby.'

He wiggles his eyebrows. 'Got everything you need?'

'We're in DNA heaven, I promise. Are you done in the attic? What did you get?'

He holds up two dolls he had tucked in the crook of his arm. 'What do you say to these?'

'One's a Chatty Kathy, the other's the kind of plastic pixie you buy at Rite Aid for under five bucks.'

'Pay her two hundred,' Ashby tells me.

'They're not worth two dollars.'

'One hundred?'

'Fifty. Anything else would be suspicious.'

'Sixty-eight.'

'Okay, sixty-eight. I can't get this razor back together.'

'*Take it*,' he whispers. 'I think I hear Mrs Pickett at the bottom of the stairs.'

⬇

I have spent so much time in the sitting room of the Jinx's suite in the Beaufort Inn that I have cultivated a favorite place for curling up. Today, as usual, I have settled on the right-hand side of the blue silk couch, with my shoes off, tucked up under an afghan because the Jinx keeps the air-conditioning turned up so high. He talks to my brother and me separately, though Ashby and I always compare notes.

We have ordered sandwiches. The Jinx is wearing expensive-looking khakis and a yellow cotton shirt. No doubt when our business is done he will be heading out to play golf. I admire the way this man has orchestrated his life for optimum personal satisfaction. His tan does not need any work, but perhaps his golf game does.

We have ordered BLTs made with maple bacon, vine-ripe tomatoes and sourdough bread. We are both starved. Silence settles as we eat. You will not find BLTs on the menu here, at the Beaufort Inn, but as always the Jinx gets exactly what he wants. Brenda isn't here today. The Jinx tells me she is in Atlanta, keeping their home office on course. The Jinx says he could not do without her – she is clearly his right-hand man.

The silver doily-lined platter is heaped with sandwiches, and I am so hungry I eat two. The Jinx takes a bread and butter pickle and crunches it between suspiciously perfect teeth.

'Want some pie?' he asks me.

It's a private joke. Ashby always wants pie when he is here.

'Just a pickle.' I wipe my hands on a thick white linen napkin. I am reminded of a man I once dated who stole cloth napkins on every dinner date we had. He did it to be funny, but he had an astounding collection next to the underwear in his top dresser drawer. We quit seeing each other about the time he moved on to beer mugs. I have always wondered what he graduated to next.

The Jinx leans forward, head tilted sideways. He has something on his mind.

I raise my eyebrows. 'What's up?'

'That obvious, am I? You read people well.'

Charm, charm. But it is not like the Jinx to be slow to the point.

He makes a steeple of his fingertips and tucks them

beneath the smooth-shaven chin. 'Georgie, the prosecution has a very weak case. They arrested Claire precipitously, almost off the cuff, probably under the influence of you know who.'

'Wilbanks.'

'No doubt. The most damaging thing they have is the statement from the waitress at the restaurant, who overheard one of you making that remark about pushing your father down the stairs. That statement, in my opinion, seems a little too good to be true. This woman, according to Ray—' He gives me a questioning look. I haven't met Ray but I know he is the Jinx's investigator. 'Ray has done a little research. This waitress happens to be recovering from a bad car accident, one she had, by the way, when driving under the influence of narcotics. Marijuana, to be exact. She's taking a great deal of medication for back pain, and her co-workers say she is moody – read mood swings – and they'll testify to that in court. We can prove she was aware of the circumstances of your father's death before she talked to the police. It is my opinion, and one I will put forth in court, that the woman's memory of the conversation she overheard was colored by the actual circumstances of your father's death. I think I can mitigate her testimony if we actually do wind up on trial.'

'Is there a chance this *won't* come to trial?'

'I'm hoping the grand jury won't indict. The prosecution has a weak case, but there's no telling what will happen. It's a possibility, but that's all.' The Jinx is clearly wary of the hope in my voice. 'Georgie, your brother was here early this morning. A matter of some letters he found in your father's things. You know about these?'

I have made a mistake. I should have mentioned them as soon as I walked in the door. 'I saw them. He called me as soon as he found them. We thought about taking them straight to the police but decided to give them to you. I know Ashby's pretty excited, but the police already know my father was being blackmailed, so I can't see how these can be much help.'

The Jinx considers me carefully. Does he suspect I am lying? Or is it my guilty conscience at work?

'As an officer of the court I can accept the letters, and of course I will turn them over to the police. But as I explained to your brother –'

I lean forward intently, but the Jinx seems to have lost his train of thought. He looks off into the distance as if an idea has just occurred.

'– as I explained to your brother, the letters are going to be suspect because they come from the family of the accused. The DA is going to think they're a little too pat.' The Jinx looks apologetic. 'They'll probably want to have them checked by an expert. Naturally, as they've been handled by your brother—'

'And by me.'

'As you say, and by you. On the plus side, I spoke with Johnny Selby, as well as one of the investigating officers in the case. Evidently, the blackmail theory is pretty strongly borne out by the records of your father's bank accounts. But as far as this Stephen Pickett being the blackmailer, Wilbanks tells me the boy was declared dead.'

'Body not recovered.'

Jinx raises an eyebrow. 'So I understand. But I have to tell you, the chances of these letters being any help are pretty thin. For one thing, there has to be some evidence, such as DNA evidence, that prove the letters were written by Pickett himself. And for that to happen there has to be something to compare the evidence to. There will be medical records, but as far as definitive proof goes, the odds are fairly slim.'

'The Marine Corps still has his backpack.'

'Do they?'

'I'm pretty sure they do. They used it as evidence, to prove he was dead. They found it out on the trail, in the woods. The theory was he fell in a trout hole. In heavy boots, in the middle of the night. Those things are like quicksand.'

Jinx makes a note on the pad that sits next to the pickles. Will he be pleased, I wonder, when the forensics bear us out, or will he be suspicious? Provided the police test the DNA. My stomach is starting to hurt.

Ever since Ashby and I raided the Pickett household, I lie awake at night and worry. If the police go to Pickett's grandmother, will she remember me and Ashby, will she think to bring it up?

Why would she?

Why does anybody do anything? She could. If somebody asked the right question. And she could pick us out in a court of law.

What the hell were we thinking? Why didn't we just break in, at night, while she slept? I have gotten rid of Pickett's razor. Thrown it in the ocean to annoy the fish. Ashby and I are geniuses or idiots. But I have huge fears that we may have outsmarted ourselves.

'There is one other matter,' Jinx says, and his voice is rose-petal soft.

I wonder what the problem is now.

'Your sister cannot be convicted unless the district

attorney has a strong motive – and this is another weak part of their case.'

I am regretting the pickle and the second sandwich. I lean forward and prop my chin in my hand. 'I have to take the blame for supplying the motive. I told the police—'

'That you think your father killed your mother. Yes, Georgie, I know.'

'I signed a permission thing. For them to exhume my mother's body and do an autopsy.'

'I understand that may be in the works. I've already spoken with the attending physician, the one who declared your mother dead. He remembers suggesting an autopsy and your father's objection.'

In my mind I am back in that hospital hallway. Why didn't I have the guts to speak up?

'The doctor will testify that he was considering the possibility that your mother took an intentional over-dose.'

'Intentional? You mean suicide?'

He nods.

'I don't believe that. Don't you understand the sequence of events? After all those years my mother was going to divorce my father. She was writing him out of her will. And meanwhile, he was being black-mailed. He was angry and desperate for money.'

The Jinx is listening, he is nodding his head, I have his full and undivided attention. Why do I feel I am being humored like a child?

'Both Ashby and Claire are ready to testify that they think your mother took her own life.'

'And you want me to do the same, is that right?'

'Lie under oath? Not at all, Georgie, not at all.'

'I'll do it. I'll do it, if you think it'll help.'

He smiles at me, and his eyes are terribly kind. 'I know you would. My concern is with your brother and sister. They seem to have a problem with you knowing what they really think.'

'What I think doesn't matter. We have to stay focused on Claire.'

Jinx places both hands on the arm of his chair. 'That's what I told them you'd say.'

I take a deep breath. Really, this isn't so hard. 'Anything else?'

'Just one.' Jinx smiles gently and winks. 'It would be best, just for the time being, if you kept those well-constructed theories to yourself. Because in spite of your brother and sister's opinions, I personally think you make a very good case.'

I stand out on my balcony in the dark listening to the cicadas and wondering if the entire town of Beaufort, as well my brother and sister, think my mother took her own life. I think of the years ahead, spending night after night wondering if it is true.

The phone rings but I make no move to pick it up, and I hear John Wallace's voice.

'Don't want anything special. Just wanted to see if you were okay.'

I wonder what it would be like to have a cup of coffee, sleepy and content, with John Wallace first thing every morning. I wonder how it would be to spend every evening with him, opening a bottle of wine or a can of beer, boiling shrimp, listening to music, telling

John Wallace about my day, listening to what he has to say about his, low-key and happy.

Could my mother have purposely taken those pills and left me behind? Could I be of so little account that she would do this to me?

I pick up the phone and call my brother.

Instead I get Reese, who says that Ashby has not come home yet, which strikes me as odd. It is 8 p.m., and Ashby should have brought *The Graceful Lady* in hours ago. When I ask Reese if he has talked to my brother today, he says no. He sounds distant and seems irritated by my questions, and I think that the Smallwood family problems are getting on his nerves. Some people slip away when you have trouble in your life, but I never would have thought Reese would be one of those people.

I know that John Wallace will call back soon, and that he will want to go get ice cream and sit on the couch and hold my hand and kiss me as the darkness falls. I close my eyes and think of him. His smile. How safe I feel when he puts his arms around my shoulders and I tuck my head just under his chin. How much I like chocolate ice cream.

I nudge my mother's dog, who is snoring though her eyes are open wide. 'Cousin?' The dog does not twitch. 'Want to go for a ride?'

Cousin stares out the open window as I drive over the bridge and to the dock where my brother keeps his boat. The sun is in my eyes. It is sinking fast, but blinding on the way down.

Ashby's Land Rover is the only car in the lot. I scoop Cousin up and gently out of the car, careful of old joints and arthritis, and we walk across the dock.

The Graceful Lady is quiet, moving gently in the wake of a passing outboard. The deck has been hosed and is still wet in spots. The equipment is stowed, the lines are in place. I smell the fishy odor of shrimp. A long seagull sits on the mast.

'Hello? Ashby?'

I think I hear something, a voice, but I am not sure. A sort of panic hits me. Cousin sniffs, and we peer in below-decks. I see a shadow, and a large shape, and I hear the noise again. My brother is crying.

He says nothing as I climb down the steps, Cousin scrambling ahead of me. She runs to him, stump tail wiggling, and Ashby puts a hand out. Cousin licks his fingers and he pats her head.

'What's going on, Ashby?' It is dim in here. He hasn't turned on a light. 'I just talked to Reese. What's going on?'

'He's leaving me.'

'He's what?'

'He's leaving me.'

'But why?'

Ashby shrugs. 'He says it's not fun anymore.'

'You're *kidding*.'

'We've been together eight years. But now he says it's not *fun* anymore.' My brother looks at me. 'He's got somebody else. That's the only thing that makes any sense.' Ashby hunches over and cries. I don't know what to do. My brother never cries.

I sit down on the cushion beside him. I think of all the things I need to say. None of them are going to take this pain away. And I don't want to believe this is real. I don't want to believe that Reese would abandon my brother when everything is going so wrong.

'Maybe it's a temporary thing, Ashby. All relation-ships have high points and low points. Maybe if you-all give it a little time.'

'We have. This has been going on awhile. I knew it was coming.'

'How long?'

'Six months.'

About the time Ashby took out the second mortgage on *The Graceful Lady*.

'Do you need a place to stay, Ashby?'

'No. Reese wants to keep the town house and buy me out – but for now we're going to maintain the status quo until things with Claire settle out.'

'Are you okay with that?'

'We've talked about it. We both think it's for the best. Tonight I'm going to sleep on the boat.'

'Don't do that. Please don't. Come home with me. I'll cook you dinner. I'll make you a meat loaf. You love my meat loaf.'

My brother shrugs. He is not interested in meat loaf. 'Can I park my grocery basket behind your shop when I'm homeless and sleeping on the beach?'

'Ashby, you're not going to be homeless. If you're in trouble, come live with me awhile. What I've got, you've got.'

My brother actually shudders. I know he is thinking of noise, teenagers, dogs, the comings and goings in my business and my life.

'Ashby, if you need money, I've got stuff I can sell. Ashby?'

'I'm afraid I'm going to lose the boat. If I do, that's it. There'll be nothing left of me. I won't exist.'

I feel a block of ice in the pit of my stomach. 'You're

not going to lose your boat, I won't let you. I'll take care of you. How many times have you taken care of me?'

A million times, I am thinking. So many I have lost count.

'I've always planned to send Hank to college. I decided that the day he was born. It's too much for you, to do everything by yourself, and I always thought I'd be able to help you more, Georgie. Now I can't even hold on to what I've got.'

'Shit. Ashby, it's only money.'

My brother's eyes are glazed and my comment goes right over his head. He is a generous person and has been since we were kids, but as far as he's concerned, *only* and *money* do not belong in the same sentence.

'I'm not letting you lose the boat. I promise. I've got stuff I can sell.'

'And we've got Claire's attorney to pay, and her kids to help, and—'

'Ashby, it's hard times with us, I know, but I won't let you lose the boat. Look, don't sit here in the dark, okay? Come home with me. Come home and take a look at all the beautiful things I can sell to raise lots of money.'

'Georgie, that's sweet. But I'm going to stay on the boat tonight.'

'Then I'll stay with you.'

He looks at me. 'If it doesn't hurt your feelings, Georgie, I'd rather you didn't. I want to be by myself.'

'I'm scared to leave you. I'm scared you won't be okay.'

He just looks at me. He seems incredibly tired. He gives me that familiar quizzical look, the mask that hides his heart. 'I'll be okay.'

'Are you sure?'

'I'm sure.'

I look around the cabin, so thick with gray light. It doesn't feel good here. I don't want Ashby here alone. But he is starting to look very irritated, and I know that tonight he does not want to be rescued by his little sister.

'Do you think Mama was afraid when she died, Ashby?'

'No.'

'What about Daddy?'

'No. He was probably mad as hell.'

'I'm not afraid. At least when I die, I won't have to worry about MasterCard ever again.'

I laugh, and so does my brother. I know he will be okay. My brother and I are very strong. I give him a hug. 'You know where I am.'

I take Cousin's leash, and she follows obediently up and out of the cabin. I know my brother loves his boat, but it is a sad boat tonight, and I don't like leaving him there all alone.

15

The grand jury meets in the municipal complex that also houses the Beaufort County Jail and sheriff's department. The clustered buildings are joined by an interior concrete courtyard and look very like a small community college.

My brother is supposed to be here for moral support, but so far he has not shown up. I think he is trying to raise more money on the boat, a new spin on the old loan. I sit outside a closed conference room. Down the hall is a courtroom with new carpet, blond wood and seats like pews in a church. It is hushed inside the hallway, and very chilly. Carla Blanchard sits across from me on a hard bench, and I recognize the waitress from the restaurant where my brother and sister got drunk. The waitress, who is named Leslie, will not meet my eyes.

Brenda Vasquez sits beside me. The Jinx is inside. Because it is the grand jury, and the courtroom is closed, I cannot go in and watch. The proceedings are secret. But Brenda goes in and out and tells me what is going on.

She leans close and whispers, as Carla Blanchard is clearly trying to overhear. My father's mistress gave her own testimony half an hour ago, and I'm not sure why she stays sitting in this hall.

Brenda's breath smells minty. 'Listen, Georgie. The

Jinx wants me to tell you to roll with the questions. He says Wilbanks is going to be offensive, and you aren't to react. Matter-of-fact and saintly when you answer, that's all you do. You okay?'

'I'm okay.'

'It's all right to be nervous. It probably helps.'

The door swings open again. Brenda goes in and comes right back out. 'They're ready for you now.' She squeezes my hand.

My first impression is of disappointment. Twelve men and women sit around a conference table, and one of the men is missing some teeth. A woman wears a T-shirt that says KICK BUTT. These people will decide whether or not my sister goes to trial for the murder, second degree, of my father. If they don't indict, Claire will go free.

The Jinx looks well. He is low-key. I see Eugene Wilbanks, and suddenly the faces of the jurors are a blur. The Jinx catches my eye and I remember I am supposed to sit up straight and look directly at the men, without flirting, and keep my eyes down when I look at the women, unless they smile at me and seem friendly.

A bailiff swears me in. I put my hand on the Bible. Wilbanks stands up.

'For the record, Miss Smallwood, please confirm that you are the daughter of the deceased, Fielding Smallwood, and the sister of the accused, Claire Smallwood.'

'Yes,' I say. Softly, just like the Jinx told me to do.

'Are you married, Miss Smallwood?'

I look at the Jinx. He doesn't smile but he looks encouraging.

'No, I am not.'

'But you have a son?'

'Yes, I do.'

'Born out of wedlock.'

'Yes.'

'How did your father feel about your having a child and no husband?'

'He was disappointed in me.'

'He was a traditional man, wasn't he? He disapproved of your situation.'

I pause. I have plans to tell other lies, so I may as well begin now. In my mind I substitute my father for my mother. 'My father wanted the best for me because he loved me. He had hopes I would graduate from college. He worried about how my life would go, as a single mother raising a son. So he helped me build my business, and he was proud of my son, and I always felt he was there to take care of me when I needed his help.'

Wilbanks is stunned, but he covers. 'And your father was aware of your sister's plans to divorce?'

'Yes, he was.'

'Did he approve?'

'My father has not liked the way my sister's husband has treated her.'

'Are you saying he approved of the divorce?'

'No.'

'Your sister has applied to Duke University, for the PhD program, is that correct?'

'Yes.'

'And she was accepted, was she not?'

'Yes.'

'How did she plan to pay for this? Divorced, with three children to support?'

'She had a grant.'

'No grant stretches that far, Miss Smallwood. Isn't

273

it true that your sister was expecting your father to support her, the same way he supported you?'

And I see where this is going. 'I don't think Claire was expecting that, no.'

'Really? Tell me, do you recognize these letters?'

'Yes, I do.'

'Can you identify them?'

'They're letters my brother, Ashby, found in my father's desk.'

'Blackmail letters.'

'Yes, sir.'

'Miss Smallwood, wasn't your father retired from the marines?'

'Yes.'

'Honorably discharged?'

'Yes.'

'Do you think it odd that he kept these letters in his desk, where anyone could see them?'

'His desk was up in an attic office. No one went up there but him.'

'Did you and your brother and your sister meet at the lighthouse on Hunting Island the night your father died?'

'Yes, we did.'

'And did your sister say, in your hearing, that she would like to push your father down the stairs?'

'No, she did not.'

He stares at me. 'Are you absolutely positive you never heard your sister say that?'

'Absolutely.'

'How about at the restaurant. Did your sister say it there?'

'No, she did not.'

'Do you think your sister might have gone back to the lighthouse, got into an argument with your father and things just got out of hand?'

'Absolutely not. I took my sister home from the restaurant that night, and she was half asleep. She was not capable of going back out.'

'Because she was drunk?'

'Yes, sir, because she was drunk. She had several beers and two large margaritas. I had to help her from the car into the house.'

Wilbanks sits down, and the Jinx stands up.

'Ms Smallwood, are you aware that your father was supporting a mistress?'

'Yes.'

'And you were angry about that?'

'Yes, sir.'

'Did you say, in the restaurant, that you would like to push your father down the stairs?'

'Yes, sir.'

'Did you have any other reason to be angry with your father?'

'Yes, sir. My son ran away from home two years ago. My father told him never to come home. I think if my father had never said those words to my son, he would have come home before two years.'

'And was your mother aware of this?'

'Yes, but only just before she died.'

'And she was going to divorce your father?'

'Yes, sir.'

'But she didn't, did she?'

'No, sir.'

'How did your mother die, Miss Smallwood?'

'She took an overdose of Xanax. She killed herself.'

'Thank you.'

Wilbanks stands back up. 'Miss Smallwood, did you tell Detective Click of the Beaufort County Sheriff's Department that you thought your father killed your mother?'

'Yes, sir.'

'But now you think she killed herself?'

'Yes, sir.'

'Did you tell your sister that you think your father killed your mother?'

I hesitate. 'I guess I did.'

'Did she agree?'

'No.'

'She didn't?'

'No.'

'But she was angry about how your father treated your son, is that right? So angry that she left her children with their father soon after the death of their grandmother, and went out and got drunk.'

'We were all upset.'

'Some of us deal with these things in other ways. Thank you, Miss Smallwood.'

I look up, and though the Jinx gives me a soft smile, most of the jurors will not meet my eyes. The prosecution has a weak case, but it is clearly more important that I am an unwed mother with a drunken sister, sponging off a loving but sorely tested father, who served his country well and distinguished himself as a marine. Ashby will testify tomorrow, and once they find the third member of the trio is a gay and nearly bankrupt son, I think we will be sunk.

⇓

This morning, just after noon, Brenda Vasquez called to tell us that the grand jury was going to indict, which is why Ashby and I are together sweating the bills. We sit at my kitchen table drinking lemonade Hank has made from scratch. Hank is on a lemonade kick, and he makes it fresh and sweet. Ashby loves it when Hank brings it in a thermos to the boat.

The windows upstairs are shut tight, the air conditioner is grinding away and condensation drips and streams down the bricks outside. Dusk is falling, but my little brick building is retaining the afternoon heat. Ashby wears loose khakis and a cotton shirt, and I wear roomy cut-off blue jeans that I stole from my brother last summer when I went out with him on the boat. I am barefoot, but Ashby wears heavy tennis shoes. I have never seen him go barefoot since the summer he was eleven and stepped on a bee. I am baking a chicken, in spite of the heat.

Hank wanders by in sweatpants. He has shed his shirt, and he heads into the kitchen for the open bag of Doritos, taking them into the living room where he can watch TV. Cousin trails along beside him and is rewarded with a nacho chip to crunch. I have bought her pig ears and rawhide sticks, and if I could get Hank to quit giving her junk food I might be able to help her take off some weight. For now, I don't press the issue. Hank and Cousin both look too happy, and I don't want to disturb their peace.

Ashby and I are trying to come up with thirty-seven thousand dollars. The Jinx is sending our letters off for private DNA analysis, which will be expensive, plus we are behind on our legal fees.

We've got five thousand dollars from Reese, two

thousand from Ashby's general expenses fund, and eight thousand is coming out of the living expenses money I have stashed.

My brother rubs his forehead. 'Fifteen thousand dollars.'

'And another nineteen for that piece I was going to sell.'

'Georgie, we don't have six months for you to search out a buyer.' My brother is hot and cranky, and my feelings are hurt.

'I *have* a buyer, Ashby.'

I sold the George III ormolu-mounted wine cooler to Burgin for nineteen thousand dollars. If I had time to sell it properly I could get seventy thousand easy, eighty if I take my time. I paid thirteen thousand when I bought it, cleaning out my savings and stretching every cent.

Ashby looks up. 'Oh. That's great then, Georgie. You getting a good price?'

'I told you. Nineteen thousand.'

'How much did you pay for it?'

'Thirteen thousand.'

My brother shakes his head and grins. 'You're good, you know it? I don't know how you pull off these deals.'

I add up the figures on the page, squinting over Ashby's impossible handwriting, and spot two places where he's inverted the figures. 'It still leaves us three thousand short.'

'What about Claire's husband? Can he kick a little into the kitty?'

'You're kidding me, right? He's hit me up for money 'for the children' twice since Claire's been in jail. He

278

wants to let his apartment go and move back in the house.'

'Don't let him,' Ashby snaps.

'It's not up to me. And I can't afford to take on his bills. I'm already paying for the girls' dance lessons and Jared's guitar lessons and keeping up with the utilities on the house.'

'You mean he won't pay for that stuff?'

'Some of it you can't blame him. Claire's divorcing him, after all. But when it comes to the kids? And I know the dance and the guitar stuff don't sound like essentials, Ashby, but their mother's in jail, their grandparents just died, and their parents are breaking up. I'm trying to keep something going in their lives.'

'We should definitely keep them in their lessons.'

I am aware of Hank, standing quietly at my side. He sets a roll of crumpled, oily bills on the table next to the papers where we are adding sums and shrugs nonchalantly.

'Barney pays me when I go out on his boat. You can use that for the guitar and the dance lessons. Or for groceries, stuff like that.'

'Hank, I can't take your money.'

'It's two hundred eighty dollars. It's not going to take care of the big things, but it'll help out some. Go on, Mom. You help me whenever I need it. And don't worry about paying me back.'

'Of course I'll pay it back.'

'You know, don't be worrying about stuff like that till Aunt Claire is out of jail.'

Hank endures a hug and Ashby stands up, stretches and scratches his ribs. 'How's that chicken coming along?'

The smell has filled the kitchen and for all I know is wafting into the street. I rubbed the chicken with olive oil, drenched it in lemon juice and white zinfandel and tucked cloves of garlic here and there. There are yeast rolls rising on the countertops, and tomatoes and peaches on the cutting board waiting to be washed.

'Not long,' I say absently. 'You know what, Ashby? I think this is close enough. We'll give Brenda thirty-four thousand, and worry about the rest another time.'

'Works for me.'

Ashby moves to the couch to eat Doritos and watch TV with Hank, and I head for the peaches and tomatoes. Something is making Hank and Ashby laugh. If Claire were here with her kids, this would be a perfect day.

I see my brother pick up the tiny gold case where I keep pictures of us when we were all kids. It reminds me that there is actually film in my camera, so I drag it out and snap shots of Cousin and the guys on the couch. They are sunburned.

After the third picture Ashby glares at me. 'Should I send out for a pizza to hold us over till we eat?'

'Set the table, if you're in such a hurry.'

Hank rolls his eyes. 'Now you've done it. She's going to order us around the rest of the night.'

'If you guys want that incredible sauce I make for the chicken, get busy.'

And they want the sauce, so they are up and moving. If you want to eat at my house, you have to earn it, as Ashby and Hank both know. If John Wallace plays his cards right, I might cook a chicken for him.

I pull out the cast-iron skillet, make a roux of flour and butter and softened garlic cloves I've taken off the chicken and add two cups of wine, peach yogurt and broth. I use more broth to steam the rice and put the rolls in to bake.

Hank and I finish the wine, and Ashby sticks to Diet Coke. Dinner isn't over more than half an hour when Ashby is ready to leave. My brother is never one to linger, and he wants to get away while there are still dishes to be done. Although it is not his usual habit, he gives me a solid hug.

'Great dinner, Georgie.'

'My pleasure.' And it is. My brother is gratifying to feed.

Ashby catches my eye. 'Don't be worried about all this money stuff. I have a feeling it's all going to work out.'

My brother's confidence makes me feel better. He is different tonight. He seems so sure that Claire will not be convicted, that the Jinx will work wonders and that all will be well. It is as if he has some secret knowledge about the future, and it is hard not to take heart. He refuses to talk about Reese, but he seems more at peace all of a sudden.

I clear away the dishes, instead of assigning them to Hank, who goes immediately to the refrigerator for leftovers as soon as I pack all the food away.

'Great dinner, Mom.'

I put on a pot of coffee to get me through the night. I have to get that wine cooler ready and make decisions about what else I can part with. I will spend the next five days working like crazy to get my quickest moneymakers up and running to sell.

⇊

The morning of a day I will remember forever begins with the smell of the chicken in the kitchen, still lingering from the night before. I put the coffee on and head downstairs.

The next few hours are spent finishing up some detail work, until I feel everything is in good order and ready to sell. I stretch and yawn and wipe my hands on a cloth. The mahogany cooler is long gone now; I dropped it by Burgin's at the beginning of the week. I also sold him the knife box, but on the plus side, I spotted an Edwardian music cabinet that I took off him for eighty bucks. The top shelf and mirror are gone, but the door still has the original pleated silk and the velvet-lined shelves are in amazing shape. The cabinet was made between 1900 and 1914, and as is I can sell it for three hundred bucks.

I find I am able to take pleasure in the small things again – my work and fitting my smaller fingers into the ancestral grooves of my grandfather's tools. I flex my shoulders, rub the back of my neck, lace my fingers together, then stretch them out. I think of my grandfather as I put away his tools. I see him in my memory, how he would set a piece on a dropcloth and back away, quiet in contemplative study.

I have a date tonight. I will check outside for the mail, go upstairs and brew a new pot of coffee, and see if Cousin would like to go out. I wipe my hands on a cloth and sling it over my left shoulder. My thoughts are on John Wallace as I step outside the door. I decide to go down the street and get my nails done. I will give myself the afternoon off for bubble baths and a manicure and remind myself I'm a girl.

How casually I approach my mailbox. It hangs

outside my shop door, and the top is ajar with the bulk of the daily mail. I tuck it all into the crook of my arm, wondering about the blue priority-mail envelope, anxious to open the Williams-Sonoma catalog, and entertaining the notion that I might buy a precious thing or two, once the insurance company pays off and Claire is safely out of jail.

I lay the mail in the center of the kitchen table, and offer to take Cousin out. Snug in the corner of my yellow couch, she turns over to allow me the privilege of rubbing her tummy. Her eyes roll backward and she refuses to budge.

'Last chance till my nails are done.'

Cousin treats me to a piglike snort. Like many people, I am ruled by a dog.

I rinse the coffeepot, measure out the grinds and sit at the kitchen table to read my mail. Behind me, the coffeemaker emits a growl and a hiss, and the first drops of hot brown liquid collect in the bottom of the pot.

No bills, praise the Lord.

The priority-mail envelope is addressed in Ashby's unmistakable scrawl, and his private post office box is listed as the return address. As I rip the tab open, I wonder why on earth my brother has sent me mail. The envelope holds three sheets of yellow paper torn from a legal pad. The writing is clearly my brother's, but the lines are jittery, as if his hand was shaking when he wrote.

Don't be mad at me, he writes, after my carefully inked name. Underneath I read *PLEASE FORGIVE ME* in huge, shaky block letters that take up half the page. My stomach is dropping like a lead weight and my hands begin to shake.

He loves me, my brother says, and he loves my son, Hank, and Cousin Beauregard. And do I know how proud he is of me, raising my son alone, building a business, being such a really big success? *I have always been proud of you, Georgie.*

My dyslexic brother who hates to write has filled three pages. Reassuring me there was nothing I could have done to stop him. Telling me how tired he is. How badly he wants to let go of the world and be with Mom. How he will watch over me and Hank, and Claire and her kids, and Cousin Beauregard, and all of us, always, and make sure we will always be okay.

My mouth is dry, and there is a peculiar buzz at the base of my skull. I grab the phone and call Ashby's house. There is no answer, just the message he leaves on the machine.

Hi, this is Ashby. You've got me. Leave a message and I'll call you back.

'Ashby? Ashby, it's Georgie. Answer the phone, Ashby, please pick up. Ashby are you there? Honey? It's Georgie, Ashby, I love you, please be okay. I'm coming. I'm leaving right now, Ashby. Please wait. Ashby, I love you, please wait.'

I am driving down the highway, hands so tight on the wheel they hurt, but I am afraid to loosen my grip. I am hunched forward, and every once in a while another muffled scream rises up and I have to fight to keep it down. Part of me cannot believe this is happening, and part of me stubbornly insists there is hope.

He might not have done anything. Ashby might have sent that note and changed his mind. Did I look at the postmark? No, I didn't.

Oh, God, Ashby, please wait.

Ashby and Reese live in a secured community of newer town houses, and I stop at the gate for a moment to think. I can climb over, buzz a neighbor or wait for another car and follow it through. I glance up and see a garage-door opener stuck in the passenger's side visor of my truck. I do not have a garage. How it got there I do not know.

I press the black plastic button and the gate swings wide, according to what I will later understand is part of my brother's master plan. It is late afternoon on a Friday, and the complex is quiet.

Where, I wonder, are the police? The ambulance? The results of my frantic 911 call? They were supposed to get there before me. They were supposed to be there to save my brother in the nick of time or tell me in irritated relief he has changed his mind.

I turn right and pull Big Mama into the street in front of my brother's place.

The town house is built like a fortress. A solid privacy fence, usually padlocked, denies entry to the house and the garage is shut tight. I get out of the truck and head for the fence. The padlock has been left unsecured. I wrestle it out of the latch and run through the courtyard to the house.

The front door is locked. A green garbage can on wheels sits neatly near the side of the house. I beat on the front door and ring the bell. No one answers. No one comes. I don't wait long.

I trample my brother's azaleas to look into the living-room window. The blinds are up, I can see inside. The room is empty. The leather couches have been cleared of newspapers, the dining-room table is empty, the television is dark. No lamps are lit, no empty beer cans litter the coffee table. Just beneath the living-room window, by the arm of the couch, is a tall pile of blankets, with the pillows stacked on top.

I toss my purse into the bushes and check the window, but it is locked. I have brought a heavy black flashlight that I keep in my truck, and I hold my breath and slam it hard into the glass. Nothing happens, except my wrist throbs. I slam the flashlight again and again, which causes not even a crack. Safety glass.

I head for the courtyard entrance to the garage, and pause, catching sight of a shovel neatly placed against the back of the house. I grab the handle and run for the window, swinging with all my strength. The window shatters in an explosion of noise and glass. Icicle shards with wicked edges stand up like lethal stalagmites along the sill.

I take a pillow off the stack of blankets by the couch – he has thought of everything, my brother. With the pillow buffering me from the glass, I swing a leg over the windowsill and drop with no grace into the room.

There are no lights on downstairs, and the afternoon light has settled, yellow and soft. It is so quiet inside this house that I do not even call my brother's name.

I move quickly. I unlock the front door and leave it open for the emergency crew, then run as fast as I can up the stairs. But my brother's presence fills this house as tangibly as a fog, and I know in my heart I'm too late.

What waits, I wonder, at the top of these stairs? If only I could go backward just a little while. I could talk to Ashby, I could change his mind.

The master bedroom is on the right and the door is open. In a scattered pile on the floor rests my brother's sweatshirt, his wallet, his shoes. The bathroom door creaks as I push it open, and I am drawn inside.

Ashby lies submerged in a full tub of water, arms and legs curled sideways as he rests on one side. He has padded the bottom of the tub with towels, his head resting beneath the faucet. A line of black ants is making a businesslike beeline from beneath the sink to the edge of the tub. Outside I can hear the murmur of traffic, but inside is so very still.

The water fills my tennis shoes and soaks my jeans as I step into the bathtub and lift my brother's head. He is not so very heavy.

There is a questioning look on Ashby's face, an expression of curiosity, and I am reminded of the way my son, newborn, shut his eyes tight to the light, sound and sensation of a world that was as incomprehensible as it was intriguing. What does he see as he leaves us all behind? He does not look afraid. It is as if he shuts us all away with the tightly sealed eyes, the clenched teeth, lips set, a man who hears what I cannot hear, who sees what I cannot see, but who yearns for something I understand all too well.

And so he goes, my brother. Leaving me behind. Placing the burden solidly on my shoulders, heavier now, with the inevitable guilt of we who survive, we who are left to sift a thousand tiny memories that hold us accountable. The logical pathways of intellect that I offer my soul must shrivel and die before the accusing inward stare of my heart.

But I am human, which deems me supremely indifferent to logic. It is this that allows me the freedom to step into this tub of water and lift Ashby's head out of the water, to offer him the sustenance of oxygen as if there were still some choice.

Later there will be an autopsy, and weeks of waiting for toxicology results, that will confirm that my brother died from a drug overdose and slipped under the water after death.

But for now I sob, and touch the wet matted hair, and whisper impossible questions to a silent corpse.

'Is there anyone in the house?' a voice calls out.

Help arrives, like me, too late, and the bathroom door is darkened with uniforms, and men with blurry faces and guns in their hands, as they take it all in – the broken window, the front door hanging open, the woman perched on the edge of the tub, sobbing over a dead body.

With a firmness that is borderline belligerent, I am separated from my brother and led downstairs to explain.

I sit in stunned calm at my brother's dining-room table. The surface is now littered with the paperwork of death. The business cards are scattered, and I have the address and phone number of all three of the uniformed police officers who responded to my call.

Another card makes its way into the pile as the coroner technician sits across from me with a clipboard and fills out a form. He has kind eyes behind rimless spectacles and is clearly an intelligent, methodical man. He has done me the courtesy of explaining the physical manifestations of my brother's death, once I manage to convince him that for me the knowledge will be a comfort rather than an extension of pain.

The men watch me out of the corners of their eyes as if I am a bomb about to go off, and they all relax visibly when a female officer arrives on the scene. She hugs me and tells me I am brave. She offers me a bereavement counselor and assures me that no one can prevent a suicide, and that I should talk with a professional very soon.

I have called home and talked to Hank and John Wallace, who joined forces to find me after I disappeared. I called Reese, who is away on a business trip, when I found his itinerary clipped to the refrigerator door. It will take him until tomorrow to get here.

How secretive my brother has been. How carefully he has plotted and planned.

The coroner technician, a Mr Benedict Clive, is asking me careful questions.

No, my brother has never been married.

Yes, I am his closest kin.

No, he has no children.

Yes, he lives with a companion in the house.

No, the companion is away on business.

Yes, you may call it an alternate lifestyle, if you mean that my brother was gay.

Together we speculate on the reasons behind Ashby's final desperation, and I dread the explanation of my sister in jail. So I explain about the recent death of my parents and try to keep it at that.

But death leaves us no privacy, and the story eventually comes out. Claire is mentioned in the suicide letter. They want to call her and see if she received a note. On the table, between myself and Benedict Clive, are the creased yellow pages of my letter from Ashby. It has been read and reread by every person in the room.

Do I know my brother's birthplace and date of birth? Do I mind if they look at his driver's license, please?

I have to sign a form, and I find I have been officially granted the power invested by the state of South Carolina to be in charge of my brother's remains.

The coroner technician pauses and clears his throat. 'Miss Smallwood, I want to ask your permission to take this note from your brother, so that I can enter it in evidence when we get our toxicology report back and assign the cause of death.' He looks at me with direct sincerity. 'I promise you that I will personally see you get the note back, as soon as we're through with our work.'

I agree. I know this is no mere request, and I suppose I should appreciate this courtesy and tact. Later, the suicide note will be swallowed by the void of officialdom, and I will never see it again.

'We'll be doing an autopsy,' Benedict Clive tells me, 'but in this case it will be a minimal procedure, involving for the most part toxicology. Those results take a long time. At the earliest it'll be six weeks.'

I nod, nod, nod. I am so cooperative. So strong. So calm. Be careful, I tell myself, to appear normal. You are at risk in a room full of cops. I have learned since the death of my mother, and most particularly the passing of my father, that to be out of the ordinary is, forgive me, the kiss of death. Law enforcement is extraordinarily influenced by patterns of behavior. God help you if you stray out of the box.

I hear an engine outside. The sliding glass doors are open to let in the air; there have been too many people and emotions in one room. Three men in dark jackets wrestle a gurney through the door. At a hand motion from Benedict Clive, one of the uniforms leads the men upstairs.

Clive dismisses the female officer, who has been working well past her shift. Police radios emit chatter; there are hushed conversations; the young officer who boarded up the broken window leaves the hammer on the kitchen counter, and I shake his hand and say thanks.

I hear my name. Benedict Clive bends close. It would seem they want me to turn my back. I am competent to break into the house, discover the body and describe its position in detail to the officer filling out the paperwork, but I am not allowed to watch them roll my brother outside on a gurney zipped snug in a bag.

I turn my chair to the wall like a child who's been set in a corner, face turning red with the indignity of this request. I am ashamed of myself for complying. I should tell them to go to hell.

I follow Ashby's progress in my mind's eye as the men in jackets bump the gurney down the stairs. No one notices as I twist sideways and watch them wheel it out of the house. I give them time to load the body in the van, then step outside for some air. The neighbors have lined up to watch in respectful silence as

Ashby makes his final exit from this house. They see me. They watch me. I feel the intrigue of their questions and I wonder what they read in my face.

Behind me, there is sudden activity, as the coroner technician and the investigating officers are rushing to leave. It is like a party that has gone on too long, and the first guest leaving starts the stampede of all the rest.

I am suddenly very uneasy. They are leaving me here all alone.

Darkness falls completely. I check all the locks in the house. Now that I am alone here, my brother's presence, dispersed like smoke in the wind, begins to return and settle throughout the house.

I walk upstairs slowly and turn on all the lights. I pause outside the bedroom, where Ashby's shoes and sweatshirt are still on the floor. In the bathroom the tub is still filled with water and a line of thwarted black ants.

I walk in on tiptoe. There are no empty pill bottles, and I wonder if the police have found them and taken them away. What did he take, I wonder? Did he suffer nausea, and spasms, or gently lose consciousness?

My brother's clothes hang with neat silence in the small closet. An ivory fisherman's knit sweater, a blue striped cotton shirt, khaki jacket, the inevitable shorts.

It was his eyes, I know, that should have told me. I am haunted by my brother's eyes, hooded and weary. And I ask myself why he would not let me into his circle of despair – why he would not give me a chance to help.

We were on our way out of the dark parts. Why give up now, in the middle of the fight? I cannot reconcile his decision. Claire is in jail. Our mother is dead. I have a son to shield and Claire's children to protect.

Did I fail to give Ashby the right words of comfort, did I let him down, did I pressure him, did I force him to see the monster our father was when he could not bear the view?

I can list all the terrible things that burdened my brother, and I would like to direct my anger that way. The quiet voice inside me, the compassionate woman who sees the pain and understands, is lost, and the angry woman wins out. Three times he begged forgiveness, my brother. You see, he knows me well.

And so I will punish him in the only way left to me. I will not mourn him. I will not cry for him, or think of him, or feel this loss.

I have this conversation in my mind. These are the words I direct to the wind and the rain and the night. You, Ashby, may not watch over me. If your ghost stands at my window, I will close the blinds and turn my back. I will not visit your grave, or speak of you, I will not celebrate your life or accept your decision to give it up. No mementos. No pictures. No thoughts of you in my head.

I hope you are peaceful now and I wish you well. But you are farther from me than the stars, and I will not call you back.

16

In a small, private anteroom near the chapel of the Ribault Presbyterian Church, my sister and I sit side by side and wait. A substitute minister has been called out of retirement to cover for the vacationing pastor, and I am annoyed that a stranger will put Ashby to rest.

How odd to see Claire in a dress. No handcuffs, no orange jumpsuit or blue denims, not a prisoner today, just my sister. This has been arranged by Johnny Selby. Out front, barely filling a pew and a half, are Reese and Johnny Selby, Hank, and Claire's three children. In the next pew are my mother's best friends, Gertrude and Ruth. John Wallace is here, looking handsome in the suit he wore on our first date. We have all signed the guest book and filled half a page.

A tall broad-shouldered man with thick silvery hair smiles and comes into the anteroom. He wears a black robe, not yet zipped, that shows the crisp dress shirt and tie beneath. His shoes are polished. He is dressed as if the church were full and all of Beaufort were mourning our loss.

'Are you Claire and Georgie Smallwood?' It is a public-speaking voice, deep and rich, like polished oak.

'I'm Georgie. This is my sister, Claire.'

'I'm Dr Morgan. I'm honored to have been called. And the deceased is?'

'Our brother, Ashby Smallwood.'

The Reverend Dr Morgan sits and takes a pair of reading glasses out of an inner pocket that is hidden in the folds of his robe. He sets a worn Bible on a small table beside a ceramic lamp. 'I noticed, on my way in, that the church isn't quite full. Maybe a time mix-up? We can hold the services back a little while, if you and your sister would like.'

'No one's coming,' Claire says blankly.

The pastor looks up.

'Our brother—' I begin.

'Had an alternate lifestyle,' Claire chimes in.

'Our brother was gay. And he killed himself. And a lot of stuff has been going on in our family. I'm guessing that no one is going to come.'

'I see,' Dr Morgan says. And he does see. He reaches out and takes my hand and my sister's, and his eyes are blue and tired. 'You know, the sad and unfair truth is that life burdens some of us more than others. And there are times when it becomes too much for even the best of us to bear. I in no way believe that God turns his back on us when we feel such despair as to take our own life.'

Claire seems to crumple and cries softly here by my side.

And so Ashby's funeral is conducted by the Reverend Morgan, who seems to understand our pain without really knowing us, who knows all the right things to say, who comforts us by answering questions that we are too wearily inarticulate to ask.

And the tone of the ceremony is altered. We are not outcast and alone. We are intimate. We are the ones who loved Ashby best, and we are not subjected to the stares of other not entirely well-wishing mourners.

We stand up, each of us, and tell stories of my brother, and so we celebrate his life, and for a while my anger goes numb. Hank makes us laugh with stories about Ashby and *The Graceful Lady*, and all three of Claire's children stand up to sing. On a tape recorder, we play my brother's two favorite songs and end with his favorite hymn.

Afterward we have lunch. No stares, no long afternoon receiving guests, no extra housework. Just our select little group.

My mind wanders while I drink a whiskey sour and wait for the food.

How did he feel, my brother, during those years when the family so carefully avoided mentioning out loud that he was gay? By the time he reached his late twenties, he was proud of who he was. How hard was it to get there in his head? What was it like, with us girls bringing home boyfriend after boyfriend, welcome to family dinners and cookouts on the Fourth of July? And Ashby always flying solo, while Daddy winked and nudged our heartbreaking brother, pointing an anxious finger at the girls who called for him constantly at the house.

It was me who outed him. Who started, in a matter-of-fact way, to invite him to dinner, including an invitation to the 'man of the week.' It was me who became exasperated with the silence of my mother, only to be told in fury that she had known all along and was waiting for him to bring it up. What a joy it was to say what was on our minds, to let Ashby know that we loved him, to make rude jokes and ask impertinent questions, to be admitted all the way into his world.

I eat very little lunch, but I drink two more whiskey

sours and three glasses of bitter dark wine. I cannot shut away the images in my head. Eyes wide, I see my brother. Eyes closed, more vivid still. I sleep and wake to his face. I drive with double vision – the road ahead competes with the memory of Ashby's face tilted upward, eyes shut tight, the left side pale, the right flushed deep purple with the lividity of settling blood.

I hug my sister good-bye and watch her climb on the back of Selby's Harley as he takes her back to jail. John Wallace kisses me gently on the forehead and squeezes my hand, and Hank drives me home in Big Mama, and I sleep the afternoon away.

Grief, like childbirth, isn't pretty. Here I sit by Cousin on the couch, and I probably smell worse than the dog in these awful sweatpants with the hole in the crotch, my hair unwashed, kicking at the pile of newspapers on the floor. I don't want to be here in my living room, but I don't know where else to be.

Wash your hair, brush your teeth, pay your bills, scrub the toilets, go to work. Join a health club, take a dance class, brush little Cousin, get along. All of it hard to do when you are too depressed to move.

In the olden days – you know what I mean – back then those people knew how to mourn. You got to be unhappy for a whole year, you got to hang a black wreath on the door and wear dark dreary clothes day in and day out, and people didn't expect you to go out and act okay. In fact, if you did, you got in trouble.

You do know, don't you, that the stuff most of us worry about isn't worth a bucket of shit? I think once

Claire is out of jail I will devote my life solely to the pursuit of the best recipe for chili.

Ashby's funeral flowers have died. It is time to throw them out. The roses have shed all over the coffee table, there are dried rose petals on Cousin's back and the white carnations are crunchy and brown.

Does my brother's death mean it is more or less likely that my mother took her own life? Did she open a forbidden door, making it easier for Ashby to follow her through? And yet, if Ashby truly believed that Mama killed herself, how could he turn this pain back again on me and Claire?

I study the picture I took of Hank and Ashby the night I cooked my peach yogurt chicken, with the two of them posed on the couch. Ashby's face is gilded red with sunburn, and he is looking up just as I take the shot. I see it now, the burden in those sad, sad eyes.

He was plotting then, I know it. He had his secret, he was making all his plans. I wonder when he put the garage-door opener in my truck. I think it had to be that night. How is it I did not notice his eyes, the look of fatigue and wear?

I have a new fear that sits like a stone at the bottom of my heart. It feels more and more like conviction.

I have always known I am not the favorite sister. I am never the favorite one of anybody, because I am too quick to anger, too self-sufficient, too prone to having my way. I don't mind. Claire is naturally sweet, and sweetness should be rewarded, but I'm not standing in that line.

But I am doubting the bond. How could Ashby do what he did and love me? It makes me question everything – our childhood, every moment, our whole family life.

The thing is, what if it's me? I could be unlovable. Maybe those things Daddy said to me when Mama died, maybe those things were true. Maybe I was nothing but a burden to her. Maybe Ashby didn't love me either, because maybe nobody can.

My sensible side tells me these thoughts are common in the aftermath of suicide. I try to tell myself that Ashby's death was not about me. But deep in my heart there are doubts.

Is my grief a sham? Am I mourning a lie?

Ashby has made me inconsequential by turning his back on me and taking his life. I am clearly not worth consideration. And the thing of it is, he may be right.

The phone rings. With a certain effort, I pick it up. It is Brenda Vasquez and she has news. Stephen Pickett's DNA is a match, and the Jinx is 'optimistic' that he can get my sister out of jail.

Today Claire is waiting for me in what we now call the family room. It is usually me who has to wait. I am visiting her twice as much, to take up my brother's slack.

'How are you, Claire?'

'I'm fine.' Her usual answer. She looks up at me, and for a second we really connect. 'It's so good to see you, Georgie.'

'Claire. I have good news.' I keep my voice matter-of-fact. I am aware of my sister's need to keep her emotions muted, and the Jinx has warned me not to get her hopes up too high. I will not make promises I'm not sure I can keep.

So I give her the story, the one Ashby and I cooked up, about blackmail letters in Daddy's desk, and she nods and looks distant because she's heard all this before.

'We just found out that the DNA matches. That the letters were written by Stephen Pickett.'

Claire simply stares. 'You mean those letters were real?'

'Of course they were real.'

'Okay,' she says.

And that is all. Claire is distanced from me now, in a way I find hard to describe. There are subtle differences and big ones. The hair, for one. She has slicked it back in a sort of asexual look that adds an air of toughness. There is a remote look in her eye. Seeing her walk through the door, seeing her before she sees me, I would almost not recognize this woman. She is guarded. She reeks of invisibility, my sister, who used to turn heads no matter what. This is a new Claire, one who is able to move about and attract little or no attention.

I think of them as her prison skills. There are times, every day, when I try *not* to think about her. Imagining her in prison, moment to moment, is unbearable. It is not the things she tells me, it is the things she does not. The dark wells beneath her eyes tell me she does not sleep. The loose orange jumpsuit grows ever more shapeless, and the wrists beneath the sleeves look breakable, brittle and fine. Her tan and freckles have faded, and her skin is almost jaundiced, as if she is suffering malnutrition.

But the worst of it is that in eight long weeks the girl who is my sister is gone, buried beneath the prison

300

inmate. If the Jinx fails, it may be one or two years before we go to trial. There is no bail for murder suspects, not in Beaufort, South Carolina.

Claire seems oddly unaffected by our progress with the DA. I know Selby is exerting some kind of influence, Wilbanks is walking a fine line and Detective Click never wanted to make the arrest. But it is impossible to read my sister's mind whenever I bring this up. And I am wary of getting her hopes up, because, as is usual in the legal system, her life depends on the whim of a judge.

There is no point in offering false comfort. A year ago, my sister and I could fall asleep at night with no real awareness of the black holes that can envelop you. We did not know how easy it is to fall off the wide sunny bridge of middle-class aspirations and concerns.

I notice a red mark on Claire's cheek the size of a quarter which tomorrow will be stained deep blue.

'Don't ask,' she says.

Claire punishes me by withholding details, because it is the only power she has. What I imagine may well be worse than reality, but Claire will not tell me about her life inside. Today, she will barely speak. So I sit with her and say whatever comes into my head, until I simply cannot sit here anymore. For the first time I cut my visit short. I am going home to a hot bubble bath, and John Wallace is taking me to a movie, and afterward we will sit out on my balcony and drink wine.

Ashby was well insured, with life policies that have been in force long past the two-year suicide clause. Claire's legal defense is secure, something I have been careful not to bring up. She still thinks we have Mama's money, and I won't let her even suspect what I know, which is that Ashby killed himself in part to make sure Claire had enough money to pay the Jinx to keep her out of jail.

❖

Ashby always told me that to catch shrimp you have to think like shrimp. How one thinks like a shrimp is something that has always eluded me, but it is second nature to cut through the water with my head swiveled backward to watch for the shrimp leaping straight up out of the boat's wake. White shrimp and brown shrimp, I can never tell the difference, but Ashby always could. What makes them jump is a mystery. Perhaps it is sheer exhilaration.

This morning I spoke with Claire – my sister Claire, not the prison inmate. The Jinx and I went together to tell her the news – her days in jail are numbered. We are waiting on the paperwork, and then she'll be free.

A ripple catches my eye as I spot the nose of a dolphin as it jumps and breaks the gentle surface of the Ace Basin Sound. It is hard to accept this moment as meant for me and me alone. I have this vision of Ashby strong in my head. His hair is cut short short and he is smiling that Ashby smile, with his eyes all squinted and his face tilted up. I place my brother here beside me in the little fishing boat he bought when he was all of twelve. I wish I had known to tell him, when he needed to hear it, that life is made up of small moments, not big events.

In the small gold case that holds my favorite old family photos, one is missing. The empty plastic sleeve is torn, and it strikes me that I picked up a small sliver of plastic that day after Ashby came to dinner at my house.

Did my brother take this picture from my house that week before he died?

The missing photo is tiny. It shows Ashby, age six; me, four; and Claire, barely two. We stand around a thin evergreen that is draped with tinsel, lights and dazzling glass balls, my sister and I with our hair cropped short by my mother's inexpert hand, Ashby's head nearly bald beneath the stubble of a military haircut. I am proud beside a new Thumbelina doll perched in a blue high chair. Claire clutches a stuffed leopard, which I believe she still has in a closet somewhere, and Ashby holds a model ship, a sailboat. Beside us, curled next to the tree, a protective hand on Claire's shoulder, my mother, younger than I am now, sits with the dog, a cocker spaniel named Nugget. My mother seems content, and we children are bright-eyed with Christmas magic.

It is this small mystery of a missing photograph that wakes me in the night. The picture was not in the pockets of the clothes Ashby died in, not in his wallet, the desk drawers, his dresser, the safe-deposit box. I could have missed it, I suppose, as I folded his life away. It could have been thrown away, become lodged in a box; it is a small scrap, three inches by three.

Are you homesick, Ashby? Do you miss me and Claire? Plenty of shrimp in heaven, I guess, Ashby, and no sportsmen's restrictions in the Sound.

How spoiled I have been all my life. How full of demands and desires and the sense of entitled expectation that my path will always be smooth. Now there are two dolphins, mother and yearling, jumping in an arc into the muddy low-country water, and like a miracle it happens. I have found the shrimp. They jump in the wake of the boat, and the white froth of churning water is thick with thin-shelled bodies – so many that they fall like rain.

❖

It is a thing that happens for a reason, coming fully awake in the middle of the night. My brain has filtered the noises that are familiar to my life: the shift and groan of wood floors; the air conditioner that automatically shuts itself off and on; the cars that move, from time to time, in night-time journey by my house. And, nowadays, the noises of Hank, rising early for work with Barney Jones, or Cousin Beauregard, who seeks my bed when her boy is gone.

The digital numbers of my clock glow red. It is 4.37 a.m.

I am wide awake, not groggy, alarmed by the memory of some noise. My heart is beating quickly enough to notice. I try to calm down. There is nothing scary in the house, I tell myself, or Cousin Beauregard would bark.

It is very quick, this reliance on a dog. They have a way of making themselves an integral part of your life within hours of the first moment they have shed on your couch. And then I remember that Hank has been taking Cousin shrimping, that she has adapted to the ocean as if there were salt water in her blood, and that they probably left together over an hour ago.

I am alone with the noise.

I hear it again. Someone is walking carefully up the stairs from my shop to the second-floor rooms where I live. The hall door at the top of the staircase opens and closes. Did Hank leave it unlocked? Did he come back home?

I sit up in my bed and reach for the phone. If it is Hank coming home, I will look like a fool.

The footsteps are slow. I hear the creak of linoleum, so I know someone is in my kitchen. If it were Hank out there, Cousin would be with him. She would be scratching at my door to say hello.

I start dialing, hands shaking, going sweaty all at once. There is no dial tone. I click down the receiver, but no luck. My stomach is dropping, dropping. I am very still. Listening. Someone is breathing on another extension. They are standing in my kitchen, breathing over my phone.

'Hello.'

The voice jolts me like an electric shock. It is masculine, pleasant in the way of a disc jockey, with the same confidence and cocky tone.

'I'm afraid I'm going to have to cut your phone line, Georgie. I don't want to be interrupted by the cops.'

I drop the phone and head for the window. Whoever this is, he knows my name. All I know is I have to get out.

The window sticks, but I put my back into it, and it creaks and opens wide. Out of the corner of my eye I see my bedroom door open slowly, and I punch the screen with my fist and pop it out. I swing one leg over the sill, feeling the void beneath my foot, peering into the dark, humid night.

The door opens wide and I see a man dressed in

black. I will take my chances and jump before I stay for whatever my intruder has planned.

'Don't go.'

It is odd how such a pleasant voice can make the sweat pool at the base of my spine. My breath comes in hard quick gasps. I look down at the pavement and brace for the fall.

'Don't jump out that window unless you want your sister to stay in jail.'

One quick swing of the other leg and I'll be gone. But I hesitate, wondering what he can mean. He takes a step in my direction.

'Stop,' I command, and he does. 'One step closer and I am out the window. One step, asshole, and I'm gone.'

'You could break your neck.'

'Beats a night spent with you.'

He chuckles, and I don't like the sound. 'Now, darlin', I'm the last person to want you to come to any harm. No, hey, put that leg back, I'm only gonna turn on the light.'

He flips a switch. The overhead fixture flickers and spills yellow light into the room. It is good to be free of the dark.

I do not know this person, or how he knows my name. But there are all kinds of people who pass through Beaufort on their way to the beach, some of them not very nice. This man is in his thirties, in good physical shape, medium to tall. He has a sharp nose and high cheekbones and a ball cap on his head.

What if he is not alone?

The man takes his time, absorbing all the details of my bedroom, the white eyelet duvet rumpled over the lace-edged sheets, the dressing table, and my bottles, jars and tubes of makeup and perfume, my bookshelves with pictures and worn paperbacks, smudged hardcovers, the antique rosewood table that I use for a desk. He bends down and retrieves a white lace bra that I tossed on the floor. Squeezes it in a fisted hand.

I should have gone with my first inclination and jumped.

'What did you mean about my sister?'

'You mind if I step closer – just a little bit, so you can see my face in the light?'

'I mind. You've got about thirty seconds to tell me what's on your mind.'

'Don't you know who I am?'

No answer on my end. This man gets no more encouragement for his games. It's going to hurt when I hit.

'My name is Stephen Pickett. I'm sure *that* rings a bell. Hey, now, take it easy there, you really are going to fall. Just let me step under the light now. So you can see my face.'

'Don't go past that dresser.'

'Yes, ma'am, Ms Smallwood, yes, ma'am, whatever you say.'

He removes the ball cap, exposing a thick shag of brown hair. He turns his head from side to side so I can study the rounded profile, a man delighted with his looks. He has a new sunburn and a stubble of blond beard. He is different from that young recruit whose face was in all the papers, but not as different as I'd like. I remember the pictures in Verna Pickett's house, the ones on the walls in the hallway and in Pickett's bedroom. The Pickett nose is distinct.

'No, I'm not a long-lost twin, and no, I'm not a

ghost. You can squeeze my hand if you want to; I'm real enough, Ms Smallwood. Stephen Pickett right here in the flesh.'

'Is there a point to all this?'

Pickett's head snaps up and his eyes narrow. 'Daddy's little girl, so I see.'

'That's right. A chip off the old block.'

He nods. 'That's just going to make this more fun.'

'I don't believe you're Pickett.'

'Get comfortable, then, and I'll prove it. Let me help you back inside.'

'I'll stay put, thanks just the same.'

He smiles, a not unhandsome man, and settles onto an eighteenth-century piano stool tucked beside my dresser. 'You went to my grandmother's house on Montgomery, and you paid her sixty-eight dollars for two crappy old dolls. You said you were an antiques dealer – I think that part's really true. You went into my bedroom and stole my razor, and you convinced the cops that I killed your dad. You on page so far?'

My bra sits curled in his lap, and he hooks a finger under the strap, running it absently up and down the shiny satin.

'That night that everybody got killed, that Hardigree Seven thing? I went AWOL instead of out on the hump. I was already in enough trouble, and your dad was promising to make it worse. I had no earthly idea things would turn out like they did: so many guys drowning, and everybody thinking I was dead. Evidently my bunk-mate got mixed up in the middle of the night and went out there toting my pack. His name was Crocker. He was one of the guys who didn't come back. I went to my grandmother's and she hid me away.'

'And collected your death benefits, so I understand.'

Pickett, if it is Pickett, crosses one leg over another and cocks his head. He's still stroking my bra. 'I know you told the police I was blackmailing your father. Did you actually know it was true?'

I think how I stood in Pickett's bedroom, apologizing to his ghost. What an idiot I am.

Pickett laughs. 'Where did you get those letters? Did you write them yourself? What, still not talking? I guess I am something of a shock. Hey, you think I'm wearing a wire or something, honey? I'll be glad to show you, just let me strip off these clothes.'

'No, thanks, I'd like to keep my supper down.'

He smiles, small and crafty. I can't tell if he's angry or just likes to play.

'It's true, you know. I was blackmailing your daddy. Soon as Nan told me about you-all inheriting all that money, I thought it was only fair for your *daddy* to share.'

All I can think is that this sociopath in tight black jeans and black sweatshirt calls his grandmother *Nan*.

'And the timing was too good. Your dad coming into that money, Wilbanks running for public office. They call him the bulldog in the papers – the man who never lets a case go. I'm sure the last thing he needs is that old business getting out.'

'Why should Wilbanks care?'

Pickett turns his head sideways. 'You don't know the whole story, do you?' He props his feet on the edge of my desk. 'See, everybody knows I went to your father. It's common knowledge I told him about Hardigree, that the guy was drunk and there'd be trouble. Your dad never liked me, you know. Didn't think I had the stuff to make a marine; he told me so that night. And I told him that if marines were like him, I didn't care.

'That was pretty much it for me. Hardigree was already looking for a reason to bust me down, so I figured I was done for. Your dad made that pretty clear.

'I hung around awhile, didn't go back to the barracks. I just stayed out of sight – it was dark and the middle of the night – and waited for your dad to do something or go back to bed. Except he didn't go back to bed. He made a phone call, and Captain Wilbanks showed up, and I thought, man, Hardigree will break my neck when he finds out I told Sergeant Smallwood, and Smallwood ratted him out to Wilbanks.' Pickett rubs the back of his neck. 'That's when I took off. Didn't go back for my stuff or nothing. But the funny thing is, nobody ever found out about Wilbanks.'

I bite my lip. 'You're saying Wilbanks knew what was up that night? He didn't do anything about Hardigree, and he let my father take all the blame?'

'Yeah. But then I hear Wilbanks took pretty good care of your dad – during the investigation, and after he got out. Getting him that job at the bank.'

'My father didn't need that job from Wilbanks.'

'Way I heard it, he did. Maybe him and ol' Eugene made some kind of deal. And Wilbanks being head of the investigation – put him in place to do both of them a lot of good.'

I take a long slow breath. 'Okay, fine. Shock – outrage – emotion. Is there anything else you want?'

Pickett leans forward, clearly puzzled. 'You don't seem to be getting my point. Let's just say your daddy died owing me a debt, and I'd like you to see it through.'

'Whatever was between you and my father is nothing to do with me.'

He smiles and I don't like it. 'Yeah, I sure would be in a jam if I didn't have a pretty solid alibi. Yes, ma'am, that I would.'

'Tell it to the police, Pickett. I'm not giving you any money, and if I see or hear from you again I'll go straight to the cops.'

'Will you?'

'You bet I will.'

'I don't think so. And let me tell you why. I was in jail the night your daddy was killed. In jail, fingerprints on file, under the name of Robert O. Myers, drunk and disorderly, out the next day.' He leans back against my door. 'Soon as the cops find that out, I think your sister goes right back to jail. But you got no cause to worry, 'cause I'm going to make you a deal. Three hundred thousand dollars, and I promise to stay dead. Your sister gets out of jail, right on schedule, and poor old Stephen Pickett, he takes the heat. As far as the cops are concerned, I'm the one that killed your dad. Otherwise, I prove it's not me, and you get to face a district attorney who's trying to put *somebody* in jail. Maybe this time your sister won't go back. Maybe you will. Or maybe that boy of yours, Hank; maybe they'll go after him. Got to go after somebody, don't they?'

Pickett tosses the bra onto the bed.

'Get the money together. I'll take it and disappear. Or you can spend it all on lawyers if you want. You'll need to, if I come out of the woodwork. Think about it, Ms Smallwood. And I'll be in touch.' He opens my bedroom door and walks away.

17

I sit in my living room with all the lights on, wondering who I can call. Ashby is gone. Hank I have to keep safe. Claire? Not only is she in jail, she needs my help, not my trouble, at least till she's safely home. I am completely alone.

I am not sure when I fall asleep, wearing my brother's big fisherman's sweater. But it is after the sun is up, and the dark is gone, and only because I feel better once it is light. I sleep hard, in retreat from the world, and I wake with the feeling that the phone has been ringing quite a while.

But it isn't the phone, because the line has been cut. The ringing comes from the bell at my shop door. I am up and stumbling into the kitchen. It is twenty-one minutes past ten. The phone cord dangles, neatly sliced, from the wall, my silverware drawer hangs open three inches, and the butcher's knife Pickett used lies in the middle of the sink. My stomach drops all over again.

And the downstairs bell is still ringing. Whoever it is will not go away.

I wander down the stairs in my cut-off blue jeans and Ashby's oversized white shirt. I have shed the sweater, because the sun is heating up my house. I smooth my hair out of my eyes. I will check and see who is at the door, but I will keep the CLOSED sign up and not keep shop hours today.

I peer through the slats in the blinds. Dust coats my fingertips and I see John Wallace at the door. I unbolt the front lock. The worried lines in his face smooth into relief. He opens his arms and holds me.

'Your phone is dead,' he says, voice muffled by my hair.

There was someone I could have called all along.

It is something of a public proclamation, hugging John Wallace on the sidewalk in front of my shop. I could not have made our relationship more official if I had taken out a newspaper ad. John Wallace has not seemed to me a demonstrative man, and I am rather awed by how tightly he holds me and how unaware he seems of the looks that we get.

He holds up a brown paper sack that feels warm next to my ribs and is spotted with smudges of grease.

'I made beignets,' he says, with a hint of a bashful smile. 'Do you have some time for a coffee break?'

He steps in over the threshold of my shop and makes no comment when I leave the CLOSED sign in place and lock the front door. He walks behind me up the stairs, hands resting lightly on my hips, paper sack bumping soft on my left thigh, and I take a deep breath and let it out because it is good, so good, to feel safe.

I listen to John Wallace talk gently to Cousin while I go to the kitchen to put on the coffee. Even using his 'animal' voice, John Wallace's speech has an edge that is whiskey rough. But Cousin likes John Wallace, and from the rustle of the paper bag I have no doubt he is feeding her a beignet.

The sun comes in warm through the windows, and only now do I notice that the afternoon is lovely and clear. I feel a comfortable domestic buzz and for a moment I am reminded of someone else: Hank's father, and the ease I felt in his arms. The memory is an old one and gives me little more than a twinge. It is almost reassuring, like the squeeze of a hand.

John Wallace stands at the edge of my kitchen. I did not hear him or see him move. He has a way of looking at me that makes me feel noticed. He has told me before that I am not like other women he has known.

He reaches across me to the telephone cord that hangs severed and loose, and I see a flicker of something raw in his face.

'Tell me what happened.' His presence fills my kitchen, and I feel cornered. I lead him to the open living room and my comfortable couch. I hear the drip and hiss of the coffeemaker.

John Wallace is awkward beside me. He takes my hands and presses them between his rough, calloused palms, and I see the thud of a pulse in his neck.

'I saw the knife. The one in the sink. What happened here, Georgie? Are you sure you're okay?' He is very still, and there is something watchful in his eyes.

I tell him everything. About Pickett, and Ashby, and Claire. About my mother, and Carla Blanchard and her horrid offspring, ending with the purloined Fiestaware, about which I know I obsess. I have hinted before, at some of these things. John Wallace has never pressed but allowed me my space.

On the coffee table beside us, beignets spill, forgotten, from the bag. Powdered sugar coats my coffee table like snow. The coffeemaker has been quiet for ages.

John Wallace pulls me close to his chest and eases backward onto the couch, so that we are stretched out with me full length on top. How good he smells. So masculine. Like cigarettes, and suntan oil, spicy soap, and the unmistakable musk of male.

He strokes my hair. Works strong fingers to massage the back of my neck.

'What are you planning to do?' His words are careful, but I get the impression he has a lot he wants to say.

'I've thought about it. I'm going to pay Pickett one time and one time only. If he comes for more after that, I figure he'll never let me be. But once – I think that might be worth the risk. I can't stand the thought of my sister not getting out of jail.'

I brace myself for the argument. I dread the inevitable male explosion of frustration, anger and ego.

But in this, as in many things concerning John Wallace, my expectations are totally off. He rubs a thumbnail gently along my forearm, and I feel a shiver course down my back.

'I think you're right.' His eyes are half shut and his voice is thick with intelligence and concentration. He has a confidence about him. 'But only the one time, Georgie. No more, no less. And make sure he understands.'

'How will I do that?'

'The first thing you do is negotiate.'

I frown. 'You don't know this guy. He's not going to *negotiate*.'

'Yes, he will. He won't expect it, coming from you, but that will make him respectful, and more careful, and it gets the point home that you mean what you say.'

I am quiet, considering. I think John Wallace is out of his mind.

'You say he asked for three hundred thousand? Can you make that?'

I shrug.

'That means he'll take two. If you're good you can get him down to one fifty. Try to get him down to half.'

'How do I know if I am good?'

John Wallace considers me. 'Offer one seventy-five, then settle on two.'

'What if he won't take two?'

'Then walk away. If he's unreasonable, then he'll never leave you alone anyway, and paying him off is no longer an option. You have to exercise some control.'

'You make me feel like I have power here. Like I have some kind of choice.'

He cocks his head. 'Who controls the flow of money?'

'I do?'

He nods. 'That puts power in your hands.'

We have been still together on the couch for a while, me thinking things over, him rubbing my back.

'Don't look now,' John Wallace says in a low voice, 'but your dog just nabbed a beignet.'

I put my head up. 'You didn't buy them? You really make them yourself?'

'Yep. What does *that* look mean?' And he traces my chin with his thumb.

'I can't figure you out.'

'No?'

I keep studying him. 'You seem to know a lot about handling a blackmailer. And you don't act all that shocked.'

In some unspoken synchronization, we move away from each other, me to curl cross-legged on one end of the couch, John Wallace to move lithely to his feet. He paces to the window, braces his hands against the glass and looks out. He speaks without turning around.

'The thing is, Georgie, I've spent plenty of time with your criminal types, some of them being my friends. Been in jail a couple times.' He looks at me over his shoulder, to see if I am shocked.

I say, 'My sister's in jail,' but it sounds odd and inane.

He smiles faintly. 'I know. But you and me, Georgie, we haven't had the same kind of life.'

'So you're not a fisherman after all?'

'I have been. I might be again.'

'I'm not sure what you're trying to say.'

He turns and sits in my rocking chair. Cousin lumbers up from her snooze on the floor and licks the back of his hand before she jumps on the couch to settle in his spot.

'I'm just trying to tell you something about me. Put us on a level playing field. Be honest with you from the start.'

'What did you go to prison for?'

'Grand theft auto, when I was nineteen. Drunk and disorderly a couple of times.'

'Were you guilty?'

'Of drunk and disorderly?'

'Grand theft auto, when you were nineteen.'

'I was with the wrong guys at the wrong time. I

should have known better and been smarter, and I take responsibility for what I did. I brought it on myself. But those days I was a pretty cocky kid.'

'So how have you supported yourself, since you got out of jail? What kind of a life have you led?'

He leans back in the chair, rocking gently. 'Bouncer for a nightclub, cooking in a diner, night watchman at a racetrack and fishing for shrimp. Done a lot of that.'

I wonder what my mother would say to all of this. Run screaming – or give the boy a chance?

'Want me to get us some coffee?' he asks.

'Sure.' I lie back on the couch and close my eyes, glad for a little bit of space.

There is no doubt I stand at a crossroad. I am trying not to think with my heart. The truth is, a few months ago, an admission like that and John Wallace would have been out of my life. But if I do not listen to what he says, and look instead at what he does, I see something bright and considerate and fine. I have myself been ground down by judgmental voices. People who consider me only in the light of my illegitimate son. I can pretend, outwardly, to be a wall of bricks, but these things can be injurious, and I have my scars.

John Wallace sees me, and he does not judge. Do I owe him the same?

He has not lived by the traditions I consider safe. He has not had money, comfort or security. I think his experiences have hardened him.

Does he care for the things he gives up? Does he care that he cannot pay with plastic, that late at night people cross the street uneasily if they see he is coming their way? Does he care that everyone I know in Beaufort is shaking their heads, as if they have seen him coming from miles away and expect no better sense from a girl who has lived with a deceptive if quiet grace but who did, after all, have a child at the age of sixteen? This is just the kind of man a girl like Georgie Smallwood *would* fall for, and if she thinks he'll ever marry her she is living in a dream.

I do not know if I am living in a dream. But I think I have fallen in love.

I am not smug. I know there is no security in any relationship, married or not. I know this is a dangerous man. These are things my head still knows.

But when John Wallace walks in with two mugs of coffee, one black, the other, for me, full of cream, I find it impossible not to smile.

We light candles behind the closed door of my bedroom. We have left Cousin alone with the beignets. I close the shutters to the rising heat of the day, and lie on my back on my rumpled bed. John Wallace puts a pillow beneath my head and sits beside me. Strips of sunlight lie like latticework on the floor, and the flickering candles cast shadows on his face. I reach out and touch the tip of his chin, and he takes my fingers and massages them one by one. I catch the scent of his aftershave, which is overshadowed by the harsh masculine odor of cigarettes.

He leans over to kiss me, and I see his profile on the wall, large and dark.

At first his kiss is delicate, the slightest pressure against my lips. He moves in closer and kisses me again, very slowly, like a man who has not kissed a woman in a long, long time, like a man who wants to imprint each and every sensation to a memory book somewhere in his head.

His tongue tastes like coffee, with the ghost of tobacco past. He sucks my lower lip gently, then puts his arms all the way around me and pulls me close and tight to his chest. He kisses the tip of my left ear, then he runs his teeth lightly over the lobe.

'Music?' he asks, as if the thought has just occurred.

'CDs in the basket.' I leave him to figure out how the player works and I am curious about the music he will choose. My collection has no rhyme or reason; I feel insecure when people go through my CDs, and brace myself for disdain.

His choice is a surprise. But this man is, after all, from New Orleans, and I smile when the strong sweet notes of Armstrong's trumpet smooth the edges of my heart.

John Wallace stands by the side of my bed. A dark shape, and he seems very tall. Just for a moment, I am afraid. He watches me and waits, like a man who can read the thoughts of a woman.

I hold out my hand, and he gives me a small nod, as if we have newly struck a deal.

His finger traces the line of my jaw, and I tilt my head sideways, mildly ticklish, as he runs his fingertips down the side of my neck and to the top button at the rim of my shirt. Little tiny white buttons, and he moves slowly, releasing them one by one, till my white linen shirt is open, exposing my stomach and bra.

The skin looks very brown against the white lace edges of my bra. On my shoulders, the straps are tiny and dear. This is not the bra Stephen Pickett fondled late last night. I cut that one into pieces and threw it away.

With one finger, John Wallace hooks each strap and slides it down my shoulders till it is loose on my arm. He kisses my throat dead center, then my neck, and then my mouth. He sighs and shudders and covers my body entirely with his. The long slow kissing reminds me of early high-school crushes, and the patient savoring exploration in every relationship that is new.

He sits back, abruptly, and takes off his shirt. John Wallace's chest is hard, dark with hair, and feels warm against my flesh. I run my fingernails up and down the center of his back, massaging his shoulders, then push my thumbs in ever widening circles on his chest.

John Wallace trembles beneath my touch. I smile and tuck my fingertips into the waistband of his pants.

'There are so many ways I want to love you,' he says, lips close to my ear. 'I hardly know where to begin.'

He is purposeful now, and puts his hands beneath my hips and pulls me close. I close my eyes and arch my back and I am wondering about the things he has in mind.

'Do them all,' I whisper. 'Every single last one.'

I feel his chest move against me. He is laughing in his throat, and clothes are now very much in our way. The frenzy begins, jeans, bra, panties – it is all stripped away.

I feel dizzy, like I am falling. I open my eyes and see that he is beautiful, like an animal. I put my hands on him and hear him suck in his breath.

'Now,' I say.

'Don't be in such a hurry.'

But neither of us wants to wait.

John Wallace has advised me on how to handle Claire's homecoming tomorrow when she gets out of jail.

'Pizza,' he told me. 'Cold Coca-Cola or beer. Keep things low-key, and don't press her to talk. She needs a comfortable bed,' he adds. 'It'll probably be a couple of days before she sleeps.'

I stand outside the Piggly Wiggly where I have bought dog food for Cousin, and the ingredients for my famous lime pound cake, and I add bubble bath to my list of things to get. This last entry is not the kind of thing John Wallace would think of, but it's the kind of thing a sister definitely would.

I glance over my list, then crumple it into the pocket of my jeans and load groceries into the back of Big Mama. It is an odd thing: I anticipate the relief of getting my sister home, but I don't feel it. I have the dark and overwhelming sensation that something will go wrong. The prison doors will open, but Claire won't come out.

The broken pavement in the Pig's parking lot is hot, and some idiot has thrown a beer can – Budweiser – into the bed of my truck. I realize I have stepped in gum, and it stretches melty and pink in a string from the pavement to my shoe. The red Keds. They're almost new.

'Whatcha step in, little girl?'

I know this voice. Stephen Pickett stands beside the truck. He is dressed in cut-off jeans, a black Harley T-shirt, a dirty brown ball cap and sunglasses with dark shades. He holds a beer in his hand, a Budweiser, pops the tab and takes a long cold swallow. He wipes his mouth with the back of his hand, grins and says, 'How have you been?'

I fold my arms. I want to shout his name to the old woman pushing a basket full of paper towels, napkins and toilet paper. I want to point and yell *Stephen Pickett is alive*.

It's an inexplicable urge that will do none of us any good. Perhaps I just want it all to be over.

Pickett glances once over his shoulder, as if he can read my mind. I notice a purple streak over his right cheekbone. Healing, it seems, but someone has given him an amazing black eye.

I grin. His sunglasses have lost their cool.

'You made up your mind, Georgie Smallwood? I hear your sister's due out of jail any time now. That true?'

'I won't make up my mind till you answer some questions.'

He smiles, but it is to cover a certain surprise, and I notice he has a bad tooth. 'Such as?'

'First and foremost, I have to know you won't come back. One payment, one time, or I take my chances with the police.'

'Just have to trust me, I guess.'

'Try again.'

'Say what?'

'Convince me, Pickett, or I walk away.'

He edges closer, and I know he does not like me saying his name. 'Look, all I want is a stake. Then I'll take off and be out of your hair.'

I think for a minute, but the truth is I am not convinced. This man is telling me what I want to hear, and he's never going to go away.

'Deal's off,' I say, and open the door to my truck.

'*Listen* to me.' He shifts his weight to his other leg,

moving back and forth. A nervous habit, I'm sure, but he looks like a little boy in need of the men's room. 'You know who I am, right? If you rat me out, I got that old AWOL charge to deal with—'

'You were only a recruit, and it's nothing anybody is going to want to dig up again. You won't have a problem with that.'

'Yeah, but my grandmother collected the insurance when she knew I was alive, and that takes us to fraud. Then there's blackmail. You know I was blackmailing your daddy, and then I tried blackmailing you. That's some serious jail time. One payment, and both of our troubles go away, and I'm completely out of your life.'

'How do I know you really have an alibi for the night my father was killed? Maybe you made the whole thing up.'

Pickett smiles and reaches into his back pocket. It seems he was ready for this. 'My arrest ticket. June sixth. On this one I've got you nailed.'

I've never seen an arrest ticket before, though I suppose my sister has. I give it a glance, but in truth it looks legitimate, and I tuck it away in the pocket of my jeans.

'I never want to see your face again.'

'Just one more time. When you make the payment. And I'll never bother you again.'

'Three hundred is too much, Pickett. One fifty is all I can do. My sister's attorney has cost me a bundle and half of the estate's tied up.'

'That's not my problem, baby doll. Your brother left some insurance, didn't he?'

Pickett does not seem surprised I am haggling. John Wallace was right all along, and I continue on with the script. 'One fifty or no deal.'

'Two fifty is the best I can do. I want to pay the mortgage on my grandmother's house.'

'One seventy-five.'

'Two fifty. Not budging.'

'The best I can give you is two.'

He does not answer. I cannot see his eyes behind those dark glasses.

'No deal, then.' I climb into my truck.

'Two, then. And I'll find you. Have the money ready by tomorrow.'

'Day after tomorrow, after my sister is out of jail. And I'll find you. Be in the Wal-Mart parking lot at three o'clock Saturday afternoon. Wear exactly what you're wearing now. No money till I see you out in the open, alone, away from any car. Any variation, anything at all makes me nervous, and I'll drive straight from there to the police. And that will be the end of you.'

'And you,' he says. He doesn't like it, I can tell.

'Cheer up, Pickett. By Saturday night you can afford a dentist to fix that tooth and buy a steak for your black eye.'

He turns suddenly and walks away. I have heard it in his voice and I can see it in his step. He is spending that money in his head.

Perhaps it is selfish, the way I have set Claire's homecoming up. But conversations with John Wallace have given me the confidence to follow my instincts.

Hank waits with Claire's children in my living room, all of them hanging balloons and arranging flowers. I go alone to the gates where Claire will appear upon her release from jail. I know that the Jinx has come personally to see there will be no bureaucratic glitches or last-minute petty cruelties to gum up the works. Just knowing he will be here makes me breathe easier.

I sit in Big Mama, an hour early. No unforeseen traffic jam, road blockage, nothing unexpected will keep me from being there when Claire comes out.

I wait in the hot silence. The windows are rolled down, and I have stretched white towels across the vinyl upholstery. I cannot read the newspaper in the seat by my side. I cannot listen to 98.1 THE BULL. I can only wait and try to empty my mind. Two long-stemmed red roses lie across the newspaper on the seat, and I check them from time to time to see if they still look fresh.

I listen to traffic move slowly up and down the baking pavement. Nothing moves quickly in the late-afternoon heat. I hear gulls, but I don't see them, then the murmur of two men talking as they walk past my car.

I look at my watch yet again. Time moves. The closer I get to the hour of my sister's release, the more nervous I get. My stomach growls, but I am not hungry. I have had nothing to eat today, except most of a cup of coffee, when I woke up, very early, with the sun.

The scheduled moment of Claire's release comes and goes. The Jinx warned me things might run late and told me not to panic. No news is good news, he told me. I'll get with you immediately if there is any serious glitch. He seems to know in advance how all of us will feel. He sent a large wreath of flowers to

Ashby's funeral, earning a permanent place in my heart.

A guard appears at the prison gate, and I see a tall older man in a suit. The Jinx. He has dressed for the occasion.

And I see Claire.

She is holding the Jinx's arm as if the two of them are out for a stroll. The Jinx puts his head down to hear something my sister says, and he and the guard both smile. Everyone seems so mannerly and carefree it would not surprise me to see Claire and the Jinx tango across the parking lot. Clearly, I should have hired a limousine.

I turn to smile at Ashby, for some reason expecting him here beside me in the truck. It is hard, still, to imagine him dead.

The blast of a Harley drifts in through the open window and I see Selby, astride his bike. He waits long enough to make sure Claire is free and on her way, then revs the engine and goes. He passes in front of me and lifts a hand. He is faceless, in sunglasses and full helmet, but seeing him makes me smile.

I step out of Big Mama and stand by the open door, waiting for my sister to catch my eye. She is turned sideways, in deep conversation with the Jinx, but she looks up suddenly and sees me from across the street.

Claire lifts a hand and gives me a neon smile. She stands on tiptoe to hug the Jinx, then turns and walks fast across the street. It is the earthquake walk, full of nervous energy and Claire-style twitches, and I cannot help but laugh.

'*What* the hell do you find so funny?' Claire is

smiling, and she gives me a tight hug. 'Come on, Georgie, let's get the *fuck* outta here, before somebody changes their mind and drags me back.'

We climb into Big Mama and wave at the Jinx, who walks with grace and barely restrained energy to his silver Mercedes Benz. I'm a BMW girl myself, or would be if I were rich.

Big Mama stalls, then catches, and Claire rolls her eyes. 'Remind me not to ask you to be my wheelman if I ever make a break from jail.'

'Wheelman?'

'I've been in prison, girl. I have a whole new set of skills.'

Relief rises so quickly inside me I feel like a helium balloon. It is the old Claire, sitting beside me on the seat.

'My God, this upholstery is hot.'

'Then sit on the towel, you moron.'

'Where are my babies?'

'At my place, with Hank, hanging up balloons. We're having pizza, and I've rented movies for the kids.'

'*Pizza*. Oh, my God, with pepperoni and banana peppers?'

'Yes, and extra tomato sauce and thin crust.'

'Bless your heart, how did you know that's what I'd want?'

'Open the bag.'

'What's in it? Georgie, did you *see* that car?'

'I can drive without your help, thank you very much.'

'Bubble bath? Cucumber and melon.' My sister speaks in reverent tones. 'And body foam, oh, I am going to soak in a tub till I shrivel.'

'And by the way, I also made a lime cake.'

'Too bad Ashby isn't here. He loved your lime cakes.' My sister smiles at me, but her face is sad. 'Would you mind if we made a stop? I want to tell Ashby hello.'

I nod. I had planned on this too.

18

The sun slants in through the open window and illuminates the motes of dust. I am curled on the couch with Cousin's head on my lap, lazily considering the word *mote*. Is a mote a thing, as in *particle*, or an actual measurement, most often applied to dust?

The door to my bathroom opens, emitting steam and the sweet smell of lotion. My sister pads into the living room wrapped in my white terry-cloth robe, belt trailing along the floor behind the footprints her wet feet make on the wood floor.

'Georgie?' comes the stage whisper. 'Are you awake?'

Claire looks younger this morning, with no makeup on her face and a post get-out-of-jail glow. I wonder if the ease will last, or if there will be depression and nightmares to come.

But now, right this minute, I feel just fine. I am cultivating the art of living in the moment, which is a brand-new thing for me.

Yes, my brother is dead. And yes, my mother is gone too. And this afternoon I will meet my father's blackmailer, hand him most of my inheritance, and hope like hell he'll go away. And the knowledge that he is out there – that will weigh down my heart for life.

But Claire is out of jail, and my son is home safe. Last night Hank gave us about an hour at the party, then spent the rest of the evening with his friends. Claire and I were still awake, talking on the couch, when Hank rolled in around 2 a.m. He changed clothes, gave his Aunt Claire a hug and made off with the last of the pizza. I think I heard him whistling as he went down the back way from the house. He has been working five days out of seven with Barney Jones. When Ashby's will goes through probate, *The Graceful Lady* will come, debt free, to my son.

'Let's go out for breakfast,' Claire says. 'My treat. I worked the whole time I was in jail. Made about a buck fifty-nine.'

'Um,' I say. There is no explaining how my day will go. 'Why don't you and the kids go on without me? I've got some stuff I've got to do.' Like put two hundred thousand dollars in a duffel bag.

'Are you going shopping?'

'I'm going to Wal-Mart.'

Claire shudders. 'Never mind. I'll call you later tonight. Right now I'm going *home*. Just let me dry my hair before we stir up the kids.'

Her son has spent the night in Hank's bed. Her two girls slept curled up in mine, and Claire just nudged them sideways when she decided at last to sleep. We've had one of those after-party sleepovers that no one ever plans – the kind that happen after too much pizza and beer.

I go into the kitchen to get dog food for Cousin and notice the crackle of paper from the back pocket of my jeans. Stephen Pickett's arrest ticket. I give it a look. My hands begin to shake, as if I understand things on a physical level before my brain catches up.

New Orleans. That's where Stephen Pickett spent

the night in jail when my father died. Arrested for being drunk and disorderly – which must have involved a great deal of disorderly in that kind of town. Is it just a coincidence that John Wallace comes from Louisiana, this man who's been frying up beignets? This man who has admitted to being in jail at least twice, one time for drunk and disorderly?

The chatter and clatter from the bedrooms is rising, and my nieces run out to give me a hug good-bye. I kiss them both on the cheek and hug my nephew, who is currently not accepting kisses. Even through my distraction I see how they shine now they have their mother back. The simple presence of my sister has put their world to rights. And it will be up to me to see she never goes away again.

Claire looks at me over the heads of her kids. *Is something wrong?* she mouths.

I shake my head no. 'I'm fine,' I whisper. I make myself smile and usher them out the door.

Cousin needs to go to the bathroom. I give Claire time to pack the kids in her car, delivered, in spite of no driver's license, by Hank, then I put a leash on the dog. Cousin is anxious, nearly pulling me down the steps, and we sneak out the side door and leave the shop closed down. Cousin finds relief on my tiny strip of backyard grass.

The dog stretches out, panting but pleased to be outside in the morning while it is still cool, and I settle in the grass beside her to think, propping my back on the freshly painted white picket fence put up by the people next door. The hard part is my inner resistance. My unwillingness to believe. But once I approach the hard-ass point of view, then everything begins to make sense. A whole lot of sense.

For instance. Stephen Pickett grew up in this town. There are a lot of places he can't show his face. For instance. Pickett needs a partner, to make contact with my father, maybe even to pick up the cash. For instance. I met John Wallace in an antiques store, a good place for anyone who knows anything to track me down.

'Let's consider John Wallace, shall we?' I realize I have asked this question out loud. Cousin looks at me seriously and licks my hand, knowing, the way dogs mysteriously do, that I am very upset. I'm going to talk this problem through with my dog.

'Think about this, Cousin,' I say, and she perks up her head to listen. 'I drive a pickup truck an idiot could recognize from a hundred miles away.'

Cousin is paying attention, but she doesn't seem convinced.

'And here comes John Wallace, who just happens to be in an antiques store, even though he hasn't got the first clue about antiques. We see each other from across the room, peering through Burgin's dust. Is this love at first sight?'

Cousin looks hopeful, but I shake my head.

'Let's not be that naive. It was too good to be true, Cousin, I should have known better and been smarter. John Wallace is going to fall for me right on the spot? Am I really all that cute?'

I hold up a finger, which Cousin licks.

'Okay, one, in John Wallace's favor, I *am* cute. But two, not in his favor, he is renting a cabin on Hunting Island, in the same state park where my father dies in the lighthouse. Point three, what is my father *doing* at the lighthouse – if not meeting the men who are bleeding him dry? Point four, what does John Wallace actually *do*, since he has no visible means of support?'

I lean over Cousin, and she licks the tears from my cheeks. 'Yes, that is one thing in his favor. *You* like him, don't you, girl?'

I stand up and look to the side door of my messy house. In three hours I am expected in the Wal-Mart parking lot to hand a huge amount of money to the recently resurrected Stephen Pickett. If he really is Stephen Pickett. Maybe he just looks like Stephen Pickett. Nobody seems to be who they're supposed to be anymore.

And John Wallace, so good and true, is supposed to go with me, to make sure all goes well. Street-smart John Wallace, who knows exactly the deal the black-mailer will make.

I have slept with this man. And revealed everything I hold in my heart. I admit it, I fell in love.

As usual, my idiotic taste in men.

John Wallace will be here in two hours. I wonder low long he will knock at my door.

'Come on, Cousin. How about a ride in the truck?'

Around about the time I am due to meet Stephen Pickett, Cousin and I are in a Sonic parking lot on the other side of Savannah. Savannah is one of my favorite places, and it bursts with charm and grace, but it also smells like old cabbage here on the remote industrial side. I am hot but have forgone a sit-down air-conditioned restaurant, because they have annoying objections to dogs.

Cousin is having iced water, a cheeseburger and fries, and I am having a cheddar BLT on Texas toast. I feed a piece of bacon to Cousin. I am on a BLT kick these days.

I picture John Wallace, puzzled at my door. Then remember him on my doorstep the morning after Pickett broke into my house. How worried John was. How tender and considerate, how supportive and kind. That fucking bag of beignets.

What will he and Pickett do when I don't show up with the money? Will they think I've gone to the police? They'll wait, of course, greedy bastards. They'll bend over backward to try and save the deal. And, God forgive me, John Wallace knows about me and Ashby writing the letters. And Stephen Pickett's grandmother will back them up. I'm going to have to pay them off.

I check my watch, then realize I am on no time schedule but my own. My anger is rising, rising, drowning all my hurt. I had thought to make a plan, to work things out very carefully, to be cool, collected, in control.

So much for plan one. I am going to take Cousin home, grab a shower and a change of clothes, because vengeance works best when you are looking good, and I'm going to confront those bastards tonight.

On the way home, I plan a quick stop at my mother's house. I happen to know where she kept a gun. I put the gun in the back compartment of my truck where Cousin can't get to it. I see she has thrown up her cheeseburger on the front seat.

335

The sun is finally losing heat as I speed down Highway 17. Cousin was so insistent on not being left behind that I was barely able to squeeze past her out the door. She seems to have decided, after our excursion this afternoon, that she will now accompany me wherever I go. It is too hot for her to sit and wait in the truck, but I almost wish I had brought her along. It is two against one now.

Most of the cars I pass on the highway are heading into town. BEAUTIFUL PLACES, SMILING FACES, as it says on South Carolina license plates. The penalty for littering here is one thousand dollars.

Anger still fuels my fire, but there is also hurt now, as well as a certain fear. Whatever happens, I promise myself I will not run. When a woman runs she becomes prey.

It is still hot outside, and I am cursed with a noticeable truck. I leave Big Mama about a third of a mile from the cabins, and lock the duffel bag up in the cab of the truck. It makes me nervous to leave the cash here in the pickup, but I have covered it over with scattered newspaper, and Big Mama, to be honest, is not overly attractive to thieves. And that much money is heavy, and I am not hauling the duffel bag for miles through the woods. I need a chance to scope the place out.

From here I cannot see the ocean. I pass the ranger station, with its wood walkways that skirt the pond. The surface of the water is heavily coated with a green scum, the official name of which is duckweed. I watch where I walk and stick to the paths, taking a second look at a thick brown log. Alligators are an ever-present nuisance, another reason I'm glad I left Cousin behind.

The no-see-um bugs sink their minuscule stingers into my flesh, and I slap my arms to relieve the itch. It's a funny thing about Beaufort. The tourists arrive in the miserable heat, and the locals who can afford it spend their summers somewhere else. The bugs alone will drive you out.

In five minutes of winding through the palm trees and undergrowth, my shirt is sticking to my back and I am shiny with sweat. The wind is blowing now; I must be getting closer to the beach. A thick layer of pine needles, pine cones and palm fronds covers the dirty white sand. The picnickers have gone home.

The rental cabins are tucked away and private – within sight of each other, but just barely, hidden as they are by the palms and the pines. My face feels flushed and I am queasy in the humid heat. I take a clip from my purse and twist my hair up on my head. No doubt the bugs will bite me, but for now I savor the freedom of having my hair off the back of my neck.

Right away I see what I am looking for: John Wallace's Coup de Ville. The cabin beside it looks unoccupied. No beach towels drying on the porch rail, no cooking smells, music, children screaming. But the windows are open, the screens shut tight, and I slip closer, moving from tree to tree.

The dusky evening is perfect. I would be hard to see if anyone looked out a window. A bit of movement, and then I am still. But there is plenty of light for me to find my way, and I move ever closer, walking as quietly as I can. I wonder, as my foot crunches a pine cone, how the Indians ever pulled this off.

Voices. Male. I move close in, then duck, because

John Wallace is standing in front of the window at the kitchen sink.

'. . . call her again, but later. Or I might just go by.'

'Come on, man, I need the car. I told you, I got a date.'

'You need to keep your mind on business.'

I sag against the tree. I realize that I have been hoping, like an idiot, for some reasonable explanation, a few magic words to make it all go away. There is no possibility of doubt. John Wallace and Pickett are working together, and I have been utterly betrayed.

My plan of storming in and giving them both hell is beginning to seem ridiculous. I will be angry again tomorrow, but for the time being the avenging angel better go under wraps. There are two of them. And one of me.

And I admit to a weakness concerning John Wallace. I never want to see him again.

'Okay, fine, take the car. Who is this girl? Is she safe? Who did you find to date you anyway?'

My plan begins to form. Simple and direct. Follow Stephen Pickett on his way out for the night. Hand him the money and go. And then it better be over. If God is good I will never see either man again.

Are victims of blackmail all alike? Do we feed on a thin but dangerous diet of hope, optimism and the words we want to hear?

'*Who* did you say?' John Wallace's tone of voice has caught me up. I hear him laughing, and it is not very nice. 'It's your neck. But if you're going out with Papa Le Marc's daughter, you better treat her nice.'

Pickett says something that I imagine is crude, but I don't know what it is because I am already moving back to my truck. If Pickett is going out tonight with Nicola Le Marc, I know exactly where he is heading.

I stand on Frogmore Island, half hidden behind a tree, close to the front bumper of my truck. Every year the United States Post Office in conjunction with various local organizations tries to change the name of Frogmore to St Helena. Frogmore is on the other side of the bridge from Beaufort, in more than physical reality. Frogmore is the foremost seat of voodoo in South Carolina.

Perhaps you associate such things with New Orleans and Haiti and parts of southern Florida rich in the heritage of refugees. But voodoo has a real presence here in South Carolina, and a sexist one as well. Voodoo queens may practice in New Orleans to their heart's content, but here in Beaufort the women are sidelined and the priesthood is the sole province of the men.

One of these men is Papa Le Marc.

I pass through Frogmore hundreds of times a year, but now, at dusk, on this gravel back road, it looks different. The last light of the day is tangible and active, rippling across my shirt, which I have pulled out of the waistband of my jeans to cover the gun.

I feel strangeness here, and I know I do not belong on this property that is not posted but is private nonetheless. There are stories that come out of the low-country islands. It is said that lost souls are trapped in the gray tangle of Spanish moss that grows in the twists of the live oak trees. There is no denying that out here the black nights are totally black. The islands are steeped in the sufferings of slaves, Indians, Civil War soldiers and Scottish pioneers. Like all beautiful havens, Beaufort has history.

The last of the light filters through the screen of moss. Here, out on this island, so close to dark, the limbs of the live oaks look tortured, and the light that sifts through the branches undulates like ocean waves. The motion makes my head ache. A soft wind is rising.

I am several hundred yards away from Papa Le Marc's house. It is a bright white wood-frame and, to my imagination, seems unnaturally still. I smell the lush tang of wood smoke. In spite of the sweltering heat I see smoke rising from the chimney of the house.

A screen door creaks and I look up in panic, but it is only the breeze, which has set the wind chimes ringing. Crushed plastic milk cartons hang from the trees in front of the porch. Seashells and polished stones and polished wood are arranged altarlike down the side of the house.

Dusk thickens into dark and I wait, sweat rolling down the center of my spine, for Pickett and the Coupe de Ville. One by one the lights go on until the house is glowing. I feel lonely out here in the dark.

I see headlights, at long last, and hear the tires popping the gravel as the Cadillac moves down the drive. I move fast for Big Mama, lean into the open driver's window and flip the headlights. Off and on. Off and on. Off and on.

The Cadillac stops, then inches forward. I move closer to the side of the road. The Cadillac keeps going until it is back behind the trees. Pickett parks it between my pickup and the road that leads out. But the grass is level here, the sandy soil packed in hard. I'm not trapped no matter what he may think.

The Coup de Ville's engine shuts down, and the headlights flicker off. The driver's door opens and closes. I see a dark shape get out of the car, hear a heavy step in the grass. I lean through the open window of the pickup and again switch on the lights.

Pickett flinches and squints and holds his arm up to ward off the light. 'Hey, enough of that, turn them off.'

'Just stay where you are and don't move. I mean it, I've got a gun.'

I fish the pistol out of the waistband of my pants and point it, hands shaking, his way.

'So it is you. What happened this afternoon – you stood me up.'

'A guy like you ought to be used to that by now.'

'How'd you know where to find me?'

'You want the money, or you want to talk?'

He is wondering what John Wallace has told me. He is expecting a double cross.

'Turn the lights off. Do you want the attention of the people in the house?'

'Let's just get this over with quick. You go and stand over by the trunk of your car. Go on, move it, I don't have all night.'

'You got it? You got the money?'

'I'm not here for your company, dude.'

I watch him as best as I can over one shoulder, then reach into the truck for the duffel bag. It catches on the stick shift. I am aware of noise from Pickett's direction, and I yank the bag free and swivel around.

He moves so fast I can't believe it and dives for the bag. My gun goes off, ricochets off my truck, and I go down, under Pickett and the cash.

The money is heavy on my chest, and I can't breathe. My legs are pinned and tangled beneath Pickett's knees and he moves swiftly, holding my shoulders down.

'I got to say this is sexy. All this money and you and me.'

The bad tooth makes Pickett's breath rancid, and sweat rolls off his face to my neck.

'Take your money and go.'

'You sure about that, Georgie? I think that might be a little unfriendly, just to take the money and run.'

'You stink.' I am struggling like crazy, trying to push him away, but he is heavy and I can barely move.

'Looking for your sweetie, now, Georgie? Is he the one told you where I'd be? What are you and him up to, anyway?' Pickett moves off me and grabs the duffel bag. I see his hands move, hear the heavy zipper. His legs are still tangled with mine. I wait two seconds for him to be distracted by the sight and smell of my beautiful cash. He will not be able to resist touching it, he will want to hold it up to the light.

I shove Pickett backward with everything I've got. He's off balance, and grabs instinctively for the bag.

I am no more than ten feet from my truck. The door is ajar, but the latch is engaged, and it takes me an extra three seconds to get inside. I slam the door, lock it. Window or keys? I crank the window up, but Pickett grabs the top of the glass with both hands and holds it down in the tracks.

We struggle. Me to crank the window up, Pickett to keep it down. It is like arm wrestling, and I am going to lose. Pickett reaches one hand in to the lock, and I lean down and bite him as hard as I can.

'Fuck you, little bitch.'

He tastes salty.

No way do I have time to start the engine. I'll go out the other door and run for the house.

I change direction in an instant and have the passenger's door open before Pickett sees what is up. I am out, I will make it, but then his hand closes over my shoulder, and his other arm moves in a choke hold over my neck. I kick but he's got me, and he drags me back into the truck.

'Take your money and go, you son of a bitch.'

Pickett laughs and pins me down on the seat, wedging my head between the cushion and the steering wheel. He fumbles for the zipper of my pants.

'You stupid little bitch, do you think I'm ever going to leave you alone? You want to keep your sister and sonny boy safe, you'll do just like I say and when I say. Old Mitchell's been nailing you good, no matter what he says, and I get half of everything he does.'

I twist from side to side, and he is sweating, trying to get a grip. He is pushing my jeans down over my hips. Can this be happening to me?

Pickett's head explodes, a miraculous thing, and for a split second I imagine it happens by the grace of my rage. Blood, pinkish-gray clumps of brain and bits of bone splatter against the windshield and the side-view mirror; dripping down the open window to the door of my truck. Pickett slumps on top of me, and his blood soaks into my shirt.

'It's all right now, Georgie. I'm right here.'

John Wallace sounds oddly calm, voice scratchy and soothing, and I cry because he has saved me, but he has also put me here.

He grabs me under the arms and pulls me out from

under what is left of Pickett. Then he is holding me, and stroking my hair, and saying things I'll remember at night, in my dreams, where all things are possible, even a bad and dangerous love.

I hear shouting, men's voices from the house, the slam of a screen door. A dog is barking. He sounds penned up.

'Go,' I tell John Wallace. I can barely see his face in the dark. 'Take half of the money and go.'

'What are you saying?'

'What gun did you use, yours or mine? You do have a gun?'

'Yours.'

'How'd you find me?'

'I saw you watching us from the kitchen window. I went to look for you after Pickett left. When I couldn't find you, I got worried that maybe you followed him.'

'What took you so damn long?'

In spite of everything, he laughs. 'I had to steal a car.'

In the distance, I hear a siren.

'Hurry,' I tell him. 'Take the Caddie, and leave the car you stole. Take half of the money. Half. Then never bother me again. Nobody knows you were here. Nobody knows you're a part of this. As far as the police are concerned, Pickett killed my father, and Pickett was blackmailing me.'

'That won't hold up, Georgie. How could he blackmail you if he killed your dad? Say this. Say he told you he had evidence. Evidence that your dad killed your mom, and he wanted a payoff before he'd let it go.'

'Good. Fine. Just go, for God's sake, will you?'

'Can I call you? Just to see if you're okay?'

'Never again, John Wallace, or Mitchell, or whoever the hell you are. No phone calls, no letters, no surprises at my door.'

He says nothing and moves quickly, working in the headlights from Big Mama. He is smeared with blood and bits of tissue. John Wallace has dead eyes now, like a shark. Did he always look at me this way?

It would be easier to believe that, to see myself as blind to reality, duped during vulnerability, taken in by evil. But I have seen his other side. The part of him that rests uneasily in the core, a sweet lover who brings me coffee and beignets.

19

Eugene Wilbanks is smoking in this room full of men, though signs posted frequently throughout the police station make it clear that tobacco is not allowed. He sits next to Detective Click and directly across from me in this refrigerated conference room, looking like a crocodile in a Geoffrey Beene suit, right down to the leathery sunbeaten skin and malevolent smile.

The Jinx sits beside me, in a silk and wool Armani, and he puts a fatherly hand on my shoulder. The tap of feminine heels sounds from out in the hallway, and Brenda, Jinx's assistant, walks into the conference room alongside Sondra Mannelli, the Beaufort County DA.

Mannelli is a tall blonde, with short, seriously sprayed hair, sensible beige shoes and a skirt that reaches below her knees. Her presence seems muted, but the way heads turn when she enters the room makes it clear who's in charge.

The Jinx signals Brenda, and she opens her thin, expensive leather briefcase and passes papers to Sondra Mannelli, Eugene Wilbanks and Detective Click. Mannelli sits directly across from the Jinx, and he addresses himself to her.

'These are signed and notarized statements from my client. We've provided copies to both of your offices.' The Jinx acknowledges Click with a nod. 'You should have received Ms Smallwood's statement early this week. We wanted to give you time to digest the material, and we'll be happy now to address any questions or concerns, if there are any.'

Wilbanks taps a pencil on the edge of the table. 'Has it been established that the murder victim was, indeed, Stephen Pickett?'

Jinx considers Captain Wilbanks but his reaction is mild. 'Ms Mannelli, please note my objection to the term "murder victim."'

Detective Click clears his throat. 'We have our forensics reports back from Columbia, and it has been established that the man who was shot was Stephen Pickett. It has also been established that Pickett's DNA matches the samples found in the blackmail letters sent to Fielding Smallwood some months ago.'

Wilbanks leans back in his chair, and addresses me directly. 'You fired two shots that night, is that right? Would you please explain the circumstances concerning those shots.'

'The first shot was fired by accident. I was getting the bag of money from the floor of my truck, and Stephen Pickett tackled me. The gun went off but no one was hit. I fired the second shot, the one that killed Pickett, when he attempted to rape me on the front seat of my truck.'

'I find the angle of that shot very odd.'

Click raises a finger. 'I was present at the scene after the residents of the Le Marc household called nine-one-one. They heard the shots, they saw headlights and they heard Miss Smallwood scream. We have samples taken from under Miss Smallwood's fingernails, skin fragments that came from Pickett. There were scratches on his body as well.'

Wilbanks turns sideways in his chair. 'How is it that you came to bring a gun with you that night?'

'Pickett was a blackmailer. I was afraid of him.'

'Let me be clear. You met a man who was blackmailing you, alone, in a remote location. You took a gun with you. You shot and killed this man.'

'Pickett wasn't blackmailing me.'

'Then why did you agree to meet him?'

'Stephen Pickett said he had information regarding my mother's death.'

Click seems to come alive. He is frowning his way through my official statement, for this information that Pickett had. He won't find it in the papers he's got now.

'Exactly what information?' Mannelli asks, leaning forward.

'Just a minute,' Wilbanks says. 'None of this appears in your statement, Ms Smallwood.'

'That's right,' the Jinx says. 'Brenda?'

Brenda once again opens the elegant briefcase. The Jinx has orchestrated this meeting like a dance.

'This is an addendum to Ms Smallwood's statement. You'll understand, once you're familiar with the contents, why I wanted to turn it over in your presence' – the Jinx nods at Mannelli – 'and yours,' he says to Click. 'I want to make certain that nothing gets lost in any kind of paperwork shuffle.' He looks at Eugene Wilbanks. 'I want reassurances from you, Ms Mannelli, that all of the issues in this addendum will be properly addressed.

'For starters, we have a sworn statement from a private detective hired by Fielding Smallwood that Eugene Wilbanks gave him a money order for half of his fee.'

Wilbanks comes slowly to his feet, but the Jinx continues.

'This detective was hired for the express purpose of determining whether or not Marine Recruit Stephen Pickett was actually alive. Which makes it very clear, Captain Wilbanks, that you were aware of the blackmail and the circumstances surrounding it from day one.'

'Sit down, Eugene,' Mannelli says softly. 'Is this true?'

He sits slowly, gives me a quick glance, then turns to Mannelli. 'About the money order? Yes, that's true. I lent a friend some money. Fielding Smallwood has been my best friend since we were in the service together.'

'And you were aware, weren't you, that your friend was being blackmailed?' the Jinx asks.

'Of course not.' Wilbanks leans back in his chair. 'Fielding was obsessing. He thought he'd seen one of the recruits who was supposed to have died during that terrible Hardigree incident. He was sure he'd seen Stephen Pickett. At the time, of course, I thought it was ridiculous. Pickett was declared dead along with six other boys.'

I wonder if anyone else knows as surely as I do that Wilbanks is lying. He is good at it.

'Fielding just couldn't let go of it, so I suggested he hire a private detective to look into it, for no other reason than to put his mind at rest.'

'That's one possibility,' the Jinx says. 'Maybe even believable, except that Stephen Pickett was alive. Believable if there weren't blackmail letters from Pickett to Smallwood. Frankly, Captain Wilbanks, I'd like to know why you didn't excuse yourself from this investigation, as ethics demand. Why, in spite of strong evidence, if not personal knowledge, that your best friend Fielding Smallwood was being blackmailed by Pickett, did you push a marginal case against his daughter Claire?'

'Gentlemen.' Mannelli holds up a hand. She glances across the table at the Jinx. 'I want to interview this private detective personally, in my office, tomorrow.'

'I'll have him there tomorrow morning,' the Jinx says.

Mannelli does not look at Wilbanks. 'At this time, my office accepts Ms Smallwood's statement of self-defense and has no plans to pursue any charges against her. Is there anything further, Mr Radcliffe?'

The Jinx looks contemplative. 'Are there any plans to further investigate my client, Claire Smallwood, or any members of the Smallwood family for the death of Fielding Smallwood?'

'No, there are not.' She gives him a hard look. 'Are you satisfied?'

The Jinx puts a hand on my arm. 'Yes, Ms Mannelli, I'm satisfied.'

Mannelli is on her feet, motioning for Wilbanks and Click to follow. The Jinx turns to me.

'Do you understand what just happened?'

'You talked to her already, didn't you? This was just a formality, what went on here today.'

The Jinx stands and closes his briefcase. 'Many things become possible during elections.'

'They're not going to do anything. To Wilbanks.'

'We just made a deal, Georgie. You and your sister, your family, are off the hook. Any repercussions for Wilbanks will be private and swift and will not embarrass the office of the district attorney.' The Jinx smiles down at me. 'Revenge rarely works in the court-room, Georgie. Be content with what you have.'

It is the end of October when I leave Beaufort, just as the weather turns cool. Wilbanks has resigned from the district attorney's office, Sondra Mannelli has a new assistant and the results of my mother's autopsy were inconclusive.

My shop bell rings, and Johnny Selby stands on the front steps, helmet tucked under his left arm, leather jacket open and hair slick with sweat. He takes his sunglasses off and tucks them in a pocket as I run to open the door.

'Hello, Georgie.' He follows me in, head turning this way and that. The shop is empty, and his boots echo loudly on the oak floor. 'I understand Hank's not going with you.'

'He's a fisherman now. He's going to stay and follow the shrimp.'

Selby nods, wanders to the scarred wall where my grandfather's tools used to hang. 'And Claire's going off to Charleston. It's a good thing Hank's staying. At least there'll be one Smallwood left in Beaufort.'

'You'll look out for him, won't you, Johnny?'

He smiles and his eyes crinkle up. 'Same way I always looked out for you.'

I run and hug him, and I have a moment of doubt. 'You're the only reason I'd stay in this town.'

He holds me tight, then lets me go. 'There's lots of reasons to stay here, Georgie. Any chance you'll let me talk you into staying around?'

I shake my head.

'Opinionated, like your mother.'

'There's too much stuff here, Johnny.'

'Just remember we're not locking the gate behind you. You can always come home.' He smiles, heads for the door, then turns back around. 'Can I ask you a personal question?'

I go very tense. 'Go ahead.'

'Hank's father. Was he my son? Was it Vincent?'

I lean backward and prop my back against the wall. There are gouges in the plaster where my pictures have hung. 'Why ask me now? All these years, the way people have been whispering about me, it never did seem to occur to anybody there might be a man involved.'

He touches my shoulder. 'It occurred to me. I just hoped maybe one day you'd tell me yourself, if you wanted me to know.' He looks intently into my face as if the answer will be written in my eyes. 'Was it him? Was it Vincent?'

'Yes, it was Vincent.'

'I'm so sorry, my dear.' He hugs me with the arm that is not taken up by the helmet and kisses the top of my head. 'Did he know?'

'Yes, he knew.'

'How did he feel about it?'

'Believe it or not, he was happy. He wanted to marry me. He said it gave him direction and purpose.'

'I'm sure he was happy, Georgie. He loved you very much.' Selby looks out the window. 'Think how different your life would have been if he hadn't flipped that Camaro.'

'I'll never understand why this stuff happens if I live forever.'

'There never are any answers, Georgie.'

'Maybe so, but it's still hard to forget the questions.'

He smiles and ruffles my hair, then checks his watch. 'Got to go to work. You keep well, in the wilds of California.'

I touch Selby's arm. 'Remember to look after Hank for me, okay?'

'You bet. Does he know? About Vincent?'

'Since he was eleven years old.'

Selby hugs me one more time. 'You ever need me, Georgie Smallwood, you know where I am.'

EPILOGUE

And so they pass, eleven years, slipping away silently and fast, my time in exile. Hank will be married tomorrow, and I have driven through New Mexico, Texas, Arkansas and Georgia to be there.

I do not return alone. My dog, Lincoln, and I have driven from the California desert to the high, hot humidity of July in South Carolina in a 1994 Jeep Wrangler. Lincoln is panting, nose pressed to the window, drool smearing the glass. He was six years old when he found me, a white German shepherd with wise brown eyes, a habit of taking off for private excursions and a past he will not reveal. No one challenges my dog, and I am always safe.

We spend a lot of time on the road together, going to auctions, flea markets and estate sales. I have filled up five California storage units with pieces that will keep me, on down the road. Someday I will settle down, fix them up and sell them off.

It is an odd thing, the way my spirits lift the minute I cross the South Carolina state line, and see BEAUTI-FUL PLACES, SMILING FACES on the majority of license plates. I have been more homesick than I know.

We take Highway 25, the last stretch home. The asphalt sparkles with bits of silicate, and the land is flat, soft

354

with brown pine needles, and shaded by tall, thin pines.

I come upon Beaufort gradually. It has not been made at all shabby by my time away. Every bend in the road is familiar. The town rushes in on me, the tide of my past rolling in. I am eager, now, for Waffle Houses, pickup trucks and the twang of country music. I imagine the end of summer, the crispness of fall, the feel of leaves underfoot. I want blue jeans and self-sufficiency and communal distrust of the government. The South is the only place I know where eccentricity is run-of-the-mill, kindness is as common as it is casual and the summers are as miserable as hell.

I drive on autopilot, heading without thinking for my old shop. I am trying to decide if it will still be an antiques store or if it has been converted into an art gallery or coffee bistro.

I pull the Jeep next to a familiar, worn concrete curb.

My shop is empty and abandoned. It has the desolate, dust-ridden and unpainted look of a building that is not loved. Strips of lettering on the display window have peeled and faded to the point that I cannot piece together any sense of the words. The sandy beige paint is peeling off the clapboard, the balcony still sags. The excitement in my stomach dies away.

My shop is empty.

This is a prime spot. A beautiful location. One block down from Ribault Street, two blocks from the main drag. And right next door to the ever-elegant Beaufort Inn, where I have a reservation for the entire week.

I look at Lincoln, who is still panting in spite of the air conditioning, leave the Jeep engine running so he can stay cool, and get out of the car.

The soles of my boots scrape the sidewalk, and I

stare through the front bay window. The glass is dirty; I can't see very much. Just for the hell of it, I try the door. The knob is frozen and locked, but the door gives. Whoever left it last did not pull it completely closed, and no one has ever fixed the cranky latch that will not catch unless the door is all the way shut.

I step inside and take a breath.

I am not quite eighteen years old again, too young and inexperienced to know how the world is stacked against me, feeling accomplished because I have graduated from all of my adult education classes in small-business management and woodwork. I am ready to look for a job in the antiques business, a possibility that beckons to me with the comfort I associate with my grandfather and the excitement of being on my own.

My mother has taken me to lunch like she does every Tuesday, but today she has an air of secrets and self-satisfaction. She has suggested The Big P, where we can have an iceberg salad in a brown plastic bowl, our choice of four dressings, a baked potato and a thin grilled steak. The restaurant is actually a Golden Corral, but Mama calls it The Big P for the size of the potatoes.

At this time in my life I am so young I do not realize she is eccentric.

My mother stops in downtown Beaufort on a side street that is one block over from Ribault and next to the Beaufort Inn. The area is respectable and houses a handful of attorneys, an ocean properties realtor, a museum and a place where you can buy surfboards, swimsuits and beach towels. On the corner over the crumbling concrete curb is an elderly sagging building with a big bay storefront window, faded white shutters and battered oak floors.

On this day a stained, weathered banner hangs over the door promising an art gallery in May. The banner has been there for eighteen months. In the window is a newish sign, black background, red letters, that says SALE OR LEASE, over the top of a phone number.

Mama parks so close to the curb she scrapes the tires. She is always either too close or too far away.

'I always wanted to go in this old building. Georgie, haven't you always wanted to see inside this place? Come on, let's peep in the windows.'

'Mama, that's embarrassing, looking through people's windows. What if there's somebody inside?'

'Oh, come on, Georgie. They aren't going to put us in jail for looking in a window.'

I am ashamed to remember how irritated I was, climbing out of the car – unfastening Hank from his carrier and settling him over my left shoulder, watching my mother stand on a concrete block to look through the old grimy windows. I am thinking that when she trips and falls off that concrete block, as she is very likely to do, she will probably break her ankle, as her bones are delicate, and I will spend the afternoon in the hospital emergency room and never get my lunch. That's how you think when you are not quite eighteen and shallow.

But when I press my nose to the storefront window, I sigh. Inside is an expansive L-shaped showroom, long down one side and wide open to the sunlight. Someone has torn out the interior walls, and wires are exposed on the north side. The floors, solid oak, are scarred and faded beneath the debris of fallen plaster, and a six-foot step-ladder, spattered with green and yellow paint, is stuck in the corner, going dusty from the neglect of someone's good intentions.

'Georgie? *What* do you think?'

'It's a neat old building, isn't it, Mama?'

'Very old. Doesn't it remind you of New Orleans? It's turn of the century.'

'Like you, Mom?'

She is working the door latch. 'Don't be smart.'

'Mama, what are you doing? Breaking and entering *will* land you in jail.'

But she manages to get the door open, and I see she has a key. She heads right in without a backward look.

We stand together, hushed and seeing things in this building that have more to do with what could be than what actually is, and my mother asks me what I think.

'I think it is the most beautiful building I have ever seen.' In my mind I can see my worktable covered with bolts of fabric, and the wall where I can hang all my grandfather's tools. I see myself in worn cut-off blue jeans, up to my elbows in glue, customers loading and unloading their couches and chairs. I can make a little play area in the corner by the window, perfect for Hank. Maybe there's a back room where I can put a daybed, and Hank and I can sleep over sometimes, and take a break from our dreary, sticky, ant-ridden apartment.

'Come on, Georgie.' My mother is on her way upstairs.

This is the first time I see the staircase, but my mother clearly knows her way around. She leads me up the creaky wood steps framed by walls I am suddenly aching to paint. She stays one step ahead, dressed as always in navy blue polyester pants and a huge sweater, her gigantic purse a lethal six inches from Hank's head.

The staircase leads to a second floor that is separated

from the downstairs by a door that was obviously not an original part of what was once somebody's spectacular town house. The door leads to a great room, with a ribbed ceiling and windows on opposing sides. Someone has put in a small kitchenette, a bathroom and two tiny, open-beamed bedrooms. The back wall is all windows and a French door leading out to a balcony that does not look safe.

'You could live here,' my mother tells me. 'We can fix it up really cute. See, this can be Hank's little nursery. It's tiny, but babies like that anyway. And here, you can make this into your room. There's a window seat, and you could put your bed there and get a wardrobe to use for a closet.' My mother wanders slowly, making plans, then turns to me, eyebrows arched. 'So? What do you think?'

I am enveloped in an odd, shy humiliation. I know that having a baby at the age of sixteen has separated me from the future I was supposed to have, and that I am no longer in a position to want things or accept help. 'I can't afford this, Mama.'

'It's very reasonable.'

I shake my head, pushing away the vision of how I would live in this space. Even reasonable is out of my reach.

'I think you should take it, Georgie. If it's really what you want.'

'How much is it?'

'That's not for you to worry about.'

'What do you mean it's not for me to worry about?'

'I mean the first month's rent is paid and will be till you get on your feet. We got a three-year lease with an option to buy.'

'Three years?'

'That gives the owner a secure income without worrying about losing a tenant. I gave him a three-year commitment, and he gave me a bargain.'

'It's too much, Mama, I can't take it.'

'Georgie, your father and I have discussed this; it's something both of us want to do.'

'Daddy hates me.'

'No, he doesn't. He loves you very much, Georgie, but you know how he is. He's been too hard on you, he's very well aware. Don't let his shortcomings be your problems. There are times in your life to take help, and this is one of those times.'

My mother is making it easy to do what I want to do, and to have what I want to have. She is not giving me a charity income. She is not taking all my problems away. She is giving me a chance to make the kind of life I want to make.

She holds out the key, and I take it.

It is suddenly too much to stand here, after all these years have passed and my mother and father are both gone, and to be confused about whether my father ever really loved me and why he did the things he did, if he did them. I go back to the Jeep and my dog.

I am doubting myself. I am thinking that because no one else seems to love this place, perhaps it is not so wonderful. I put the car in drive and pull out onto the narrow, quiet street.

I could actually come back here. Reopen my shop. Fix that sagging balcony and sell, piece by piece, my collection, which has grown enormous over the past eleven years.

The urge to come home is strong, sudden and surprising. I have never once felt this way till now. Beaufort has been such a dark place in my heart. How odd to see it once more without the old agonized resentment. To see it fresh and clean and with affection.

I am home.

I sleep well my first night home in Beaufort, take Lincoln to walk along the waterfront in the morning when it is cool, have a late breakfast in the dining room. My son will be married today in the old brick courtyard at the back of the Inn.

There is a loud knock on the carriage-house door. 'Mom?'

It is startling, matching this grown male voice to my son. I open the door to see him grinning at me, and I smile because he is so handsome in his black tuxedo. He is holding a small white box, and for the first time in my life I understand why mothers cry at weddings.

'Trip okay?'

'Yeah, it was fine.'

'Oh, hey, I got you something.' Hank opens the cardboard box and I can just catch the faint but sweet fragrance unique to orchids. 'It's a wrist corsage, Mom. I hope it's okay.'

'How beautiful, Hank. I love it.'

How different my son is now from the fifteen-year-old boy who ran away.

He did try school from time to time, those months

after I left South Carolina, but he was drawn, as always, back to Beaufort and a life as a shrimp fisherman on *The Graceful Lady*. It is a hard business, shrimping, but Hank is thriving. He could buy a new boat but he stays with *The Graceful Lady* and his luck at finding the shrimp is a matter of local renown. I like to think that Ashby is there with him, keeping him safe and spotting the shrimp.

Cousin Beauregard lived three years after Mama died, going out every day on *The Graceful Lady* with Hank, rarely leaving his side. One afternoon, as Hank pulled in on a sun-drenched day with a full catch of shrimp, Cousin Beauregard curled up at his feet, closed her eyes and never woke up again.

I've tried to talk Hank into another dog, but he always says no.

'I have something else for you, Mom.' Hank pulls a stained and crumpled envelope from his breast pocket. 'I found it on *The Graceful Lady* about a month after you left. I wasn't sure what to do with it. I probably should have given it to you, but . . . you know how upset you were then. I thought you should just get away and not think about stuff.'

He hands me the letter and kisses my cheek.

'Anyways. I better go see if my best man remembered the rings.'

I grip the letter and smile at my son. 'Be happy.'

2 June

Dear Ashby,

Honey, I am worried about you. I have the feeling that things are getting away from me, and I know

362

I need to write you this letter tonight.

You are so sad, Ashby, even though you put up a good front. I am your mother, and I know. I think things are not going well with you and Reese. I hope I'm wrong. Remember, all relationships go through highs and lows, and be patient with him.

I see you still trying to please your father, and it bothers me because you never realize he can't be pleased. If you understood your father better, you might realize that whatever is lacking between the two of you is his failing, not yours.

Your father very much wanted to finish college. He applied to the University of Virginia and the Citadel, and was so thrilled to receive acceptance to Virginia. You didn't know him then, Ashby. He went to a small high school, had a 4.0 grade average and played on the high-school football team. He worked two jobs in the summers to save for college. He was going places.

And then he fell in love with me and pursued me like he did everything else he wanted. But a man can't support a wife and a baby and pay tuition, and your father joined the marines, for housing, health care and a military career.

You know what happened. You know about that night when Stephen Pickett went to your father for help. What you don't know is that your father took the matter right to Eugene Wilbanks. Hardigree had been getting way out of hand, and Eugene was supposed to handle things unofficially, but with enough authority to get Hardigree back in line. Instead, Eugene decided to speak with Hardigree on a semi-official basis the next day. He purposely did not interfere with the forced march through the swamp because he felt it would give Hardigree enough rope to hang himself, which, tragically, it did.

Your father took complete responsibility for what happened. He never reported Eugene for his part in this mess, and always told me he should have handled it himself and not passed the buck. He and Hardigree were such close friends his loyalties were conflicted. That was his mistake, he always told me. His duty was clearly to the recruits in Hardigree's platoon, and when the corps was going to discharge him for dereliction of duty, he was not going to lift a finger to fight it.

Eugene, much as I hate that man, never let that happen. And he got your daddy that bank job when the other offers fell through. You know Hardigree died in prison, but what you don't know is your daddy and I supported Hardigree's family financially during a lot of years when it was all your father and I could do to support ourselves.

But your father was never the same. He was tired, Ashby. He tried to do the right things all his life, but honor for honor's sake is harder to live with than he realized.

My point is this, son. You cannot live by what others tell you to do. You cannot live by the rules of the people around you, even when they happen to be your father. Everybody has an inner voice, Ashby. You listen to that and you'll be okay.

Things are going to get bad for a while, and I have no idea how your father is going to react. There are some new complications, and it looks like we might be dragged through the whole Hardigree mess all over again. If it comes out that he shielded Eugene Wilbanks, your father thinks that people will think he did it so that Wilbanks would get him the bank job, that he did what he did for personal gain. I personally don't think these things can hurt us any more than they already have, but your father is not himself. So I have made the decision to end this charade once and for all.

Just remember, whatever happens, that I am proud of you, son.

Love, Mom

The last of the afternoon sun comes through the trees, a blinding contrast to the shadows that will soon gather into dusk. The air is soft with humidity and tinged with ocean and salt marshes. I shade my eyes against the light's brilliance as I walk slowly down the steps of the carriage house to see my son take his vows. The parking lot is full, and there are voices, and knots of people milling. The chairs are filling, and a piano sits on a dais to the right of the heavy white canopy.

I pause at the edge of the courtyard. In a minute I will thread my way through the groups of people and smile, and I'll find friends I haven't seen for years. But for now, I hesitate.

The letter has set the memories loose.

The thing I remember the most about the night my father died is the echoes. Echoes of footsteps on the lighthouse stairs.

I didn't mean for it to happen. My mistake was to go back. I went for my sweatshirt, an old favorite, worn and frayed – my lucky sweatshirt, the sweatshirt I shed when I drank beer with Ashby and Claire, the sweatshirt that fell into that select category of comfort clothes you cannot live without. I knew that if I didn't stop by and get it that night, the lighthouse tours would start in the morning and the shirt would disappear.

I climb the steps slowly, use my flashlight carefully and hear a car engine just as I grab the shirt. I think it is a park ranger making the rounds, so I turn off the flashlight, put my back to the wall and stand very still, holding my breath.

The car engine stops. I hear the ocean, the crickets, the scuff of someone walking in the sand. Downstairs, the door creaks open, and I hear footsteps. I flash my light just for a moment, and see my father at the foot of the steps.

I do not know why I am so afraid. My father glares at the light. He is holding a thick brown mailer, the padded kind that costs two dollars and twenty-five cents at Staples. He clamps the packet to his side and comes up to the second level, then stops and waits.

'Who is it?' He sounds angry. 'I know you're there. What are you doing up on the landing? Get down here now, or I'll come up and get you.'

It's an ingrained reaction, the way I panic. It is as if I am a child again, caught doing something very wrong, and my father is righteous and angry. He cannot see me, but he knows, he knows it is me.

I could tell you that I didn't think to warn him that the railing was loose, but I am facing things, and I remember the thought did cross my mind. But I didn't call out. I listened to those swift but heavy steps, the clang of my father's shoes on the spiral stairway. And the rasp of his breath when the rail loosened and swung away.

I did not warn him. I did not.

I lunge forward and see him just as he falls. He sees me too, he meets my eyes, and it is odd the look he gives me. I am not who he expected at all.

It is only now that I see what others know, that my father is older and slower and no longer the strong, young, invincible marine. No one to fear after all.

He puts out a hand, but I don't take it. The weight of him will pull me forward – my father outweighs me by two hundred pounds. So I step backward and away, out of reach.

And he falls. And falls. And falls.

I hear him hit the bottom, and his scream echoes off the walls.

I am running, running down those steps, flashlight bright. When I reach the final level I see that his shin-bone is splintered and has torn a jagged path through the flesh, exposing a white shaft of bone that shocks me and sends my imagination into overdrive where I try to comprehend such pain. He lies at an angle, his eyes wide, suffering, and clearly the eyes of a man who lives.

The look he gives me has an animal-like quality, yet he has never seemed so completely human. I clock his progress toward eternity by watching his eyes, the life slowly draining away, until they close and I am convinced that my father is dead.

I was quiet when I could have spoken. I withdrew when I could have offered a hand. And when I looked at his broken body and thought he was dead, I did not call for help but went home instead. How great is the sin of omission?

In the South, they say your relatives come for you when you die.

In a certain light, my mother's letter to Ashby reads like a suicide note. Yet if that were truly the case, why was there no letter for me or for Claire? And why would my mother not wait to welcome Hank, when he'd been lost for two long years?

That, for me, is the clincher. That is the final piece of logic that assures me my mother did not take her life.

And when she tells my brother that she is finally going to 'end the charade,' I know that she means she will no longer stay quiet. She will tell what really happened, the night all those boys died, and let my father and Wilbanks deal with the truth.

I hear my father's voice . . . *I checked her at four-thirty, and twenty minutes later at ten to five* . . . a litany that can only make sense if he was expecting my mother to die. And I think again, as I often do, of that bolted bedroom door. I picture my father feeding my mother pill after pill, until she is groggy and close to death. I picture him holding a pillow over her face, speeding her on, his thumb bruising the fragile skin of her throat.

My sister's voice brings me back. She stands on the back porch of the inn, just under my son's wedding canopy, and she has all her children around her. Claire wears little round spectacles now, for close work, and keeps her hair swept back in a chignon. There are new lines in her soft oval face, and if the sparkle died in prison and she seems oddly still from the inside out, the effect enhances rather than detracts.

Where have we gone, my siblings and I? I see us so clearly in my heart. Will our voices always echo? Will the imprint SMALLWOOD FAMILY exist as an entity somewhere? My family cannot be lost. We are so real, so lively. How can we ever be gone?

If I could go back in time I would return to my childhood of twilight evenings in a suburban South Carolina backyard, on a night when summer surrenders to the crisp clear promise of fall. I'd be out in the dark with Claire and Ashby, playing kick the can, hiding behind retaining walls and pine trees, running into the circle of packed-down orange dirt beneath the basketball goal where the grass does not even try.

I would go back to the Thanksgiving weekend where my mother curled up in the living room with Hank and Claire's three and left my sister and brother and me free to play ping-pong and pretend to do the dishes, me slinging soapsuds at Ashby while Claire did all the work.

You do not see them, these moments, when they flow through your life. You live them, you move on and later you cast backward and see it for what it was: an oasis of happiness and security where you lived totally in the moment, unaware and unafraid of what went before or what would come to you later. In my heart we are still there, in an endless loop, and if no one else can see us or hear us or know us, it cannot matter.

At times when I least expect it, I look into my mirror and catch a glimpse of my brother's face, as if his ghost stands forever at my back. He is gone so soon that I am never sure I see him, and I never meet his eyes. I am not afraid when I see Ashby behind me. It is not his presence I fear, but the lack thereof. My brother has put his shadows in my closet, and they will be with me for the rest of my life.

And yet, I am glad to be Georgie Smallwood. All that has happened has made me.

Nothing really matters, you know, except the way the sun slants in through the window and warms the curve of your back. All else falls away.

LYNN HIGHTOWER
THE DEBT COLLECTOR

Praise for Lynn Hightower

'Suspenseful and psychologically sound, with a fierce, frazzled quality to the writing which gives it edge and credibility. Astonishingly good' Philip Oakes, *Literary Review*

'Genuinely fresh and exciting' *Observer*

'A cracking tale told at a stunning pace . . . the characterisation is great, the suspects are 10 a dollar and the dialogue worth a million' Frances Fyfield, *Mail on Sunday*

Predators at Play

Home invasion – the kind of call every homicide cop dreads.

Cincinnati detective Sonora Blair is called to a small house at the end of a cul-de-sac, and finds the brutal decimation of an average American family – deeply in debt.

A high-profile search brings two ex-convicts, both murdered in prison within twenty-four hours of their apprehension.

Evidence points to a third man at the murder scene – a man called the Angel, a man who runs a collection agency that can turn a debt into your worst possible nightmare.

HODDER & STOUGHTON PAPERBACKS